# THE FALLEN HUNTERS

SPACE MARAUDER CHRONICLES
BOOK THREE

LORENA PARA

eBook May 2025
Paperback May 2025

*Book design by Lorena Para*
*Cover Image by Ronnie Jensen*
*www.tegnemaskin.no*
ASIN (eBook) B0DNQ1LMQD
ISBN (paperback) *978-1-7375253-3-2*

Get a free bonus story at
TheShortWriter.com

*For my Grandpa Ronny.*
*Thank you for your sacrifice,*
*love, and memories.*

# CONTENTS

# PROLOGUE

$\mathcal{F}$our weeks had passed since Arsenio Anton failed to kill his sister. Four weeks of silence. Twenty-eight days spent under investigation by the Earth Confederate, stripped of his title as Commissioner of the Galactic Marauder Hunters. Too much time to dwell on the numerous mistakes he made; the ones he could not come back from.

Life blurred into monotony since his return to the New Cruces Republic. The walls of his penthouse were confining. His only source of information came from the news reports on the social net and whatever Adora chose to share with him. Neither provided much. He was not only trapped inside his home. His mind and body became a far crueler prison than any other he could imagine.

Arsenio looked out the expansive window of his bedroom at the sprawling city below. Thousands of hover cars flew past his building, going about their lives completely unaware and unconcerned about his. As the sun dipped behind the desert mountain, he watched lights blink to life throughout the world from which he was disconnected.

*You could be in actual prison,* a voice said inside his head.

He closed his eyes in lassitude, trying to block out the room around him.

*Remember, it's because of me you aren't,* the voice added. *I pulled favors to keep us under house arrest rather than shut away in a cell. Where they'd cut us off from each other. Then you'd really be alone. Things could be much worse for you.*

*Worse than what, Adora?* Arsenio thought back to his twin via their telepathic link. *This is already pretty bad. We've lost our jobs, integrity, and power. And it could've been avoided. But no. You had to take it too far like always. You never know your limits when it comes to Orinthia.*

There was a long pause. He knew better than to mention his youngest sister's name to Adora. But he was tired. Yes, she kept them out of prison, but for how long? The stress of waiting was eating him alive, and sleep had not come to him most nights. The skin on his face had gone patchy grey. He wished something, anything would happen.

*If you had let me kill her, this wouldn't be a problem,* Adora responded. The anger in her words stung like a burn, even if it was only imagined. *She was in my hand and sentenced to death, but you had to drag it out. We should have executed her on the deck in front of the crew. There would've been hundreds of witnesses. This is not my fault, but yours.*

Arsenio leaned forward and pressed his forehead against the cool glass. His eyes still closed, he pictured Orinthia in her prison cell, burned but defiant. *It was protocol, and I did what I was supposed to do. I've always taken this job seriously. It meant everything to me. We were doing good, protecting the EC's interests from marauders. You used it as your jackboot. It's a miracle we weren't investigated sooner.*

A long sigh passed through Arsenio's lips. The air bounced off the window, brushing his face on the way back. He had not realized how much he missed the simplest sounds, like breathing or the swishing of fabric as he moved.

There were many things he wished he could have done differently, though he was not entirely sure it would have changed anything. Orinthia was their enemy, but not without reason. They had made her that way, all of them. It did not absolve her, not by a long shot. But it made it harder to pretend she was the only one to blame. Neither party was innocent in their feud, and everyone involved had much to answer for.

Arsenio slowly pushed himself away from the window, careful not to move too fast and get dizzy. He opened his eyes and faced the rest of the room behind him, focusing on nothing in particular. His fingers drifted to the patch of skin above his right ear where his father implanted the connection between the twins. The stone marauder dislodged it when he swung Arsenio over his shoulder onto the floor of the *Mathias'* prison deck. The impact had caused swelling near his temporal lobe, and as Adora described it, dislodged the implant and severed his auditory nerves.

According to her interpretation of what the physicians told her, there was no way to repair it. He would live in silence for the rest of his life. It had been a shock at first, realizing he would never hear again. But it was a comfort to know he still had Adora. He would not be completely alone. She promised they would continue as they always had: sharing information in the way only they could.

*Has anyone come in with you?* Adora asked, abruptly changing the subject. There was a hint of something in her voice; tight, brittle. Panic maybe, so rare he almost did not recognize it.

Arsenio made a wide scan. The door was still shut. *No, it's only me in here. Why?*

*There're new guards. Messies.*

*Is it shift change?* He glanced at the clock near his bed. They were not scheduled to swap for another two hours. *Adora, what's going on?*

There was no reply. He called to her again. Still, nothing. Arsenio paced the length of his bedroom. A tight fist built up in his chest. His imagination spiraled with visions of a feral Adora tearing through anyone who dared to lay a hand on her.

Her apartment was only the level above his, but he could not tell if there had been a struggle. No guards had entered his room. No one came to alert him to a change. There were no signs anything out of the ordinary had taken place.

*Adoracion, what's wrong?* he asked one more time.

*Uri,* was the only reply he received.

*What does that mean?* He tried to decipher her code. Did they have a failsafe word he forgot about? Was she being questioned about Uri's death? Arsenio did not understand. He ran his fingers through his hair, tugging at the roots. The pit of his stomach bubbled hot and the tightness in his chest grew.

Fifteen minutes passed before he received a word back from Adora. *Things are more complicated than I thought,* she said.

*Tell me what's going on,* Arsenio demanded. He was on the verge of convulsions and could not handle the anticipation any longer.

*I'm about to be arrested. Properly this time,* Adora replied in a flurry of thought. *They're coming for you n—*

Arsenio had not stopped the trek around his room until

that moment. The tension in his body exploded, leaving him cold and numb. *I don't know what to do.*

Movement to Arsenio's left caught his attention as the door slid open. Two GMH officers stepped in, their white-and-teal uniforms were crisp, leaving no doubt as to their ranks. They were not his usual guard, though he recognized their faces.

Messies.

Officially, the Marauder Hunter Elite Squad, the GMH special forces. He knew them well, trained them, and commanded them once. The ones they sent when things were about to get serious.

Arsenio straightened himself and made his face as steely as possible, though his heart pounded in his throat. One officer pulled a PortTab from his white coat's breast pocket and typed something before crossing the room to show him the screen.

> *You have to come with us, sir. We've been*
> *ordered to detain you and bring you to*
> *High Station.*

"What are the official charges?" Arsenio answered out loud. His hearing may have been taken, but he still had a voice. The words vibrated over his tongue; an almost foreign feeling as of late.

The officer pulled up a list.

> *Per the Confederate Tribunal Doctrine 35-M,*
> *you are hereby charged with falsifying*
> *information, unlawful imprisonment,*
> *attempted murder, abuse of power...*

It went on for three lines.

Arsenio narrowed his eyes and squared his shoulders. He knew the law better than anyone else. He, the now-former Commissioner of the GMH, had once been the arbiter of the law in open space. It sent a hot needle through his core to read what he had spoken hundreds of times before.

"I demand legal counsel," he said, without finishing reading the charges.

The two men turned toward each other and spoke. Their mouths moved in silence, like watching a film with the volume turned off. Arsenio's stomach twisted. He could see their expressions shift, their gestures tightening, but he could not read them. He was cut out from that world.

The officer closest to the door shrugged and leaned into the hall, waving someone else to come forward. He stepped aside to let the newcomer enter the room.

Arsenio stumbled back. His knees buckled, and he gripped the side of the chaise at the foot of his bed to keep himself up.

*Uri's alive?* he asked Adora.

She did not reply.

Uri joined the first man in front of Arsenio and gestured for the PortTab. He typed quickly before turning it for Arsenio to read.

> *Adora lied to you. About me, about Orinthia,*
> *all of it. Your world is about to fall apart.*
> *Don't make it harder than it has to be.*
> *You've got every right to counsel. I suggest*
> *you use it, and say nothing until you do.*
> *But you need to understand something.*
> *She's played you.*

> *We both know Adora's the one who shot me,*
> *not Thia. I've already given my statement.*
> *The reckoning is coming, Arsenio. I can't*
> *stop it. But you can make it easier on your-*
> *self if you come on your own. She'll use*
> *you as a shield for as long as she can. So,*
> *get your story straight before you end up*
> *on the gallows beside her.*

Arsenio looked up from the PortTab and met Uri's eyes. Unlike Arsenio, who took after their father, his brother and sisters resembled their mother in so many ways. The few memories he had of her were weak at best. Even then, he could not be sure if they were real or the imagination of a heartbroken little boy. Uri, however, had always been the kind one. The eldest who bridged the gap between the twins and Orinthia. He was gentle and caring, loving them all even when his own life had nearly been cut short.

"She found him, didn't she?" Arsenio asked, the weight of his question pressing on his shoulders. "Then, she's still alive?"

Uri nodded.

He did not understand why, but a warm wave of relief rushed over him. Maybe it was the peace of knowing he no longer had to guess when their lies would catch up. Perhaps it was the comfort of seeing his brother again, alive.

Or maybe even knowing, against everything they put her through, Orinthia was safe somewhere in the galaxy. For a fleeting moment, his breath caught. She was not the fragile child she used to be. There was something unshakable about her. And maybe, in trying to break her, he had a hand in making her that way.

Whatever he felt was cut short when the officer nearest him pulled a pair of mod-dampening cuffs from his hip. Arsenio surrendered, accepting his circumstances, and held out his hands. The cold metal cuffs snapped shut around his wrists and tightened against his skin.

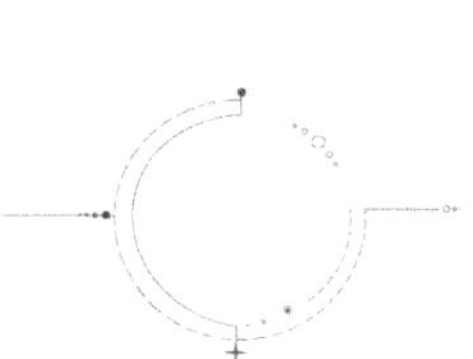

## 1

*A* streak of lightning cut across the sky like a cracked glass. Thunder rumbled through the open window, filling the small space with vibrations. Large drops of water pelted the ground three stories below, kicking up dirt and spreading its fragrance like incense.

Orinthia leaned her head on her arm that rested on the back of the couch and watched the mid-afternoon downpour. It was always summer on Buscoch, and Orinthia came to learn it brought rain. The seasons never changed on the tiny moon as it orbited the gas giant, Kren. They were the perfect distance from the system's sun to stay warm enough to grow green foliage all year long.

Time slowed in the early days after Elendoras, when she learned how to be alive in her new skin. Kos had not let her out of his sight during her recovery, and the farthest she went at first was to the balcony of Mimi's apartment. He set her up with a cup of tea that first time, watching her close. But Orinthia? She breathed in the life around her.

Every building, far taller than the four story complex they stayed in, was covered in shades of emerald. Vines climbed walls, wound their way into natural trellises, making homes for hundreds of other vegetation like moss, ferns, and flowering bushes. The homes were one with the wilderness.

Orinthia had not known such a perfect place could exist. Warm in the sun, surrounded by hues she could not name. Everything she ever wanted was before her. Uri was alive, her friends were together, and she was safe. She wished there was a way to bottle up those days and hold onto them forever.

But, time could not stand still for long. Once they were sure Orinthia was healthy enough, the group split in different directions.

Uri had gone back to Earth. Resurrection was a logistical nightmare. It was simple enough to prove he was alive; all he had to do was show up. The hard part was in the paperwork. It was only the first step in getting his life back and clearing Orinthia's name. But seeing as she was a fugitive, the courts were in no hurry to clear her of murder charges. There were also rumors they were waiting to see the outcome of Adora and Arsenio's trial before moving forward with her case.

Another flash of lightning danced through the dark clouds. Orinthia's skin was electric. She lifted two fingers from beneath her chin, without moving her head, and flicked them in a small circle. The window nudged open a few inches. Warm, wet air blew in, brushing her face like a whisper.

Orinthia's mind wandered again. She smiled softly as Thrutt's face appeared in her thoughts. He changed her life, maybe more than he would ever realize. But then again, he probably knew. Thrutt had a way of seeing things no one else saw. Maybe it was his age, or a gift his species possessed. Whatever made him who he was, it was missing from her life since he left.

"I won't be gone long," Thrutt had told her the day he

boarded Mimi's bounty ship. "Mimi's team took a hit while she was away. I'm only helping her out until she can hire more people. It's the least I can do to repay what she did for us."

*Us,* she thought. *Not what she did for me, but us.*

An unease settled on Orinthia's heart from then on. She did not like the idea of Thrutt clearing another one of her debts.

Orinthia returned her attention to the drops of water that fell from the terrace above. The pouring turned to a drizzle, through there were still echoes of thunder afar off. *Even after the murder charges are dropped, I'm still wanted. They aren't going to overlook my death sentence for marauding, even with Adora and Arsenio locked away in prison. The EC hates marauders, and I being the traitors' sister, will be made the highest example possible.*

The rain came to a complete stop and the thunder drummed farther in the distance. With a final deep breath of tepid air, Orinthia stood from the couch and walked to the kitchen, returning to the half-done dishes she had abandoned to sit by the window when the rain started. A glass of water sat on the edge of the counter across from her as she crossed the living room. Orinthia paused, planting her feet where she stood.

With an outstretched hand, she pictured the cup coming toward her. Water sloshed inside the glass as it lifted from its spot and settled into her palm. Her fingers curled around the glass and she grinned. Using her new mod became a habit, growing easier each time she did.

Uri made her promise not to practice unless someone else was home with her. Unfortunately for him, Orinthia was not one to take orders. Yes, it would have been safer to have a set of eyes on her in case she passed out. But that only happened when she pushed too hard. Even then, she was getting stronger and controlling it for longer times before wearing down.

She sipped her water, the reward for a job well done. But, a knock on the door startled her, and it slipped from her grasp. The glass shattered and scattered across the floor.

Again, the knocking came.

"Hold on," she shouted, calling a towel to her, and tossing it over the water to soak it up. Orinthia crossed the kitchen and opened the door.

A small delivery droid swung its arm back to knock a third time, but froze before striking Orinthia in the thigh. It had a flat trailer attached to its backside with a large brown box strapped to it, both were damp. "Miss Anton?"

Orinthia glanced down the breezeway to be sure they were alone. "No, but I can take the packages for her," she said, returning her attention to the droid.

Mimi and her crew held the market on bounty hunting in that sector, and promised she was safe at her house while they were away. But Orinthia did not want to risk being caught over something as silly as accepting a parcel. Her time with Celso made her cautious.

"Thank you," the droid said. The arm swung behind its back, unhitched the trailer, and rolled to pick up the box. It carried it to the threshold and set it down before returning to the trailer and reattaching it. Then, it gave a forward tilt for a bow and rolled away down the walkway, splashing through pooled water that gathered beneath the railing where it dripped from the upper levels.

Orinthia grabbed the box and kicked the door closed. She read the label as she walked to the couch and set it on the floor in front of her.

"Oh, Uri," she said with a smile. Tucking her fingers into

the tape, she tugged the box open. Paper popped out and she tossed it beside her. Beneath it was a white spacer's helmet with a pink tinted sun shield. She brushed against the smooth top and pulled out a note tucked into the visor.

*Saw this on the social net. Thought you'd like to have it in case you have any more adventures ahead.*
*Love you, Uri.*

She took the helmet in her hands and lifted it for a better view. Her face looked back at her in the reflective cover and smiled again. Kos had offered to buy her a space suit, but she declined. He already worked hard enough to keep them fed and save to buy parts for *Freya*. She could not ask him to spend that kind of credits on her. Though he had plenty in his marauder accounts, he had not found a way to access them without the risk of alerting any watching eyes.

Ahto's death had caused a stir amongst the outlaws. Whispers of the *Fera's* new captain reached them through local pilots. There was no confirmation on who it was, however. News traveled slow to Buscoch, and marauders were not frequent visitors to the moon. Still, Kos kept his head down to avoid unwanted trouble.

But Uri had no such restrictions, and she felt no shame in accepting gifts from him. He had always taken care of her and loved her like his own. Though in the light of Desidario's revelation, she wondered if Uri being programmed with her mother's memories played a part in that. He had hardly been home long enough for them to discuss how he felt about being a synthetic human.

She could not help but worry about how he was dealing

with it. Especially being so far away, facing more world shaking situations on his own.

A dull ache settled in her chest. They were only together for a short time before he left. Orinthia had fought the galaxy to save him; then he was gone. It was hard to be upset with him, since part of the reason he did was to help her. But that did not change how much she wished she could have basked in her victory a little longer.

Heartsick and grieved, she set the helmet back in the box and stood up. Taking the package on her hip, she carried it to her borrowed room and set it on Mimi's bed. There were clothes piled in the corner and the blanket had slipped halfway onto he floor. She looked over the mess and, forgetting all about her previous task of dishes, began tidying up the best she could.

Tossing clothes into a basket, she eyed the three half dead plants on the end table near the foot of the bed. They were all that lasted from the original eight Kos had bought for her. She was proud to have kept them alive for as long as she did, though she assumed Kos had watered them when she put it off for too long.

Her new life was far from perfect, but it was close and more than she pictured her future could be. She held her breath, deep in her chest, afraid to let go; worried that if she looked too hard, it would vanish. For the first time in her life, she had something worth losing. And the thought of that nearly undid her every time.

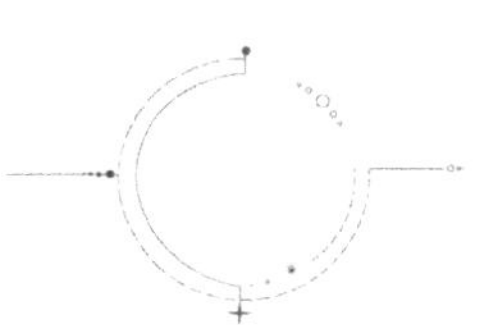

## 2

*K*os grunted and hissed as he yanked a spanner against a rusted bolt. It slipped from his hands, and with a clang, echoed through the garage. Sighing, he retrieved the tool and examined it. The jaw was chipped and misshapen from the force used to unsuccessfully pry the bolt loose. Frustrated, he took the busted instrument and laid a few heavy swings into the hull of the ship he was crouched under.

"I hope you don't treat all my ships like that," a man's voice called from behind him.

Pulling himself out from his cramped position, Kos looked behind him to see a tall, broad shouldered human man walking toward him. "Just the ones that don't cooperate, boss."

"Why don't you get Elio to loosen it for you?" The man leaned against the side of the ship, crossed his arms, and looked down at Kos. "That's what I bought these droids for. Put them to work and stop wasting my money."

Years of hard labor had caught up to Kos. It was made evident by his joints cracking as he stood. He had spent half his childhood on the streets followed by six years of military service, and another half dozen of marauding. He physically and mentally felt every minute of it.

"I like doing things myself, Jari," Kos said, rolling his neck a few times. "Just need a better angle and I'll get it out. What brings you down to the lowly hovels?"

Jari grinned and shrugged. "Closed a deal with some high paying clients a bit ago. They're up in procurement signing the docs. Fancy a trip off world? Shouldn't be more than a few weeks."

Kos tilted his head back. "I did that out of system job as a thank-you for the opportunity to work. Can't do anymore."

"You're the best pilot on my roster," Jari said. He waved his hand in the air. "I can't trust these plebes with a task like this. Hear me out, okay? There's an auction for decommissioned ships coming up this weekend in the far-side city. Take the job and I'll see what I can find for your old girl."

The offer caught Kos' attention. He chewed his bottom lip and cupped his hands around the edges of his sleeve while he thought. Parts for *Freya* were hard to come by. Her hull was pretty much intact, but most of her internal workings had been blown during the journey from Elendoras. A good portion of the aftermarket parts he put on had burned up or fallen off in the few days it took to get to safety. In the time they'd been on Buscoch, Kos had only managed to get his hands on basic scrap.

*Someone with Jari's connections and knowledge of classic ships could secure at least a few useful parts.* He weighed the decision.

"What's the cargo?" Kos asked.

"Couple tons of don't-ask-questions," Jari said with a twist of his mouth. "My job is to get the contracts, your job is to transport them. That's how this works."

"Where then? You have to give me something to work with."

"The Lyngor System." Jari sighed.

Kos bent down and pulled a rag from his work bag and wiped away the grease. The conversation was lasting longer than he was prepared for and his shift was almost over. "That's outside EC territory. Need clearances and licenses to go across borders. I'm not dealing with illegal cargo."

Jari let out a grunt and rolled his eyes. "It's not illegal. Humanitarian aid or something. There's a civil war brewing on a few of the outer rim planets and my clients are sending medical supplies. At least that's what we're putting on the docs. Happy? No licenses needed when you're carrying stuff like that."

"It's also why I need you on it," Jari continued, shifting his stance. "No one else has seen action and I need someone competent to get this done."

"Are they looking to set up a trade route?" Kos asked, thinking of ways Jari might try to wiggle more trips out of him. "Or is this a one and done type of thing?"

The man in the three-piece black suit avoided Kos' eyes. It was nice enough for someone who wanted to be taken seriously, but cheaply made. The jacket had been tailored to look custom, but the buttons pulled tight across his waist. Kos couldn't tell if it was poorly measured or if Jari had gained weight since getting the work done, but he knew many other men just like him. Those who put on the air of wealth because they believed it boosted their authority.

It was Kos' turn to sigh. He didn't want to get wrapped into anyone else's fight. But, he did need to parts for his ship. "I have to run it by Thia first."

"There you go!" Jari thrust off the hull and moved to slap Kos on the back, but stopped mid-swing and eyed the greasy jumpsuit. Instead, he shoved his hands into his pockets and rocked on his heels. "That ship of yours is one-of-a-kind. She deserves to be flown. I'd be more than happy to take her off your hands if you'd like. Be easier than watching her rust into oblivion while you drag your feet to get her fixed."

Jari paused for a moment and cocked his head to the side. When he spoke again, his words were a little drawn out in a pseudo singing tone. "Or, you can take the job and be that much closer to having her back."

Defeated, Kos tossed the rag back into the bag. Jari had been after *Freya* since Kos first approached him looking for work. He allowed Kos to keep her in the spare garage for a fee he gladly took out of Kos' pay each week. It was better than leaving her exposed to prying eyes and the near-constant rain, but he never quite felt like he got the fair cut of the deal. "Give me time to talk to Thia, okay? She's been through a lot in the last few months, and doesn't have anyone else on planet. I don't really want to leave her on her own if I can avoid it."

"Tell the missus that the offer's good until closing tomorrow," Jari said, already walking away from Kos toward the stairs leading up to his office. "You don't want to miss an opportunity like this."

Kos waited until Jari was behind closed doors before collecting his tools and packing up for the day. His hands moved on autopilot while he thought. *Freya, have I let you down? Will Thia understand how important this job is?*

His comm sat half-tucked into a side pocket and he wondered if he should call Orinthia to let her know he was heading home soon. Not their home, of course. Mimi was gracious enough to allow them to stay at hers while she was away. She insisted it was a favor to her as much as it was for them. But Kos didn't believe it for one minute. He knew her better and she wouldn't have turned them away. They were family and comrades, bearing the burdens of one another.

*If I get Freya fixed soon, we could have a home of our own,* Kos thought. He closed his work bag and carried it to the break room where he removed his coveralls and donned clean clothes. He pulled a long-sleeved shirt over his head and tucked it into a fresh pair of pants. They were relatively safe on Buscoch, but he took on the discomfort of humidity to keep his tattoos hidden. The less people knew about his or Orinthia's pasts, the better. Jari only knew as much as Kos felt necessary to secure the job in the first place. He left out the part of being a former marauder, having no official records on his name, and talked up his time spent with the Navy.

They were working on a new life together. One that didn't involve killing just to survive. One he and Orinthia could be proud of.

He smiled, losing a battle of will to call Orinthia. It would only be another half an hour before he was home with her again, after getting groceries for dinner and maybe another plant to add to her dwindling collection. But he wanted to hear her say his name, his favorite sound in the galaxy. Kos flipped the comm open and tried to connect with hers. His first try went unanswered.

So did the second.

A tingle built up in his spine. *Don't panic,* he told himself. *Everything's fine. No one is hurting her. She's fine. The comm is probably lost again. Be calm.*

It did little to keep his heart from racing. He couldn't help but think of Caytoo. Losing her there sent him into a spiral. Up until then, he hadn't realized how much he cared for her. How much she brightened his life and anchored him to something real. He'd regard leaving her behind as the worst decision he ever made.

*How am I going to leave her to go to Lyngor?* he thought. *I can't even handle when she doesn't answer her comm.*

Kos steadied himself and called her one more time. The light went green, signaling the connection.

"Thia?" Kos said, breath catching.

"Sorry," Orinthia said on the other end. Her voice was light and playful. "My comm was tucked under the bed. I could hear it but had no idea where it was. Glad you called again, because I found it."

A wave of relief washed over his senses, replaced by the crash of embarrassment. "You didn't answer, so I th—"

"Thought that I was kidnapped again?" Orinthia finished his sentence, softening her tone.

He didn't answer.

"We're safe here, Kos. No no one knows we're here, so you don't have to worry."

"You were supposed to be safe with Vandra, too."

Orinthia let out a puff of air that made the speakers sound like static. "Vandra was a hustler. We shouldn't have trusted her in the first place. That isn't the case here. Adora's in prison. Things are finally settling down for us. Enjoy it."

Kos did like what they had. He didn't always know if he was doing the right thing, or enough, but he cherished every moment with her. He promised all his love and was determined to give it to her.

"Did you need something? Or was it just a welfare check?" Orinthia asked, the playful tone returning to her words.

He realized he was stuck in his head and hadn't said anything for a few seconds. "No. Just wanted to let you know

I'm gonna stop at the market on the way home. Want anything?"

"Can you make something cool tonight? It's so humid and I think it would be refreshing."

"I'll see what I can stir up," Kos said. "See you in a bit. Love you."

"See you, soon" Orinthia said. The light dimmed and the call disconnected.

## 3

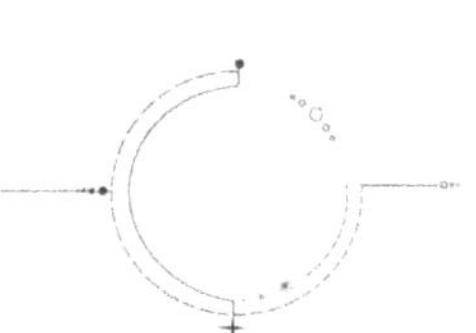

The kitchen smelled of fresh herbs and citrus as Kos put the finishing touches on dinner. Orinthia sat on the edge of the counter, swinging her feet while he worked. She liked watching him cook. It was domestic, something she never dreamed she could have or want. Her heart was warm and full.

Kos glanced over his shoulder at her. "What's that look for?"

"I like what we have here." Orinthia slid off the ledge and wrapped her arms around his waist, resting her cheek on his back, and soaking in the warmth radiating off him.

"So do I," Kos said, setting the knife down on the cutting board. He put his arms over hers. His voice was low when he spoke, like he was afraid if he spoke too loud, she would run away. "This can be our forever. Tell me what you want and I'll get it for you."

Orinthia's cheeks went hot and she thought for a moment. The idea of forever was huge. Nothing lasted that long, but she hoped this would. Her words came out rushed, spilling out the images of her heart. "I want a house of our own. Full of plants. Or a garden outside we can sit in the sun and watch life happen around us. Lots of pets, too. We can live in the middle of an open field, surrounded by green grass and clear skies for miles. Thrutt, Uri, and Mimi can visit sometimes, but it will be our home. No more shared spaces."

Kos turned in her arms and faced her, placing his lips to the top of her head. "How about a warm breakfast every morning?"

She took in a deep breath, calming her racing heart. Never had she allowed herself to dream that big. But with him, it was safe. "Maybe not every morning. That's too much of a commitment to wake up early. Weekends and special occasions."

Their bodies shook as Kos chuckled. "I can live with that."

Orinthia straightened herself to look at him better. She twisted her mouth and frowned. "We have to get *Freya* back first."

"I might have a way to do that," Kos said, running his hands down the sides of her arms. "Jari's offering to get me some parts for her."

Orinthia pulled away, keeping her hands on his hips, and squinted. "What's it going to cost you?"

"No credits. There's an auction this weekend and he's going to scope out some of the older ships."

Her mod was silent, but she did not need it to know he was hiding something. He kept eye contact without blinking and spoke like he rehearsed the lines for a while.

"Don't do that," Orinthia said. She dropped her hands to her side. "You're lying to me without lying. Jari doesn't do anything for free. What's the real cost?"

Kos rubbed the back of his neck. "He asked if I could take

a shipment off world for him. I won't be gone too long. A few weeks."

"All your shipments are off world. Why will this one have you gone so long?"

Buscoch was one of eight moons orbiting Kren. While the planet was uninhabited, the moons made up the Kren Collective. They shared resources between the other moons, importing and exporting goods. Kos' boss, Jari, owned shipping depots on three of the moons. His routes reached every surface in the collective, taking whatever contracts he could get.

"It's out of system," Kos said, a little less firm as before. He was testing her reaction. "But he's paying me and getting parts for *Freya*."

"Did he say he was paying you?" Jari had a habit of wording his deals in a way that made it sound good at first, but in reality, worked in his favor.

"Well, no. But it'll be during my regular work schedule, so I'm sure he will."

Orinthia shook her head and stepped back from Kos. "I don't like how he uses you. It's dirty."

"Am I not using him, too?" Kos asked. His voice pitched higher, not yelling, but close to desperation. "He has connections I don't. It's a good deal whichever way you look at it."

Silence hung in the air between them. His argument was valid. It was what he had to trade that was the issue. But how could she deny him in good conscience? Freya gave herself to save them. Orinthia lowered her gaze to his chest. "I'm sorry I broke her. She was your home. Your companion."

Kos' eyebrows pinched together. "What? You didn't. I know I've made a big deal about losing her, but *Freya's* damage isn't your fault in anyway. Ahto would never have stopped looking for us. Whether or not we fought him on Elendoras, the outcome would've been the same."

"We took her to find my father, Kos." The words caught in her throat.

"And you stopped Ahto from hurting anyone again." Kos reached for her hands but she took another step back.

*I killed him*, she thought. It did not sicken her like it used to. There was not much she remembered from the night they were on Elendoras. The memories usually came in flashes when she was too tired to focus on anything else, or in the form of nightmares. Mostly what she remembered was the pain that coursed through her body for what felt like hours, and Desidario skewered on Ahto's tail.

When she did let herself think about it, she did not dwell on the ethics of killing Ahto. He was an AI, manmade machine. Not born. Not human. Not alive. But he was living. He had thoughts, emotions, and memories.

Just like Uri.

That was usually where the train of thought ended. She did not like thinking about her brother not being her brother and what that meant in the grand scheme of things.

Kos opened his mouth, but was cut off by knocking at the door. He and Orinthia threw their attention at it. The sun had set over an hour before, and it was dark outside. They had not made friends on Buscoch and had no reason for more packages to be delivered at that time.

The knocking sounded again. Orinthia stepped out of Kos' way as he walked to the door, his hand hovering over his hip. He touched it, opening the compartment, and retrieved his golden blaster.

"Orinthia?" a muffled voice called from outside. "Orinthia Anton?"

"Get rid of them before someone hears," Orinthia said to Kos.

Kos turned the doorknob with his free hand and held the blaster at chest level. He cracked the door open and craned his head through the opening. Then he shouted, trying to slam the door shut again, "Thia, run!"

Orinthia's heart seized in her chest and her arms ran hot. She turned for the back door, but there was nowhere to go. They were too high up to land safely if she jumped off the balcony.

There was a thud behind her, and she looked in time to see the door smack Kos and knock him back. A Galoric forced himself inside, ducked out of the way of the blaster aimed at his head, and pushed up on Kos' arm.

Static pricked at Orinthia's body. A fire lit inside her chest and her vision tunneled. In one movement, she threw out her black blade and reached into the air in front of her with her normal hand. In her mind, she grabbed the intruder's shirt and yanked him toward her. Just as she imagined, it happened before her in reality.

With a yell, Orinthia cleared the distance to the edge of the kitchen where the man lay. She placed the tip of her blade against Kian's throat as he looked up at her.

His skin shifted to green and his eyes bulged.

Kos slammed the door shut and came around the other side of him, pointing the golden blaster at Kian's forehead.

"I'm here as a friend," Kian stuttered. "Friendly."

Orinthia's mod detected no lie, but she was not going to take a chance. "Are you here to arrest me?"

Kian shook his head.

"Answer out loud," Kos said through his teeth.

"No," Kian replied. His empty hands were open wide near his face.

Silence. She looked at Kos and nodded. He lowered his blaster but did not put it away. His eyes were fixed on the man, twitching with every move he made.

Orinthia took a step back and gave Kian room to get to his feet.

He rolled to his knees and stood, straightening out his civilian field jacket. His arms dropped awkwardly to his side and he looked between the two humans before him.

"How did you find me?" Orinthia asked, recalling her blade. She trusted him well enough, but even if he made a move, Kos would be the quicker draw. Her arms were weak from the effort of dragging a grown alien man through the air, but she held herself steady.

"Uri told me," Kian said, flexing his fingers as he fidgeted.

Orinthia's heart jumped into her throat at the sound of her brother's name. "Why? Why would he give up that information? Is he in trouble?"

Kian shrunk a little at her rapid fire questions. "He's fine. We have him in protective custody."

Another jolt through her system. "Protective custody? So he is in trouble. With who?"

Kian reached into the pocket of his canvas jacket.

Kos lifted the blaster again and held it an inch from Kian's face.

"Just look," Kian said in a strangled voice. He pulled out a holopad and activated it. The twin's images appeared in the air, rotating mugshots. "Adoracion and Arsenio escaped prison."

A breathy laugh passed through Orinthia's mouth. Her head was heavy, and she fought through the fatigue.

"Then, why are you here?" Kos asked. "Warning us?"

Kian eyed the blaster, no doubt choosing his words carefully. "I need her help."

A hot poker jabbed Orinthia in the base of her neck. Her head spun for a moment and she tried to keep standing. "What do you need my help for? They've been in your custody for weeks."

"Give me a minute, okay?" Kian swallowed hard and replaced the holopad in his pocket. "I had this all worked out, then you ambushed me." He took a few deep breaths and spoke in a tone that indicated he had indeed rehearsed the speech before.

"They were on transfer to a hearing," Kian began. "Like you, they had help escaping. There are still many Hunters loyal to them. We had sixteen Hunters guarding the convoy. Half of them turned on the other eight, killing them. Some you knew."

"How come I haven't heard about it?" Orinthia's mind was running at a slower pace, her words felt far away from her ears. "There's been nothing on the social nets. Not even Mimi has said anything."

"The EC's trying to keep this as quiet as possible. You've caused a lot of issues for them. Now the two heads of the GMH are dirty and on the run. Everything they've touched is under fire. It could shatter the entire legal system, and all the marauders we've put away will go free. This is bigger than just a blemish on the EC's face. The rule of law is at risk. I need your help to get them back."

"Why me?" Orinthia asked.

"Can you call off your guard dog?" Kian asked, barely keeping the panic out of his voice. "I'm about to go into convulsions."

Orinthia nudged her chin at Kos. He lowered his weapon but kept a shadowed eye on Kian.

Kian swallowed hard. "You three have been at war for as long as I can remember, and probably way before that. No one knows them better than you. No one cares about this as much as I do."

The words landed soft against her mind. She took a moment to inspect Kian. Though he was not in his GMH uniform, she put the pieces together and guessed why he was coming to her personally. "You've been promoted."

Kian's skin changed hues and his eyes darted to the side. "Commissioner."

"I see. So that's really it. Your new job's on the line, isn't it?"

"Yes, but that's besides the point." Kian locked his focus on Orinthia's face. "Adora is a danger. She's already amassed a small army. For what, I don't know, but I can guess. And it isn't just former Hunters, but marauders and mercenaries."

"I'm not her keeper," Orinthia said, shaking her head. "They're your problem. We have a quiet life here, far from where Adora can get to us. Send Uri back here and we'll keep him safe."

"When you were in that cell, I believed you when no one else did. I didn't have to help you then, but it was the right thing to do."

Orinthia's chest ached from the thought. The wounds were healed, but the memory had not faded. She chewed the inside of her cheek.

"Please, I'm coming to you as a friend." Kian lowered his voice. "Yes, my position is in jeopardy, but so is the security of the EC. The twins have already recruited or killed almost everyone I've sent after them. The EC is giving me one last chance to capture them before they combine the GMH with the rest of the military and go after Adora themselves. I believe in the good the Hunters have done and continue to do.

We've made mistakes, but that's what I want to fix. Unless they're back in prison, I won't get the chance."

Kos spoke up for the first time. "The EC doesn't know you're here, do they?"

Kian shook his head, glancing at Kos. "I have a team in orbit, though. They're keeping watch in case Adora caught wind of me trying to recruit Orinthia."

A crack of thunder shook the apartment. Heavy drops of rain hit the walls.

Orinthia looked at Kos, who cocked an eyebrow. His brown eyes were shadowed and mouth clenched tight.

"I want a full pardon," Orinthia said, setting her focus back on Kian.

The color drained from Kian's skin, leaving him a dark grey.

"If I agree to go after them, my payment is my freedom."

# 4

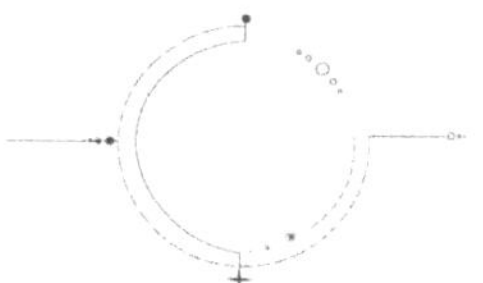

Kos paced from one end of the living room to the other, running his hands through his hair and shoving them in his pockets on a loop.

Orinthia sat on the couch and watched him. Her knees were tucked against her chest and her arms wrapped around her legs. Neither of them had said said anything since Kian left. The rain came in waves, going from downpours to drizzles for an hour.

*We were so close to getting a normal life,* Kos thought. *It was all right there. And now, because the EC can't do their job and keep prisoners locked up, it's all gone. They can't have her. I won't let them.*

The room slipped away in splinters, moments folding into each other, and darkened around him. His heart pounded like a fist against his chest. Each shaky and shallow breath sent him deeper into the void. He fought against it, clawing his way through his mind, trying to hold onto reality. It was a losing battle, like every time he blacked out. The world was gone, and he was left in chilling emptiness.

Hollow faces and burning worlds flashed across his mind.

People he would never see again, others he hoped he could forget. He could hear the voices of men and women he served with, mixed in the cries of lives he cut short. He could feel the icy fingers of fear tug at his nerves.

Duty.

Betrayal.

Death.

His body, used as a weapon and wielded by the Earth Confederate. Claiming systems in the name of peace. Killing all in his path, enemy and civilian alike. Hot hatred rolled through his body. Hatred for the EC. For Mod Bleyers. For himself.

A soft hand touched his face. Cool and gentle, it pulled him back from his waking nightmare. Fresh air filled his nostrils as he took deep breaths like coming out of a frozen pool of water.

"There you are," Orinthia said in a hushed, almost reverent tone. She stroked pieces of hair from his eyes, brushing light fingers against his cheeks.

He stood in the living room again, pastel pink walls surrounding him. The smell of rain wafted through an open window and melodic thunder rumbled in the distance. Kos was home. He was safe.

"I wish I knew where you went," Orinthia said, removing her hand from his face and taking him by the arm. She led him to the couch and sat him beside her.

"It's not a place for you," Kos said, forcing himself to breathe normal.

Orinthia frowned and looked away. "Sorry, I didn't mean to pry."

Kos laid his head on the back of the couch and listened to the tinking of rain against the balcony floor.

"I don't care about your secrets," Orinthia added, taking his hand and sandwiching it in between hers, stroking the back of it with her thumb. "You can have those. But if I could help you stay out of the darkness, keep you here with me, I would."

"You can't," Kos said. His mind was still in a haze and the ghosts lingered outside his vision.

Her hand twitched in his.

Kos sighed and cursed himself for being short with her. "What I mean is neither can I. But having you here to guide me back is better than going through it alone. There's no stopping it, but this does help."

Orinthia took her hand from the top of his and set it on the side of his head, pulling him to rest in her lap.

Kos stared toward the kitchen, but didn't focus on anything. His mind was still recovering from the whiplash it had received. They happened less often in his peaceful new life, but more than he liked.

Before Orinthia came crashing into his life, Thrutt used to stay with him during his episodes. He sat quietly and waited, making sure Kos didn't hurt himself while he was being tormented by his mind. Then, he'd give Kos his space while he came down from it. It had been the two of them for more than half of Kos' life. The giant's absence was felt in more than just the space he took up in a room.

"I'm sorry all this is happening," Orinthia murmured, caressing his hair and pressing her fingertips against his scalp. "I'm sorry my family upturned your life. First in meeting me, then Uri's injury and having to find my dad, and now the twins."

Kos rocked his head against her leg. "I know you feel like everything's your fault all the time because that's what you've been told for so long. But you didn't directly do anything wrong. Your family is just the worst and that's bound to spill over into the rest of the galaxy."

She let out a puff of air from her nose and chuckled. "They really are the worst. Well, except Uri." Orinthia paused. The lightness to her touch faded and her hand rested on the top of his head. "I think I have to do this, Kos."

"You don't. Let the GMH and EC figure it out. There's no need for you to fight their battles for them."

"It's the only way I can be free. And not just legally. But free of the twins. They've haunted me my whole life. I finally have a chance to be rid of them and I'm going to take it."

Kos sat up and faced her, tucking his knee against him on the couch. "We can be free now. We are free. If we asked her to, I'm sure Mimi could get us new identities. As soon as *Freya* is fixed, we can go anywhere. That was the plan. Why change it?"

"Because I want to be me," Orinthia said, looking at her hands where his head had been. "It's taken a long time to become this person. I can't switch into someone else. You fell in love with me." She emphasized the last word with a touch to her chest.

He grabbed her hand and held it close to his face. "And I will always be in love with you. A new name won't change that. But Adora almost killed you last time. We can stay here for a while longer. *Freya* is my top priority, then I'll take you anywhere you want to go. Far beyond the reaches of the EC and the twins. We both deserve to start over. To be together. I can call you whatever you'd like, just don't go."

Orinthia blinked hard. A tear rolled down her cheek. "I have to do this. But you're not hearing what I'm saying. This won't end with them in prison. They've escaped once. Adora is too dangerous."

The rain no longer ticked against the walls. A heavy

silence swallowed the room. Kos didn't want to believe what she insinuated. That wasn't like her. And it wasn't the path he wanted her to go down.

*I have to take her away,* Kos thought. *This isn't her life.*

"I'm doing this for us," Orinthia continued. She lifted her head but didn't meet his gaze. "We'll always watch over our shoulders, waiting for her to take this away from us. I have to kill her. For my freedom. To know we're safe and happy. I love you, Kos. And I love the life we have. She can't have it."

Her words smacked him in the chest. It was the first time she'd said she loved him. The sound was bittersweet. *How can I tell her not to do this out of love, when I would do the same thing for her?*

"I want quiet nights after work," Orinthia said, perhaps unaware she'd said the words that came so naturally for Kos, "listening to nocturnal sounds through the open window. Planning our weekends and having no worries of what's going to happen next."

"We have that now," Kos said, swallowing hard. He was mixed with joy and desperation. "Isn't that what we're doing right now?"

Orinthia shook her head. "I have worries. Kian came here. He found me. If he had arrested me, or worse… I have no peace. And him coming here only confirms what I've been afraid of. Adora and Arsenio have taken everything from me. Don't I deserve to be free of them?"

"And you're going to do that on your own?"

"I never wanted any of this, Kos." Orinthia's voice shook. She yanked her hand back to herself. "When I left that stupid planet, all I was looking for was an escape and to make some credits. This was not part of the plan. There was no plan. Not once did I picture myself with you. If I could go back in time, I would stop myself from getting on that ship."

For the fist time in almost a decade, Kos felt a chill roll through his body. His breath hitched, caught between a gasp and a whimper. "Do you regret this?"

"Of course not." Orinthia put her head in her hands. "That's why I would rewrite time, so I wouldn't know how good life could be. There are so many parts of my life that are in danger. I've never had people to care about or who cared about me. Losing any of this will kill me. So since I can't change the past, I need to protect the present. But it has to be on my terms."

Kos reached across the couch and pulled her to him, locking his arms around her. "Can you really do this? You think you can kill your sister?"

"I hope so," she whispered. "I don't see any other way."

"And Arsenio?"

"She has the bit in his mouth, but that doesn't make him any less guilty of what they've both done."

"How long have you thought about this?" Kos took her long silver hair and bunched it over one of her shoulders, trying to give her comfort. "This can't be a decision made in the time since Kian's been here. And what about the consequences of killing them? Not just morally, but legally?"

"If it's a justified kill, no one can question it, right? They don't have to know it was planned. As long as it looks clean, it is clean as far as the GMH is concerned."

"Can you hear what you're saying? Do you think killing is easy?" He pushed, desperate to shake her loose from the spiral tightening around her.

"I've done it before," Orinthia said. Her voice choked.

His words came out fast, too fast, as if speed could undo the weight of them. "That wasn't the same. Those were all in defense. This is premeditated. That takes you down a path there's no coming back from."

She didn't move. "Ahto wasn't in defense. I killed him out of anger."

Kos gripped her tight, afraid if he let go she'd run away and follow through with her plan right then and there. "He had just killed your father." His voice dropped, almost a whisper. "He was going to kill me. That's defense enough for me."

But the words didn't sit right. They echoed hollow in his chest. Because in that moment, he hadn't been fighting. He hadn't been standing. He'd been unconscious. Vulnerable.

And she'd made the choice.

His chest tightened. She had done it before then, too. Before Ahto. "And Neve," he whispered. A weight settled in his stomach. "That was in my defense, too."

Two bodies. Two kills. Both for him. She carried what he could not. And she had done it alone.

"And now I have to do this for me. Adora will never stop hunting me. I'll always look over my shoulder expecting to see her. There'll be no peace unless she's dead."

Kos' breath hitched. The knot in his stomached twisted to where he could almost not breathe.

"And what will I do while you're gone?" Kos asked, his voice shaking. "Worry alone in this tiny house, not knowing if you're coming home or not. How can I save you if we're so far apart?"

"Kos, I don't always need saving." Orinthia tried to push away from him, but he held firm. "I can take care of myself. You saw what I did to Kian. My mod is getting easier to control."

That broke him. He let her go, but gripped her forearms, not in restraint or anger, but to ground her. To let her know this mattered more than anything he had said before. "And that's another thing. I wish you wouldn't use it anymore."

"I can control it, Kos. I've been practicing."

His heart jumped like it wanted out of his chest. The room around him darkened, but he fought to stay in the moment.

*No. Not now. Not with her like this.*

His hands shook and he let go of Orinthia, worried he'd grip too hard and hurt her. "You said you weren't going to use it when you were alone. Why have you hid this from me?"

"Because look at you right now." She tossed a hand in his direction. "I knew you'd be upset."

"Why, Thia?" Kos got to his feet and flared his fingers at his side. "Why can't you just listen to me for once?" His voice cracked, louder as he fought to keep the calm he was losing hold of. "I'm trying to protect you."

Orinthia stood, too, and pushed her shoulders back. Her voice raised in volume. Not in a yell, but to be heard. "The only time I have peace inside me is when I use it. You don't know what it's like to have these mods. My head is never quiet as it is. Now neither is my body." She touched her chest, then her arms. "I can feel the world spinning around me, and every atom is pressed against my skin. It's like I'm trapped in a bottle someone shook too hard. If I don't learn to control it, then it will control me. And I won't let anyone control me ever again."

The tension snapped as realization settled on Kos like the walls toppled on top of him. It wasn't about her mod or him.

He relaxed his muscles and stepped forward, touching under her chin and making her look at him.

She softened but didn't meet his eyes. "If I can master this mod," she said quietly, "then no one can hurt me, or you, or anyone we love ever again."

"Be careful," Kos said, surrendering but heartbroken. "If you won't listen to anything else, listen to that."

"I will. You have to trust me, now."

5

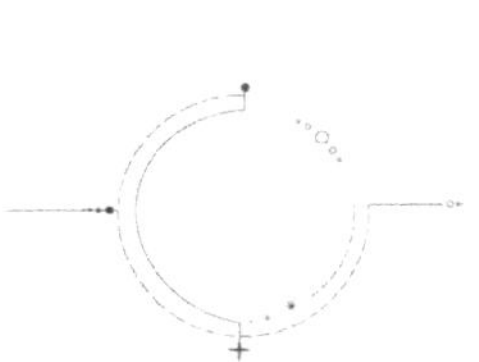

*I*t took half an hour of arguing for Orinthia to agree not to make any decisions before the morning. Another hour passed before he managed to get her into bed and sleep. Kos, however, stayed awake.

He sat in his room across the hall and watched her. She changed so much from when they first met. No longer was she the angry, bitter woman standing toe-to-toe with him on the decks of a marauder ship. Sure, she still had a temper and lacked anything resembling a normal amount of self-control, but that was what made her who she was. Orinthia was different in other ways. She showed selflessness, and it scared Kos more than anything he could've imagined.

He couldn't think of the words to talk her out of leaving with Kian, but there was one person in the galaxy who might be able to do it. Unfortunately, Thrutt was several systems away, farther than a regular comm could reach. Kos' only option was to use the long range link on *Freya*.

The idea of leaving Orinthia alone made his skin itch, but he didn't have a choice. She was going to find Kian in the morning and agree to go with him. There were no other options but to hurry as fast as he could.

Kos walked through the wet, mid-night streets until he found a cab to take him to the spaceport.

He hadn't been aboard *Freya* since Jari had her moved to his hangar. Sometimes, after work, Kos took a lap around the ship itself and looked for things he could patch up with the scrap he managed to find. But the courage to face Freya properly evaded him. With as much time as they'd been on Buscoch, he regretted waiting so long.

Using the manual lever in the panel on her hull, he disengaged the lock and lowered the ramp. The doors hissed open and dry air flowed out. Kos' steps made a dull echo through the hold as he entered. It was dark and he activated his visor to see better. Though he could have walked with his eyes closed, it was safer and quicker with a clear vision.

Kos climbed below deck and stopped at the foot of the ladder, his feet settling into the dent at the base. A familiar sensation set on his body. Like an overly worn coat, he felt comforted to be there again. He looked at the quiet galley where he'd eaten hundreds of meals.

The doors to the crew quarters were open, too. Uri's makeshift restraints were still on the floor beside the bed, where they'd been since Elendoras.

Everything of importance in either cabin had been removed before putting the ship in storage. He did not bother looking in his room, but instead went to the cockpit.

To save as much of Freya as possible, Kos had shut down all the systems. Her AI was still fully intact when they landed, from what he could tell before the computers malfunctioned. But the ship was in complete ruin. Kos bent down and activated the control panel. One by one, the lights came to life on the console. He opted to keep Freya in stasis for a little longer, unsure if the power could run communications and her at the same time.

It'd been a long time since Kos had to hail a ship on his own. He thought through the steps one-by-one, but Freya's assistance would've been appreciated. The windscreen lit up as it waited to connect with Mimi's ship, the *Yama*. It was a solid three minutes before anyone answered. A pinch of guilt built in his back for interrupting whatever they had going on on their end, but it was not a call that could wait for a better time.

A pink haired woman peered at him with one eye open. The other was behind the blanket that half covered the rest of her face. "Rogue? What are you doing calling this late?"

"Sorry, Mimi," Kos answered, pulling at his sleeve. "I didn't know what time you'd be in right now."

"Yeah, whatever," Mimi said, rubbing her eyes to open both. "Are you in trouble? Did you get *Freya* working?"

"Not exactly." Kos sat in his captain's chair. He rubbed his beard then clasped his hands together. "I'm using auxiliary power. But, that's not why I called. I was hoping to speak to Thrutt."

"Oh, good. I'll get him on my way back to bed. Tell him to shut the thing off when he's done."

"Good seeing you again, Mimi," Kos said.

Mimi waved her hand as she walked away. She mumbled to herself, but Kos caught most of it. "Haven't talked to him in six years, and all of a sudden he's calling all the time."

Kos grinned as he waited for his friend to join. It was a strange feeling on his face, knowing what he was about to tell Thrutt. The situation couldn't have been farther from smile-worthy. He cleared his throat and leaned back in his seat. Kos didn't know how to tell Thrutt he wished he hadn't left. How much he missed him. For the better and worst part of twenty years, Thrutt was always there beside him. Thrutt was more than his friend. He was his brother, uncle, and father all at once. This was the longest they'd been separated since Thrutt took in Kos and his aunt. Even during the war, they served on the same ships, only apart during specific missions. It was strange not to have his looming, overbearing, wise companion close by.

*You no longer need me to watch over you,* Kos remembered Thrutt saying when he agreed to go with Mimi. *I've stayed with you to make sure you were safe and never alone. But you're not alone anymore. You and Thia can take care of each other. This part of your life doesn't have enough room for an old boulder. And that's okay.*

It didn't take long before Thrutt's giant face appeared on the screen, pushing the ache from Kos' chest. "Rogue, my boy. I've missed you."

"Heya, Thrutt." Kos gave a spread-finger wave. He couldn't help but smile again. His mind eased seeing Thrutt. There was never a problem that Thrutt couldn't solve and Kos knew he would have the answer to this one. "How's bounty hunting?"

"Not too bad, actually," Thrutt said with a wide grin. "Doesn't hurt that most people are shocked to see a boulder chasing after them." He gave a booming laugh that would've shaken Kos' core if they were together. "Racking up good credits while also having fun. It's a great time."

Thrutt placed his hands on his hips and nodded a few times. "Anyway, I don't think you called just to pass the time. What's going on? Has something happened?"

"Nothing too serious, at least not yet," Kos said. He retold the entire story of what happened that day. Everything from Jari's offer of parts and the job he'd have to do to get them, to

Kian's news and offer to Orinthia and what she planned to do if she went with him.

"When does she leave?" Thrutt asked when Kos was done.

"She's not leaving," Kos said. "I'm not going to let her."

Thrutt chuckled. "When have you ever been able to control her?"

Kos briefly ran through their time together. From the moment they met in the NCR, to their time on the *Fera,* and even facing her father and getting a new mod he didn't want her to have. Very rarely had she obeyed what he told her.

Thrutt made a clicking noise with his mouth. "You should let her go."

Kos scooted to the edge of his seat, his hands balled in his lap. "What? No. No way is she going with them alone."

"Take a breath and listen to me," Thrutt said. There was a long pause. He tapped his lips together and they made a tinking sound. When he spoke again, his face was more serious than Kos had seen in a long time. It was the face of Kos' childhood, when he was about to teach him a life lesson. Kos braced for what was to follow.

"You called me for advice," Thrutt started. "The GMH isn't going to let you go with them. No matter which way you try and spin things, you're a marauder. And not just any marauder, but the quartermaster of the *Fera.*"

"They can't prove that," Kos said. "We were never caught. And Thia is the one who was convicted of marauding. Doesn't that put her in a worse position to work with them?"

Thrutt put up a hand. "It won't matter, they still know who you are. But it remains that they're offering to clear Thia's charges. At least for now, she's not in any danger with them. And, she's a former Hunter. She knows how they work. You will be too much of a liability."

Kos narrowed his eyes. He had never heard such terrible reasoning coming from Thrutt before. "You expect me to sit around waiting for her to come back with no idea of what's going on?"

"I didn't say that." Thrutt shook his head and took a moment to sort out the next thought. "We'll follow her. Mimi can lend me a ship and I'll come for you. It'll take a few days to get back, but I'll leave as soon as I can. There are a lot of things to figure out in the meantime, but if it's true that Adora's building her own army, then Thia is going to need one, too. We can give that to her. The GMH has rules and protocols to follow. We don't."

"If you're coming back, then why can't we just take Thia away from all of this?"

"She's already told you why. This is her last stand against her sister. I'm not happy with it either, but I understand what she needs to do. You would, too, if you looked at it from the outside."

"This is insane," Kos said. He was on his feet, leaning forward on the console with his head hung low. The hope of Thrutt fixing his problem faded into stardust. "Why does it have to be like this? Why couldn't we just have a normal life?"

"Is Thia a normal woman? Are you normal, for that matter? What life is worth living if Thia isn't in it?"

"She needs you now more than ever," Thrutt added. "This's what you signed on for when you chose her. She's not easy to handle. Nothing worth having is. We can protect her. This is something only we can do for her. Not the GMH and not the EC. Us. We have the friends and allies to give her."

Kos closed his eyes and thought about what Thrutt said. "I don't want another war."

"War is here whether you want it or not," Thrutt said.

"You and I have the chance to fight it on our terms and for our girl. I swear I'm going to do whatever I can to keep you both safe."

A weight that felt like someone stepping on him filled his chest. Kos looked around the dark ship, taking in the details. "I thought there'd be more time to get her fixed. Now I'm going to have to leave it behind."

"We were never destined for regular lives," Thrutt said. "I'm sorry, my boy."

Kos lifted his head and twitched his mouth in acknowledgement, but didn't say anything back.

"I'll tell Mimi I'm leaving. It shouldn't be more than —" Thrutt leaned over and looked at something off screen. "— three days before I can get there. Just hang tight. I'll see you soon, bud."

The screen went black and Kos looked around his empty cockpit again. Like Thrutt, Freya was his constant companion. Her walls were his sanctuary when on the *Fera*. Leaving her hurt almost as much as the thought of losing Orinthia. But, there was a way he could save part of her in case Jari had any ideas of his own while Kos was away.

He typed something on the console and a panel slid open. Kos leaned farther over and reached into the compartment they used to store extra equipment. He retrieved a data disk and placed it on the open panel. Lights flashed in a pattern around the console until a steady blue light blinked on both the center of the dash and the data disk.

"Freya, can you hear me?" Kos asked.

There was no answer.

Kos stood, typed a few more lines of code, and waited. "Freya?"

"Yes captain?" A silvery voice called from around the room. "Where have you been?"

Kos let out a sigh. "I've been away, old friend. But it's time you come with me."

"You've found a better ship for me to live in?" There was an artificial hope to her voice.

"There's no new ship," Kos said. "I'm going to store you in the data disk until I can repair this one."

"Captain, you can't be serious." The hope was gone. "This ship was already too small for me. When you found me, I was the flagship in a fleet of battleships. And now I'm going to have to compress down into a data disk?"

"I don't like it either," Kos said. "But it's to keep you safe. There's a man I work for who would love to have the ship for his own. I have to go away for a while and can't risk him taking you, too."

There was a pause. "It's dark when I'm in stasis. I'm not frightened, but I also don't like it."

Kos' stomach turned and he pinched his eyes closed. He recalled Orinthia asking if *Freya* dreamed. At the time, he didn't have an answer. "Freya, do you ever dream?"

Another long pause followed his question. Longer than Kos expected. He opened his eyes and looked at the lights on the data disk. She had not downloaded herself yet.

"I don't know what a dream is," she responded. "There are no emotions, not like you'd have them. Nor feeling. But I'm floating through a void when in stasis. There's no input nor output. Nothing. My code hits the edge of the void and without external connections, it is as if I don't exist. It's like being whipped around by a current and not moving all at once. Loud and quiet. Is that what it is like when you're sleeping?"

The ache in Kos' stomach grew. "Sometimes, yes." He took a few deep breaths. "I'm sorry, Freya. It'll only be for a while, I promise. Once we get back, I'll repair your ship and we can be in open space again."

"I need a bigger ship," Freya said. "My code is limited with this one. It doesn't have to be a warship. But something I can roam freely through. I never liked this one. I'm confined to the cockpit. Give me space, please."

"I'll see what I can do," Kos said. "Ships like that are no longer in my power to get. We're not in the marauding business anymore. I can't just commandeer ships like we used to."

"Give me more to work with. That's all I ask. My abilities are squandered." She paused. "Be safe, captain. Whatever it is you're doing out there."

The data disk lit up in a flurry of flashes. When it was done, the console lights dimmed. Kos retrieved the disk and placed it in his pocket. He somberly smiled to himself and patted the disk. "Sweet dreams."

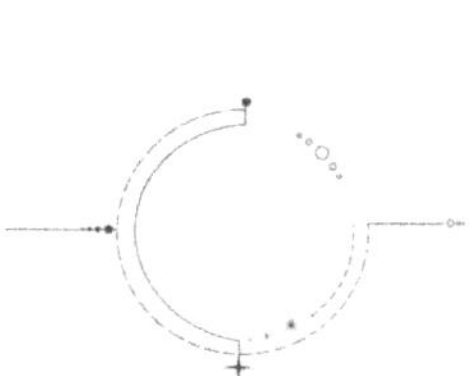

# 6

Faint morning sunlight illuminated the bedroom, casting light on a half-packed bag on the foot of the bed. Orinthia glanced across the hall to Kos' quiet room. She heard him leave in the middle of the night, but fell back to sleep before he came home. He had not stirred when she got up to shower and throw whatever she could find into a pack to take with her. The last time she ran away, she was sorely under-prepared and was determined to not let that happen again.

As if summoned, Kos stepped out of his room and leaned against his doorway with his arms crossed. "You weren't planning on leaving without saying goodbye, were you?"

"I wasn't, but I also didn't realize you were home," Orinthia lied, shoving the last pair of socks into her pack. She had sensed him across the hall, knew his frequency like her own skin. But she was not about to tell *him* that. "Where did you go?"

Kos kicked out his leg and stood straight, clearing the corridor in two strides. Tattoos ran the length of his thick arms, fully exposed and stretched tight as he moved. Though

Kos tried to leave that life behind, he still looked every bit a marauder. "I went to get Thrutt's opinion on things. There's no talking you out of doing this, is there?"

Orinthia swallowed hard and lowered her gaze. "No, I have to go."

"Okay," Kos said, settling beside her. He stood close but did not touch. "Then we're going, too."

His statement hit Orinthia like a punch to the ribs. It took effort not to burst into hysterical laughter. "You're going to try to stowaway on a GMH ship?"

"Well, no," Kos said. "But we won't be far behind. Thrutt's going to get me and we'll be wherever you need us."

"What about *Freya*?" Orinthia asked, cocking her hip.

"The ship can be replaced. I'm going to go by today and pay Jari to keep her safe until I come back. Whether he does or not can't be helped at this point. This is what I choose to do." He inched closer and ran the back of his fingers down her arms. "You could've asked me at any moment and I would've sold *Freya* and bought us another way out of here."

Orinthia pinched her eyebrows together and looked him in the eye. "There are some things I couldn't ask you to give up for me."

"You're the best part of my life, Thia. I'd give it all up for you. I just wish you didn't have to go."

"We can't have our wishes. If we could, I'd wish a hundred times for Adora to be back in prison and *Freya* to be fixed. I'd wish for your episodes to go away. But we can't *will* these things into place. They are what they are and we have to face them as they come."

"That's more or less what Thrutt said, too." Kos smirked and let his hands rest near hers. "You're more like him than I realized."

Orinthia let out a humorless chuckle, but it did not reach

her heart. She ran through the events of the previous year. Her life turned upside down, pulled apart, and stretched thin like falling into a black hole. She had been forced to duel for her life, shot, poisoned by a sadistic sequencer, kidnapped, imprisoned, and parts of her DNA were rewritten.

"Kos," Orinthia whispered his name and turned her face from him. She put her arms around his middle and held onto the last bit of him that she could. "This hurts. I'm scared, so let's not pretend like things are okay. I don't want to go. I don't want to fight anymore. But I have to. Please, understand that."

"I'm going to fight for you," Kos said back, holding her tight. "You're not going to be alone for long, I promise. If I could go with you, I would. But there's no point in poking the GMH when they're already on edge. Everything's going to work out, just give me time. If I thought you'd fail, I would've taken you away. But you're right. She'd find us. I don't fully understand this rivalry, but I know she won't give up."

Orinthia took in a shuddering breath, like the weight of the galaxy filled her very bones. "I love you, Kos. I'm sorry I didn't say it sooner, and now we're going to be apart. But I do love you, more than I ever thought I could love anyone."

Kos took her chin and kissed her, holding her as close as he could without hurting her. His mouth burned her skin. "I'd die for those words," he said once they parted again, resting his forehead to hers.

"Just live for them," Orinthia said. Her heart raced. She was terrified and full of love, anxious and grounded all at once. It was hard to hold onto reality. A second longer in their kiss and she would have let him take her away, unable to leave him ever again.

"Nothing in this galaxy or any other matters more than

you," she whispered. "Adora is fighting for herself, but this, right here, is my purpose. I have so much more to lose."

—❊  ❊—

THEY SPENT their last hour together eating a breakfast Kos insisted on cooking. It was the final gift he could give her until they were reunited. Orinthia knew their lives were going to be changed again, no matter the outcome. She would come home a killer or not come home at all. It was hard to keep the panic out of her chest, but she focused on the present as long as she could.

When they were finished, Kos carried her bags to the street and hailed a cab for them. They held hands in silence until the hover car stopped at the entrance of the dock. Orinthia stepped out first, holding her spacer's helmet under an arm and looked around.

Storage and commercial buildings surrounded the port. Kos worked for one of the ten shipping companies that ran cargo throughout the Collective. Non-commercial hangars filled the open spaces in-between buildings, owned by hobby sailors and day-trippers. Though Kren was uninhabited by sentient beings, it did have plentiful wildlife. The planet was home to many creatures that had become delicacies in the system. Buscoch was the smallest of the moons and did not see many sportsman, but they were common enough it had a growing tourist community.

Hobby crafts and sports vessels lined the bays, sailors and their captains readied the ships for another day's work. Aside from them, the two ships closest to the entrance were a Kren Collective transport ferry, and a cargo freighter delivering goods from the system's central market. At the far end, in Docking Bay Six, sat the worst-built ship Orinthia had ever seen. It was dull grey in the overcast light. Dark burn marks and dents marred the hull, making it look like it had hit every piece of debris it could find.

"There's Kian," Orinthia said, pointing in the direction of the trashed ship. As she and Kos neared, she read a faded name near the tail. *Tertion.*

The Galoric stood out in his crisp black and teal GMH uniform beside such a degraded hunk of machinery. He tucked his arms behind him and held his chest out. "I didn't think you'd come," he said, as they approached.

Orinthia thought about the first time she met Kos, in the NCR port beside *Freya.* Thrutt had told her the same thing. This time, her answer was different. She put on a brave face and lifted her chin. From that moment forward, she had to keep her fears and worries locked away. No one would be on her side once she stepped aboard. "A chance to clear my name? I wouldn't miss it."

"And you?" Kian asked Kos, eying the luggage in his hands.

"Seeing her off," Kos answered. "And to make sure you're going to keep her safe."

Tourists trickled into the port behind the group. Some wandered around, examining the various ships, laughing and talking loudly. Passengers passed their travel kits off to service droids who loaded them onto the ferry. Transport pilots set off on their voyages, one-by-one, to avoid the congestion of the travelers. The clouds moved in over the sun, casting a haze over the ground.

Kian rotated his shoulders. "Oh, I'm not going with her. Things are shifting too rapidly for me to be away from the NCR that long. I'm risking a lot just being here. She'll be working with the best the GMH has to offer, though. Messies."

Orinthia gave the ship a closer examination. It did not look like a typical GMH ship. Most of their vessels were military surplus with some custom makes. None of them were as decrepit as the one before her.

"What are Messies?" Kos asked, leaning closer to Orinthia so only she could hear.

"They are the best of the best," she whispered back. "Their official title is the Marauder Hunter Elite Squad, but they're known for the dramatics. You only call in the Messies when whatever you're fighting needs to be turned to ash."

"Have you worked with them before?"

Orinthia shook her head and glanced at Kian, who checked his watch every few seconds. "There was no way someone like me would have ever been near them when I was a Hunter. I was a mess but in different ways."

Kos ran his tongue over his teeth and nodded. He pulled himself straight and they both faced Kian again.

"Ready?" Kian asked, raising his eyebrows.

A voice in the back of her mind told her to stop, to walk away and ask Kos to run with her. That Adora was not worth the fight, not worth losing herself over. And, maybe Kos was right. Maybe she would not be able to come back from the path she put herself on.

She breathed the voice away, clamping shut the flutters in her chest. The life she wanted with Kos, that was worth fighting for. She would hold onto herself for as long as she could. But she had to go. It had to end.

"Yes." The word carried all the weight she could manage. It was not just a signal to Kian, but a vow to herself. She was ready to face the brewing storm, to leap feet-first into whatever came next.

Kian pounded on the hull of the ship.

A small group of white and teal uniformed Hunters emerged onto the ramp and stepped down to file behind Kian. They each stood with their arms crossed behind their backs and stared above Kos and Orinthia's heads.

In a formal pace, Kian stepped aside, waving a hand in front of the crew, and spoke to Orinthia and Kos. "This is Op Cell 9."

The three officers clicked their heels in unison.

"Grenadier Cliff Ward," Kian said.

The tallest man at the front of the line gave a curt nod. His hair was shaved to the scalp and left iris was a pale green, ghostly in contrast to his vibrant colored eye. White scars stretched from the corner of his pale eye up through his hair-line, almost matching the wounds on the ship behind him.

"Comms and Intelligence Specialist, Annatilla Dai." Kian continued down the line.

A woman about as tall as Orinthia smiled at them. She wore a full spacesuit with her helmet sealed over her face in the Messies' white and teal colors. There was a bubbly expression to her stance. Not rigid like the others, but closer to a dancer poised ready for her cue.

"Lastly, Zero-gravity Combat Specialist and Away-team Lead, Marius Armitage."

The third man did not move, nor acknowledge his intro-duction. He pinched his lips tight and his nostrils flared.

"Your mission is to bring Adora and Arsenio back, nothing more," Kian said, speaking to the group as well as Orinthia. "Remember who the enemy is. I expect civil conduct between every one of you." Kian first pointed a finger at the crew behind him, then landed on Orinthia. "Cap-tain Masood is waiting on the bridge. He's not a patient man nor is he thrilled about you being here, so I wouldn't keep him waiting much longer. Dismissed."

The three officers climbed back into the ship without saying anything. Kian did not wait for them to be fully inside before he approached Orinthia. "Stay here," he said to Kos before putting a hand on Orinthia's arm.

Orinthia ran her fingers against Kos' hand before following Kian. They moved several feet away and he leaned closer to her. He spoke low to keep their conversation private.

"Stay on your best behavior," Kian said. "They're looking for an excuse to end you. You represent everything they hate. A Hunter who left her oath, then turned marauder? There's no worse offense in their eyes."

"I didn't leave my oath." Orinthia bit back. "Adora fired me."

"It doesn't matter what the truth is, she never spun it that way. Look, just keep your head down and get the job done. That's going to be your best bet."

"What's going to happen to me if we don't catch them?" Orinthia asked. "If I don't succeed in getting my pardon?" The thought woke her up a few times during the night. She would be in the wolf's den with a death warrant over her head. An easy kill in the middle of open space.

Kian cleared his throat and looked over his shoulder then back to Orinthia. "Don't fail?"

Orinthia's breath caught, but she masked it with another question. "How long do I have to not-fail?"

"A month. Six weeks, tops."

Cold hands moved down her spine. "Perfect. I have six weeks until I'm back and hanging from the gallows."

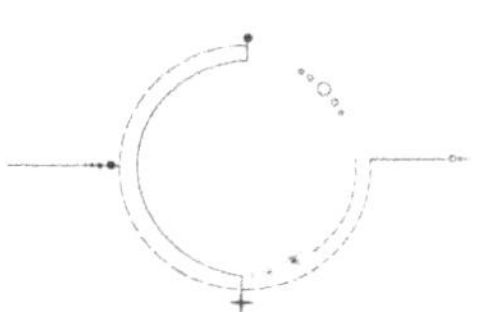

$\mathcal{A}$ mist fell over the spaceport, damping the already sour mood. Orinthia's braided hair, the only thing keeping it tame in the humidity, grew heavier by the minute. Lighting flashed on the horizon, followed by a low rumble of thunder.

Leaving Kos was the hardest thing she had done. The look on his face nearly sent her running away from the *Tertion* onto the first charter off the moon. She knew he would have fought Kian to let him go with her if she asked. But the GMH was not his place. As much as it hurt, being apart was their only choice.

"I love you," Kos said, kissing her forehead. "We'll be together soon." He slipped a comm into her hand.

"What's this?" she asked. The box had half a dozen extra wires sticking out of the back, running in circuits and looping around each other.

"It's hurried work, so be gentle with it," Kos said and pulled a matching one from his pocket. "I modified them to reach outside the normal systems. It's the best I could do with what I had in the garage last night, so there wasn't time to test it. But call me anytime. It's the only way I can marginally be okay with this."

Orinthia's lower lip trembled but she held back the sobs that threatened to overtake her. She flared her nose and sniffed. There were a hundred things she wanted to say, but her mouth could only pick one. "I love you, too."

With a soft touch, Kos pulled her into him and kissed her. It would have to last her as long as they were apart, and she did not pull away until Kos did. He ran a bent finger over her cheek, and gave her a soft smile. The kind of smile that held promises of a better future. "You better go or I'll never be able to stop."

"You say it like it's a bad thing," Orinthia whispered, memorizing his burning touch.

Kos placed her pack over her shoulder and nudged her arm.

Large drops of rain splashed Orinthia's face, announcing her time was up. She jogged away from Kos and only allowed herself to look back at him once she was at the top of the ramp. He had not moved, but covered his head with his arm. It was the last she saw of him before the door closed in front of her, sealing her inside the ship.

With a shake, she wiped her face with her arm and turned around to look at the interior of the *Tertion*. She had no idea where to find the bridge and wished Kian would have shown her around before walking away.

The *Tertion* smelled like something that had burned once, been patched together, and kept flying out of spite. The air was dry, tinged with oil and something sour in the vents. Orinthia took cautious steps, her boots giving muted thuds against the hard floor. Her eyes trailed over bulkheads scarred by years of service. Pipes ran along the ceiling, painted over so many times eventually they gave up and let the paint chip, revealing layers of colors.

There were words, with worn-down letters, embossed into the walls. The top row read: *Bridge, Med-bay, Officer's Quarters.* Beside it was an arrow that pointed forward through a small corridor. She huffed her spacer's helmet into a more secure hold and followed the signage. A light flickered overhead as she walked around the opening that led to the lower decks.

Beyond the ladder was a half-open bulkhead. Voices echoed out from inside. Orinthia stepped around the door and peered in.

An old Hydrano stood near the helm of the ship. His face was etched with deep lines over his scaly, rust-toned skin. He wore a white coat lined with official ribbons and stripes on his teal lapel and faced Orinthia with his arms tucked behind his back. The rebreather over his aquatic gills bubbled around his neck and hissed.

Beside him was a female Arachnillo. She was smaller than the few Orinthia had met before, only meeting the captain's shoulder. A single fang peeked out from the edge of her mouth. Her deep indigo exoskeleton shimmered in the lights from the console behind her. She matched the captain's stance with her four arms behind her back, and four legs in as much of attention as they could be.

"Did you leave your sense of time behind when you left the order?" The Hydrano asked. His voice was clear and deep, filling the small space with vibration. It was more a jab than a direct question and did not pause long enough for an answer. "I am Captain Masood Solvay. You will address me only as Captain Solvay. This is my Executive officer, Zegotta Talyon. If there is ever a reason I am not on the bridge, XO Talyon has command. Her words are my words and I expect every order to be kept as gospel."

Orinthia locked eyes with Talyon for a moment. She shivered from the icy stare she received back. Thankfully, Solvay continued speaking and drew both their attention to him.

"You're an unwelcome guest aboard my ship," he said. "However, seeing as the new Commissioner demands it, I am now responsible for your actions. Under different circumstances, you'd be held in the brig and not housed in one of my cabins. Do as you're told and you will be free to roam the ship. Step out of line and I will gladly have you confined until your services are required."

Static ran up Orinthia's arms as she pinched her lips together and narrowed her eyes. Her free hand was clenched tight on the edge of her helmet. A wave of energy flowed off her, uncontrolled.

Solvay took a steadying step back, but did not flinch or react anymore than if a breeze had touched him.

"The galley is stocked with enough rations to feed a garrison, but don't expect hot meals. Our chef, curse his soul, abandoned his —"

The floor shook. For a moment, Orinthia wondered if she had done it, and checked the surroundings. A cacophony rapidly grew outside the ship. No lightning had struck the ground, and the thunder was out of place. Bright orange flashed across the windscreen behind the captain and Talyon. The ship rocked again and Orinthia stumbled sideways. She dropped her helmet and braced herself on the wall.

Warning alarms sounded throughout the tight space. Rubble pelted the hull as it rained down.

Orinthia's eyes widened and heart clawed up her throat. *Kos,* she thought. He would still be on the flight line, waiting for her to take off.

"XO, damage report?" Captain Solvay shouted, jumping to his post and running through the preflight process.

Talyon's arms blurred over the screens and buttons on the console. "It wasn't a direct hit, sir. No damage."

"Where did the attack come from?"

They spoke quickly, neither looking at the other, and moved in sync with the precision of a choreography.

"Aerial," Talyon answered. "North of our position. The ship's turning back to make another pass."

Orinthia turned to run for the door, to find a way to see Kos outside, but the *Tertion* rattled hard, knocking her to her knees. She gripped the jump seat and held on as she watched the grey sky blur. The ship lifted, spiraling smoke and fire around them as the engines whipped the air.

"Strap in," Solvay ordered through the PA. "Taking fire and making an emergency evac." He glanced back at Orinthia. "That means you, too. Get in that seat and hold on."

Returning to the controls, Solvay said, "Man the weapons, XO. Keep an eye out for that ship."

"Incoming," Talyon said, rushing over his last few words.

Just as Orinthia clicked in the last buckle, another wave of missiles fell above them. Captain Solvay swerved and rolled out of the way. If she was not secured, she would have been tossed across the deck. Two of the missiles hit the ship, causing it to shake harder than before and the sound made Orinthia's eyes water.

"Who is shooting at my ship?" Captain Solvay bellowed. His rebreather bubbled faster.

"It's the *Sensiti*, sir," Talyon reported. "One of her ships."

The emphasis in her words was unmistakable. *Adora,* Orinthia thought.

Their attacker came into view in front of them. Smaller

than *Freya* and the *Tertion*, it was sleek and the white hull almost blended in with the clouds they flew through.

Captain Solvay pulled the helm and the *Tertion* shot up, leading them above the cloud cover into the clear skies. They continued to climb until a glow formed on the horizon as they neared the edge of the moon's atmosphere. The *Sensiti* followed and appeared in the window seconds later.

A pair of projectiles left the *Tertion* and sped toward the enemy ship. It dodged one, but caught the other with its starboard wing. Talyon fired another four at the ship, hitting her mark three times. In the middle of the volley, the *Sensiti* returned fire with two more of their own.

Chaff flew out along a stream of white ribbons, catching the enemy's attack and igniting it safely away from the *Tertion*. Talyon's nimble hands danced across the panel. She sent a final half dozen ranged attacks at the enemy vessel. It caught all six, sending the ship into a downward spiral, free falling through the clouds back to Buscoch's surface.

A scream stuck in Orinthia's throat as she watched in horror. The ship plummeted out of sight, leaving a trail of smoke. She let out a hushed whimper, hoping they had moved far enough away from the village that no one would be hurt.

"Do a full sweep," Captain Solvay ordered. "Find any other ships that may be out there."

"Already have," Talyon said. "Radar is clean, sir. It looks like she sent just the one. A scout perhaps."

"Calculate the debris' trajectory, then send word to the Commissioner," Solvay said. "He has a lot to clean up before he can leave."

"Aye, captain." Talyon's four arms flew across the panel, pressing buttons and moving levers for half a minute. "Done."

"Take us out, then, XO." The captain turned to face his

newest member as he spoke. "Sector hop to be sure no follows."

Orinthia squeezed her eyes closed and covered her face.

"Crying already?" Solvay teased.

"I get warp sickness," Orinthia said, her words muffled. In reality, she was also trying to keep from crying. The skin around her neck was warm, and her eyes were tight.

The old captain chuckled an unkind laugh. "Even better. Talyon, get her off my bridge."

"Yes, captain."

8

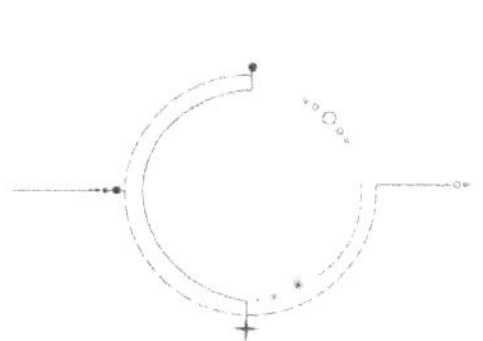

Kos squinted into the rain and watched as a white ship he'd never seen before came in close. It didn't lower its landing gear, nor did it slow. Realization struck Kos like the missile that fell from the mysterious craft. He pushed himself forward, unsure of how he would get Orinthia out of the the *Tertion*, but knowing he had to do something. Pieces of tarmac fell, forcing him to dodge the debris with each step.

Before he reached the door, the ship jumped into the air, knocking him back with the force from the engines. Kos threw himself down and curled into a ball, covering his head and neck. Smoke circled around him and he coughed as the sound of the ship drifted away.

He rolled to his knees and stared up. The enemy ship came in for a second pass. Moments before they collided, the *Tertion* barrel-rolled out of sight into the clouds. Orinthia's safety was out of his hands, and he prayed the reputation that followed the old war captain, Masood Solvay, was true.

A rush of footsteps came from behind him, stopping at his side. "What was that?" Kian asked.

Kos rose and dusted off his pants. His mind ran through idea after idea on what he could do to help her. None of Jari's ships had defensive capabilities. He turned to Kian, eyes narrowed but vision clear. "Where's the ship you came in?"

"There." Kian pointed into the sky. "I came with them. I was on my way to take a ferry to the interchange —"

Kos cursed, no longer interested in what Kian had to say. He examined the docked crafts, none of which were armed.

Kian gasped, sending Kos into a spin to see what he was looking at. A ship, ten miles out at least, spun wildly through the air, trailing smoke and locked on a crash course for the ground.

Without waiting to confirm his fears, Kos dashed for Jari's hangar. His feet splashed through puddles, drenching his legs as the rain soaked the rest of him. Breathing came in as if through a straw as he fought to stay in the present.

Reaching the edge of the port, Kos scanned his watch to get into the building. Jari was half way down the stairs as Kos skittered in. He blew on a steaming cup of drink and called out a morning greeting.

Kos ignored him, and jumped into the transport ship he was meant to fly out that day. He flicked on the ignition and pressed the controls to open the bay doors. As they slid apart, Kos ran through the minimum round of preflight he could get away with to get the ship off the ground. As soon as he was cleared, Kos leaned on the yoke and launched.

It was no more than a few seconds before Kos relocated the smoke and positioned himself toward it. He clenched his teeth, sending shocks up his skull, and forced himself to have no thoughts.

Plumes of smoke came from the bottom of a hill, signaling him like a beacon. In less than five, heart-aching minutes, he set the transport down beside the smoldering vessel. Leaving the engines on, Kos rushed out and forced his legs to move as fast as they could.

Mangled pieces of the wreckage jutted out of the ground and lay scattered across the field. The downpour suppressed any fire that may have erupted, but it only made the thick smoke worse.

Kos tapped on his temple, activating his HUD and scanned the debris. Three lifeless bodies were still strapped to their seats inside the ship. He pulled up his sleeves and called on his armor, pressing his wet clothes between him and the steel. Once shielded, Kos ventured closer to look for any indication of who the ship belonged to.

A scorched GMH emblem caught his eye, half buried in the dirt and charred through the middle. Kos swallowed down a rush of bile. Away from the wreckage, nestled in the grass, a single blip lit up on his visor. He followed it. There were no signs of other survivors, and he didn't know what he would do if it was one of the crew Kian had introduced.

Flat on his back, a man in a blood-red jumpsuit coughed and clutched his middle. Burn marks spattered the fabric, and soot darkened his face. Kos scanned him quickly. He had several broken ribs, a fractured femur, and internal bleeding.

"Where is Orinthia?" Kos asked, crouching to get closer to the stranger.

The man coughed again and took in sharp breaths. He flinched as the rain pelted his face.

"Are you a Messie?" Kos yelled, trying to get some type of response.

"No," the man said, swallowing hard.

Kos stood and recalled his armor. He placed his hands to his hip and pulled out his golden blaster. Lifting his head, but keeping his eyes on the man, Kos aimed the barrel at the man's face. His finger was steady on the trigger.

"You're going to tell me everything," Kos said.

THE TRANSPORT SHIP touched down inside the hangar, its landing gear hissing as it settled. Through the cockpit, Kian and Jari came into view, standing on the second level. They descended to the garage floor and met Kos outside the ship's bay doors.

Jari stood silently behind Kian, red-faced, but in control of his temper. Kos was glad to not be yelled at. He wasn't sure if he'd be able to hold himself back if he were pushed. It was hard enough to keep from killing the injured man, but there was no guarantee it would last long. Someone needed to die, and it almost didn't matter who.

"Adora sent them," Kos said to Kian without looking at him.

"How do you know?" Kian asked, stuttering. His gaze trailed down to Kos' hand, but it was Jari who spoke next.

"Why are you bloody?" he asked, low and cautious.

"Talking," Kos said. His hands were loose at his side, and he didn't look anyone in the face while he spoke. The world around him was wrapped in a haze.

"Who?" Kian asked.

"Sylvanio Mellic. We've become… close."

"What did you do?" Kian asked, each word measured and spaced. He stepped around Kos and climbed the ramp. A heavy silence followed. "Did you kill him?"

"No," Kos answered, not looking back. "But if you're going to arrest him, you'd better get him to a hospital first."

Jari studied Kos, his focus picking over every inch of his favorite employee. He stared at Kos' hands, too.

Kos knew what he saw. Bruises and cuts.

"You're not who I thought you were," Jari said, shaking his head in slow passes.

"This is exactly who I am," Kos said. His voice was deep in his chest. Every breath called him back from the darkness that danced around the edges of his vision. "It's just been tucked away and I had hoped to never be him again."

"Rogue, stay right there, and don't move," Kian called out from inside the ship.

Kos turned his head but did not look over his shoulder. "Are you going to arrest me, too?"

Kian sighed as he stepped closer. "No, this is wildly out of hand. But I need you to tell me what he said. Jari, can you call a medical droid to get this man? Have the authorities keep an eye on him until I can sort this out."

"What is going on?" Jari asked. He waved his hands around in front of him. "What is all of this?"

"It's a matter of EC security, that's all you need to know. You'll be fully compensated for whatever it takes to clean this up. Let me get through this first." His voice had a hint of formality, but came out rushed and breathy.

Jari looked between the two men and lowered his shoulders. "Use my office. Kos has been good to me and whatever this is about, I don't really want to know." He pointed at Kos. "Just don't touch anything."

Kian thanked the man and led Kos out of the ship, up the stairs, and into the offices. The secretary shrieked as they walked in, but Kian pushed Kos through to Jari's office and locked the door behind them. He set Kos in the middle of the room, scooting the furniture away to avoid getting blood and dirt on anything.

"Walk me through what happened."

Kos' mind slipped in and out of reality as the adrenaline

faded. He watched memories play over his eyes, blending in with the crisp white walls and black furniture surrounding him. Faces, whispers, and smells swirled together. They were nearly engulfing him, attempting to take him down. It took the last bits of his strength to find the parts that were not nightmares. Orinthia needed him to tell Kian what he knew, and Kos focused on that, using it to pull himself back to the real world.

"Adora sent them," Kos repeated, taking in sips of air. He flexed his fingers. They still ached from giving Sylvanio "incentives" to talk.

"How'd they know she was here?" Kian asked, taking notes on his PortTab.

"There's a spy somewhere in your ranks," Kos said. "You have to call them back. She's not safe."

"No," Kian said, holding up a hand to keep Kos from jumping at him. "We have to follow through with this as planned. There are very few people who know about this mission, and most of them are on that ship with her."

"That's even more reason to bring her back," Kos yelled.

"We can control this from the outside," Kian said. "The twins think they have a stacked deck, but now we have the upper hand. We can feed false information through Orinthia and weed out the traitor."

"That's dangerous. She's already putting everything on the line, and now you want her to do her own spying?"

Kian frowned. "She can't know about this."

Kos stepped forward, his fists clenched and ready to knock the Galoric across the room.

"It will keep her safe." Kian lifted his hands and moved back to keep the space between him and Kos. "If she knew, how do you think she'd react? I've known her a long time, and I have a few ideas of what she would do. Keeping her in the dark for as long as possible will keep her safe. She needs to focus on the job at hand and if she's playing her own spy games, it'll fall apart."

"I'm not going to keep secrets from her," Kos said, still ready to strike.

"Yes you will. We both have to. If Adora found out we knew, she'd have the spy kill Orinthia. This really is for the best."

Kos yelled and swung his fist, making contact with a conference chair. It flipped over and slid across the floor, smacking the wall. He spoke through gritted teeth. "If anything happens to her, you're the one who has to answer for it."

Lowering his hands, Kian let out a long breath and his shoulders sagged with it. He shook his head once, glanced at the wrecked chair, then tapped something into his PortTab. "I'll have plenty to answer for anyway, so add it to the list."

9

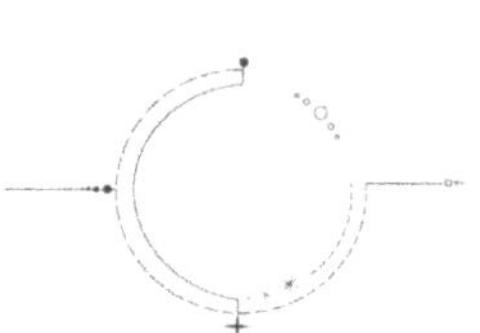

***

*F*rom one desert to the next, Arsenio thought, staring across the cracked, red horizon. Dust clung to his skin, absorbing whatever moisture he had left. It itched. He hated the taste in his mouth and the ever-present crunch every time he pressed his teeth together. This was not the empire he was promised. Far from it. But then again, at least he was not locked away.

The floor vibrated beneath his boots in steady pulses from ordnance detonations beyond the walls. It had been a week since he and Adora took over the compound, but the locals had plenty left to say about their arrival. These things never lasted long. Arsenio expected the siege to end any day. Eventually, they would either starve or surrender.

That was not what worried him. A knot settled in his spine, tightening like a snake. The *Sensiti* had yet to report in at their appointed hour. He knew it was a risky move, directly going after the Messies. But Adora insisted on a quick end to their sister. All he could do was wait for a mission report, and who it came from would tell him the outcome.

Arsenio did not like putting one of their own in danger. It

felt wrong to sacrifice a loyalist. Not one of the many who just followed orders; they had plenty of those. One who truly believed in the vision.

But he understood the importance of a backup plan. And so did she.

The air in the room shifted, followed by a slight draft as the door opened behind him. He turned on his heel, slow and deliberate, and faced the newcomer. An ensign stepped in, carrying a tray; his lunch, still steaming from the kitchen. Nothing grand like he was used to, but still better than what they had outside the gate.

The young man moved with stiff, rehearsed movements and walked straight to the table. He set the tray down with care, then stepped back, his eyes locked at Arsenio's feet. Not once did he look directly at him. It was the kind of avoidance that drew more attention than if he had stared.

Arsenio rolled his eyes and waved his hand to dismiss the ensign.

With a curt bow, the man backed out of the room and disappeared down the hall.

The scent of the meal lingered in the air, spicy and sour. Arsenio sat, and picked up the fork, turning over the cuts as if inspecting them. Then, he set the utensil down again. His body wanted to eat, but his mind was caught in a loop of anger and fear.

He pushed the tray away from the edge of the table and leaned forward, placing his head in his hands. The movement made his head spin for a second, which only deepened his frustration.

*Are you pouting again?* Adora asked, her voice clear in his mind. *You've been shut up in this room too long.*

Arsenio tilted his head to see his twin sister leaning against the doorframe, keeping the auto door from closing.

*Where else am I to go?* Arsenio thought back. *I've seen how they look at me, or don't look at me in most cases. Staying up here is better than being a talking point.*

*You're Arsenio Anton.* Adora kicked off the wall and moved closer. Her steps were steady and timed. *Show them the only thing that's changed is your hearing. Remind them who you are.*

*What do you want, Adora?* Arsenio leaned back in his seat and crossed his arms. *I'm in the middle of lunch.*

Adora smirked without looking at his tray. They both knew he was lying. *Any word from the Sensiti?*

The question hung in his mind. It was an hour past their check-in. Not too alarming on its own, but pitted against Masood, they were likely to never call. Still, Arsenio stretched out his leg and retrieved the PortTab from the pocket on his thigh.

*Nothing.*

*And the other one?* Adora asked, resting her backside against the edge of the table. They were almost the same height when he was sitting. *Send word to check.*

*Are you afraid?* Arsenio smirked.

*I'm cautious.* Adora's words simmered around the edges. *She's not a threat on her own, but if they poke around too soon, we'll be found out before the pieces are fully in place. I want them to come, to cross that line. Just not yet.*

The smirk faded from his face. He was in a constant state of uncertainty about Adora's plan. Yes, the EC turned against them and they deserved to fall. But all they had worked for, all the years spent keeping the galaxy running, seemed wasted. Any victory that came felt hollow. Once Adora cut off the heads, it would be on him to keep the body from collapsing into chaos.

It was a solid plan, one they toyed with for years. But he

never dreamed it would actually happen. There was something to her recent methods, though. Something too smooth about the transition he could not pin. Like it was not just a plan, but as if there were an unseen hand moving through the background.

The PortTab vibrated in his hand, tossing all other thoughts aside. He checked the message. A single word came across the screen.

*Failed*

Arsenio cursed through his breath. A rush of heat ran down his head to his feet as he braced to tell Adora.

*Mission failed.* He turned the screen to her, as if to prove he told the truth. *Looks like you were right to keep the secondary in play.*

She slowly lifted her head, but did not respond for a few seconds. Her eyes moved back and forth, not seeing anything, but in thought. A smile danced around the edges of her mouth. *Let's hope you picked a good one.*

There was no anger in her words. If anything, she was amused by the news. Like a game piece moved in her favor rather than tipping off the board. *Make sure they stay back for now. Get more information before we react to the change.*

Her calm unsettled him. Adora was not one to scream, but their first big move had gone sideways. Arsenio expected some disappointment from her.

He narrowed his eyes and studied her. *What are you playing, Adoracion?*

She shrugged a shoulder, but her grin widened. *It'll all work out. This was more of a test than anything.*

Arsenio placed the PortTab back in his pocket and cocked

his head. *A test for what? Loyalty? They've already left every-thing behind to be here.*

Adora shook her head and took a chest full of air. She looked out the window at the setting sun. *I have a secret.*

All the heat rolled out of his body. His stomach twisted. If he were standing, the words would have knocked him back. *Since when do you hold things back from me?*

She did not look at him, but continued to stare. *I wanted to see how this panned out before I came to you with it. To make sure I wasn't wasting our time. But, it's happening like he said it would.*

*Who?* Arsenio slid the chair back and got to his feet. His heart raced and his cheeks burned. *And for that matter, when? We tell each other everything. That's how it's always been.*

Without moving her head, Adora made a long blink then turned her eyes back to Arsenio. *A sequencer. He came to me shortly after we escaped. What he showed me, it was too good to pass up. But I'm not a fool to blindly trust something this delicate to an overrated fortune teller. So, I sent the Sensiti ahead, to tempt fate. The way I saw it, I won. Either he was a liar and the Sensiti would destroy the Messies, or he was right and following his plan would bring us victory.*

Arsenio could do nothing but gawk at his sister. How could she keep something like that from him? Something as big and risky? He did not want to believe what she told him, but it was too farfetched for even her to make up.

*Then what is the real plan?* Arsenio asked. *What is it he told you that makes you believe him?*

There was a long pause between them. One that stretched for minutes, with each one feeling like it was longer than the last. They stared at each other, neither moved. It was a battle of wills, one Adora almost always won.

Those outside their family thought Orinthia was the stubborn one, but it was Adora who held that title. It was the cause of most her beatings. Though, those only pushed her deeper inside herself.

*Are you going to tell me what's going on?* Arsenio tried to control his mental volume. Aggression toward her would get nothing done.

*We're taking a trip,* she told him. It was not an answer to his question. *I need to speak with The Sheriff.*

Arsenio laughed. It rippled through his chest and up his throat. There was no humor to it, just the release of a broken man who had no control. *Why? What could he possibly do for us?*

*It's the next step in the plan,* Adora said to him.

*You say that like it's a grand prophecy.* Arsenio set his hands on his hips. *Sequencers are dangerous. There's a reason the EC put a stop to the practice in the core territory.*

*And they're trying to put a stop to us.* Her words were sharp, and made Arsenio flinch. *I'll do whatever I need to to get back on top.*

*To get us both on top.* Arsenio narrowed his eyes.

Adora's face softened. Not in elegance or as an apology. That was not her. There was something behind her eyes, more than what she already admitted to hiding from him.

*I've kept you from your lunch for too long.* Adora straightened from off the table's edge. *I'll call for you when I'm ready to leave.*

The smell from his meal puffed up as she turned and walked out the door. Arsenio let his eyes travel to the tray. A weight pressed on his shoulders, and if he let it, would bury him. For the first time in their lives, he was unsure of where he stood with her.

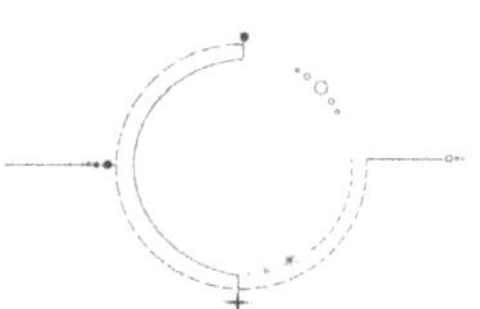

## 10

The *Tertion's* decks were unusually quiet. Though the GMH never manned full crews for any ship, Orinthia found the lack of activity out of place. Her mind had nothing to distract her as she followed Zegotta Talyon down the barren halls.

Seeing the Arachnillo stirred up emotions in her she had buried. Xyla, the Master Gunner of the *Fera*, was the catalyst to the end of her short stint as a marauder. Her death changed the course of Orinthia's life, though she had not realized it until much later, when the minutes ticked away like hours. She liked Xyla, even if their acquaintances were short-lived. A slow chill ran up Orinthia's back and her thoughts wandered through the events after Xyla's death.

It all unfolded in front of her as if it were happening in real time. The walls of the *Tertion* disappeared from around her, and not even the thumping of her footsteps broke through the memory. The duel with the unnamed sailor. Her unwillingness to murder him. Kos' duty to a dying and crazed captain. A dead body laying in a pool of blood. The fire in Kos' eyes as he yelled at her.

Cold barbs dug into her bones, chilling her core.

Xyla's death shook her more than she realized. At the time, Orinthia had ignored it, shoving the thoughts deep inside with everything else she kept hidden. Behind anger, pain, and bitterness. But she was no longer that person. Almost everything about her had changed, and her old coping skills no longer worked in this new life.

From Xyla, her mind moved to Neve. She died by Orinthia's hand. Her first kill. As she lost her sword, she also left a piece of her soul behind. It was another memory she had locked away. Uri and Elendoras took precedence. The only time she thought about her was after she blew up the sloop, when the *Fera* attacked them near Sarv'on.

*I've killed before*, she repeated to herself. *It's cost me, but I've done it. I can do it again with Adora. This means more than the others. I have to. I have to.*

Orinthia plowed into Talyon, who stopped in the middle of the hall. Her visions vanished, and she shook herself back to reality. She peered around the XO and saw the woman in the spacesuit, Annatilla, standing beside an open door to the left.

"I thought I heard footsteps," Annatilla said, beaming like she had heard some hilarious joke. "Don't see you down here much, XO."

"Captain Solvay ordered me to show Anton to her quarters," Talyon said with a slight hiss to her words.

Annatilla placed her hands on her hips. "That was some quick shooting out there. Can't imagine Adora will be that brazen again for a while. Why don't I take this one off your hands? There's nothing else for me to do and I'm sure Captain wants to debrief with you."

She turned her attention to Orinthia. Her white spacesuit hugged her body like a second skin, sleeker than the standard

GMH issue. Teal lining traced the seams along her arms and knees, accenting the suit's sharp angles. Rounded cuffs at her shoulders bore a painted Hunter emblem, barely visible beneath the soft gleam of the corridor lights. Her helmet remained sealed. Thin lines of circuitry pulsed along the sides of the glass, glowing gently from yellow to orange; alive like the suit itself was breathing.

"Thanks, actually," Talyon said. "Captain Solvay was already on edge when I left, so it's best to get back quickly anyway." She nodded at Annatilla, then Orinthia, and left the way they had come.

When the two human women were alone, Annatilla took Orinthia's spacer's helmet and examined it as she spoke. "Despite what the others might say, your addition is a relief. I'm sure you've noticed how few we are. Any living body is a welcome one."

"What happened to everyone else?" Orinthia asked, taking back her helmet. She wanted to be polite and start off on a better foot than she had with Kos and Thrutt, but she also did not want her things handled by strangers.

"Adora." Annatilla shrugged a shoulder. "She's charismatic and has convinced most of my friends to work for her. Those who didn't, died. We're all that's left."

*If they all failed, how am I going to do this?* Orinthia thought. A heavy feeling settled into her stomach. No one but the best and dedicated Hunters were enlisted, and it was by invitation only. They took more lives than prisoners, and were reserved for the most dangerous missions in open space. Though, it was not much of a surprise to hear they would side with the twins. Most were handpicked by her.

*But, they weren't trained to fight her.* She pushed the thought aside. *She's not the enemy they know. Hunters haven't dealt with her like I have.*

"If she has so many Hunters on her side, then why is she outsourcing? Kian said she's been recruiting marauders, too."

"It seems like an enemy-of-my-enemy sort of deal," Annatilla said. "They have a common enemy in the EC. She might have headed the GMH once, but now she needs new allies. Isn't that what you're doing here? We're all working toward one goal. Troubling time, really. Everything is backward and mixed up. I liked it when we knew who was on the right and wrong side."

Orinthia held her tongue. She stood in the middle of both sides. Though she understood there was never a right or wrong side. It boiled down to survival. Not all marauders were bloodthirsty murderers seeking to topple governments. And not all Hunters were altruistic. Most were trying to live the best way they knew how.

"Well, let's show you around," Annatilla said, clapping her hands together. "Captain will be upset if he finds out we're loitering in the halls. Though, they don't come down here much, so it usually isn't a problem."

They walked in silence for a few feet until stopping in front of the last door in the hall. Annatilla waved Orinthia forward. "This is your room."

"How do you know?" Orinthia asked. There were no name placards or anything to differentiate one door from the next. She knew Annatilla had not lied, but needed to be sure it was going to be the right room.

"Captain told us to stay away from you." She lowered her head and scrunched her face, then spoke in a distorted voice. "Don't go making friends with the scum. She's not one of us, no matter what the Commissioner has promised her." Her face returned to normal and she rolled her eyes. "So he made sure we knew which cabin was yours as a warning."

"Gee, thanks." Orinthia popped her mouth a few times.

"I'm not a marauder, though. I haven't been for a while, and I wasn't even a good one. That's why Kian's working with me to clear my name."

Annatilla twisted her lips. "Was that not Kos Rogue, the quartermaster of the *Fera,* with you earlier?"

Orinthia grimaced. "Well, yes. But he's not with them anymore either. We left at the same time."

"Okay," Annatilla said, no emotion across her face. "Anyway, I'll let you get comfortable. And don't worry about what the captain said. I tend not to listen to his orders when they aren't directly related to a mission." She turned on her toes and glided back to her cabin.

Standing alone in the hall, Orinthia faced her door again. She braced herself to be met by a giant window depicting the warp outside the ship. As she stepped in, Orinthia lowered her head and kept her eyes on the floor, searching for the space where it met the wall. Slowly, she followed it all the way up and found there was no window at all.

The door closed behind her and she dropped her things at her feet. Rotating her arms and stretching her neck, she took stock of the space around her. Nothing but dull grey metal greeted her. A narrow bunk was built into a recessed cubby near the door, dressed in crisp white sheets and a thin black blanket worn with age. Looking at it made Orinthia's skin feel dry. Two recessed lights glowed overhead, casting the room in a muted yellow haze.

To the left of the bed, a built-in desk stretched across half of the back wall. A lamp with an adjustable arm sat on top, its neck angled to one side. In front of the desk was a bucket seat bolted to the floor. Its single leg and muted color blended seamlessly with the stark metal walls. Beneath the bunk were two narrow drawers which offered enough space to stow a few belongings.

The rest of the cabin, lifeless and devoid of personality, weighed heavy on her senses. Even her prison cell on the *Mathias* had more character. It was drab in a way that ached her bones, as though it had been designed to snuff out any trace of individuality.

Orinthia had very little references, as she had only been on a few, but the *Tertion* was the worst GMH ship she had seen. At least she was in her own room. She took in a deep breath, holding it until her lungs shook, then let it out in a slow stream. In the quiet, the first few thoughts of Kos crept into her mind. There had been no time until then to let herself think of him, or worry what might have happened to him in the port.

She crouched down and looked in the side pocket of her pack for the comm Kos had given her. It seemed to have survived the thrashing from the bridge, but then again, she did not know the difference. With her thumb, she flicked open the comm and moved to her bed. It gave way very little as she placed all her weight on it, scooting until her back touched the cubby wall.

"Hope this works in warp," she said out loud. Orinthia punched in Kos' comm code and waited for a sign that it connected. The light blinked and blinked, but there was no answer. She tried again, but the outcome was the same.

"Don't panic," she whispered. Her heart rate ticked up a few beats and she assumed it was how Kos felt when she had not answered all his calls.

*He said he hadn't tested it yet,* she reminded herself. *Maybe it just doesn't work.*

It did little to help, but the more she forced herself to repeat the thought, the more she believed it.

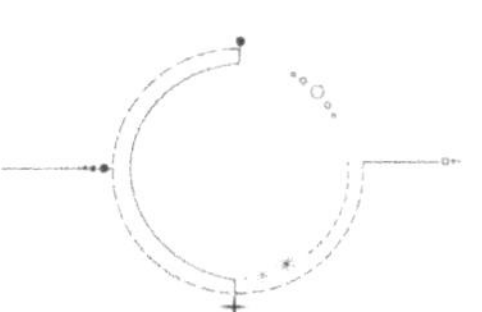

*V*ibrations from the ship's engines lulled Orinthia as she lay on the bunk, on her side, with one arm tucked under her head. She stared across the drab room at the wall. Nothing brightened up the space; she had not brought anything personal with her, afraid it would end up abandoned like what was left behind on the *Fera*.

Even one of the plants would have brought some color. But those, of all the things she owned, were her prized possessions and she sheleft them for Kos to tend. They were more than just plants. They symbolized their love. Kos filled her life with beauty in a way that proved he understood her.

She hoped he found a way to care for them while they were away.

*I hope he's okay*, she thought, rolling to her back. *Being away from him again is wrong. We were meant to stay together. To keep each other safe. That's what Thrutt said.*

Orinthia sighed and rubbed her face. *Why does Adora keep ruining my life, even when she's not in it? Can't we pretend like neither of us exist? The universe is big enough for us to be separated and never see each other again.*

A tingle built up in her shoulders and she slapped the bed with a huff, trying someway to disperse the tension. In the stillness, her mind wandered from the present to Uri. She had not spoken to him since before he left for Earth. And other than the note he sent with her spacesuit, there had been no word from him.

*Does Adora even care that much about him? Uri was the best of us and had the most compassion. They never had a problem with him like they did me.*

Then, another thought hit her, one she avoided when she could. *Did he only love us, love me, because of his programming?* The question stung. *If he wasn't made to be kind and caring, would have have treated me like the twins did?*

Her stomach twisted and tears pricked her eyes. Uri had been her one safe place growing up. She did not want to believe anything other than what she remembered. But even in death, her father continued to torture her with the truth of what he made Uri into.

Uri swore he loved her. That should have been enough. But she did not know if it was, and left more questions than she could form into words.

Orinthia wiped her eyes with the back of her hand, frustrated by how easily tears came lately. There was a time she did not care, when it was easier to feel nothing at all. But that had hurt, too, in its own way.

A soft beep came from beside her head. Orinthia flipped over to see her comm blinking. She rushed to open it. "Kos?"

"I'm so glad to hear your voice," Kos said with a sigh that made the speaker scratchy for a second.

"What happened?" Orinthia asked, curling her legs and closing her eyes to picture him as she listened to his voice. "I tried calling you once things settled down."

"Sorry," Kos said. "I had to take care of a few things

before I could get back to you. Things got interesting after you left, but it's better now. You're okay, right?"

"Yeah. This ship looks like garbage, but it held up well enough at least. Brought back a few memories of our last trip, though. Other than that, I've met some of the crew."

"Anyone stand out as odd?" Kos' asked, almost too quickly.

"Me," Orinthia chuckled. "The captain isn't excited I'm here, and the other two I've spoken to, in not so many words, reminded me I don't belong."

"Be careful, okay?" Kos said. There was a weight to his words. "Don't put all your trust in any of them."

"They might not like me," Orinthia said, "but I'm not who used I used to be. This is my chance to make them see that. Besides, I was wrong about Mimi, and it's okay for me to admit it when I am."

Kos laughed, a deep, bright sound that burst through the comm.

Orinthia covered the speaker to muffle the noise, but she let it fill her heart. There were many things she was worried about missing while she was away, and Kos' rare smile was of them. She held onto the image. He was a different man when he thought no one noticed. Only a handful of people were privileged enough to know that side. The side of him that loved deeper than anyone, cared more, and whose passion would put the most celebrated poets to shame.

"You still there?" Kos asked. His voice was softer than before, broken up by relief.

"Yeah, I am." She opened her eyes and rolled to her back, holding the comm close. A quiet ache settled in her chest.

"I miss you," he said like a prayer. "I'd give anything to be there with you right now. After Caytoo, I promised I'd never leave you again."

"We'll be okay, I have to believe that," she said, letting the words linger between breaths. Saying she missed him back would have solidified the distance, poked holes in her hope. Instead, she chose to reassure them both. "How long until Thrutt reaches you?"

"A few days. It's going to be hard to keep busy until then, though."

"Was Jari upset when he found out you're leaving?"

Kos took a moment to respond. "He's not pushing the issue for now. Kian didn't tell him a lot, but after the attack he figured some things out."

"Oh, you spoke with Kian after?" Orinthia turned on her side again. There was no real comfortable place to rest. "Did he have anything on who came after us? Talyon, the XO, said it was one of Adora's ship, but —"

A light flickered for a moment, cutting off her train of thought. The ship shuddered and shook, rocking Orinthia in her bed. She bolted up and held onto the edge, preparing to be tossed onto the floor. Seconds passed, the sound of the engines died down, and the walls ceased vibrating. She noted the hissing in the vents. *Well, life support is still on. That's good.*

"What's going on?" Kos' voice was on edge.

"I'm not sure," Orinthia said, sliding out of bed. Footsteps sounded outside her door. "Give me a second, just stay quiet." She put the open comm in her pocket and ventured out to see what was happening.

"Thia," Kos said in a loud whisper.

Orinthia hushed him then opened the door. The two remaining Messies she had yet to meet were already gathered in the hall. The tallest, Cliff, grimaced at her as she stepped out. He turned his face so his good eye bore into hers. She lifted her chin and squared her shoulders. "What was that?"

The second man, Marius, banged on the wall with his palm. "She's an old lady. Sometimes she needs a nap. Other times her warp drive falters."

Orinthia's mask slipped for a second. The tips of her ears tingled. "We just fell out of warp?"

Marius shrugged. "Happens all the time."

"Why is the ship so broken? For a team of your caliber, I thought the twin's would've tossed more funds your way."

The two men filled the hall with laughter. Marius let out a raspberry and placed his hands on his hips. "You're serious? We were her boot. Anything Adora wanted to never see again, she pointed us to it. That doesn't mean she cared about what happened to us."

"That's not what the rest of us thought," Orinthia said, shifting her stance. "Back in the NCR, the Messies were idols. Legendary."

"Never meet your heroes." Marius made a mock bow. "Out here, on the fringes of the EC territory, things aren't as perfect. Someone with your connections wouldn't understand."

It was Orinthia's turn to laugh. She did not mistake the bite behind his remark. "Do you know why Kian recruited me?"

Marius glared at her and straightened his back, but did not answer.

Orinthia stepped closer to him.

Cliff stiffened and scooted between the pair. "Watch it, Anton."

She stopped moving but continued speaking. "I've been on the receiving end of that boot a lot longer than anyone else. We might share a name, but that's all we have in common. I'm tired of people telling me who I am without knowing a thing about me."

"Back off," Marius said, leaning closer to Cliff as if he were going to go around the man and fight Orinthia. "I know what kind of family you were born into. Some of us had to fight the war your father profited off of."

"There's more to me than what you can read on the social net or in reports written by people who hate me," Orinthia said, clenching her fists. She did not intend to swing at him. It was to keep herself grounded.

"This conversation's enlightened me enough on who you are. Arrogant, defensive, and pushy. We don't want or need your help. The Antons are nothing but a blight on justice, all of you."

"Justice?" Orinthia chuckled the word. "What justice? The GMH as a whole is a boot. You said you fought in the war? So did most of the marauders you hunt down. The EC didn't care about you then, and it certainly doesn't care now."

Marius' nostrils flared. "The EC brings stability to the galaxy. Without law and order, there's chaos. More people die. Wars are waged. I continue to protect the EC's citizens, like I've always done."

Orinthia took a steadying breath. In her soul, she wanted to fight back, to keep showing him how wrong he was. But, like Kos not so long before, he had to see the truth. No amount of shouting would pierce through his armor. Instead, she lowered her voice and relaxed her shoulders. "I'm sorry you think that's true. My hope is you'll come to see through the lies before it's too late."

"That's enough, both of you." Cliff pushed Orinthia back with his elbow. "Go back to your room, marauder, and wait until the captain calls for you." He looked at Marius. "And we better get the engine fixed before he comes down here and throws us all in the brig."

Marius sniffed and clenched his jaw, but did not argue. He

walked around the massive man. Cliff followed him, putting a barrier between him and Orinthia.

Before they were halfway down the hall, Orinthia returned to her room.

"You really know how to make friends, don't you?" Kos asked from her pocket.

Orinthia cursed and retrieved the comm. "I forgot you were on the line. This might be harder than I thought."

"You won me over," Kos said. "Just don't make him fall in love with you, too."

"No promises," Orinthia said, rolling her eyes. She sighed. "I hope I can get through this in one piece."

## 12

THIS CHAPTER CONTAINS DEPICTIONS OF
PTSD, WARTIME TRAUMA, AND EMOTIONAL
DISTRESS, INCLUDING A COMBAT-RELATED
FLASHBACK. READER DISCRETION IS
ADVISED.

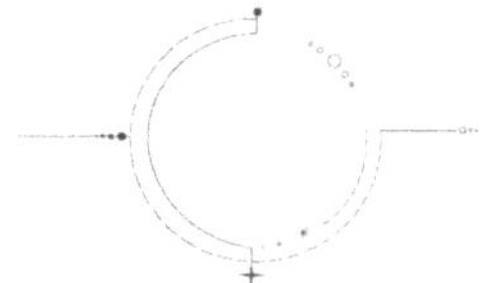

The only light in the room came from a soft glow outside the open window. Night fell and Kos hadn't bothered to get up from the floor where he had been talking to Orinthia. He laid on his back in the middle of the living room, staring at the ceiling and struggling to keep his head clear of thoughts. It was a losing battle. There was only so much abuse his mind could take before it snapped, throwing him through a tunnel into the past.

His body ached, and it served as a reminder of what he did. Beating Sylvanio to the brink of death stirred up old ghosts. They whispered to him, begging to be let out. Talking with Orinthia kept them away, but alone in the dark there was nowhere to hide them. He had considered telling her a few times, but he didn't know the words to explain it all.

*How can I tell her I see the faces of dead enemies and allies every time I close my eyes? That being alive is a reminder of those I've lost? What would she say if she knew, really knew, that killing had quickly left the realm of necessity and gave way to pure thrill? That sometimes I still enjoy it? That it gives me a power and hunger that eats at my core?*

Kos rolled to his knees and stilled, unaware he did so. His breath turned shallow. The edges of his vision narrowed. Then, the floor dropped out from under him, and he fell.

Shouting. Cries. Pain.

They came from all around him, from inside him.

His boots struck the deck as they landed through the scorched opening in the hull. The air was thick with the scent of burned circuitry and sweat. Sparks and stuttering lights lit up the corridor.

The breaching team always made quick work of disabling ships before his crew boarded. Still, the danger was ever present, and his heart pounded with adrenaline, ready to take out the first thing that moved.

His HUD scanned through the haze, searching for Mod Bleyers. The mission was simple: secure the ship and neutralize any remaining enemies.

Kos stepped forward as the last of his men filed in. He motioned to the others. "Clear left," he said in the comm.

His team followed as he raised his weapon and slunk down the passageway. Bodies dropped every few feet, yells and blaster fire echoed from all around.

They pressed on, up two decks, and stopped at a door. He signaled for his team to clear the rest of the corridor, then stepped aside as his demo tech moved in to set the charge.

A second later, the door lay in pieces at his feet.

Inside was a small room, no bigger than his shared cabin. Cramped. Walls lined with data drives and flickering monitors.

Two figures turned toward the breach. Both armed. Kos

barely had time to register the threat before the gunfire erupted.

A blaster bolt caught him in his shoulder. It would have burned through if it wasn't for the shock absorbing armor. He didn't flinch. He was too fast for them to get off a second shot.

Kos darted toward the closest of the two, tackling him to the floor. He rifle fell to his side on its sling. This was how he preferred it, close and personal. He was on top of the sailor, landing blows to the face. The sounds of his reinforced fists crunching bone with each hit.

The man gurgled, his hands beat uselessly against Kos' steel frame.

Kos didn't stop.

Boots scuffled behind him. One of his crew took a half-step forward, then stopped. No one said a word.

They had seen this before. This was why they followed him. He was the gun they aimed at the enemy and prayed never turned on them.

Kos shut it out. He shifted his weight, sliding his bracing hand up the man's throat. Their eyes looked.

The pleading look sent a jolt of shock through Kos' veins. His grip loosened for half a moment.

It was too late. The man's eyes unfocused and stared unmoving at Kos.

*They deserve this,* Kos told himself, dragging in a breath through gritted teeth. *They killed her. They started this war.*

Something stirred in the corner of his eye. The second sailor, who hadn't moved to defend his partner, watched Kos.

Kos rose, blood still pounding in his ears, and reached for his blaster.

"Please," the man said with a whimper.

Before Kos could draw, a blaster bolt cut through the air.

He followed the sound to see his newest member standing with their rifle trained where the sailor had been.

Kos stood over the bodies, panting heavily. His pulse made his head spin. The exhilaration was already fading.

*One mission. Two kills.* He made a mental note. *That's all they ever are.*

The room shrank around him. His mind slipped back to the present in a spiral of color and confusion. The screams still echoed, but they receded, folding into the background of his memory.

There were no cool hands to draw him back from the nightmare. The burning in his throat and ringing in his ears were his only companions.

Kos collapsed onto the dark living room floor, swallowing air like a man pulled from deep water without a rebreather. His stomach twisted. Every muscle trembled. Carpet fibers stuck to his lips as he panted.

The nightmare in his mind had ended. But the one in his body was about to begin.

Rain poured outside. Every drop slammed against the wall like a hammer. It made the pressure in his skull worse. His body was too weak to get up and close the window, so the tortuous sound went on.

The churning in his stomach worsened, provoked by the noise and spinning in his head. He hadn't eaten since before Orinthia left. There was nothing left in him but acid. Hot stomach acid rose up as he heaved onto Mimi's floor.

His shivers faded, though he did not feel cold. He never did anymore, not since nearing the limit of mod-intake. Same as his mother toward the end. It wasn't something he noticed until Orinthia pointed it out, while she came down from her poison-induced high.

Kos held his breath and forced himself to scoot back out

of the sick. The smell stung his nose, but it was a relief to not marinate it it anymore.

He lay still, making deliberate attempts to slow his heart rate and keep hold of reality. Episodes like this didn't always come alone. Thrutt used to keep watch. Orinthia after him. Someone was always there to make sure he was okay.

But not this time. The silence pressed in, loud and heavy. He listened to the thrumming in his pulse, waiting to see if it was over, or if he would be swallowed again.

*Thrutt, you better hurry,* he thought. *I can't do this on my own.*

After a long half hour, the world inside and around him calmed. Kos found the strength to push himself up, but only moved as far as a seated position. He propped his legs at an angle and rested his forearms on his knees.

The air was fresh and smelled of wet dirt. It made him think of Orinthia and how much she loved it. The thought of being without her was almost enough to send him into another spiral, but he refused to let it take hold. *I'll get her back. I have to, there's no other choice. Whatever I have to do, I do for us. We deserve a free life, and I won't stop until we get it.*

Kos' empty stomach growled, reminding him he had thrown up and it needed cleaning. It took a few attempts, but Kos rose and trodded to the kitchen to fetch a cleaning rag. He ran it under warm water before returning to his mess.

When it was cleared, he tossed the cloth in the sink and washed his hands. His mind wandered to food, the second love of his life. He stuffed whatever he could find from the cooler into his arms, then dropped into a seat at the table, eating until his body felt fit to burst.

The tension in his shoulders eased. The worst had passed.

Only the dull ringing in his ears remained, a final echo of the headache that refused to let go.

Kos cleaned up his eclectic meal, then filled a glass with water. He drank three full cups, filling in the gaps food couldn't reach, until even his mouth no longer craved hydration. After a long breath, he leaned against the counter, arms limp at his sides.

Rain continued. Not in hurried droves, but in taps and whispers.

For a moment, he didn't feel the weight of his past pressing against his chest. Just the thrum of the rain and the rhythm of his heart. It wasn't much, but it was better than before.

*On the bright side,* Kos thought, with an audible sigh, *maybe now my head's clear enough for a full night's sleep.*

The first one in almost a month.

# 13

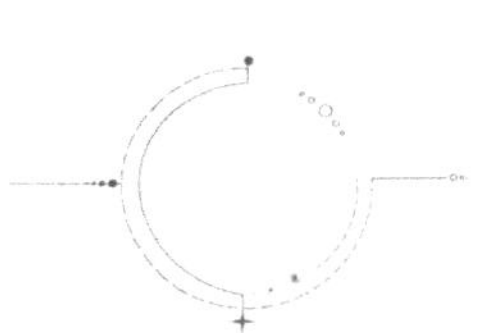

In the stillness of the half-dead ship, Orinthia stood in the center of her room, fingers wide and twitching in front of her. The spacer's helmet floated inches above the floor, turning in slow, deliberate circles. Her goal was not to bring it closer, that was easy enough. Manipulating the object proved far harder than calling them forward. With lips pressed into a thin line, she drew in a steady breath to center her focus.

It was not about strength. The key to her mod was focus. Control. She had to discipline her mind as much as the object, keeping her thoughts sharp and singular. That was not a problem in a dark and quiet room, alone. The true test would come in real time, when chaos and noise pressed in. But doing so would expose her gift, and that was not something she was ready to do. Not yet. Tensions were already high. If she wanted the crew's trust, she would have to ease her way in.

The helmet flipped backward three times, its pink visor catching the dull light with each turn. It started a fourth rotation, but Orinthia's arm trembled. She could not hold it up any longer. Holding on, she tried to slow the descent, but her grip faltered at the last second. The helmet clattered to the floor a foot below.

Strain snapped through her like a broken thread, and she dropped beside the helmet. Her mouth was dry. Her body heavy.

Something smacked the hull of the ship like a hand knocking. She flinched and tossed her head around looking for the source of the sound. A chill filled her arms and the back of her neck itched. Orinthia waited, listened, and extended her senses. Nothing but silence again.

She relaxed her shoulders and pressed her lips together, running her tongue across the inside of her mouth. Dry. Her throat felt like sandpaper. The mod drained her. Not just mentally, but her body, too.

*I need water*, she told herself. But this was not *Freya*. There was no stocked cooler. No Kos handing her snacks with a quiet, worried eye. With a sigh, she pushed herself upright. Her limbs were heavier than they should be. Boots on, hair tied up, she stepped into the corridor with practiced quiet.

The hallway was dim. Pipes and conduits exposed along the walls like veins. Her boots thudded softly against the grated floor as she approached the ladder.

A faded sign caught her attention. It had arrows listing the different decks.

↑ Bridge / Medic / Officer's Quarters
→ Crew Cabins / Armory
↓ Mess Deck / Engine bay

*Mess deck.* She tapped the words. The bars were smooth under her feet as she descended the narrow ladder with care.

Her arms shook, but she held tight. The lower she climbed, the warmer the air grew. It was heavy with the scent of fuel, oil, and recycled heat.

A second, more forceful object smacked the hull. It was louder this time. Larger than the last, perhaps. Orinthia curled and uncurled her fingers but pressed on to the galley.

The mess deck was quiet, achingly so. A handful of benched tables filled the small room. She spotted a dispenser along the back wall and crossed through the seats, her steps echoing slightly in the hollow space.

The water was warm and metallic, but it coated her throat well enough. She refilled the cup and leaned on the edge of the counter, trying to not think about what was actually in the liquid.

Voices, muffled but distinct, came from the wall to her right. She strained her ears to listen, and crept closer.

"Heard the banging," Cliff said. "Did we make it to the debris?"

There was a pause, then the crackle of the captain's voice, almost too quiet to hear, came over the comm. "Appears to be an old theater of war. Ship graveyard. Half the quadrant is covered in scrap. Can't say I recognize the battle, but it was an expansive ordeal."

Another pause.

"We're reading a larger object at the center of it," the captain continued. "Looks like an intact ship. Picking up a distress signal. Could be an old, unanswered mayday, but XO's taking us in for a closer view. I'd like to move out as soon as we clear the field, though. So get that engine running."

"I'll keep digging," Cliff replied. "Getting low on spares, but I'll make it work."

"Copy," the captain said.

Steps thumped behind the wall, followed by tools clanking.

"He's going to make us go out there, isn't he?" Marius asked. His voice was quieter, farther away.

"Not me. You," Cliff replied, with a hint of levity to it. "I've got to fix the engine. You're Away Lead."

Marius grumbled. "Not by choice. Firincha bailed with the rest of them and left me to pick up the slack. Dai can't lead, and you're always elbow-deep in repairs. Not like there's a team left anyway." He sighed. "Maybe we should've just gone with them. Better than waiting around to get picked off one by one."

Orinthia's breath hitched. She covered her mouth and took slow steps toward the door. Her body tensed. *If they catch me listening, especially to talk like that...*

The ratchet stopped turning.

"Deserting now, too?" Cliff asked, his voice unreadable.

"It's not like I want to," Marius snapped. "But what's the point, man? Don't tell her I said it, but Anton's right. The GMH doesn't care about us out here. Look at this rust trap. You think that's going to change with new management?"

"Don't much care if it does," Cliff replied. "I'm doing my job. Trying to keep things a little safer, a little longer."

Their voices were almost completely blocked out by the distance. Another step closer to the door.

*Screech.*

The floor shuddered, followed by the grinding of the engine.

Orinthia flinched. Her fingers clenched around the water so tight, the cup nearly crumpled. Her heart thudded against her ribs. She set the cup down on the nearest table and turned for the door. Moving the last few steps to the ladder, she prayed they had not heard her above the noise.

As fast and quietly as she could, she climbed up rungs, keeping her breath as steady as possible. The middle deck opened above her and she pulled herself through. Before both feet were securely on the landing, Orinthia broke out into a sprint.

She only made it a few feet before colliding with Annatilla, sending them both to the ground.

Metal rang out as Annatilla hit the floor, her helmet slapping hard against the ground. She gasped and bolted upright, fingers flying over the seams to check the latches.

Orinthia rolled to her knees, caught somewhere between guilt and adrenaline. She watched the woman's eyes dart in straight lines, perhaps doing a visor scan. A beat passed. Annatilla gave a slow, relieved blink.

"You okay?" Orinthia asked, unsure what else to say.

"What is wrong with you?" Annatilla snapped, voice sharp and raw.

Then, just as quickly, she blinked again, composing herself. She let out a shaky exhale.

"Sorry," Annatilla said, voice smooth. Almost forced. "I just… Watch yourself, yeah?"

The tone tried to soften her reaction, but Orinthia read something else. Like the truth had been swapped out last second. All she could do was nod short, quick shakes.

They looked at each other for a long moment, neither moving until Annatilla pulled herself to her feet. She checked her backside with a tight twist then turned back to Orinthia.

Orinthia joined her, gave an apologetic bow, and stepped to the side to pass Annatilla. The woman did not move.

"Captain's looking for you," she said.

This made Orinthia pause. Her mind raced with reasons why he would want to see her. She could not pin one thing down.

"He's on the bridge," Annatilla said when Orinthia had not acknowledged her first statement.

"Right, thanks," Orinthia said. She put one foot behind the other and turned back to the ladder.

When she reached the bridge, the bulkhead was already propped open. She stepped through, still feeling the sting of Annatilla's tone and the unease of what she had overheard in the galley.

Captain Solvay did not need to look up when she came in. He was facing her directly, arms tucked behind his back, as if to say *finally.*

"Anton," he said. "I believe I saw you carrying a spacesuit when you arrived."

Orinthia nodded once, unsure if it was a question or accusation.

"Now is the time to show your worth," Solvay said. "There's a distress call from a vessel dead ahead, but we're too deep in the debris field. I cannot take the *Tertion* any closer, and they are not responding to our hails. You and Armitage will go over and investigate."

"Me?" Orinthia asked, brow furrowed. "Why me?"

"Because those are my orders," Solvay said with a flat voice. "If you're going to be on my ship, you'll work like the rest of my crew. Suit up. You leave in twenty minutes."

# 14

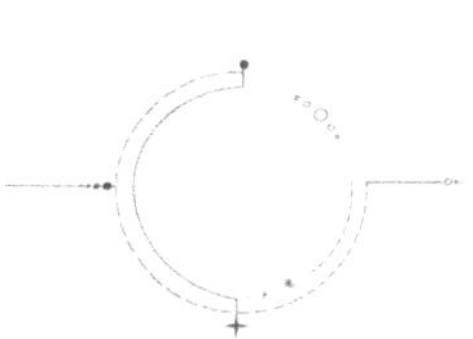

*A* steel door was all that stood between Orinthia and the inky black vastness of space. Stars blinked in the distance through the porthole beside the airlock. She craned her head to get a better look out as the *Tertion* aligned itself with a mysterious starship. Hunks of debris in various sizes and shapes floated by, like discarded puzzle pieces. Larger ones, such as whole sections of fuselages, hung suspended throughout the mess.

Marius shoved a jetpack against her arm. "Put this on."

Orinthia looked at him and grabbed the pack. "What happened out there?"

"War," Marius said, strapping his jetpack to his suit. "Won't be surprised if we see summies."

"What's a summy?"

"Space mummy. Bodies don't decay out there. Moisture boils out in a few seconds, and the vacuum preserves them. Lots of old theaters have summies, especially if they were this far out and undocumented."

Orinthia's pulse was in her teeth and her mouth felt like it was full of static. She had seen a handful of dead bodies before, but none like Marius described.

Marius clicked on his helmet and tapped twice near the base of the visor. "Do you copy?"

"All clear," Orinthia replied, shoving away the knots in her stomach. Her jetpack weighed against her back and she adjusted to keep the straps from digging into her shoulders. The inside of her helmet had a faint chemical scent that marked its first voyage into space.

Marius tapped once more. "Captain, do you copy?" he asked over the broad channel.

"We do," Captain Solvay responded in Orinthia's helmet. "Keep on your toes and report anything you find."

With a nod toward the airlock, Marius pressed a switch and the doors slid open with a hiss.

Though the suit was insulated against the freezing temperatures of space, Orinthia felt the warmth bleed from her body. She stepped to the edge of the opening and looked out. Nothing waited beneath her feet but the void. Her breath quickened, and she touched a small spot on her abdomen, an old ache that never quite went away.

Neither of her spacewalks had ended well. One left a blaster hole through her, changing everything about her. The other earned her time in a marauder brig.

Being on the edge of the void did not frighten her. But part of her, an ancient and human part, still wanted to hold back.

Without his own hesitations, Marius pushed past her and leaped out. He spun to look at her, jabbing his thrusters to slow his momentum. He stopped ten feet from the hatch and called out to her. "Relax, Anton. It's only open space. Not like you haven't walked out on bigger things."

His turn of phrase burned a fire through Orinthia's gut.

She narrowed her eyes, snuffing the hesitation out like a match.

"I haven't walked out on anything I miss," Orinthia said, lacing her words with cool flames. "I just learned to stop wasting my time on the wrong side."

As she pushed out of the airlock, away from the power of the gravity generator, nothing held her back. A sense of power washed over her. Stillness. Quiet. It was as close to perfection as she could imagine.

For a minute, Orinthia was transported back to the Glass Shard, flying through its center. The last moments of her old life ticked away. Before the truth shattered her reality, ripping her apart like the wound in her side. Tearing through what she thought she knew and launching her into the person she was in that moment.

Marius gave a sharp whistle over the comm, dragging her attention back to the task. He turned toward the drifting ship ahead.

With a blow of air from her nose, Orinthia angled herself to follow him. The pair moved quietly through the mess of ships. They dodged smaller pieces and climbed over larger ones, shapes blending into one another in the void.

A distant star cast sharp beams across the debris, light bouncing off twisted metal and fractured hulls. It was just enough to illuminate the path ahead, and a single step more. Light in space did not fill the dark, only cut through it. It should not have been beautiful, but it was. That made it worse.

She pushed herself up and jumped over a section of fuselage. As she did, a crooked pipe floated toward her. She raised a hand to swat it aside, waiting to meet it. But, drifting closer to each other, she saw the truth.

Frayed cables jutted from one end, bent and curved like a claw.

Her breath caught somewhere between a gasp and a scream.

A dismembered arm, stained a smoky green, spun past her. She nudged her thruster, enough to avoid it, and turned to follow it through the wreckage.

Her visor lit the path in stark cones of white. Without it, she would be blind. The wide circle landed on the hull she had climbed over, illuminating the nightmarish sight. Without counting, Orinthia made out at least fifteen bodies strapped to seats. Most were intact, but others were ripped apart, their limbs orbiting like an asteroid belt.

Orinthia pinched her lips to keep from yelling and throwing up at the same time.

"Hey, you don't have to look at them," Marius said in her comm. His tone was softer than before, not friendly but understanding. "Just keep going. There's bound to be more, so stay focused on the ship and don't turn back."

The momentum of her thrusters used a second before kept her floating forward, but she could not take her eyes off the dead. They shrunk as she moved, and the hull rotated away from her. But they stayed in her mind like a graveyard of fabric and bone.

Something touched her arm. The scream she had held back ripped through her throat. She turned to see Marius.

"Yeah, this was a great idea," he said, shaking his head. "Come on. We're almost there."

They continued their journey, reaching the ship and activating their mag boots to secure them.

"*Tertion*, we've made contact with the distressed ship," Marius said, tapping his comm. There was no response. He tried again. Nothing.

He turned to Orinthia. "Sometimes thick debris like this jams the signal." Though his tone suggested he did not fully believe it. He pointed to a raised square door near the center of the ship. "Look, there's a hatch. We'll go to the bridge and try their comm link. They called for help, so we should be able to get a message to the *Tertion*."

His boots scraped against the steel as he led the way and tested the hatch. It did not budge. Without a word, he pulled a plasma torch from his belt and rapped the handle on the door, then paused. Silence. Marius ignited the torch and pressed it to the seams, carving slow lines until the hatch groaned loose.

The door drifted open and Marius sheathed his cutter, grinning to himself. After deactivating his mag boots, he lowered himself inside feet first. His movements were smooth. Efficient. Like second nature.

Orinthia watched in barely-hidden awe. It was not more than a minute before they were inside the hold. She would never give him the satisfaction of a compliment, but was impressed nonetheless.

"Scared of ghosts?" Marius asked, looking up at her.

The shaft was lit by a slow blinking orange light. Orinthia slid in, turning off her light, and stood shoulder-to-shoulder with Marius in the tight space. In front of them was an airlock door that led to a sealed passageway. She did not think there was enough room for both of them to fit through.

"Looks like a repair access hatch," Marius said. He pointed forward. "Those doors are to keep the ship pressurized to not interfere with the life-support and artificial gravity. I'll go first and check things out. If it's clear, you come in behind."

He did not wait for a response before activating the switch and opening the first door. It hissed and groaned, like it had not been used for years. Once inside, the first door closed behind Marius, who sunk to the floor. A bright light flashed six times in his small room before the second door opened. He stepped through and surveyed around. Without looking back at her, he waved a hand for Orinthia to follow.

Repeating the process, Orinthia joined him in the main hall of the ship. It looked abandoned in the sense that the ship was empty, but no more antiquated than *Freya*. She did not know what she expected. Maybe sparking wires, holes ripped through walls, or at the very least discarded contents left on the floor from its passengers rushing to safety. Nothing gave away why they would have called for help.

"This is Officer Armitage of the Galactic Marauder Hunters," Marius called out over his helmet's speaker. "We received your distress signal on our ship, the MHS *Tertion*. I'm here to help."

No response. No noise. No movement.

Marius moved to the left side of the wall and walked another few feet before repeating his statement.

They passed an open door. Orinthia hesitated, then leaned her head in. The room was poorly lit, shadows swallowing the corners. Her eyes strained against the dark.

For a second, no more than a blink, someone stood in the corner.

She flicked her helmet's light back on and swept it across the room. Empty. Tiny pin pricks moved up her spine. The kind she felt when someone stood behind her. She swallowed the saliva filling her mouth and looked back.

"Scare yourself?" Marius teased, moving farther down the hall.

"I'm not scared," Orinthia lied, grateful he did not have the same mod she did. Her chest beat against her thermal undershirt. "I just thought I saw something and it surprised me. Ship's too quiet."

"Agreed." Marius nodded. "Let's find the bridge. Maybe someone is holed up in there."

They passed more open doors, and Orinthia took her time looking inside. She kept her light on and waited for her eyes to adjust before making a sweep. The farther they went into the ship, the deeper the pin pricks dug, radiating through her arms and up her neck. She tried to shake off the feeling and rotated her shoulders, thinking the new suit was applying too much pressure.

Nothing worked. A deep sensation pushed down on her, and she spun around. Another shadow darted across the hall. She nearly sprained her neck following it. Her hands, beneath two layers of spacer gloves, froze.

"Marius," Orinthia whispered to hide the tremble in her voice. "I know I saw something."

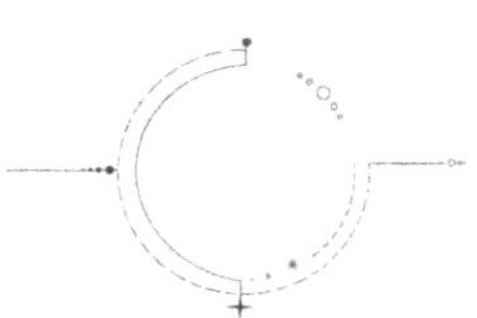

## 15

*K*ian had dismissed the shifting shadows on the *Mathias* as tricks of isolation and exhaustion. But on this ship, Orinthia was not alone. She knew what she saw behind her. The circumstances were different.

The feeling was not.

Still, Marius did not believe her. "Don't," Marius said, not bothering to look back at her as he kept moving toward the front of the ship. "Deep space is not for the weak. Lots of things can make shadows move. Angles of your flashlight, reflections of mirrors, a smudge on your visor. You're letting your imagination run wild." He paused long enough for the words to settle. "Frankly, it's almost embarrassing."

Anger flashed through her, burning away the fear. She opened her mouth to snap back, but the words never came.

Marius froze mid-step as they rounded the corner into the main corridor. Orinthia slammed into his back, stumbling to stay upright.

Then she saw why he stopped.

Dozens of bodies filled the corridor. Some were slumped

in piles, others propped upright, held in place by the weight of other corpses. A few leaned against the walls, their jaws unhinged, eyes locked in distant, glassy stares. Like statues carved in the middle of their final scream.

Orinthia let out a shuddered whimper.

Each body wore a different uniform or spacesuit, but none matched the callsigns or insignias of the ship they were on.

Marius stepped forward and crouched beside a few of the corpses, examining them closely. He shook his head. "This doesn't make sense."

Orinthia found her voice. "What doesn't?" As if staring at a hall full of dead people made sense in the first place.

"I know some of these sailors," Marius said. "Not personally. But their faces and names." He pointed to a trio crumpled in the corner, suits streaked with grime and frostbite. "Most of them were aboard ships reported missing. These three?" He gestured to three bodies clad in teal. "They're Hunters."

Marius wrung his hands together and slowly scanned over the area. His helmet tilted to the side and his shoulders rose steady as he took in deep breaths.

"*Tertion*, do you read me?" He tried again, voice clipped and tight. "There's a situation I need advice on. Do you copy?"

Orinthia's stomach turned. For a man so smug, so certain, even a crack in his words felt like a warning siren.

She lowered her gaze and stepped through the group, careful to find clear footing. Crouching down, she examined one of the GMH uniforms. The name of the badge was familiar, but only in a vague sense, like one she had heard in passing or during a briefing.

Still hunched over, a low hum sounded in her head. She

popped up straight and looked around. "Marius." Her words were sharp in her mouth. "Did you say something?"

"No," he answered, not looking up.

A tingling sensation built up in her right arm followed by a second, louder hum in her mind. She focused hard on the surroundings. Her breath shook as she exhaled from her nose.

"You're sure they're all dead?" she asked, her eyes moving over every inch of the room.

"They're all very dead. Not a single freshie. I'd say at least a few months since the last one was alive."

Another, more prominent shadow shifted in the corner of Orinthia's right eye. She snapped her head toward it, hand flying to her hip, only to grasp air. There was no time to curse herself for leaving the blaster behind. A wave of static prickled down her arms, crawling in a line from the right side of her body, wrapping across her back, then trailing down the left. She stiffened, breath tight.

Marius did not notice. He was still hunched over his wristlet, noting names and affiliations.

More dark shapes, like when she was in prison on the *Mathias*, danced slightly out of her view. She stared above Marius' head and tried to concentrate on what she could not see. Her head hummed again, louder.

"Slowly stand up," she whispered.

He lifted his head and frowned.

"There's something in here with us," Orinthia said, no longer restraining the panic in her voice. "I think whatever did this —" she waved an open hand over the bodies, "— is still aboard."

Marius stilled, his attention steady on her. For a long second, they stared at each other through their visors. She could not read his expression, but something in his posture changed. He moved slower, more deliberate, like he finally believed her. Without a word, his hand slid to his side, and unlatched the blaster from its holster.

Every nerve in her body lit up, alive and alert. Like she was surrounded by a crowd. She did not see them, but she felt them. More than five living forces moved in slow, calculated circles around her and Marius. Predators sizing up prey.

She shut her eyes and drew in deep, steadying breaths, trying to decipher what her body told her.

Whatever stalked them had no form, none of the weight or movement of beings covered in cloaking tech. The energy radiated off them in ebbs and flows like a gas. No mass. No gravity. They drifted through the room untethered to the same plane she and Marius stood on.

The pieces clicked into place, and her eyes flew open with a jolt.

"This is the Spectral Scow," she said.

Marius let out a nervous chuckle. "That's a deep space tale. Specters aren't real."

"We are in deep space, Marius." Orinthia bit back. "Ghosts may not exist, but whatever these are, they are very, very real."

"I don't see or hear anything. So either you're in shock from seeing all this, or you're lying to me."

"This isn't shock," Orinthia said, her breath shallow, forehead damp. "Listen to me. I can't fully explain it, but I know there's something in here. They're listening to us. Talking to each other. I can feel it."

Marius opened his mouth to respond, but froze. His body lifted off the ground, feet dangling, arms thrashing in wild strikes at something unseen.

"Stop it!" Orinthia shouted. She flung her hands out, searching for space between atoms, reaching with everything she had to find whatever held him. A mass of energy surged behind her. Before she could switch her focus, she was yanked upward. She kicked, her lungs were being crushed under invisible pressure. Not just in fear, something had wrapped around her insides, squeezing like a vice.

Her heart pounded. Stars burst across her vision. Her ears rang. Heat climbed her throat.

Still, she searched. Her mod crackled beneath her skin as she cast her awareness outward, desperate to grasp whatever force was doing this, even as her body began to fail.

The walls of her mind slowly caved in, blocking out the room with bright white. Inch by inch, the tunnel narrowed, swallowing her.

Then, her mod found it. It made contact with a form. The being was weak and fluid, unlike anything she had felt before, but it was enough to grab hold of. She imagined the particles, tiny but plentiful, and took hold of each one. With a gasp, Orinthia forced the entity off her, and fell a foot down to the ground.

Her body trembled and she struggled to stay conscious. Marius' face turned purple, his movements slowing and he slapped helplessly at nothing.

Again, Orinthia closed her eyes, this time with an idea of what to look for, and grabbed hold of Marius' attacker. She yelled as she pulled her hand back toward her body.

Marius roared as he inhaled deep breaths of air from inside his helmet, followed by choking.

The room darkened around her, but she could not let it pull her in. If she passed out while they were still surrounded, it would have been for nothing. With everything she had left, she extended farther out and connected with every spectral form in the room. Her arms shook and tears dripped down her cheeks from the strain. It was the most she had ever used her mod, and it drained her. With one final shove, she forced them past the walls, away from her and Marius.

Weakened, she collapsed forward. Fatigue overtook her and she crashed headfirst into the ground, laying beside the body of a GMH officer whose life ended long before. His hollow eyes bore into her and it was the last thing she saw as the darkness closed in.

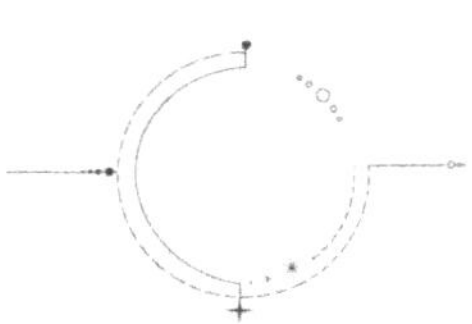

Kos adjusted the overhead lamp and reached for the spanner, his mind focused and clear. Each ratchet, hiss, and beep of the hangar dulled his restlessness, but not enough to make him forget why he was passing time and pocketing a few extra credits. Thrutt would show, he always did. It was the "when" that made him anxious. But, elbow deep inside the inner workings of a ship, even one that wasn't his, was when Kos was most at peace.

Being a marauder was a way to make money. It was never about conquering the stars or building a name for himself. If he had found the right opportunity, he would have liked nothing more than to rebuild machines full-time. That was what drew him into Jari's doors to begin with. But after Jari learned he was a pilot, it all went out the window. Sure, he got to fix things here and there, but it wasn't the same.

*When this is all over, I'm getting back to the NCR and cashing in some of those credits from the restaurant,* he thought. *I'll get whatever we need to fix Freya, then use what's left over to buy a repair shop. There's places all over the galaxy I could set up, and every one of them will need someone to fix ships.*

Neither Thrutt nor Orinthia knew anything about machines. They were the best part of his life, but not ones he could talk about his passion with. Still, he knew they'd support him, whenever he got around to telling them about his new dream. Once Orinthia was pardoned, and their worries were parsecs behind him.

"Rogue," Jari called out, his voice echoing through the garage.

Kos pushed off the compartment edge and twisted to see him approaching. "Yeah?"

"Climb down here," Jari said, motioning with his hand. "We need to have a chat."

*Those words are never good*, Kos thought. He filled his lungs, letting the tension ease out with a slow exhale. The spanner clipped against his thigh as he hooked it back onto his belt and started down the ladder. Jari was waiting at the base by the time he hit the ground.

Wiping his hands on his coveralls, Kos asked, "What do you need?"

Jari twisted his mouth, but didn't look Kos directly in the face. He cleared his throat. "How are you?"

Kos almost laughed. It was not what he expected to hear. "I'm good. Thanks." He paused and looked sideways for a moment. "How are you?"

"That not what I meant. How are you? After your..." He balled his hands into fists and made a boxing motion.

The lightness drained from Kos' chest like someone flipped a switch. He looked at Jari's shoes. "Oh. That. Yeah, I'm okay. Sorry if your ship is messed up. Did Kian get it sorted?"

Jari didn't answer right away. The silence stretched, thickening the air. Around them, the garage stayed alive with motion. Tools clanked and pounded, echoing off the steel walls like distant thunder.

Kos stood still, focusing on everything but the man in front of him.

"How about I take you to lunch?" Jari finally said. He twitched his eyes to meet Kos' for a second, then lowered them again. "Get changed and I'll meet you out front in ten." The man turned and walked away before Kos gave an answer.

*Perfect*, Kos thought. *I'm getting fired on my last day.*

THE STREET outside the port wore the same face as every other port Kos had seen. Food stalls sizzling with oil and spice, trinket shops hawking cheap memories, and windows filled with imported luxuries no one truly needed. He and Jari walked along the fringe of it in silence, the buzz of life around them fading into background noise.

They stopped in front of a modest eatery, its doorway spilling warmth and the scent of seared meat onto the street. Jari gave a small nod to the server lingering at the back, then led Kos to a table pressed against a broad window.

A Leynin waiter hurried over, his tiny, clawed feet ticking against the floor, with two tablets in hand. "Usual today, Jari?" he asked, voice high pitched and smooth.

"What's today's catch?" Jari asked reaching for the menu.

"Green daxel. Brought fresh from Kren yesterday."

Jari twisted his mouth. "I think I'll pass this time. Daxel is one of those meals that doesn't always sit right with me. Got a busy week ahead." He looked at the tablet and scrolled. "I'll have the grilled tandri skewer."

The waiter took Jari's menu and tapped a few times before turning to Kos. "And you, sir?"

Kos hadn't fully gone over the menu, but had spotted a few things that sounded interesting. He made one more quick pass, then said, "The yulen and grain stew, thanks."

With a polite nod, the waiter accepted Kos' tablet and moved off.

Tension worked through Kos' hands, his fingers clenching and releasing as he waited. The more he sat with it, the less it felt like a firing. That kind of thing usually came behind closed doors, not over a shared meal. Unless this was damage control. Jari's way of keeping things calm and casual.

"Don't worry about the ship," Jari said, scratching his neck. "That's what insurance is for. Besides, there was no damage done. I told you, you're the best pilot I have."

"Thanks," Kos said, chewing his bottom lip for a second, and tugging at his sleeves. "What's this about?"

Jari let out a low sigh. "I'm not as young as I look. Was in university when the war started. Awful thing that was. My brother…" his voice trailed off, followed by a shaky breath. "Tanzal joined up against our parents' wishes. He was gone for ages, only coming home for a few weeks here and there. Every visit, he was a little less himself. Until the last time. Tanz wasn't the man who left. He was unrecognizable as the best friend I grew up with. He was angry, all the time. Spent hours alone in his room, just laying there not saying anything."

"We did our best to help him, but none of us knew how," Jari continued. There was a softness to his voice. Like if he spoke louder, it would break his soul. "Tanz didn't talk about what he went through. But we could guess. His body was scarred and tattooed —"

Kos tugged at the cuffs of his sleeves.

"— and when he did sleep, if he slept at all, it was broken."

Kos sat still, every breath tighter than the last. Jari was pulling back parts of his past he had never told him. He might as well have swapped out his brother's name for Kos'.

"I won't tell you what happened to him, but I'm sure you know plenty like him." Jari pinched his lips together and drew in a deep breath through his nose. "But I decided then I'd do anything I could to help others who came back like that. That's part of why I hired you. To give you a safe environment to work in, with a steady income so there'd be one less thing to worry about. Had I known you were battling other demons, I would've done more."

"Jari," Kos said in a whisper. "I'm sorry about your brother."

"Me, too." Jari nodded. He cleared his throat. "You're leaving, I know. And even if I don't fully understand why, I want you to know you have a place here if you decide to come back. No questions asked. No time limit. We'll just pick up right where we left off."

The chair creaked under Jari's weight as he leaned over and reached into his pocket. He pulled out his hand and tossed a credit chip on the table. "I'll keep her safe until you come home."

Kos opened his mouth, but Jari kept speaking.

"If you need anything, I'll take care of it. Best I can. Just call and I'll answer."

"Jari, I want to pay for *Freya's* storage," Kos said. "It's the least I can do for taking up the space."

"You could always sell her to me," Jari said with a wink and a grin that didn't quite reach his eyes. "She's a gorgeous ship. Still think she deserves to fly."

Before Kos could respond, the waiter returned with their

meal. Jari pushed the credit chip aside to make room for the food.

"Enjoy," the waiter said as he set down the trays.

The food steamed, fragrant and warm. It filled Kos' nose but did not touch his soul. All he could do was stare. His stomach turned.

"There was no offense meant," Jari said, leaning on his elbows. "But as you're out of here tomorrow, I didn't want to miss my chance. You're not a man of many words, which I respect. Just know you don't have to go through it alone."

He leaned back in his chair and picked up his fork. With a wink he said, "Eat up. Don't want the boss to get after you for taking too long of a lunch."

Kos managed a ghost of a smile, but it didn't stick. He looked down at the food again, steam curling around his face like a fog, and picked up the spoon with a hand that felt foreign to him.

*You don't have to go through it alone*, he repeated.

Maybe he could believe that. Maybe someday.

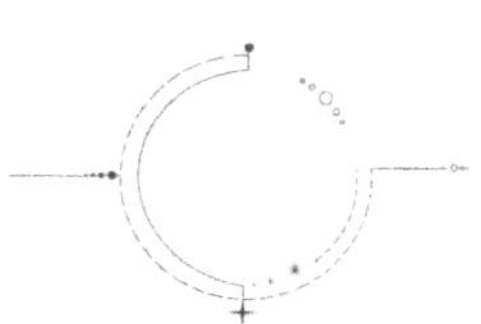

## 17

*A* weight pressed on her chest. Something shifted nearby, soft and subtle. Orinthia flexed her fingers. She could not move her arms.

*The basement.* Her breath shuddered. She could not open her eyes or Desidario would know. A needle tugged at the crook of her elbow. The burn would come soon.

*Kos,* she thought, searching for his sound. *I need to tell Kos I'm okay, before Desidario sees. How long was I out this time? He has to be worried.*

Her nails tapped the surface beneath her. Not metal. A cushion. She shifted her weight. Not a table. Mattress, maybe.

*Not the basement.* Her mind scrambled to make sense of the setting. She searched for something to anchor her. *My bunk. On Freya. Okay, that's good then.*

Orinthia shifted again.

"Oh, hey. The stimulants are working." The voice was not Kos'. It was a woman's.

"Mimi?" Orinthia whispered, her throat burned.

"Nope," the voice said, a little too casual. "Annatilla.

Remember me? We knocked heads when you ran me over in the corridor."

The voice moved closer as she spoke. A gloved hand brushed her cheek.

Orinthia tried to sit up. To pull off her restraints. Nothing happened.

"No, no. You're okay." Annatilla said. "Just open your eyes."

"I can't," Orinthia said. Her heart worked its way up her chest.

"You can. Take it slow."

Orinthia stilled her body and listened, focusing on the pulse in her ears. She peeled her eyelids back like they had been glued shut. A blurry face behind a transparent visor hovered above her. The light behind the woman's helmet framed her like a halo. It took another handful of seconds for Orinthia's vision to clarify and Annatilla's large brown eyes came into focus.

"Annatilla?" Orinthia asked. Her head swam trying to grab hold of reality.

"Yes. Don't worry. You're back on the *Tertion* in the med-bay. Marius dropped you off. Didn't say more than you had passed out."

Orinthia looked down at her arms, startled to find they weren't strapped in place after all. No pressure on her chest, either. Just the phantom weight of something that had never been there. Slowly, she rested her head back and reached for reason.

The ache was real, though. Something, or someone, had crushed her lungs from the inside. She shivered as the memory crawled across her skin.

"I'm running a blood panel to rule out any chemical or biological contaminants," Annatilla added. "Armitage is quarantined in his cabin until you're both cleared. Shouldn't be much longer."

"How did we get back?" Orinthia asked, dragging through her mind, trying to piece together what happened.

"Marius," Annatilla said, moving to bring a chair closer to her bed. "Do you remember anything?"

"We almost died," Orinthia answered, hollow. "They got Marius first, then me."

"They?" Annatilla crossed her leg over her knee and leaned forward.

Orinthia paused and let the memory wash over her. The energy radiating off her attackers clung to her nerves. "There's something on that ship. Murderous. Unrelenting. At first, we found dozens of bodies scattered across the main cabin. Looked like they were ambushed. But there were no wounds.

She drew in a shaky breath. "While Marius was inspecting one of the fallen Hunters, we were attacked. I tried to help him, but whatever it was… it got me, too."

Annatilla froze. Not rigid, but still. Like a statue carved out of marble and plastina. There was a grace to her, evident even in the silence. "How did you get free?"

Orinthia forced herself into a coughing fit, stalling for time as her exhausted mind scrambled for a lie. Improvisation was usually her strength, but the toll her mod and her brush with death took left her drained. She continued coughing until Annatilla gestured to the sink and offered her water.

It was not any better than the one from the galley. Still, Orinthia took it and scooted herself into a seated position. After a sip, she set it aside. "I don't know why we lived when the others didn't. Maybe Marius saw something I couldn't." It was the best she could come up with in her current state. She thought she would have had more time to work up a story about her mod, but it would have to do for the moment.

Annatilla eyed her for a beat. "Once I know you're not going to keel over I'll check on Armitage and see what he knows."

"Can I talk to him first?" Orinthia almost jumped off the bed as she asked. Then, she relaxed her posture and added, "He may be more open to talking about it with me since I was there. The whole story sounds crazy as it is."

There was long pause between them. Orinthia hoped she would not push the issue further.

"Let me know what he says," Annatilla answered.

IT TOOK effort to convince Annatilla to let Orinthia leave the med-bay. She had to promise not to push herself or move around too much, but in the end Annatilla agreed that being in her own quarters would suffice. Orinthia's labs were clear. No contaminations and no threat to the crew, so there was no real reason to keep her confined any longer.

Annatilla escorted her back to the cabins, but broke off at her own room. Alone, Orinthia continued until she stopped in from of Marius' door. She did not now what to say to him, or even what he would ask when he saw her.

*Does he realize I saved us?* she wondered. *Or was he too busy fighting for his life to notice anything else?*

The anxiety of not knowing what he knew finally got to Orinthia, and she rapped her knuckles against the steel. No sound came from the other side, but she waited anyway, knocking again.

"What do you want?" Marius asked as the door slid open, tugging a shirt over his head.

"Can we talk?" Orinthia asked.

"No." Marius moved his hand to close the door again.

"Then why did you open in the first place?" Orinthia asked, pinching her eyebrows together.

"So I could tell you to leave me alone. Go."

"Thank you for bringing me back." Orinthia rushed the out the words before he could put the barrier between them.

It made him pause. Marius wiggled his jaw. "Thanks for doing whatever it was you did to save our skins."

"You do know it was me, then?" Orinthia lowered her voice, not in shame, but to keep their conversation as private as she could.

"I don't know what I know," Marius said. "Just that it wasn't anything I did. So it had to have been you."

"Can I come in?"

"Don't you already have a boyfriend?" Marius asked, slow blinking. "You and that marauder. Or does he not mind sharing?"

"You know that's not what this is. I need to talk about the *Scow*."

Marius sighed and shook his head before stepping to the side. "Whatever."

His room had more personality than hers, which she expected. Like *Freya* was for Kos, the *Tertion* was the Messies' home between ports, and Marius likely spent more time aboard than wherever he claimed residency.

Orinthia stepped into the center of the room and tried to make herself small, not wanting to impose more than she already had. She understood how the presence of an unwelcome stranger could steal the peace from a room. Still, she hoped to win him over like Mimi had done to her.

"What did you feel when you were —" Orinthia mimed being choked, unable to find the right words for what happened.

The man across from her did not answer. He closed his eyes for a second, hard lines spread across the creases. When he opened them again, he focused on a space behind Orinthia's head. "Am I supposed to say scared?"

"You say whatever you want," Orinthia said, her voice soft and even. She did not like him, not really. But she understood what war could do to a person. She had seen it in Kos. Even if she did not know Marius' story, she knew enough to give him the space to talk if he needed it. The stress of almost dying would have set Kos off into a spiral, and she worried Marius' might have done the same.

He lowered his gaze and his voice. "I was scared. Thought I'd…"

Marius' words trailed off. Then he shifted and stiffened his shoulders. "What is it you did?"

Orinthia saw it. The broken armor. It closed up as soon as it appeared. She took a deep breath and asked, "Do you know who my father is?"

"Of course I do. The great Anton patriarch," Marius said, sarcasm thick in his voice.

"You also know I was charged with my brother's murder, which since he's alive, I clearly didn't do. But I found Desidario. Made him fix Uri after Adora shot him. It came with a trade."

She glanced down at her hands, as if the truth were something she could hold. "Not willingly. I had to help him with one last experiment. What I did on the *Scow* was the result of that. It's a new mod, something he spent the last years of his life perfecting."

"Last years?" Marius asked, cocking his head.

"He's dead."

The words fell flat. It was the first time she had said them aloud. She had thought them many times, circled around them, tried to make them digestible, but never spoken them. There was a pain in her chest she did not not understand, nor like. He had treated her poorly her whole life, never truly showing love. Never cared for her more than the obligation required. They had fought more than they spoke. Peace had never existed between them.

And yet, she mourned him.

She mourned him, and the mother she never knew. Worst of all, she mourned him alone. The others did not know him like she did. She was the last to see him alive. To speak to him and hear his voice. The thought twisted in her stomach.

Orinthia pushed the ache down before it could overtake her. "That's not the point of this. I don't want to talk about him. But there are very few people who know about my mod, and I'd like to keep it that way. I've been forced to share my secrets for too long. Please. Help me hold onto this one."

"What does it do?" Marius asked. He crossed his arms and spread his stance.

"I'm still figuring it out," Orinthia said. She could not lift her gaze to meet him. "Ahto killed him before he could explain it to me. But I can control things, like make objects move. My body can sense energy on a cellular level. That's all I really know or can put into words."

"Why keep it a secret?" Marius asked. There was no accusation to his question, only curiosity. "It sounds like a great power to have."

"Because I've been used as a weapon before," Orinthia said quietly. "And the twins don't know about this mod. The fewer people who do, the better. If I'm going to use it against them, I need it to stay a surprise."

Marius took in a deep breath and let it out in a slow stream. "Fine. I guess that's what I owe you for saving my life. But don't think this makes us friends. We're barely allies."

Orinthia lifted her head and locked with his eyes. "If that's all you think of me, then you've got a lot to learn. I'll show you I can be trusted. We all make mistakes. We all have our past. I *have* changed."

Marius did not blink. "We'll see."

## 18

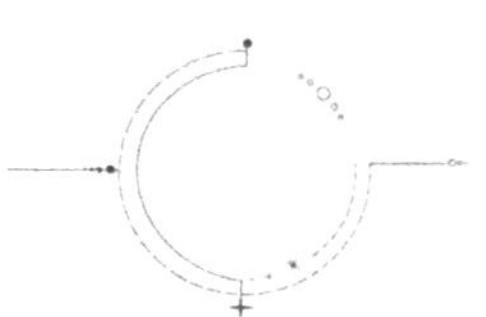

The ship vibrated around Arsenio. It was cold, colder than he was used to. Their vessel was outdated and worn, built to function and nothing more. A disguise wrapped in steel. The grey, unpainted walls pressed in on him, leeching the room of life, of warmth, of anything human. It drained him.

But not Adora.

She sat with one leg crossed over the other, reviewing briefs and data. Unfazed like nothing had changed. Too calm. Too settled. Like she was moving with the current. A far cry from the woman who usually fought to dam the flow.

They had not mentioned the sequencer since their argument in his quarters. But Arsenio knew it was on her mind. It had certainly not left his. Though, not for the same reasons.

He had fully believed, with unwavering faith, that there were no secrets between them. Every win, every failure, every fracture, Arsenio had laid himself bare to Adora. There was nothing she did not know. He thought it was the same for her.

Now, he was not so sure.

For years, he had done her will, thrown her weight around because it was his, too. They were a team. Bound by something sacred, closer than any two people could understand.

News of the sequencer had poked holes in that truth. Where she floated with the current, Arsenio felt swept away by it, his head just above the water. He would hold on as long as he could, watching and gathering before deciding what to do.

*You're brooding again,* Adora thought to him without looking up from her PortTab. Her voice was clear, soft and almost bored. She did not need to see his face, though. The stillness of his hands, the slump in his shoulders, it all said more than his words could.

Arsenio did not answer right away. He stared at the barren walls, only made more drab by the yellow lights.

*I don't like this ship,* he told her back. It was not a lie, though it was not entirely what set him on edge. *And I don't like the idea of turning to the detritus for help.*

*Trust the plan,* Adora replied, as if it were the simplest thing in the world.

Arsenio stood abruptly, fists clenched. Not to strike, but to center himself. The vibrations from the engine rolled up his feet to his legs, rattling his bones. It only made his mood worse. On a good ship, a properly plated ship, you would never even notice there was an engine. Everything was all wrong.

*I've always trusted the plan,* Arsenio shot his words to her, watching for a flinch. There was none. *When it was your plan. This? I don't know what this is.*

Adora's shoulders rose and fell. Calm. Controlled, but with a hint of fire in her cheeks. The scar darkened a shade. She set the PortTab in her lap and looked at him. Her eyes pierced through his. *I've done everything for us. Taken your hand and led you to where we are now. If you want to start questioning my methods, you're more than welcome to leave.*

That cut. Cut deeper than any plasma torch could. Leave? Arsenio could never. They were two halves of a whole. Even when separated by systems, they were still connected. Leaving was not an option. So why had she offered it?

*How could you say that?* Arsenio brought his eyebrows together. A heat rushed through his veins. It crawled up his collar and stopped at the tips of his ears.

Adora's face was not hard. She did not glare at him or twist her lips. She lifted her chin slightly and tilted her head. *I need to know you trust me. Everything I do, I do for us. I need you Arsenio, but if you think this is too big for you to handle, I'll understand if you want to back out.*

The temperature in his body shifted. Anger drained to something colder, heavier. Shame. He blinked at her, chest tight. Her words still echoed in his mind. *She needs me,* he thought to himself.

How could he have doubted that? Doubted her?

Adora had never let him fall. She had always known the way forward, shielded him from the worst of their father's fists. Every step they had taken, every tear shed, she had carried them through it.

Another rush of shame flowed through him. She was not offering him a way out. She was giving him a reminder to stay. To choose to do this. To choose her.

Arsenio unclenched his fists, the tension in his shoulders melting away. He nodded once.

*I trust you,* he told her.

Adora smiled at him. The scar on her cheek moved closer to her eye. Long and deep. It was not only a reminder to her, but to Arsenio, too. Orinthia was not always as weak as they thought. And they were not untouchable.

Quickly, she turned her head away from him and looked across the way. Arsenio followed her gaze. A service droid rolled in, vocal line moving in rhythmic pulses as it relayed information. There was a pause, then the droid dipped forward and backed out of the room.

*We're nearing the station now,* Adora told Arsenio. *The captain will send word when we've docked.*

Arsenio returned to his seat and faced the window. The stars outside the viewport stretched thin, warping light into long silver lines. Bits of anxiety crawled up his spine. Not as sharp as before, but steady. Familiar. The kind of pressure that lived on his shoulders.

They would soon be in Mon Claven's den. Claven, the self-appointed sheriff of a broken star station. Once a fellow Hunter. Someone Arsenio had trusted. And someone he had personally fired.

His stomach twisted at the thought of crawling to him, hoping he would play the part in Adora's plan. There was a humiliation to it. He did not like owing favors, and he especially did not like asking for them.

The ship shuddered as it slowed. Smooth black replaced the stream outside the window. In the distance, lights from the station blinked like a lighthouse.

More sputtering that felt like a pipe shoved between gears shook the ship. *Reverse thrusters,* he thought. *Must be coming in to dock.*

Arsenio looked toward Adora. She was already standing, feet apart to steady herself during the transition, and smoothing out the front of her jacket. Regal. Poised. Ready to do what she had to do.

*She has this,* he told himself. *We have this.*

Even as he repeated the thought, he could not shake the feeling they were walking into something much larger than either of them were prepared for.

Moments later, he followed his twin to the airlock shaft. Together, they stepped out of the ship onto the narrow platform connecting the ship to the station.

A crowd had gathered.

Arsenio set his hand on the butt of his pistol. His other ready to activate the charges embedded in his palm. Breathing came in sharp through his nose. He would not flinch.

His eyes swept over every face. Dozens he recognized from holoposters and flagged manifests. Marauders. Smugglers. Exiles.

They could not have inched closer to Hell if they had tried.

At the end of the platform stood a single guard. He wore an orange plastina coat, left open to reveal a rifle strapped across his chest. With his arms tucked behind his back, he nodded as they approached.

The guard and Adora exchanged words, then the guard swung out a hand and stepped toward the crowd.

Adora held her head level. She did not exaggerate her presence. No grand show. Just her.

Arsenio moved like her shadow, his hand never far from the trigger of his blaster. He met eyes with everyone who dared to stare back.

The press of the bodies on either side of the trio kept a constant itch beneath his skin. These people were not civilians. They were the worst the galaxy had to offer. Scum. Criminals. Any one of them would have torn him and Adora apart if it were not for Mon Claven's escort cutting a path ahead.

Arsenio was not scared. He hated the word echoing in his mind. *Powerless.* They should have feared him.

Some still did, he noted, catching flickers of recognition. The way a few faces turned away too quickly. But it was not enough. Not here. Not like this.

Groveling. That was what they were about to do. He wanted to spit.

The corridor opened into a long chamber, and at the far end stood an ornate bulkhead door. Their guard stopped, offered a curt gesture, then stepped aside.

Inside, Claven waited. He sat behind a wide desk made of real, solid wood. Heavy. Deliberate. A statement of control. One Arsenio did not miss.

Security screens lined the wall behind the sheriff, grainy footage flickering across each one. Arsenio scanned the displays out of habit, then shifted his attention to Adora. He stepped to the side to better read her posture.

She held herself steady. No tension was found on any part of her body. This was her role. One she stepped into well, like she was bred for it. Maybe she was.

A wide grin spread across the aged man's face. His sharp chin wagged as he spoke to Adora. He waved a hand in a half gesturing motion, casual and mocking all at once.

*He's welcomed us to his station,* Adora spoke in Arsenio's head. *Said he isn't surprised to see us darken his halls.*

Arsenio waited for more, watching twitches of hands, nods of the head, and shoulders move. He tried to fill in the gaps between Adora's interpretations but it moved too fast.

*I've asked him to stand with us,* Adora told him. She moved her hands in front of her. Her palm came down in a slicing motion.

Arsenio looked to Claven. He narrowed his eyes, studying Adora. Then he shook his head and pointed to himself.

The flow of information paused. Adora leaned forward on

her tiptoes. Her mouth moved quickly. She tapped her fingers one by one, listing off pieces of her plan.

Claven tossed his eyes to Arsenio. His brow lifted and he nodded in Arsenio's direction. There was a question on his lips, but Arsenio did not catch it.

*What did he say?* Arsenio asked.

Adora did not respond. She waved her hand in front of him and dragged Claven's attention back to herself. Her head shook once, and she pressed a finger to her chest.

*No, wait, let me answer for myself,* Arsenio told her. *I want to know what he asked.*

A beat passed. Then her voice was back in his head. *He wants to know where you stand on the plan to overthrow the EC.*

Arsenio straightened himself, and spoke. "I stand with her."

The sheriff slowly moved his eyes to Arsenio.

"Adora's plan will bring a balance where there is none," Arsenio continued. "The EC is corrupt, bloated, and dying. She's the only one who can cut through the rot."

He paused. Heat traveled up his neck. "When there's nothing left, we'll rebuild something better. Something new."

Claven's gaze did not move from Arsenio. A slow smirk curled one corner of his mouth. He said something, tight and quick.

Arsenio caught the shift in Adora's posture before he could focus on her face. A clench of her hand. A twitch of her jaw.

Then Claven turned his head, fully, toward her. Amusement flickered in his eyes. His head wagged from side to side as he spoke, lips smooth and slow.

Adora did not give up what the man said.

Arsenio opened his mouth to further push his belief, to

make sure Claven knew he was part of the plan, but was cut off.

Adora went still. Like a breath would knock her over.

*What did he say?* Arsenio asked, more urgency to his words. His breath came in quicker.

She did not answer right away. Then, in a tight clip she told him, *He's not going to help.*

A shock blew through Arsenio's limbs. *That's it? All of this and that's what he said?*

*He said this is his slice of heaven, and he doesn't want any part of our troubles.*

Across the desk, Claven leaned back in his chair like he had won a delicious game. He pressed his fingers together and made eye contact with Arsenio. There was a knowing look behind his face. Something that made Arsenio's insides squirm.

Adora turned and moved for the door. Waves of fury rolled off her. *We're leaving,* she snapped at him.

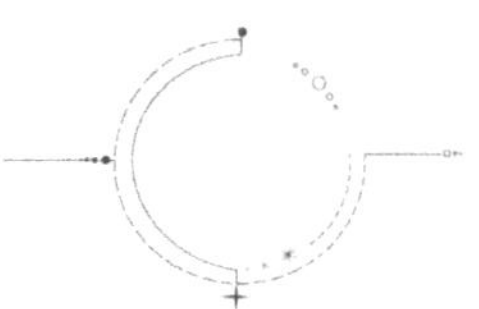

## 19

*P*acking a kit bag was a routine Kos knew by heart. It was the same bag he used during his time in the Navy, and the smell of rough canvas under his hands stirred memories. Not all were bad. He had made good friends, some he continued to serve with on the *Fera.* Many valuable lessons about life were learned while living out of his kit. Lessons about discipline, self-reliance, and how little a man really needed when everything else was stripped away.

Beside the tightly folded clothes, Kos packed everything he thought he might need while away from civilization. After months of cooking for himself on Buscoch, going back to rations would be hard to stomach. So, he stuffed half the bag with packaged food and familiar snacks. Nothing fresh that could spoil, but enough to make the distance from home a little more bearable.

Before sealing the bag, Kos stepped over to the table by the window. Two plants sat in mismatched pots. Orinthia had left them in his care, and cared for them he had.

They were half dead when she gave them to him. Now they looked… still not good. But alive. Stronger and growing.

He stared at them for a moment, then picked both up with gentle hands and tucked them in between two shirts. If he was going to be away for a while, the plants were coming with him.

In spite of himself, the closer it got to Thrutt's arrival, the more excited he became. Of course he looked forward to seeing his old friend again. But that wasn't all he longed for.

Kos was a sailor. And no matter how hard he tried to fight it, open space still called to him. Traveling from one moon to the next wasn't the same as carving a path through the stars. Back in the Navy, navigating systems, plotting their way across entire quadrants, had been the only part of service he truly loved.

He sat on the edge of his bed and opened his palm, swiping the tattoo with his other hand and activating his holomap. The Kren Collective flickered to life in electric blue. Moons orbited the gas giant in a slow rotation, glowing softly as they drifted through the void. It was beautiful.

For ten minutes, he watched them move slowly, calming his mind and giving him a moment of peace. After a while, he pinched and pulled the image with his free hand, moving it to another location. The map blurred across the galaxy, stars streaking past, until it landed on the system he was looking for. With a movement of his fingers, Kos expanded the image and stared at a single planet.

Mars.

The first world colonized by humans. His birth planet and resting place of his mother.

Kos hadn't been back since his aunt took him away to the NCR, but the pull was still there. It tugged at something deep in his chest. He tried to picture his parents' old apartment in the underground city of Ostia. There weren't many memories left, only specific images like the green carpet that lined the hall and living room with tattered spots by the front door. Rooms without windows. The constant hum of pipes in the walls.

Before the war, his father had been a miner. A hard-working man, trying to provide. But credits didn't stretch far when mods were involved. Every week brought newer, faster, more powerful implants. The wealthy upgraded. The rest, like his mother, bought what they could secondhand.

There were no regulations back then. No safety nets. Just a market flooded with unstable tech.

Kos had been too young to understand it, but he remembered how it tore his family apart. He remembered the sickness in his mom. The way she shook from the fevers that burned out her body. There was never an official count on how many she had, but he knew it was more than one person should have.

Then she died. She left him and his dad with nothing more than a broken image and debts she stacked up to pay for her own death.

Kos closed his hand, the map with it, and pulled himself into the present. The dark apartment in his mind faded away and light shone in through a window, scattering the last of the Martian dust. His heart was heavy. He rarely thought about that part of his life. The years before moving in with his aunt were lived by a different person.

The comm chimed from the inside pocket of his jacket. Thankful for the distraction, Kos flipped it open and was greeted by Thrutt's deep voice.

"Thought I'd see you waiting for me at the docks when I came in," Thrutt said, teasing in his voice.

"It rains too much for that," Kos replied, standing. He took hold of his bag and tossed the straps over his shoulder, leaving the room without a glance back. After three long days of waiting, he was finally setting off to help the woman he loved. There was nothing left to do but chase. Nothing mattered more.

"I'm picking up my luggage from the ferry's hold," Thrutt said. "Going to head to the shops and grab some last minute things. Mimi's lending us her ship, so we gotta get that moved from storage, too. How about we meet up for lunch before we head out?"

On any other day, lunch before departure would've sounded perfect. But Kos had already waited long enough. Another hour, maybe more, of just sitting still? The thought made his stomach twist.

"I'll wait for the ship in the hanger," Kos said, rotating his shoulders. "I'd rather get going sooner than later."

"Moping around while the droids do all the work isn't going to make things go faster," Thrutt said. "You might as well spend it enjoying a good meal and great company."

Kos sighed and pinched his eyes closed. "Where are we eating?"

KOS TAPPED his foot against the canvas sack beside his feet as he waited for his old friend. He was on his second round of sweet drink before the giant walked through the door. Thrutt pulled off his dripping coat and hung it on the rack with the other patrons' and joined Kos at his table. A smile etched across Thrutt's stony face.

"My boy, how are you?" Thrutt didn't wait for Kos to stand before scooping him out of his seat and pulling him into a crushing hug.

"Hi, pal," Kos managed, voice strangled.

Thrutt set him on his feet and lowered himself into the chair across from him. The seat groaned under his weight, but he didn't acknowledge it. "I'm sorry things are the way they are," he said, "but I'm very glad to be back. Been away too long. This is where I need to be."

Kos had forgotten how much energy Thrutt bought into any room, and how contagious it could be. It only took a few seconds for a smile to warm his own face, for the fog of his mind to lift.

The situation hadn't changed. But Kos' outlook had. He was ready to face what came next. And this time, he wouldn't be alone.

A woman in a soft lavender apron stopped by their table to take their order. Two meals, two drinks, and something sweet for Kos to save for later. She offered a polite nod and disappeared without another word, leaving them to catch up in peace.

"So," Thrutt said, leaning with his elbows on the table, but not putting too much weight. "I need to hear how you're dealing. You're looking a little pale and, if I can be so bold, ragged."

Kos didn't try to deflect the question. He'd seen himself in a mirror. "It sucks. I thought this would be the place Thia and I could finally start over. The house has been empty for days, and I've been in my head for longer than I'd like. And then there was the dogfight."

Thrutt stiffened and cocked his head. "What dogfight?"

"Did you see the half destroyed tarmac?" Kos asked, twitching a thumb toward the window. "Thia's ship was attacked before they even left port. They managed to take out the other ship, but I didn't know that until I got to the crash site."

He paused and shadowed his eyes. "There was a survivor."

"What did you do?" Thrutt asked, saying each word in its own beat, like he already knew the answer.

"Exactly what you're thinking I did." Kos stared at a smudge on the table. He could feel Thrutt's gaze land on him.

"That's why your hands look like that," Thrutt said. It wasn't a question.

Kos nodded once.

"Was it bad after?"

Another nod.

"You should have called me," Thrutt said. There was no accusation in his voice. Only comfort. "I couldn't have gotten here any faster, but at least you would have had someone to talk to."

"Couldn't," Kos said. "*Freya's* pretty much scrap. It was a gamble getting the call out to you in the first place. I made it through, though. Painfully, but it's done."

"We're together now," Thrutt said. "There's no need to be alone anymore. Once we get Thia's life in order, we'll stay together again."

The waitress returned with their food. Thrutt slid his arms off the table and leaned back against his chair. He smiled, a genuine warm smile, at the woman before she walked away.

"Have you worked up a plan on how we're going to wrangle up our own forces?" Kos asked, stabbing a piece of cooked vegetable with a fork and lifting it into his mouth.

Thrutt tapped his lips together but did not answer. The silence made Kos look up.

"We start with the *Fera,*" Thrutt said.

The cooked root lodged in Kos' throat and he choked on it from inhaling in surprise. It took a few hard coughs to clear it and he spit the chewed food into his napkin. "Have you gone insane?"

Thrutt held up a hand. "Listen, if we can convince them to join us, then we have a greater chance of finding others to follow. Our fight wasn't with the crew. And now that Ahto's gone, we can show them we mean no harm."

"They tried to kill us," Kos said. He struggled to control his volume. The restaurant was busy with a lunch rush and there were people close enough to hear their conversation if they tried hard enough. "More than once. The crew voted to have Thia and I marooned after we tried to stop *them* from attacking a civilian ship."

Thrutt nodded and shrugged a shoulder. "Under Ahto's orders, yes. But these were our brothers and sisters. The new captain may be more understanding."

Kos scoffed, the bitterness too quick to hide. The edges of his fork dug into his palm. "Yeah? And who is that? I was quartermaster. I should've been captain."

A flash of jealousy sparked through his chest. He'd daydreamed about captaining the *Fera* back when he served under her flag. He didn't care for marauding anymore, but the thought of someone else sitting at the helm made his stomach turn.

"Ignio Tryn," Thrutt said.

The name cut through the weight in Kos' chest. The heat drained from his thoughts, letting him breathe again.

Ignio had served with both him and Thrutt during the Mod War. A kind, steady man who genuinely cared about his crew. Back in the Navy, he'd been a commander, a rare one who actually looked after the people beneath him. Kos remembered that. Respected it.

"At least someone with sense is running the show," he muttered.

Thrutt nodded, then took a sip of his drink. "And he's eager to talk with you," he said with offhanded ease.

Kos narrowed his eyes. "How do you know?"

"I had three days of travel time to kill," Thrutt said. "There wasn't much else to do. So I reached out."

Kos cursed louder than he meant to. He let out all the air from his lungs and placed his hands over his face, dragging down and rubbing his cheeks.

"It's opening the conversation before we get there." Thrutt took another sip of his drink. "I've done the legwork, now all you have to do is show up and present the argument."

"What did you tell him?" Kos asked, his hands still on the sides of his face.

"To start with, I did my best to explain why we left. Ahto really talked up the betrayal, so it took some work to smooth things over. That was as far as I got before he agreed to meet with you."

"Meet?" Kos' stomach flipped and knotted. "In person?"

"On neutral ground." Thrutt took a large bite of his food and chewed it before speaking again. "Casandor."

"The marauder haven?" Kos flopped back in his seat. "That's hardly neutral. We won't be welcome there. Especially not in a registered bounty hunter's ship."

"It's the best I could work out," Thrutt said. "And Mimi's ship isn't part of her fleet. It's her personal hopper, registered under an alias."

"I guess you've got it all figured out." Kos sighed. "Looks like we're going to Casandor, then."

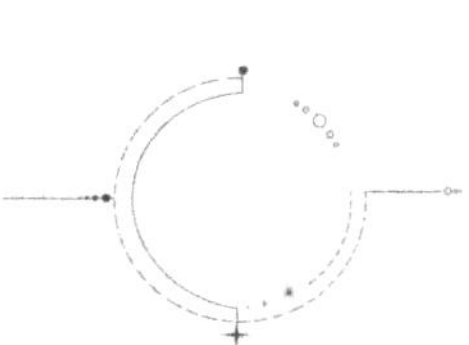

## 20

Space moved by in a blur as the star hopper warped to its destination. Kos sat in the pilot's seat with his hands tucked behind his head and let the lights from the console wash over him. It would be the last moments of peace he had before stepping into recruiting mode, and he wanted to absorb as much as possible.

Mimi's ship was half the size of *Freya* with just the one deck. *Freya* the ship was a long haul transporter made to carry people and goods across the galaxy. Almost everything about the ship was modified and retrofitted, including weapons and drives. The ship Kos sat in could not have been any less like this own.

It was as custom as one could get from a manufacturer and every part matched. The four cabins were not as roomy as *Freya's*, but built to fit single occupants.

Kos' favorite part was the galley. He had expected to eat stale, shelf-stable food for the duration of their trip. That was not the case. The kitchen came fully automated with pre-programmed meals.

He had thought about plugging Freya's AI into the

console, but decided against it. She complained about not fitting in her old ship, and this one was much smaller than that. The data chip stayed in his kit bag, safe and secure until he could find something suitable for her.

As cool as Kos may have looked, a restless energy coiled up his spine, sending electric pulses through his nerves. He tapped the heel of his boot to the floor and stared at the streaks of space in front of him.

*The Fera*, he thought. *I did betray you, didn't I? We were supposed to live and die together as a crew. And I left. Our bond is as shattered as my oath to the code. I shouldn't expect anything less than to be gutted on the spot.*

The tingling in his back prompted him to stand. Kos rotated his shoulders and flexed his hands, trying to work out the sensation from his body. It wasn't the same feeling as slipping into the past, but dread of what laid before him.

People he once cared about now hated him, and for good cause. He, Thrutt, and Orinthia went against the marauder's code. Kos led the mutiny and aided in the death of the captain. He had no right to speak to them and didn't take the permission lightly.

Kos let out a breathy laugh. *Then I left with her.* He finished a half formed thought. *The very woman I voted to cast out when she failed to complete her first task as a marauder. And fell in love with her.* He shook his head. *But, then again, they had more grace than I didn't they? They chose to give her a second chance. Maybe I can earn one, too.*

"You okay?" Thrutt asked from behind him.

Without turning, Kos said, "Yeah. Getting anxious, that's all."

"I've smoothed over as much as I could," Thrutt said, joining him. He tapped Kos' arm with his knuckles.

Kos looked to see Thrutt offering a hydro-sphere and he took it. "I played myself thinking I could keep that life behind me, didn't I?"

"We are who we've always been," Thrutt said. "Every moment and act builds on the last, shaping us into who we become. It never stops. Even this, right now, will lead you to a newer version of yourself. I see a great man. A loyal man. Others do, too."

The corners of Kos' eyes twitched as he fought tears back. Thrutt had always been the best of them. Kos knew, without a doubt, he wouldn't be the man he was without him. "Thank you for being there for me," he said without moving. "From the very beginning until now. I wouldn't have anyone else to call for help, and I'm glad I have you."

Thrutt slid an arm around Kos' shoulders and pulled him close to his side. "You are my son," he said. "I've always loved you, and always will. It's my honor and privilege to stand with you."

He let a pause follow his words. "Your aunt loved you, too. She'd be proud of the man you are now, even if you were lost for a while."

The mention of his aunt broke his hold, and a few tears slipped free. Kos didn't think about her much, but the pain of losing her had never gone away.

She had taken him in when he had no one else. Gave up everything to care for him. His father's only sister had loved him more than her own life. And showed him that every single day.

Kos could never quite understand why so many people loved him. Cared for him. He felt the least deserving of the affection his circle gave him. But he wouldn't squander it. He'd show them his gratitude through service.

He took in a deep breath and cleared his throat. There

wasn't time to be a blubbering mess, not with his former crew on the horizon. The hour called for courage and clarity. He would have to muster up as much of both as he could.

"Can you check the nav computer?" he asked. "How much longer 'til we come out of warp?"

Thrutt dropped his arm and leaned down. "About three hours." Then he straightened and crossed his arms. "Have you worked out what you're going to say?"

"I've got some ideas," Kos said. "But everything depends on how we're received." He exhaled through his nose and counted out his fingers as he listed off his thoughts. "First, I have to apologize for leaving. Then for the deaths of those we fought on Sarv'on and Elendoras."

He blew out a raspberry and pressed his fingertips to his forehead. "And if they don't take the opportunity to murder me… I have to convince them to fight Adora. For Thia. And for the GMH."

"You'll do fine," Thrutt said with a shrug. "Don't frame it as fighting for the GMH. Keep it simple. Make them see that a galaxy at war is bad for business. Fewer places to hide. More military patrols. More chaos to get caught in."

He shifted his stance. "Most of them served. They'll remember what it felt like. No one wants to go through that again. They're not on the GMH's side, and neither are we."

Kos let his hand fall from his face and took a long sip of his hydro-sphere. "And if I can't convince them?"

Thrutt didn't hesitate. "Then we keep trying. Until we run out of allies."

"We don't have many of those left as it is," Kos muttered.

"Then we hire mercenaries," Thrutt said, tension rising beneath his usual calm. "We both have enough credits to fund a battalion if we had to. Why are you doing this to yourself?

Thinking you'll fail before you even tried. This isn't like you."

Kos bit the inside of his cheek and sighed, eyes cast toward the console. He searched for something solid to hold on to.

"I don't know." His throat tightened. "We've been through so much change in the past year. And somewhere along the way, I think I lost myself." The words filled his mouth before he spoke them. "I don't know who I am in all of this."

A long pause followed Kos' words.

Thrutt shifted in his spot and fidgeted for a second before speaking. "You've followed strict rules for too long, Rogue. This is your time to decide what kind of man you want to be." His voice was low and clear. "Are you going to keep letting others dictate your every step, or are you going to do what you believe is right whether or not anyone is behind you? I see a man who has been scarred by doing what others have told him to do. A man who followed orders without question."

Another pause.

Kos' shoulders tensed.

"Maybe you're used to hiding behind authority, having been in a submissive role for most of your life," Thrutt continued. He didn't look at Kos, but ahead at the empty space outside the window screen. "It is easier to follow orders than to fail on your own. Poverty. The Navy. Even Ahto, all forced their will onto you. But look where that led you."

He shook his head. "You're a good man. I see it. Thia sees it. My hope is soon you'll see it, too. You haven't lost yourself because you never had the chance to know who that was."

Thrutt fully turned to face him.

Kos pulled his lips between his teeth and locked his gaze on the dash.

"This was not a criticism, just the truth," Thrutt said, softening his tone. "And I hope it gives you something to think about. Laid out before you is the opportunity to have something amazing. A fresh start. Begin it on your terms. Make today the first day of who you truly are."

Thrutt set a hand on Kos' shoulder. "You're not a marauder anymore. You can greet them as whoever you choose to be."

Kos had no idea how to respond, so he stayed silent. Only Thrutt could make accusations sound like compliments that still managed to sting. His mind raced, replaying the words and trying to hold onto the truth buried in them.

Thrutt had a rare gift. He said a lot, and meant every word. And while there was plenty of times Kos wished that old giant would keep quiet, there was always value in what he said.

"Have you called Thia since we left?" Thrutt asked, easing the conversation away from Kos' moral compass to his personal life.

"No," Kos said. His mouth was dry and he took another sip of his hydro-sphere. "But I should touch base before we dock. Let her know what we're walking into. Or at least the plan."

"Give her my love," Thrutt said with a smile. Then he winked. "Though I'm sure she has enough of yours."

Kos wiped a hand over his arm and cleared his throat. There were few secrets between him and his oldest friend. Not even romantic ones.

But Orinthia was different.

She was more than a fling or someone to pass time with in some cold port town. Kos wanted to spend the rest of his life with her, and somehow it made talking about her with Thrutt uncomfortable.

Maybe it was because Thrutt cared about her, too, just in his own way. Or maybe the idea of forever was too heavy for him to speak out loud. He didn't respond, just waited quietly for Thrutt to leave.

Once alone, Kos pulled out his comm and adjusted the dials, tuning it to Orinthia's modified comm. A moment of hesitation stopped him. He hadn't told her about the spy the last time they spoke, keeping his word to Kian. At the time, it felt like the right move to keep her safe, but it didn't sit right. He was already keeping his ghosts secret, adding this made his gut twist.

Kos sighed and waited for the comm to chime. He settled into the pilot's seat, expecting to have to try a few times before she picked up. So, it surprised him when her link connected after the first few seconds.

"Hey, I was just thinking about you," Orinthia said. Her voice fell soft on his ears. "You okay?"

"We're good," Kos said, soaking in the sound with his eyes closed. The weight he carried lifted, just a little.

"We?" Orinthia asked. "Thrutt's with you?"

"He picked me up two days ago. It's been a scramble to get everything together, so I hadn't had the chance to call. How are you? Any progress on your end?"

Orinthia took longer than usual to respond. "No progress toward Adora, yet. But we did have a run-in with something I don't really know much about."

"What does that mean?" Kos' heart jumped up his throat. All other thoughts vanished. "Were you hurt?"

"Not really," Orinthia said quickly. "I'm okay now. Promise." A beat passed before she added, "Have you heard of the *Spectral Scow?*"

"I have." He drew out his words.

"What do you know about it?"

"Only legends I can barely remember. Why?"

"Would Thrutt know more?" Orinthia asked.

She brushed past her injuries too quickly. And now she was asking about a ship that didn't exist? "Don't dodge the question. What happened?"

"I'm okay, now," Orinthia replied. "But this has to do with all of it. I will tell you, just not yet."

Kos shook his head and leaned toward the door, calling down the hall for his friend.

Thrutt popped out of his quarters and looked at Kos with with eyebrows together.

"Thia's asking about the *Spectral Scow,*" Kos told him.

The giant emerged from his room and made his way back to the cockpit. He took the comm from Kos. "Hey, kid."

"Thrutt," Orinthia said with such ring to her voice that it made Kos' heart ache. "I miss you so much."

Thrutt smiled then looked down at Kos.

Kos made a circular motion with this finger, encouraging Thrutt to hurry along with the call so he could get back to talking to her.

"The *Scow,*" Thrutt said, low and steady. "Marauders tend to stay away from her. These are rumors mostly. But I have heard she's a lost warship. One that never got the message that the war ended. Some say it was an experiment gone wrong in the early days of battle. Others say they were testing new tech to tip the scales. Whatever it was left them wandering through the stars in search of their enemy. Those who have seen it make no official reports, but there are whispers and warnings to stay away."

Kos watched Thrutt tell the story. His words were measured and even. He could not tell if Thrutt was retelling the legend or if he truly believed what he said. Either way, there was a charge in the room that hadn't been there before.

"She looks like another old wreck, drifting through the black," Thrutt continued. "No one who steps foot on the ship reports in. Though, from what I've heard, plenty of scrappers and bounty hunters have tried to claim her, thinking she's a prize stocked with wartime weapons and tech. Only the void waits for those who cross paths with the *Spectral Scow.*"

The room was silent for a long minute. Kos' skin prickled.

"I was on the *Scow,*" Orinthia said.

2 1

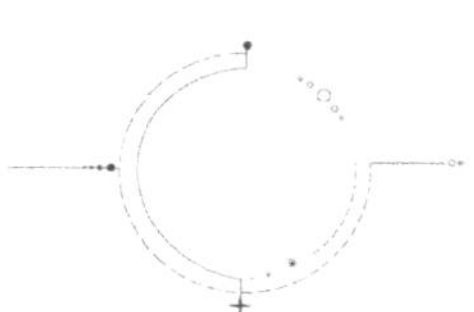

Reliving the experience on the *Scow* took effort. Orinthia's voice wavered as she told them what happened. About how close she had come to dying. She left nothing out, even knowing how it would land. By the time she finished, her throat was raw and her limbs heavy. The memory drained her.

She waited in silence, not sure who would speak first. The ship hummed around her. Her cot was hard under her, and her muscles ached.

"Are you okay?" Thrutt asked, his voice full of concern.

"That is not a little thing, Thia," Kos said louder. "You told me weren't really hurt, but then you almost died?"

Orinthia flinched at the sharp edge in his voice. "Everything's fine now. I'm sore, but no worse than I've been. My mod left me more drained than the actual attack."

There was a thud on the other side of the comm, followed by a string of curses.

"Oh, yeah," Kos said, "that makes it so much better."

He was not yelling, but she could feel it, the heat in his

words. Kos did not lose control often, but she could hear he was getting close.

"You need to be careful with that," Kos added.

Orinthia did not roll her eyes, like she would have in the past. Using her mod like she had on the *Scow* was unlike anything she had ever experienced before. A new high. A dangerous one, but still. Pride burned warm in her chest. She had saved them.

She was the one who sensed the danger. She fought them off. Held back long enough to escape. And for the first time in twenty-something years, she did not feel cursed by something her father gave her.

Desidario had been many things to her, a good father was not one of them. But this mod, this power coursing through her? It was a greater strength than she ever knew. And it was hers. "It saved me," she said.

"And it's a huge risk every time you use it," Kos said, his voice still rough.

"Are we always going to argue about this?" Orinthia asked. "This is who I am now, Kos. I'm not going to say it again. You have to trust me."

"I do trust you," he snapped. Then he sighed. "But that thing, whatever Desidario put in you, it killed everyone before you. And it's horrifying that it makes you feel like it does."

He paused, breath unsteady. "Sooner or later it's going to cost more than you can give it."

"I have to decide what's worth the risk," Orinthia said. A boldness rose in her chest, steady and fierce. "This makes me formidable. No one can take advantage of me, or hurt me, or make me feel powerless ever again."

She paused to take a breath, not to leave room for comments. "I hate Desidario for what he did to me. But this?

This almost makes up for it. Adora doesn't know about it. She can't use it against me. So I have to learn to control it. It's the only way to beat her once and for all."

"We worry about you," Thrutt said. "That's all this is. Love and concern. You're too far from us to keep an eye on. Not to baby you, but because you're important to us." He paused. "But it is yours to wield and you have to use it the way you see fit. No one can control it for you, no matter how much we wish we could keep you from getting hurt."

Thrutt's voice softened. "Look, we didn't call to berate you. I'm glad you're safe. Now, you two have a moment alone. We'll be landing soon and won't have time to chat for a while. Take care of yourself."

Orinthia gave Thrutt a moment to leave before she spoke again.

"I'm sorry," she said, pouring all her regret into those two words. "I don't like fighting. Especially not now, when there's already so much going on."

"We'll get through this," Kos said. There was still an edge to his voice, but it was broken, jagged. "Thrutt and I are working on something we hope will help."

She rested her head against the wall of her bed cubby and closed her eyes. Her pulse was fast, but not from the anger. It was hurt. Hurt that they were apart. Hurt that he was upset with her. Hurt that even as much as she wanted peace, she still had no control over anything.

"Where are you going?" Orinthia asked almost in a whisper.

"A marauder haven," Kos answered.

"And you're okay with that? How are you feeling about going back into that world?"

"Probably about as good as you felt rejoining the GMH."

Orinthia scoffed. "I didn't rejoin. They've made that

clear." She softened, just a little. "Most of them anyway. Annatilla, the one in the spacesuit when we met them, she's been friendly. Helpful. I think she'll be a good ally when it comes down to it."

"Thrutt thinks we have a few of those left, too," Kos said with a half chuckle. "He reached out to some of the old crew."

Orinthia's eyes flew open. Her breath caught. "Wait, you're meeting with the *Fera*?"

"The new captain is eager to speak with me, as Thrutt put it."

"Do you know them?"

The faint thumping of the engine pulsed through the wall behind her. She shifted and crossed her legs and stared at the wall, imagining what Kos was doing while they spoke.

"Yes, very well, too. Ignio Tryn," Kos said. "You probably don't remember him, but if anyone was going to lead that ship, I'm glad it's him. It's the rest of the crew I'm worried about. Marauders vote on everything and I'm not sure I can convince all of them to join our cause."

The pipes above creaked and groaned. There was never real silence on the *Tertion*, and Orinthia had yet to adjust to the bumps and knocks.

"You don't have to do this," she said, letting the weight of her words fill her mouth. "I know you think you have to protect and save me, but this isn't your fight. There's no need to go through with something than can put you in danger."

Kos was silent for a long beat. She heard a soft rustle over the comm, maybe the shift of fabric or the sound of his thumb brushing the mic.

"Protecting you is all I want to do," he finally said. "I spent years defending a Confederacy that didn't care about me. This is my chance to put myself toward something I truly believe in. No, fixing the GMH's mess isn't my fight —" he exhaled, and Orinthia could picture his brows pinch, "— but standing beside you is where I belong. And if I can't do that literally, I'll provide whatever support I can."

Orinthia said nothing at first. Tears streamed hot down her face, and for once, she let them fall. No hiding, no swallowing them back. Just her, clutching to the voice of a man lightyears away, and a hitching breath in uneven bursts.

Seconds stretched. Her shoulders trembled. She was not sure how long it lasted, how long she unraveled under the weight of his honesty.

When the wave passed, she took in a few shaky breaths and said, "That's the most ridiculous and wonderful thing anyone has ever done for me. Maybe even for anyone at all. You're trying to build an army to prove your love to me? Kos, that's insane. Incredible. And deeply, deeply you."

"You're worth fighting for, Thia," Kos said. "It's why I get upset when you're hurt. I hate not being able to stop it."

A sharp beeping cut through the comm.

"That's the proximity alert," Kos said, his voice a shade tighter. "We're about to come out of warp. I'll let you know how things go when we're done."

"Be safe," Orinthia said, meaning it with her entire soul.

"I lo—" the line went dead before Kos finished his sentence.

Orinthia knew what he was going to say, but not hearing the last words left a hollow feeling in her chest.

The hum of the ship's engines filled the quiet, underscored by the ringing in her ears. Alone, she shifted into a more comfortable position and reached into the drawer beneath her bed, pulling out the PortTab she'd borrowed from Mimi's room.

Still no news on Adora and Arsenio's escape. Just a few

vague mentions of civil unrest trickling in from the Outer Zone. The galaxy was quiet, for now.

She flicked through her messages and typed up a quick note to Uri. He had not responded to any of her previous updates, but part of her did not expect him to. Not while under the watchful, heavily encrypted eye of the GMH.

Uri was the best of the four Antons. No matter how much Adoracion hated Orinthia, she could not imagine the twins targeting him. He was the eldest, after all. He carried more burdens than he shared.

And even though he had always preferred Orinthia's company, and not shy about his feeling toward how they dealt with her, Uri never treated his two middle siblings lesser.

His softness was missed in the cold, sterile halls of the *Tertion*. Uri understood her, stood by her, even when she was wrong.

Orinthia knew he would be able to convince Kos her new mod was not a weakness. If only she could could talk to him. Hear his voice.

She let out a dry, snorted laugh. *I spent the better part of a year thinking the same thing,* she thought, setting the PortTab beside her and pulling her knees to her chest. *He's safe. Alive. But I still don't have him back.*

Two weeks. That's all they had together before she lost him all over again.

*I fought so hard to save him. And there's no reaping of my efforts. Two weeks wasn't enough.*

A gentle knock on her door pulled Orinthia from her melancholy thoughts.

"Orinthia?" Annatilla's muffled voice called from the other side as she knocked again. "I'm sorry if you were sleeping, but Captain Solvay is ordering you to the bridge."

With a sigh, Orinthia swung her legs out of bed and

stepped barefooted onto the cold ground. It ached her already sore muscles. She shook it off, not wanting to admit Kos could be right about the mod costing her more than she could give. The door slid open as she pressed the button.

Annatilla stood with her arms behind her. "Captain says there's a message for you. Also —" she pulled her arms forward and held out a light grey coat with fine teal lines, "— he wants you to wear this before you 'set foot' on his bridge, as he said."

Orinthia's heart sank. "I'm not wearing a GMH uniform."

"It's not the full uniform," Annatilla said, offering a small, apologetic smile. "He said you need to at least look the part if he's going to take you seriously.

The coat hung in front of her like a relic of everything she left behind. That part of her life was over.

And yet, there it was, calling to her again like a recurring nightmare.

She reached out and took it. The fabric was stiff in her hand. Rigid like the regulations she had fought so hard to escape. Coarse like the treatment from her fellow officers. It smelled stale, like someone had left it in the back of their closet only to resurface to taunt her.

"Come on." Annatilla nodded her head in the direction of the ladder.

Orinthia breathed through her mouth as she slipped on the jacket. It was heavy and too big for her frame. Her hands barely reached the end of the sleeves, and it flowed over her body like a tent.

Shaking her head, she stepped into her boots and followed Annatilla to the ladder.

The coat hung down to her thighs, brushing against her legs with every step up the ladder. Each swish hit a nerve, made her skin tingle with irritation.

By the time she and Annatilla reached the bridge, Orinthia was ready to rip the tortuous garment off her body and launch it through some exhaust tube.

Annatilla opened the door and waved Orinthia to go in. "You're on your own."

## 22

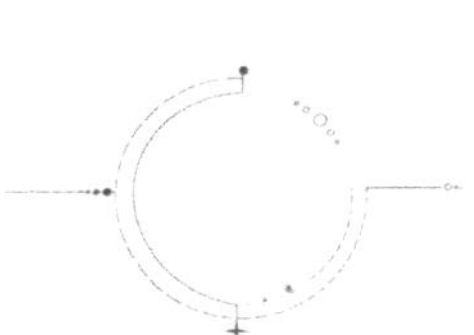

*O*rinthia cupped her fingers around the cuffs of her sleeves and kept her eyes low, avoiding the windscreen and the warp beyond it. Her stomach churned, anticipating having to look up and see the galaxy blurring around the ship.

"Anton's on the bridge, Captain Solvay," Talyon announced as the door closed behind Orinthia.

"About time," Captain Solvay said. His boots ticked across the floor as he moved a few feet from where he stood. "It's not decent to keep your commander waiting."

"You're not my commander," Orinthia muttered.

"But I am," Kian's voice said near the front of the room. He sighed. "Have you all been like this the whole time?"

A shock passed through Orinthia's chest at hearing him speak. She risked a glance up. Her shoulders straightened when she saw Kian on the visual comm blocking the window and space warping beyond it.

"You know what?" Kian made an exaggerated face and shook his head. "I don't care and don't want to know. Let's just get down to it. We've caught word the twins have been trying to recruit at an outpost orbiting Hedphin. Brul Star Station. There's an ex-Hunter out there who's set up shop as the sheriff. He's not too friendly with most Hunters, but you'll have to convince him to share what he knows. Find out why they're recruiting and what they're trying to accomplish."

"And if Adora *is* recruiting?" Orinthia asked. "What do we do if she finds out we're there?"

"She won't," Kian said. "I'm sending out an extra patrol sweep in the Viyaz sector. We flagged some background chatter that might've come from one of her old relay routes. Probably nothing, but it'll keep her eyes off Hedphin if she's watching traffic patterns. Let her chase ghosts while you're out there."

Orinthia cocked her head. "Viyaz is a dead sector. Wasn't that a Mod Bleyer stronghold?" She silently thanked Kos for the history lessons.

"Maybe she's digging for old tech." Kian shrugged. "I just have to follow whatever leads I have at this point."

She gave a small nod. The mission was clear, even if she hated digging around anywhere near Adora's trail. It was what she was sent to do and the sooner she got it done, the sooner she could end it.

But her chest tightened as she watched Kian. He was her one chance to reach across the stars and ask about Uri. "Can I talk to my brother?"

Kian's skin went maroon. "He's not here. We've moved him to a safe house where we can keep him more comfortable longterm."

"At least tell him I've been sending him messages. Let him write me back."

The Galoric exhaled and shook his head. "He's under blackout. Two guards, off-grid, no comm access. I don't even have a direct line. I get updates when they remember to drop them. We're stretched thin as it is, so I can't stay on them constantly. Besides, if he pings the net, the twins could track him."

"Why do you think he's so important to them?" Orinthia asked. She held herself steady, but inside she was burning. "Or that they would even hurt him? He was the only one who got along with each of us."

"Adora's already shot him once." Kian spread out his arms with the palms toward the center.

"That was an accident." The words slipped out before she could stop them and regretted defending her sister. "She was trying to kill me."

"Him coming back from the dead was what finally nailed the twins to the wall." Kian stared at her with eyebrows together. "They also know he's your biggest weakness. A survivor from the ship that hit you on Buscoch said Adoracion wants you dead. Not captured. Dead."

The words hung for a minute as he let them settle on Orinthia. "Uri is the easiest way to get to you. He might have built the case, but she blames you for toppling everything. She's not chasing you because she thinks you're dangerous, though that's part of it. She's trying to end you because you got away. You represent everything she's lost. The reason the EC turned on her. The reason Uri's alive to being with. Do you think she's going to let that go?"

Orinthia's ears rang. Her pulse was in her throat. She had not thought of it that way before.

"That's so typical of her," Orinthia said. "Neither of them ever owned the consequences of their failure. She wants me dead? Fine. That's the only way she'll be able to stop me. I'll go to the outpost and find out whatever I can."

She clenched her fists around the cuffs again. "But if anything happens to Uri, I'm done playing by everyone else's rules."

Kian closed his eyes and pinched his nose. "Please don't say things like that over comms. These conversations are recorded."

He waved his free hand toward the screen and did not look up. "If the tribunal doesn't have my badge before I get more news, I'll keep you posted on what we find. Let me know how the visit goes."

Solvay made a salute but the screen cut off before he was finished. The warp was in full view and spiraled around the window.

Orinthia spun around and smashed her eyes closed, taking deep breaths to stave off any sickness. She concentrated on the sounds around her. Talyon typed on her screens. Captain Solvay's rebreather hissed every few seconds in a steady rhythm.

The ship quieted to a dull hum.

"Did we fall out of warp again?" Orinthia asked, turning to see a clear line of stars in front of her.

"No," Captain Solvay said. He had his fingers tucked into his pockets with his thumbs hooked out. His white coat bunched up around his wrists. There was no gruffness to his voice like there had been a moment before. It had been replaced with something else. Something close enough to pity it made Orinthia's skin crawl. "We're changing course to Brul Outpost. We should be there within a day, as long as the old girl can hold herself together. Tell Armitage to see me. Dismissed."

The change in his tone caught her off guard. She did not

stay long enough to let the feeling take old. With a dip of her head, she left the bridge. A weight settled on her shoulders she could not shake or name.

Annatilla greeted Orinthia with a tilt of her head when she stepped out. Her large eyes moved with Orinthia as she walked by. "You look to be in one piece."

"Did you hear any of it?" Orinthia asked, not stopping to chat. She made her way to the ladder and began her descent to the middle deck.

"The door is thick," Annatilla said, following behind her.

"Adora's stirring up things," Orinthia said, reaching the bottom rung. "Some recruitment effort. They want me to poke around and see why."

"Where?" Annatilla said as she, too, touched the landing.

Orinthia did not answer by the time they reached Marius' door. There were too many thoughts crowding her head at once and she could not sort them out until her task was done. She knocked hard a few times and waited, almost bouncing on the balls of her feet. Her new companion stood behind her to the left.

Marius' door opened and he rolled his eyes before fully looking at Orinthia. "What is it now?"

"Captain sent me to get you," Orinthia said.

"Cliff needs to get that PA system fixed for the whole ship and not just the places he likes to hang out," Marius grumbled, shaking his head. He leaned to the side and grabbed his officer's coat. "Is that all?"

"As far as I know," Orinthia said. She stepped aside to let Marius move, but he was already pushing past her. He buttoned his coat as he walked, then climbed the ladder and disappeared.

Orinthia turned to head to her room, but Annatilla stepped in front of her. She tilted her head slightly and pressed her lips together, as if trying to shape a difficult thought into words. "Why are you here?"

The question struck Orinthia as odd, and she was not sure how to answer. "I'm assuming for the same reason you are. To stop Adora from taking over the EC, or whatever it is she wants to do."

"But why you?" Annatilla emphasized the last word, softening her voice. "What's in it for you?"

Orinthia sighed. "Can we talk about this inside? I'm still a little fatigued and would like to sit."

She expected Annatilla to follow her, but instead, the other woman turned and headed in the opposite direction. Her own cabin door slid open, and she stepped inside, gesturing for Orinthia to follow.

The room was cold and had a chemical smell to it, like cleaning products were used constantly. Shelves with drawers lined the walls, each labeled with numbers and symbols Orinthia did not understand. Pictures of dozens of different worlds hung above the shelves in a gallery style. At the end of the room, on the built-in table, sat a computer screen secured to the top.

Inside the bed cubby were purple rope lights that faded off and on in slow blinks.

"Have a seat," Annatilla said, motioning to the chair under the table. She lowered herself onto her bed, hands planted behind her for support, and leaned back. The purple lights reflected off her faceplate as she leaned her head back.

"What's all this for?" Orinthia asked, sitting on the chair. It spun without her influence and she had to walk it back to face the right way.

"I asked a question first," Annatilla said, still in the same position.

Orinthia thought about how best to answer without

revealing more than she wanted to. She stared at a spot above Annatilla's bed, not focusing on anything.

"Kian thinks I'm the only one who truly has a shot at stopping the twins from doing whatever it is they're planning," Orinthia said. "We've been feuding our whole lives and he's under the impression that insider knowledge gives me an edge."

"Is he wrong?" Annatilla asked. Her voice was wispy, like she was speaking from a dream.

"Probably not." Orinthia chewed the inside of her cheek.

"Why've you been fighting?"

A tightness built up in Orinthia's chest. Not like on the *Scow*, but a slow pulsing ache.

Of all the things in her life, her childhood was the last thing she ever wanted to talk about. She had relived moments in flashback and nightmare. In whispered fragments with Kos when neither could sleep.

Annatilla had not earned the right to glimpse into that part of her life.

"If we're going to be a team, you're going to have to trust me," Annatilla said. She lifted her head, her eyes meeting Orinthia's.

The words were not sharp, but they still stung. For a brief moment she remembered Mimi and how she had misjudged her at first. Mimi was the type of friend who threw aside every plan to help Kos and Thrutt when they needed her. Maybe Annatilla could be that for her.

Orinthia set her jaw for a moment, pulling in the strength to open just a little. "My father liked to pit us against each other. I was useful to him and he abused the naivety of a child."

"What does that mean?" Annatilla asked. "Useful how?"

Orinthia let her mouth move without her mind, holding

herself apart from the pain. "It means Desidario didn't have favorite children, he had favorite experiments he used us for. I was too young to realize I was a tool, and by the time I figured it out… the damage was done. The twins took their anger out on me, doing their own *fun* experiments to see how much I could take before crying, passing out, or whatever it was they were looking for at any given time."

"Maybe they were just scared children, trying to hold on to whatever power they were denied," Annatilla said.

"And I wasn't a child, too?" Orinthia gripped the sides of the seat cushion. "You're defending them after what they've done to your friends?"

Annatilla straightened and lifted her hands, palms out. "All I'm saying is maybe Adora can't control herself anymore. Founding the GMH gave her the authority and power she always craved. Now it's gone. Fighting for her life might be the only thing she knows how to do."

Orinthia could only stare at the woman, who had thrown her head back to bask in the light above her again.

*The galaxy is full of downcast and abused people*, she thought. Her chest rose and fell quickly. *Most of them don't go through the stars on a rampage, killing all who stand against them. Adora has never shown remorse for her actions. She goes out of her way to come after me and hurt the ones I love.*

"They aren't attempting to survive," Orinthia said, finishing her thought and getting to her feet. Static danced around her hands and she clenched them tight to keep her mod from acting on its own. "They're attempting to tear down the galaxy and rebuild it in their image. This is not self-preservation. It's the refusal to accept responsibility."

Annatilla smirked, her face awash in violet light. "Now I

see why the commissioner chose you. He's right. If anyone has the drive and chance to stop them, it's you."

The drawers, and whatever filled them, no longer concerned Orinthia. Their conversation left her drained and hollow. She did not wait for Annatilla to ask her anymore ridiculous questions. She turned and left the room, storming off to her own.

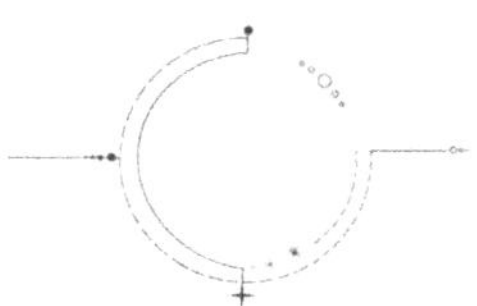

## 23

Kos stared at the face looking back at him in the washroom mirror. It was older and rougher than he remembered. Grey hairs streaked his dark beard, lightening the color.

He had gained weight, too, from eating until his heart's content on Buscoch. His cheeks were fuller than they'd ever been. Thin lines formed across his forehead, making way for future wrinkles.

Aging didn't bother Kos. It meant he survived everything the universe threw at him, and he wore his new features with pride. Living long was a privilege he didn't expect to earn, and a few extra pounds meant he achieved the life he fought so hard to reach.

The ship rocked around him, making him sway into the wall. Kos placed a hand against the sink to steady himself and waited for things to settle before exiting to join Thrutt.

A clock near the entrance of the ship spun its digital numbers until the reflected local time, syncing with the docking bay's data network. Kos and Thrutt were an hour early for their meeting with Ignio and his crew, which was less time than Kos had hoped for.

Ideally, Kos would've liked at least half a day to prepare and scope out the area. This was different from when he and Orinthia met Mimi on Sarv'on. She had been an ally. Linking up with uncertain collaborators without prep work left Kos on edge.

He stood with his coat in his hands, debating whether or not to cover his tattoos. Anyone he met outside the ship would know who he was. Or, at the very least heard of him. Some of them would have similar details on their own skin. It wasn't so much wanting to hide who he was, but unsure of how he wanted to present himself to the marauders he left behind.

Was it better to play into the role he once knew, a hardened marauder with the taste for blood? Or should his appearance reflect what he felt inside: a man trying to find peace, ready to leave the world of senseless violence behind?

*I'm about to ask them to fight with me,* Kos thought, staring at the maroon jacket. He'd had it for years, back from his Navy days, but had stripped it of anything that would resemble its old purpose. *How can I say I'm trying to leave this life behind when I keep running back to it? Maybe I wasn't meant for anything else other than fighting. It's what I'm good at.*

A long, warm sigh passed through his lips. He held onto why he was there. For Orinthia. For freedom. For peace. *That's worth fighting for. I have to believe that. Now's the time to make them believe it, too.*

"Ready?" Thrutt asked, his heavy steps growing closer as he came up to Kos.

Kos nodded, tossed the coat on a hook and opened the

door. Cool, damp air rushed in through the opening, filling the compartment.

Casandor was a cloud city, suspended high in the atmosphere, hidden by clouds and impossible terrain. The elevation kept the marauders safe, harder to spot from orbit, and nearly impossible to reach without previous knowledge or invitation. If Hunters were nearby, they would not easily find it.

The haven was familiar to Kos, having sought refuge among the ships many times during his six years under Ahto's command. A few things had changed, like vendor stalls and shop names. But the layout was the same.

His feet moved on memory alone, leading him to Ahto's favorite bar. The Irelad didn't need to eat or drink, being fully machine, but he had always enjoyed the views from the Skylander Cantina.

Thrutt and Kos stayed close as they loaded into the lift. Three marauders stepped in behind them, each casting a long, hard glance their way. Kos wiped nonexistent dust from his arms and shifted into a wider stance.

The air thickened as the newcomers adjusted their positions, too. Subtle, but unmistakable.

The elevator began its slow climb, twenty levels to the highest point of the fabricated city.

One of the marauders, a four-armed Frunch, slid a hand toward his hip. His companion coughed, a poor attempt to cover the sound.

In the same breath, Kos reached into his belt, pulled his dagger, and pressed it to the base of the alien's skull, just enough pressure to make his point.

"Don't," was all Kos said.

A second marauder, his scraggly locks tied back with a

strip of leather, swung his arm wide, revealing a blaster. He moved to aim for Kos at the back of the lift.

Thrutt's arm snapped up, catching the weapon midair.

The marauder screamed as Thrutt's diamond-plated hand crushed his. The blaster clattered to the floor.

The third marauder dove for it, but Kos kicked him in the face the moment he got close enough.

With the dagger still pressed to the Frunch's spine, Kos stepped on the fallen blaster and kicked it toward Thrutt.

The other two growled and reached for backup weapons.

Before they could get them, Kos drove his foot into the back of his captive's knee and kicked hard. The alien collapsed forward, slamming into his companions and pinning them to the wall.

It was enough space for Kos to pull his blaster and stand his ground in the small lift. He clenched his teeth and waited for his vision to completely darken. His breathing was shallow and rapid.

Thrutt rose to his full height and placed himself between the group and Kos.

"Move outta the way," the scraggly-haired marauder said. "There's half a million credits on his 'ead."

"Not anymore," Thrutt said, making his voice reverberate around the lift. "Ahto's dead. The bounty's void."

The group traded glances before glaring at Thrutt and Kos.

"We ain't heard nothing o' that sort."

"Saw it with my own eyes," Thrutt said, moving just enough to keep their attention on him.

Kos' pulse beat in his ears. His head swam in the noise.

"Well, may'haps the new captain will pay up," the scraggly one said. "We don't much care who the credits come from, s'long as we get paid."

"I'll be more than happy to ask him when I see him in about fifteen minutes," Thrutt said. "That's who we're here to meet."

The marauders dropped their bravado, scrambling for a response that didn't come.

A chime sounded overhead, followed by the elevator doors sliding open to the top level.

Thrutt moved without urgency, setting a hand behind him to usher Kos through. He continued to block the others, his bulk like a wall between Kos and danger. Once Kos was clear of the lift, he stepped aside and waited for Thrutt's next move.

The giant reached into his pocket and pulled out a pair of red credits. "Buy yourselves a drink in the lower level and chalk this up to a story to tell your buddies." He turned to face them and backed onto the landing.

Just as the doors began to close, Thrutt tossed the credits into the lift. All three men dove for the chips, scuffling to grab one. The door sealed shut and the light indicated their descent.

Kos' chest rose and fell with deep, steadying breaths. He hadn't felt like he was in danger, just afraid he might have had to kill one of them. Killing was easy. What scared him was how much he wanted to.

How he'd hoped Thrutt would let them come at him. How ready he'd been to turn the dagger on the Frunch and watch the light drain from his eyes.

He'd held back with Sylvanio, but only because they needed him alive for questions. That restraint? It felt thinner than he wanted to admit.

"You good?" Thrutt asked, holding his hands in front of him, reaching for Kos' blaster.

It took a second for Kos to crawl back out of the tunnel.

Then, slowly, he lowered the weapon and slid it into his hip. He stuffed the dagger back into its sheath and he straightened himself.

Thrutt watched him for a beat, lips pressed together. Concern flickered in his eyes, but he did not voice it. "Come on. Let's get inside before we start drawing too much attention."

Music thumped around them as soon as they opened the door.

The cantina spread out in a wide half-circle, lined with panoramic windows that curved from wall to wall. Beyond the glass, the planet's upper atmosphere shimmered in blue, fading into black. Stars blinked above through the dome overhead. Close, cold, and endless.

Private tables lined the outer edge, each one fitted with a miniature dome that could lower over the booth at the push of a button, sealing the conversations off from prying eyes and ears. Without them down, the place was alive with sound.

It wasn't hard to see why this was Ahto's favorite place to spend leave. He was built for space battles, to wage war among the stars. But war didn't afford taking in the beauty. Not like this.

Even Kos, jacked up on adrenaline, couldn't ignore the wonder of a place like this. Though he moved with shadows over his eyes and a hardness to his step, the view was undeniably incredible.

Thrutt motioned for him to take a seat at a table tucked in the back, while he made his way to the droid bartender. Kos navigated through groups of patrons who leaned in close, shouting over the music to be heard.

No one glanced his way as he passed. Not here. Everyone had their secrets to carry.

He slid into the booth with his back to the window and scanned the room.

Lavishly dressed marauders lounged on plush sofa-like benches. Some wore silks and leathers, others glittering jewelry and neon-threaded fabrics that caught the shifting light. Holograms flickered on tables throughout the cantina. Some were entertainers, dancers cycling through programmed routine, while others displayed flickering digital games, space races, or spinning galactic maps.

The dome above his table shimmered with the option of privacy, just a touch away if needed.

There couldn't have been a more distracting place to meet, but it was also the perfect location. No one would hear their conversation, nor pay attention to them with all that was going on around them. Kos never really liked the Skylander Cantina, but it didn't hurt to be there.

The giant took a longer way around, finding wider openings to pass through the crowd. He set down two drinks on the table when he reached Kos.

"Take the edge off," he said, sliding one to Kos.

Kos didn't make a habit of drinking. His mind was broken enough without alcohol making it worse. He glanced up at Thrutt, confused.

"It's a tea," Thrutt shouted over the pulsing music. "Something to calm the nerves. Need your senses about you and I don't think that's something you can do on your own just yet." He used a finger to move the glass closer to Kos.

A faint steam caught a glint of light and wiggled like a ghost escaping the mortal world. Kos grabbed hold of it and pulled in a swig of the liquid. It had sweet and floral notes with a woody scent. The perfume wafted from the cup and filled his mind with a rush of ease that was so intense it almost backfired and sent him into a panic.

With another sip, he allowed the herbs to do their job and settled in to wait.

He finished the drink in long sips and rotated the empty cup on the table, balancing it on the edge of its base. Kos kept an eye on the door, but no one came in after them. Ten more minutes passed. Still nothing.

Then, the door opened.

An all-too-familiar human woman stepped inside, short, with one side of her head shaved. She squinted against the low lighting and rotating colors, scanning the room. Her eyes fell on Kos and she froze. They stared for a long moment before she turned and bolted out.

"They're here," Kos said, leaning in closer to Thrutt.

Thrutt rolled his shoulders and fixed his eyes on the door.

Ignio Tryn stepped in, a wide-chested Undu with deep grey scales and a stare that locked on Kos the moment he stepped over the threshold. He moved through the crowd without pause and dropped into the seat across from him.

The human woman, Yamalin, settled beside him. Three more marauders took up positions behind them, each one watching and waiting.

It was time for Kos to prove himself a worthy ally or nothing at all.

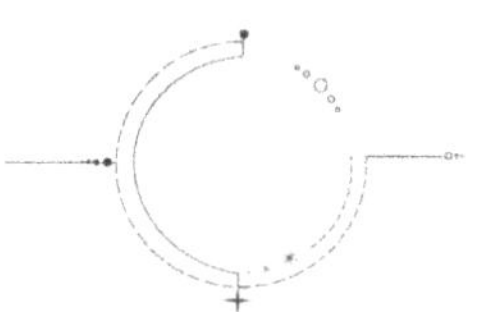

"You're looking well, Rogue," Ignio Tryn said. He leaned back in the seat, one hand propped loose at his hip, the other resting near the grip of his gun. His leg stretched out beneath the table, and he bobbed his head slightly to the beat pulsing through the cantina.

The right side of his face was tattooed to resemble a skull, an x-ray image of the bone structure beneath his skin. His eye on that side wasn't real. A high-grade monocular implant sat in the socket, capable of zooming across city blocks and locking onto heat signatures. During the war, Kos had seen him take out enemies quicker than most could draw a weapon.

"Last time we saw each other, I had a broken nose from a cell door slammed in my face," Kos said. He tried to ease his posture, but was too aware of the eyes on him. "Looking any way is better than that."

Ignio grinned and let out a puff of air from his nose. "We're grown men and can skip the small talk." He flicked an eyebrow up. "Why are we here?"

Kos smoothed out his shirt and nodded to Thrutt to close

the dome. In a moment, all they could hear was the back beat rattling the bracers in the glass. He leaned forward with his elbows on the table, pulling at every marauder root he had to fix himself as the man he used to be.

"The galaxy's shifting," he said. "Adora and Arsenio Anton escaped GMH custody and are quickly building a force out of anyone who will join her."

"We've heard the rumors," the woman said. "She's the EC's problem. Not ours."

"That's what I thought, too," Kos replied. "But right now the GMH has jurisdiction over the situation and their numbers have been skinned to the bone with almost nothing left. They don't have the manpower to stop her. And the EC doesn't want to get involved because they know it'll start another war. If the GMH doesn't control the situation, though, the EC will step in and take over. You might think it won't affect you, but it will. Military ships and fleets will patrol open space again, claiming territories that currently belong to marauders."

Kos shifted and put his hands flat on the surface. "There'll be no neutral side to it, either. The twins have spent years hunting us down, breaking crews apart, destroying lives. You think they're going to stop? That maybe Adora will let you scrape from the heaps of her empire?"

Ignio fanned his fingers in front of him. "Hunters are our sworn enemy and you're a traitor." He licked his top teeth. "I don't see a reason to side with either of you, yet you say there's no benefit in neutrality. So tell me, why should we join your cause after you abandoned us?"

Kos glanced at Thrutt who gave him a low nod. "I never turned my back on the crew. I left because Ahto went down a path I couldn't follow anymore. He lost his way and in the end turned against all of us. I can't change what happened, but know it was only between Ahto and I. As for Adora, she will only use you like you've always been used: as bodies. Is that what you want to be? Fodder? I don't. I want to stand on my belief that what I'm doing is right."

The woman stood halfway out of her seat and slammed her hands on the table near Kos'. "My brothers and sisters are dead because of you."

Kos curled his hands into fists and dropped his gaze, casting a shadow over his eyes. "Because of Ahto. We won't pretend Sarv'on and Elendoras didn't happen, but let's be honest. You were trying to kill us, too."

Ignio raised a hand and pulled his quartermaster back, keeping her from arguing more. He gave Kos a silent nod and allowed him to finish.

"You don't have to forgive me," Kos said, drawing in a breath to center himself. "But if Adora succeeds, she'll burn everything in her way. I know her. I've fought her when she was still bound to GMH regulations. There's nothing to hold her back now. Stand with me and make the galaxy see how you've survived. Remind them who holds the real power. We didn't just survive a war, we're here to pave a path to our own future."

Thrutt's seat creaked as he set his hands on his knees, elbows bent.

Four of the marauders across from them murmured to each other, masked by the soft thumping.

Ignio hadn't moved. He studied Kos in the commotion.

Kos stared back.

Ignio stood, and the hushed conversation of his crew ended. "You've given me a lot to think about, Rogue. There's one more thing I need to know."

"Ask," Kos said, standing, too.

"Did you kill Ahto?"

Kos stared at Ignio, weighing which answer would serve him best. The truth. Always the truth. "No. Orinthia Anton did."

"Antons," Ignio said with half a grin and a shake of his head. "Ahto's obsession somehow won't die with him. That family may very well bring destruction to our galaxy." He tipped his head toward Kos. "I'll take your argument to my crew and present what you've given me. They'll have their chance to vote."

Thrutt opened the dome again, signaling the meeting had ended.

Kos reached across the table. The music almost drowned out his voice. "I look forward to hearing back."

The captain took Kos' hand and gave a firm grasp, then turned to leave. His crew followed without looking back.

Once alone, Thrutt slapped Kos on the shoulder. "That was splendid."

"I'm not sure it'll be enough." Kos sighed.

—❋　❋—

OUTSIDE KOS' window, ships came and went; landing, lifting off, and vanishing into the blue haze above the haven. There was nothing to do but wait for Ignio to send word.

Knowing he'd go crazy sitting at the controls, Kos left the cabin and cockpit doors open, just enough to hear if the comm chimed. It was better to to step away until the last possible minute.

Thrutt didn't share the same anxiety. He spent his time in his own quarters across the hall, cleaning weapons and repairing a tear in his coat from his most recent bounty hunting gig. His door laid open, too, but the men stayed in comfortable silence, having no need to speak in order to feel the other's presence. It was an old familiar routine they fell into over the years.

An hour passed before the comm chimed, sooner than Kos expected. He rolled to his feet and darted toward the cockpit. After composing himself, he took a second to slow his breathing and flipped the comm channel. Ignio appeared before him and stood with his arms loose at his side, not stiff like Kos who had his hands gripped behind his back.

"The crew wishes you to come aboard so they may see you before casting a final vote," Ignio said. "We're holding steady outside the planet's orbit. I'll send coordinates to meet us and welcome you when you arrive."

A head butt from Thrutt would've been easier to recover from than an invitation back on the *Fera*. Kos tried to control his face, but Ignio's grin told him he wasn't as smooth as he'd hoped.

"Thank you, Captain Tryn," Kos said with a sharp nod.

"I look forward to hosting you soon." Ignio gave a bow. Then the channel disconnected, leaving Kos to stare at the dusky sky spattered with glittering stars.

"Did you hear all that?" Kos called out to Thrutt.

"Of course I did," Thrutt answered as he entered the cockpit. He moved through the pre-flight checks, flipping switches and entering the data that appeared on the nav computer. "How do you feel about it?"

Kos didn't answer. Instead, he chewed the inside of his cheek while checking the life-support readouts as the ship sealed itself, letting his mind search through his emotions. He settled into the pilot's seat and took hold of the yoke. The ship lifted gracefully off the dock and hovered for a second as the engines warmed. A thump under his feet signaled the landing gear had secured itself and they were clear for flight. Kos eased the ship forward, then pulled up to face the sky.

"I never thought I'd see the inside of the *Fera* again," Kos finally answered once they cleared the atmosphere. "We left in such a frenzy that I didn't make peace with it all. I loved that ship, almost as much as I love *Freya*, though each in their own way." He paused and checked the computer. "How about you?"

Thrutt lowered himself into the seat beside Kos. It groaned under his weight. "Doesn't matter much to me. I was only on that ship because of you. And I left because of you. My sole allegiance is to you and our Thia. So, going back is no different than being on any other ship."

Kos thought over Thrutt's words. It wasn't just another ship to him. It should've been his legacy. He helped design the *Fera*, and knew her better than anyone else. But his priorities had shifted in the year away from her decks. And he was barely the same man who left.

They reached the coordinates quickly. If Kos hadn't known what to look for, he may have missed it. The deep black ship absorbed all light and radar, and there were no signs it existed according to their screen readouts.

The *Fera's* port side bay doors opened, revealing room for the smaller ship to land. Kos eased the vessel into place, the movements coming back to him like saying his own name: natural, effortless. The landing gear knocked against the deck and decompressed. He stayed at the controls for a moment, looking out the window at the familiar sights. He was a stranger in his old home. A ghost come to haunt at last.

Thrutt said nothing while he stood and tapped Kos on the shoulder. He left the cockpit and activated the ramp. Kos rose and followed Thrutt to the exit.

Two dozen marauders stood behind Ignio who waited

near the base of the ramp. All eyes were on the men, watching their movements. Whispers spread through the group, but no one spoke up.

"Welcome, Rogue and Thrutt," Ignio said, waving his hand to the side. "Please, join us on the observation deck."

They didn't need Ignio to lead, but followed at his pace anyway. The rest of the crew fell in line after them, still murmuring to each other. Thankfully, they stayed far enough back from Kos that he couldn't make out what they said. He wanted to wait to hear their official decision and not rely on hearsay and speculation.

The winding corridor opened to an expansive chamber. The ceiling above them opened, revealing the void of space. A rush of memories washed over Kos. Orinthia was the center of them all. His mind played each back, overlaying them against reality. He watched her fall from the ledge, helpless and shocked. Saw her screaming at him, cursing his name for taking the life of an unarmed man. And he remembered standing beside her when he realized surviving wasn't the same as living.

Orinthia Anton, the most frustrating woman he had ever met, had changed his life, and it was his turn to repay part of that gift.

Crowds had gathered, filling in all available space. Some watched from the balcony and stairs. Others parted to let him and Ignio through. Kos held his head high and face steady. His giant companion walked two steps behind him, not as a shield, but in solidarity.

Ignio led them to the center of the floor and turned to him. "Stay here," he said before joining his quartermaster on the upper level. A hush fell over the room as the captain took his place. All eyes were split between watching their leader and Kos.

"Kos Rogue, former quartermaster of this vessel," Ignio began, his voice booming through the chamber. "You stand accused of mutiny against our late captain, Ahto the Irelad. How do you plead?"

Every face turned to Kos, rustling like wind across tall grass. Thrutt widened his stance and lowered his chin, ready to defend his friend.

"Guilty," Kos said, his voice clear.

He had imagined this moment a hundred times. There was no point in denial. By definition, mutiny was exactly what he had done.

The silence held.

"All who find Kos Rogue guilty of mutiny, vote now," Ignio ordered.

Half a dozen hands went up. Kos braced himself for the rest to follow. Several heartbeats passed.

No one else voted.

He let out a quiet breath and gave the audience a bow at the waist. A gesture of thanks for their faith, and the second chance he hadn't expected.

"There are no further accusations against you, and we, the crew of the *Fera*, hereby declare you clear."

Ignio's expression softened as he shifted into a less formal tone. "Ahto betrayed us all in the end. He didn't seek the will of the crew and pushed us past the limits we agreed to. His death was no one's fault but his own, and we owe him no loyalty. Now —" he swept his eyes across the room then back to Kos, "— there was a time you led this crew, fought beside us, and kept the code with honor. All in favor of recognizing that commitment and standing beside our one-time quartermaster, cast your vote."

Nearly every hand rose, save the few who voted against him in the first place. Kos looked around. Pride filled his chest to see men and women he fought with join him once again.

"You have our crew at your command, sir," Ignio said with a click of his heels.

In a wave of motion, the crew snapped to attention, filling the air with a flurry of movement.

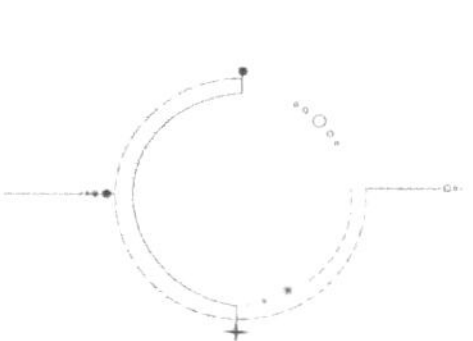

## 25

Something was wrong with Adora. Arsenio had seen her angry, seen her cold and cruel, but this was different. Since leaving the station, she had moved like Claven's words were still lodged under her skin. No fury, just tension. Tighter than usual. They had not discussed what Claven had said. Arsenio knew he had missed something in the interpretation, but could not think of what.

*More secrets,* he thought to himself. *More things I'm left out of.* Part of him, one that visited late at night when the world was dark and still like tonight, wondered if there had always been secrets. If Adora had left things out or done things he was not aware of. The thoughts stuck to him, even when he tried to bury them. He wanted nothing more than to believe this was the first time.

She had not interacted with him much since their return. Only answering him as much as she needed to. A divide grew between them, and Arsenio hoped it was the stress of the plan that kept her to herself and not irreversible damage.

The moment did not last. A low buzz rattled against his side from the PortTab. He picked up as a message appeared.

## *Moving*

— was the first word to come through. The light from the screen barely reached the red clay walls, as it was only bright enough for him to see the words. He read the intel, rolling upright with his legs over the edge of the bed. A warm string of curses flowed over his mouth and he mentally called for Adora.

*I need you to look at a report that just came in,* he told her.

*Can't you just tell me what it says?* Adora's words were bitter. Had she been sleeping? It was late enough, and truthfully, he should have been asleep, too.

*No.* Arsenio wanted to see her. Force her to come to him instead of shutting him out.

No response. Maybe it was not worth getting out of bed for. Maybe she would ignore it until morning. It did not matter to him, though. He would keep pushing as long as it took. This was not just an intelligence report. It was a way in. A chance to find whatever Adora was hiding.

*It's Orinthia.* He risked the fire, dropped her name like a match, just to goad Adora into action. Either she would berate him or she would show up. Whichever way it went, something had to give.

*I'm already on my way,* Adora told him with ice in her words. *Just wait.*

Arsenio grinned and stepped into his slippers, flipping on the light switch beside his bed.

*Finally,* he thought. *Maybe now I'll get some answers.* He pulled on his robe, though it was not needed. The nights were almost as warm as the days, but old habits and creature comforts died hard. With the PortTab tucked under one arm, he moved to the table and waited for his twin to arrive.

A few minutes later, the door slid open. Adora stepped in. If she had been asleep, it was not on purpose. She was fully dressed, boots strapped tight. Her hair was pulled into a messy bun, but not for style. It was purely to keep it off her face.

*Give it to me.* Adora stuck out her hand before she finished crossing the room.

*They're paying an old friend a visit*, Arsenio told her, passing the PortTab. *The one we just came back from.*

Adora's eyes flew over the report. The scar on her cheek brightened with each line. The light from the PortTab created harsh shadows across her face. Then she looked up. *I've never told Kian about her gift. But if she asks Mon Claven the right questions, she'll find out whats going on.*

*Then what do we do?*

*Go after her*, Adora replied, shaking her head as she shoved the tablet toward him. *Stop her before she can report it. Bring her to me and don't lose her again. I want to be the last thing she sees.*

A chill ran down Arsenio's arms. He knew it was the play all along, they had tried to kill her before. But something about Adora's tone was off this time. It was not controlled anger like usual. This was vengeance. Orinthia was the one who survived. She was proof that the twins were not invincible. And that made Adora furious. Dangerous. Unstable.

*Is this part of your grand scheme?* Arsenio asked. *Did your sequencer foretell this would happen*? He stretched out the sentence, putting weight where he knew it would sting.

Adora glared at him. The scar pulsed. *He told me Claven was the turning point. That the moment I stood in front of him, everything would start to fall. He said I would light the match, but not how big the flames would be.*

The light flickered overhead. Arsenio noticed her flinch but she did not react further than that.

*This is the issue with sequencers, Adora.* Arsenio threw his hand at her. *They cannot be trusted. No one can predict the future. He's playing you and watching you react, because you can't let anything go.*

*It's going to work,* she told him. The words came out steady, measured. *Perhaps Claven was never supposed to join me, but draw her closer. To put her within arm's reach so I can snatch her up. This is merely a trap she doesn't even see.*

Adora stepped closer and lifted her chin. *I know what I'm doing Arsenio. I've always known. You think he's playing me? Never. But if he is, he'll be the next to go once I'm back on top.*

Arsenio blew out a puff of air through his nose and lowered his gaze. *How much of this did you actually build yourself? How much of it did he whisper in your ear?*

His twin narrowed her eyes more and crossed her arms. She did not answer and turned her back to him instead. There was no hot anger coming off her, but Arsenio still sensed the rage beneath.

Her shoulders were drawn so tight they looked like they might snap. Her boot heel twitched like she was keeping herself from running. She hated being questioned.

*That's why she kept it from me,* he thought to himself. *To keep it inside where doubts couldn't prod at the plan. Still, there's more to this than she's giving up. I can see it.*

He watched her for a moment. Her tantrum would have been amusing if they did not have more to discuss.

*Did you read the whole report?* Arsenio asked.

Adora's fingers stopped drumming. She did not respond.

*Kian's also sending a patrol to the Viyaz system,* Arsenio added.

That got her to look back at him. Her eyebrows were pinched together. *The Mod Bleyer facilities? What's he looking to find there?*

Arsenio shrugged.

Adora's eyes moved from side to side in thought. Her lips were in a line. *He's trying to see how we react. Maybe to see if we're listening. Checking for leaks or a mole.*

The grin slipped from Arsenio's face and he thought about their leak. *Do you think he knows who?*

*No. If he did, he would have jumped already. I don't think he's sure we've got someone on the inside. Could be testing.*

Arsenio's hand tightened around the edge of the PortTab and readied to call the spy back, away from danger if he needed to. *Then we stay still then, right? We pretend like we didn't hear anything?*

Adora turned to face him again and shook her head. *Keep moving like we planned, just quieter. You go after her and bring her back to me. I'll send a team to retrieve the asset. Then we pull the trigger. Let them scramble through the wreckage and draw them out completely.*

*Why do we need to grab them both?* Arsenio asked. *Taking him was meant to draw her in when nothing else worked. But if we have her, then why do we need both?*

*To make sure she stays put this time.* Adora took a step forward. *And to make sure she stays down. Kill them both, I don't care. No loose ends left. Neither will stand in our way for much longer.*

Arsenio did not respond. But in the beats that followed, he realized something had shifted in his sister.

This was no longer a strategy. It was not just vengeance. She was about to burn the whole thing down and did not care about the fallout.

He faced Adora and thought to her, *I'll get her. Whatever this is, I'll trust you.*

But, as his sister left without as much as a single more word between them, he could not shake the feeling that he was about to get caught in the storm. He would have to tread carefully and make sure he was watching his own back. Adora was about to snap, and the results were going to be ugly.

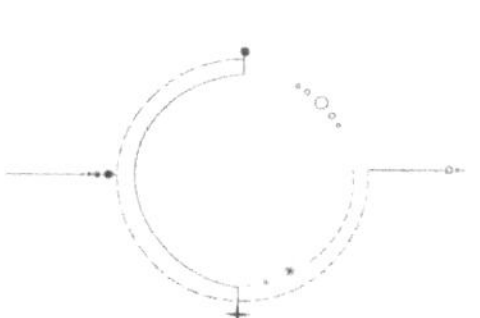

## 26

*E*verything about the Messies contradicted Orinthia's image of what they were made up to be. They were meant to be the best of the best, but their equipment was worn, and the Hunters themselves looked just as battered. It made her wonder if they were as expendable as Kos and his comrades had been. Good at what they do, but nothing more than a living weapon meant to kill and destroy at any cost. The skiff that transported her and the rest of the squad from the *Tertion* to Brul Station only confirmed her suspicions.

Condensation from the air filtration system leaked down the walls of the small bunk, leaving streaks of rust in several places. Orinthia laid on a wispy thin mattress with see-through sheets. The bars of the bed frame dug into her back and reminded her of the closet she stayed in while Vandra held her semi-hostage. Cardboard boxes would have been preferred over unmoving metal, however.

Stuffing poked out from the mattress above her, making neither of the two beds in the room more appealing than the other. Even the space was too cramped and could have been repurposed from a storage room like Vandra's. It was not much bigger, and a few loose bolts were all that held down the bunks.

Annatilla had insisted Orinthia stay sequestered for most of the journey. She was convinced she needed more rest after the ordeal on the *Scow*. Though she did not know the truth about why Orinthia had passed out, Orinthia was happy to let her believe it was solely from the attack.

Marius kept his word and offered no evidence to suggest otherwise. He had not spoken to her about the incident, nor had he said more than a handful of words to Orinthia since they left. She was glad to keep her mod secret for a while longer and purposed to only use it when completely necessary. No matter how much she disagreed with Kos, she understood the toll it took on her body, and being in the heart of an enemy stronghold was not the time to overdo it.

Early in the trip, Annatilla spent time with Orinthia and gave her a brief rundown of the station's history. The system housed eight planets orbiting twin suns, though most were too cold or too distant to support life. Instead, several hosted floating colonies.

Brul Station was one of them, a second generation Earth colony founded centuries before the war and abandoned as newer and better tech replaced it. In recent history, it had become little more than a black-market trading hub. Slavers, chem manufacturers, and assassins all called it home.

"Mon Claven is the self-proclaimed sheriff," Annatilla hold told her, showing an image of an old man on her Port-Tab. "Like you, he couldn't cut it as a Hunter. After the twins fired him, he fled to the darkest corner of the galaxy."

She had tapped on the image for emphasis. "Sheriff is a very loose term for what he does, though. His word is the only law that matters and he uses favors as currency. Those who don't pay usually get swept up by bounty hunters or turn up dead on some distant moon."

The man's face burned into Orinthia's memory as she laid on her cot. His sharp grey eyes not dimmed by the years his face clearly showed. No part of the man held a delicate feature, and every inch of his face was angled and thin. He would be easy to spot if she needed to find him on her own.

Orinthia had been alone for hours after Annatilla left. She thought about her mission. *Don't make it complicated. Get in, get the information, and get out.* But she could not shake the weight in her chest that nothing she ever did was easy. And given Claven's reputation, she did not fool herself into thinking their task would be anything but difficult.

The door to the cabin slid open, getting stuck halfway. Marius pushed his body through, and shoved it into the pocket. He wiped his hands on his pants and looked at Orinthia who had propped herself onto her elbow and watched him.

A dusty grey shirt hung loose over a black jumpsuit, replacing the Messie uniform he had left the *Tertion* in. The white Hunter boots were gone, too, swapped for clunky black combat boots, their leather peeling around the eyelets.

Marius tossed a pile of clothes at Orinthia. "Nap time's over. Put these on."

Orinthia flinched as they hit her, but she rolled to her side and sat up, her body stiff with discomfort. The rags were not in much better shape than Marius' and did not smell like they had ever seen the inside of a washbasin.

Marius did not wait for her to ask questions before leaving. He slammed his fist on the "close" button and let the door separate them again.

A sour funk lifted from the fabric as she changed into the disguise. Once dressed, she pulled Kos' old blaster from her travel bag, along with the holster Mimi had given her before Elendoras. She strapped it on, slid the blaster into place, and snapped it closed. After a quick adjustment, she tucked the belt out of sight to avoid an argument with Marius.

Nose scrunched and breathing through her mouth with lips pressed together, she left the cabin to join the others.

None of the Messies acknowledged her presence as she moved closer to them. Marius sat at the pilot's chair with his arms crossed and feet on the console. The lights illuminated his face from the side.

Beside him was a shadowed figure wearing earthy brown coveralls, and a hooded sweater. If Orinthia had not seen Annatilla's face plate sticking out of the hood, she would have not realized it was her.

Orinthia took a seat beside Cliff, who sat behind Annatilla. He looked nearly the same as he always did: a tank top and black pants. Only he wore an even harder expression on his face than usual.

The windscreen in front of Marius was black and blocked out all views of the hyperdrive. Celso did the same when Orinthia was on his ship. For a moment, she wondered what he was up to and what he spent his credits on. If he moved on to a quiet life, or was getting plastered in a loud bar somewhere everyone knew his name. In the end, it mattered little, but it would have been nice to know, since she was traded to fund that lifestyle.

"Don't get too comfortable," Marius said without looking back. "We'll be making our approach in about fifteen minutes."

"I understand why we left the *Tertion*," Orinthia said, "because a Hunter ship coming up on radar would blow any cover we could have. But won't the skiff read as the same?"

Annatilla turned in her seat and propped an elbow on the

back of her chair. The hood shadowed her face and made the circuitry on her visor brighter. "It has a scramble code. Most outlaws out here do, so it won't be out of the ordinary. The *Tertion* is large enough that it would stand out or be recognized by anyone we may've come across before. But the skiff is just another generic craft that no one will think twice about." She shrugged a shoulder. "Everyone has something to hide, so we'll hide among them."

Marius pushed buttons and pulled a lever on the console. The constant whirring of the ship's engines died down to a puttering hum.

The lack of noise made Orinthia's ears ring.

"Brul Station, this is *Nova Deep,*" Marius announced over the comm as they came out of hyperdrive. "Looking to dock in Sector Five."

The skiff's windscreen opened to reveal a massive space station. Five rings circled themselves, each one larger than the one before it. Three of the five were intact, though burn marks scarred the outer walls. The two farthest from the center were in worse shape with large chunks missing in almost identical spots. There were gaping voids where an asteroid, or maybe an ion cannon, had torn through.

Along the station's hulls were rows of dimly lit windows. It was not unlike the Moon's old space station, the first colony Earth established after taking to the stars. Though that had been updated, repaired, and maintained over the centuries. The one before them had not. Its original occupants long forgotten, replaced by the hardened masses of society.

Clusters of small ships moved around the station, coming and going like insects from a hive. Most were battered freighters or retrofitted fighters, no doubt belonging to marauders and smugglers. Their hulls were scrawled with symbols and scorch marks that told stories of their deeds.

Despite the disrepair, the station dominated the view of space. The scars bore witness to its survival, a reminder that it lived through countless battles and served as a reflection of those who called it home.

No one on Brul's end had responded to Marius' hail. Orinthia shifted in her seat and chewed the inside of her lip.

"Business?" a voice replied.

"None that concerns you," Marius said. His voice was even and clear. "Heard this was a no-questions-asked sorta place to lie low. That's the kind we need right about now."

Another long pause followed Marius' words. The other two Messies did not look as tense as Orinthia felt. Their skiff continued to drive toward the station.

"Take bay nine in Sector Five," the man on the other side of the comm said.

A massive cannon followed their path as they pulled closed to the station. Marius flicked off the comm and punched information into the computer. The skiff shuddered and rotated on its axis, and the artificial gravity kept the passengers secured to the floor rather than falling to the side. Using the yoke, Marius guided the ship to the docking bay, activating course-correcting thrusters as he did.

Orinthia's nails dug into her sweaty palms and she unclenched them. The ship made one last loud thump and hissed into place.

Stretching his neck and standing, Marius turned to his crew. "Ward, stay with the ship. Make sure none of these lowlifes take off with our only way out of here. Rest of you, time to go to work."

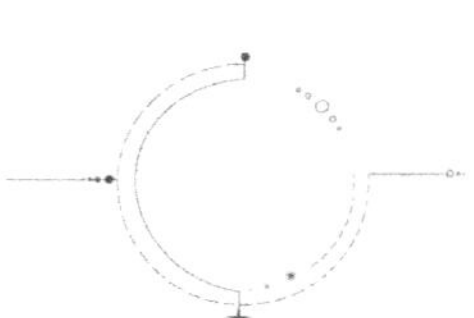

It took all of thirty seconds for Orinthia's head to fill with humming once inside the station. She fought to ignore it, and stayed closed behind Marius and Annatilla. Vendors lined the corridor, all shouting to passersby, banging on wares, arguing with customers, or repairing a variety of objects. Men and women of multiple species huddled together, laughing, drinking, and doing who-knows-what type of chems. Caytoo was civilized compared to Brul.

Marius walked through the station as if he owned it, forcing himself through tight groups and not stepping aside when someone came from the opposite direction. It was difficult to know if this was his normal personality or a persona he built to show he belonged in that type of atmosphere. Either way, he was good at it. He convinced Orinthia enough that a few times she forgot they were not all marauders on a stroll.

The hood over Annatilla's helmet covered most of her face. She had also activated the sun visor, blocking out her features altogether. Black leather gloves and thin boots hid the rest of her spacesuit. No one passing by could tell she was a Hunter underneath her clothes. Plenty of residents on the station wore life preserving gear, as not all came from oxygen planets.

Even Orinthia's braided silver hair was not unique among the crowd. There weren't many, but she spotted a handful of silver-haired, violet-eyed rapscallions. Their overly exposed tech told her they were Mod Bleyers and not just someone like her, who received mods too young. She wished she had a hood to hide behind, like Annatilla.

Marius led them to the first open stall and picked up a trinket from the table, turning it over in his hand until it caught the owner's attention.

"Seventy-five credits," the gangly alien said. It had a raspy, thin voice and sucked in air as it spoke. Large yellow eyes sat in the middle of its linear face, the edges bumped out past its skull. Its speckled, slimy green skin reflected the white light above it.

Marius pulled a pouch from his pocket and tossed credits on the table. They added up to three times the amount the vendor asked for. "Where can I find the Sheriff?"

The vendor gathered the chips with one eight-fingered hand and dropped them into a satchel on its waist. It looked back and forth on either side of Marius and the crew. "Check the haven. He's got a bartender there he cozies up to on cold nights."

Without a further response, Marius pocketed the trinket and continued on his way. The other two followed, falling back into the formation from before.

The group walked for ten minutes before Marius turned left into an adjoining hallway. Brightly lit signs illuminated the space. Orinthia could read a handful of words written on the boards, but most were jumbles of shapes and letters in languages foreign to her. Instead of open-air stalls, storefronts lined the corridor, their doors set into the walls that reminded Orinthia of the Shard. Smells of food, strong drink, bodies, and perfumes from the different businesses mingled together. Orinthia's stomach flopped as she attempted to keep each scent separated. Again, she breathed through pinched lips.

Orinthia glanced at Marius and noticed a shield over his eyes, one that matched Kos'. He barely looked at the signs and walked straight into a bar as if it were his favorite haunt. To her relief, the air was tolerable inside, though the patrons were no less savory than those near the docking bay. The sting of alcohol overpowered most everything else. At the back of the room was a long bar counter with two empty seats.

Marius recalled his visor and looked over his shoulder at Orinthia, then nodded for her to follow. Annatilla veered off and took a table near the entrance. As Orinthia moved with Marius, she did her best to check every face around her, searching for anyone who may look familiar. She wished to avoid any run-ins with sequencers or blackmailed bounty hunters.

Once seated, Marius folded his arms on the counter and knocked twice to get the bartender's attention. Orinthia matched his posture. She knew her way around a watering hole, and though she intended not to drink, it was natural to her.

The human female behind the bar ignored Marius' first attempts. She glanced at the pair, then continued to run a rag through a glass before setting it down. A few more drinks were served to the patrons closest to her. One drained his cup and staggered out the door. Then, the woman came over to Marius and placed both hands on the bar. Her chestnut hair was streaked with thick grey strips, and deep crows feet lined her eyes, etching the years of life into her rich ochre skin.

Her glare was harsh, but there was a warmth to her. With only the single impression, Orinthia knew this was a woman who did not suffer fools, and her presence alone would be enough to break up fights.

"Two drink minimum for bar seats," the woman said. Her voice was strong and clear, sweet in a way. "No tabs and pay upfront."

"I don't drink," Orinthia said, lifting her hand for emphasis.

"Don't care," the woman said. "Do whatever you'd like with the drinks. It's still a two drink minimum."

Marius pulled his pouch out again. "Four of the cheapest liquor you got."

Without missing a beat the woman said, "Want cheap drinks? Try the stalls outside. This ain't it."

Marius laid out a smooth grin and cocked his chin. "How about I get two shots of Zotto's and buy a round for everyone at the counter to make up for my dry friend here?"

The woman eyed Marius for so long, Orinthia thought they were blown.

"She takes a shot, too, and you got yourself a deal." The bartender looked Orinthia straight on.

A heat rose up Orinthia's neck, but she kept her face even. Inside, her stomach was in knots. *It's just one shot,* she told herself. *Get it down and move on. Don't. Puke.*

She had not drank since Dumalth. Kos did not care for it much, and she felt her new life was one worth staying sober for.

A handful of credits fell on the counter, followed by the clanking of a shot glass hitting the surface. Liquor splashed over the side as the bartender poured and slid the glass toward Orinthia.

With a deep breath, Orinthia took the glass, put it to her lips, and threw her head back. The liquid might as well have been cold flames going down her throat. Her eyes watered and she suppressed a cough.

The skin around her ears warmed. Her past self would have been ashamed, disgusted that she could not handle a single shot without wanting to be sick. The current version of herself agreed, but smoothly set the glass down and tossed it away with a flick of her wrist.

Marius slapped Orinthia on the back and laughed with a single burst of sound. "Now, drinks all around."

Another five minutes passed while drinks were served, ending with Marius' two. Orinthia stayed as composed as she could, though her stomach threatened to spill and her head was light. The humming in her head only added to the discomfort. She glanced around for complimentary snacks or anything she could eat to soak up the alcohol.

Her company took no time to swallow both his drinks. He wiped his mouth on the back of his sleeve and sighed loudly.

The bartender, who had not gone more than a foot away, turned her attention toward him. "Another?"

"Looking for work, actually," Marius said, fiddling with this empty shot glass. "Heard there's a new crew starting up. Massive fleet, from what I understand. Show that large is gonna need a lotta hands."

"Sure are throwing around credits like you already have a job," the bartender said cooly.

"Call it my resume." Marius winked.

The woman turned around all the way. "The Sheriff deals with work like that. Likes to vet recruits himself to see if they'd be of use to him instead."

Orinthia's ears perked up. She fought through the haze and noise in her head to listen for anything they could use.

"Sheriff, huh?" Marius clicked his tongue. "Know where I can find him?"

The woman leaned forward, putting weight on her elbows, and flashed him a devilish grin. Her voice was barely above a whisper when she spoke. "Already sent for him."

A wave of adrenaline shot through Orinthia, serving to sober her up a bit. If he had already been notified about the crew, then it was very likely their cover was blown. She stayed still and waited for Marius to react, though she slid her hand into her lap near the hidden blaster. Whichever way he went, she would follow.

Marius was as calm as if the woman had announced the time. He had not flinched or showed any indication of inward emotions. "Appreciated."

The humming in Orinthia's head died down as a hush fell over the room. A metal jingle replaced the chatter, followed by the solid thump of a boot heel. The tink and thump took turns, alternating with each step. Some chairs slid across the floor, followed by scurried exits. The sound grew louder until it stopped behind Orinthia and Marius.

"Well, well," said a deep, scratchy voice. "If it isn't the Golden Screwups."

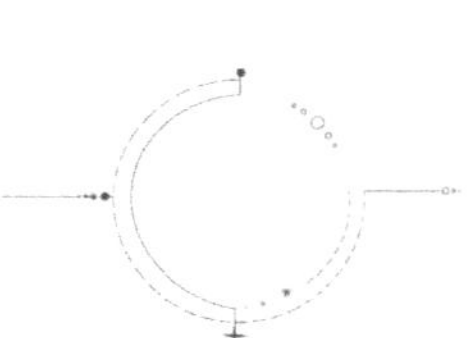

The galaxy had shifted. The crew had changed. And Kos wasn't sure where he fit anymore.

Walking through the *Fera's* corridors was natural. He spotted familiar scuffs and burn marks from battles and skirmishes in the past. Welcome nods greeted him, but the warmth didn't reach their eyes. It was no longer home.

His things has been emptied not long after he left. None of the automatic doors opened like they used to. Almost all evidence of his presence on the ship was gone, cleansed like dirt from a wound.

He and Thrutt were given access to the galley, observation deck, and the hangar. Anywhere else on the ship was restricted, needing an escort from one of the crew. It was degrading to be led around a ship he had designed, but Kos kept his opinions to himself.

*At least we're making progress,* he thought. *They very well could've stolen our ship and marooned us first chance they had. Things could be much worse.*

On their second day aboard the *Fera,* Ignio invited Kos to eat lunch with him in the captain's quarters. Thrutt, who quickly fell back into good graces with the others, stayed back.

Kos stood outside the large doors of Ignio's cabin and waited to be let in. As Ahto's code degraded, he became more paranoid and set up surveillance outside his room. No one could come near without alerting him. Unless Ignio had them removed after Ahto's death, he'd see Kos soon enough without having to knock.

The door opened, and Ignio greeted Kos with a warm grin. "I'm glad you agreed to join me." He made a sweeping motion with his hand and beckoned Kos to enter. Inside, Kos realized he wasn't the only one scrubbed from the ship. Nothing of Ahto, save for a portrait of him on the back wall, remained. The room had completely changed.

A lavish, overstuffed mattress on a wooden frame replaced Ahto's nest of blankets and cushions. The lights were dim and inviting, more cozy than the harsh white bulbs from before. Deeply colored carpets covered the floor, dampening steps as the men walked across.

Ignio led Kos to a solid wood, round table set with matching chairs. He took the one closest to the bed, with a canvas bag propped against the leg, and gestured for Kos to sit.

"You're probably thinking this is overdone," Ignio said, taking a platter of meat and setting strips onto the plate in front of him. "The crew voted me captain, I didn't push for it. I much rather would've stayed quartermaster, but I serve my men's wishes. This —" he flapped his hand around, "— is the only perk I truly enjoy."

"So, you took over as quartermaster after I left?" Kos asked. He waited for Ignio to finish serving himself before filling his own plate.

"Again, not by choice," Ignio replied. "Given my history

with Ahto, he was more comfortable with me than he was with the rest. His mind, if you could call it that, had gone shortly after you did. He locked himself in here, leaving me to take over as many duties as I could. That said, I was also assigned your quarters."

The captain set his utensils down and retrieved the canvas bag. He swung it at Kos. "Ahto ordered me to destroy all your belongings, but I couldn't bring myself to do it. You were our brother and I knew in my heart there was a reason you left. I hid these hoping to return them to you someday. Or at the very least to honor your service."

The bag was heavy. Kos opened it and peered inside to find notebooks, photos, trinkets, and more from his old cabin. He dug through and found a silver picture he didn't recognize.

Turning it over in his hand, he saw a woman and toddler staring back at him. The woman looked strangely familiar, but he couldn't place where he'd seen her before.

"This isn't mine," Kos said, showing the photo to Ignio.

"No," he said, nodding. "I found that under Anton's bed. She had little worth keeping, but I made sure to store it safely with your things."

*This is her mom,* Kos thought, touching the edge of the frame. *That's Thia as a baby, then. Look at that brown hair. No wonder I didn't recognize her.* His stomach twisted knowing what she went through to get the silver locks. "Thank you," Kos said, swallowing back the lump in his throat. "We both greatly appreciate it."

"You love her." It was not a question.

"I do," Kos said, his voice just above a whisper. "She's not why I left, I hope you understand that. No matter what Ahto may have said, this wasn't a lover's passion. That didn't happen until much later, when I realized she made me a better man. Even if she's hardheaded and stubborn."

"And you're building a war band to fight for her? Is she worth it?"

Kos placed the photo back in the bag and set it on the floor. "She is to me. What man wouldn't want to rip the galaxy apart for the woman he loves? And I can. I have the ability to to do just that."

His gaze hardened. "Her brother and sister have torn her apart multiple times. And they'll do the same to the rest of us if we don't stop them."

"I have to be honest, I don't care what happens to the EC," Ignio said, cutting into his meal. "If Adora's as dangerous as you say she is, why aren't they doing more?"

"They probably don't realize how bad it is," Kos said. "But I do, because of Thia. That whole family's a nightmare. Their father was a traitor who secretly worked with Mod Bleyers during the war. The twins used the GMH as their own private navy, all under the guise of security."

He paused and shook his head. "The EC deserves what's coming. But I took an oath to protect its citizens. War's coming, again. And once again, it'll be the innocent who get caught up."

Ignio took a moment to respond. He pointed at Kos' plate with his fork, a silent order to eat. When his meal was half gone, he finally spoke.

"You would've made a terrible marauder captain," Ignio said without looking up.

The words hit Kos, but he waited to hear the full matter before reacting.

"You're too honorable for our kind," Ignio continued. "Too willing to throw yourself into the fire. But you are a great man. A man that I've proudly fought beside, and will gladly do so again. Remember this, though. You can't carry the whole galaxy on your back. It'll crush you before you notice. Sometimes we have to let sins atone for themselves."

"Thank you, I think," Kos muttered.

Ignio tipped his head and placed another bit of food into his mouth. "What's your next plan of action?"

"As much as I appreciate you standing with me, we need more ships if we're going to have a chance at fighting back," Kos said, poking at his food. "Thrutt said he reached out to some crews, but you're all we've met with so far."

"I'll take care of that," Ignio said. "What do you have to offer them in return for their service?"

Kos sighed. "Not much. If I had access to my credit accounts, I could offer more. But even then, I'm not sure that would be enough."

"Men do crazy things for credits." Ignio chuckled. "But perhaps there's something else we can use for incentive."

Kos leaned back in his seat and tapped his foot on the carpet. He thought of anything else he could exchange for their alliance. "We let them have whatever Adora's gathered. Ships, weapons, the lot. If we win, they have first dibs."

Ignio twisted his mouth and nodded. "That could work. I'll see what I can do."

"Thank you for your help," Kos said. "I know I'm in over my head, but this fight is important to me."

The men ate in silence a while longer.

Kos listened to the creak of the walls and the soft hum of life pulsing through the ship. His thoughts drifted forward in time, to the battle waiting ahead.

*Would it be quick?* Kos thought. *A single decisive strike? A surprise attack might be enough to cripple their forces and make them surrender. Or, would the battle drag out, a war of attrition? And if so, how long could they sustain it?*

"You look troubled," Ignio said.

Kos shared his concerns.

"That's valid," Ignio said. "And one we'll need to address sooner rather than later. You have my crew's hands for as long as you need them, but I can't speak for others. We'll need to be clear this could be a long fight. Everyone should know where they stand, and what's expected."

He leaned back in his chair and folded his hands, tilting it onto two legs and rocking. "I'll bring it up when I start feeling out who would be best to talk with. See who's willing to commit long-term. For now, get some rest. We won't solve this in one day. I know you're short on time, but there's only so much you can do on your own."

Kos nodded. He poked at a few scrap pieces of meat and vegetables that laid close to the edge of the serving tray before setting down his fork. "Appreciate the meal. And for holding my things."

With a sigh, Kos pushed himself away from the table and gave a quick bow. He collected his bag and left the cabin. Outside the room, Kos took his time walking back to the hangar, thinking over their conversation. Whether the battle would be quick or long, one thing was certain: it was coming.

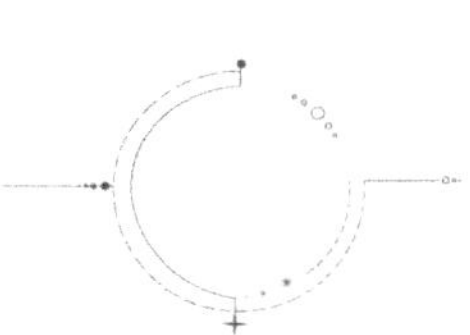

Claven's office was a tattered mixture of wealth and wear, the kind of setting that reeked of over-importance. A massive, polished desk dominated the space, its dark wood gleaming under the harsh outdated lights and clashed with the decrepit metal walls of the dying space station.

Dishes of food were arranged on the desk in a display that would send any of the outlaws on the main decks into a coma. Rare meats, glazed fresh vegetables, and breads that still steamed their yeasty scent into the air sat between Claven and the Messies.

Orinthia kept her hands folded in her lap and did not let her focus linger on the food, though her stomach begged her to eat. She recognized the game Claven played, having lived it before. Desidario had perfected it when she was a child, using silent meals and lavish displays as a punishment, a way to remind her who held the power. The grotesque spread, deliberate silence, and even calculated glances were all familiar. But familiarity bred immunity. If he was hoping for a crack in their armor, it would not come from her.

A wide-brimmed hat that rested on the ear of the tall-backed chair flopped up as Claven leaned back. It resembled a throne, though not as ornate as those from ancient Earth used to be. He kicked his feet onto the edge of the desk and crossed an ankle over the other. Folding his hands across his stomach, he finally spoke. "To what do I owe the pleasure of hosting the Golden Screwups in my humble abode?"

"Save the dramatics, Claven," Marius responded. His face was calm, but his voice held an edge. "You know why we're here. Adoracion."

A toothy grin spread across Claven's face, though it was not friendly. More like a predator savoring the moment his prey ventured too close. "Now, why would I know that? Wasn't keeping her locked up your job?"

Orinthia watched Marius through the side of her eye.

"Lots of marauders come through here," Annatilla said. Her black visor was up and she showed her face. "Heard she's been building a rather large crew. Someone out here has to have passed information. Man of your quality would be up on all of it."

"I don't associate with that scum." Claven raised his eyebrows in a shrugging motion. "You're more than welcome to ask around yourself, seeing as that's the type of company you keep." His eyes darted to Orinthia and fixed on her.

Orinthia lifted her chin and stared right back, refusing to show any sign of weakness.

"You and your sister are cut from the same cloth, aren't you?" Claven asked.

"I'm nothing like her," Orinthia said as smoothly as she could.

Claven placed his feet back on the ground and stood. "You believe that, don't you? There's nothing special about you. She's who you could be if you let it all, the hate, the fear, the strength of your family, consume you."

"There is no point in playing word games with each other," Orinthia said, also standing. "Do you know what she's planning?"

"No," Claven answered.

A faint humming sounded in Orinthia's head. "Do you know where she is?"

"I do not," Claven said.

Again, her mod revealed his dishonesty. "Tell me where she is. I know you're lying."

Claven did not flinch at the accusation. He stayed silent for a full minute. "Aye, perhaps I am. But I'm not giving up any information for free. You're going to have to work for it."

Orinthia tossed her hands in the air. "Of course. Everyone always wants something."

The man leaned down and slid open a drawer. He pulled out a data disk and tossed it at Marius. "Some no-name marauders have been causing trouble for my... interests. They're not worth the effort for me to handle myself. Bring them in and I'll tell you what you want to know."

Marius pocketed the disk and stood from his seat. "Where do they run out of?"

"Hold on," Orinthia said. "We didn't agree to anything."

"Marauders are marauders," Marius said, barely looking at her. "Take a few out and get the information we came for? Sounds like a good deal to me."

Orinthia's upper lip curled in disgust. "Is that all you are? All law and no justice?"

"My job isn't justice. That's for the courts. I bring them in. That used to be your job, too."

Ready to unleash every ill thought she had about him, Orinthia opened her mouth but was muzzled by a gloved hand. "This isn't the place to hash this out," Annatilla said.

"We were sent here to do this job, and if that includes a detour, fine."

Claven spit on the floor. "Good night, that was nauseating. You're all too wrapped up in the EC's protective packaging. The farther you get from the core, the more clear things become. This —" he waved his hand in a wide half-circle above his head, "— is the reality of things. The meager and less fortunate left to scrape a living off the bottom of the boots that kick them down."

Orinthia yanked her head free from Annatilla's hold. "And you? What are you, then? Nothing more than another boot."

"I, young Anton, am the order in the chaos," Claven said, lowering his voice and straightening to his full height. His words were slow and punctuated with venom. "The vulture that eats the dead and dying, ridding the ecosystem of disease. I am the top of the food chain, because no one makes it out alive and they all have to go through me."

A chill ran up from Orinthia's lower back to the top of her head. She was not easily shaken, but the image he painted in her mind showed him as a sharp beaked creature, tearing flesh and sinew from rotting bones.

Claven returned to his seat, tossing his hands at the crew like shooing away bugs. "Now get. I won't say another word until you're done."

ORINTHIA SAT behind Annatilla back on the skiff with her mouth pinched shut. The smell from her clothes did not help her mood, but she left it until they were undocked from the space station and well on their way. Once clear to move around, Orinthia retreated to the bunk room and tore off her disguise, wishing she could burn the foul rags, but settled for shoving them under a pillow. She looked under the washbasin for a cloth to clean herself with, but there was none.

*Perfect,* she thought. *It's pretty clear why they're all miserable all the time. This place sucks.*

Instead of scrubbing herself clean, Orinthia settled on scooping water that trickled from the faucet onto her skin and rubbed as hard as she could. It helped less than she would have liked, but at least she felt better. After she redressed with her own clothes, Orinthia sat on the edge of the lower bunk and struggled with what to do next. Staying holed up in the tiny bunk room was less than appealing, but the idea of spending more time around Marius did not excite her either.

*He's worse than Kos when we first met,* she thought, setting her head in her hands with elbows planted on her knees. *How do I make him see we're on the same side? That I'm his ally and we can trust each other?* She wanted to flop back and get comfortable, but knew there was no use trying. *I have to show him. We don't have to be friends, but he needs to see I'm not who he assumes I am.*

With a deep breath, Orinthia got up and joined the rest of her crew. Cliff stood at the weapons locker, organizing things to suit his liking. A bright light reflected off Annatilla's face shield as she sat cross-legged in her seat, typing into the PortTab in her lap. Marius sat with his arms crossed and legs propped on the console again. It was clear this was his normal position while traveling. They all continued on with what they were doing and paid no attention to Orinthia as she moved closer to sit behind Annatilla.

Orinthia sat straight-backed with her hands folded in her lap, the silence eating at her after spending so much time chatting with Kos and Thrutt. Her friends were a joy to be around, and she missed them. It was good to hear Thrutt's voice, even if it was for a short time. She was eager to finish the extra mission and call them in the privacy of her room.

Sick of the quiet, Orinthia spoke up. "How long until we're there?"

Annatilla glanced up from her PortTab and turned it to the side, as if surprised to see Orinthia beside her. She looked at Marius, then back to the nav computer. "Soon," was all she said.

The ship's engines knocked and thumped, shuddering the walls. No one flinched except Orinthia. They stayed in one piece, and Orinthia let out a quiet sigh.

"What're you reading?" Orinthia asked Annatilla, trying to make conversation anyway she could.

"News net," Annatilla said quickly.

Orinthia's head hummed. "Anything interesting?" she asked.

Annatilla swiped a few times on the screen before responding. Her eyes moved back and forth as she read what was on the tablet. "More reports of unrest in the outer zone. Looks like there're a few factions that are rebelling against the planets in the Lyngor system. There's talk about it spilling into the EC territory, but nothing too alarming."

Her answer did not trigger Orinthia's mod, but she could tell Annatilla was reading the article for the first time. Orinthia eyed Annatilla and wondered what she was looking at before she was noticed.

"Did you know I can't live outside this suit?" Annatilla blurted out, drawing all attention away from her tablet. "During one of my first missions as a Hunter, we boarded a marauder ship. They funneled us into a corridor and blew it up. I was toward the back and survived, but was severely injured. My captain found me and dragged me back to our ship. They didn't tell me how they kept me alive until we reached the Moon. All I remember was waking up inside this three weeks later."

Orinthia stared at Annatilla. The idea of sharing something so vulnerable with a stranger made her stomach twist in knots. Many times in the last year she had been forced into spilling the truth about her mods. She could not recall a time where she willingly spoke about them, and never to someone she barely knew.

"That was a deeply personal thing to share with a stranger," Orinthia said.

She caught Marius watching them from the side of her eye. His eyes were narrowed and brows pinched together. Even Cliff had stopped tinkering with the cage behind her.

"We're not strangers, though," Annatilla said flatly. "You knew me before I looked like this. But, I consider her dead. She's who I had to bury in order to survive."

Orinthia was unsure how to respond. Annatilla had a different version of herself, like Orinthia did. Though the instances that led them to their current lives were unique, Orinthia understood the desire to leave the past behind.

The proximity alarm sounded, making Orinthia jump and draw back from such an intense moment. Marius straightened and flipped switches until the engine died down. "Buckle in. We're here."

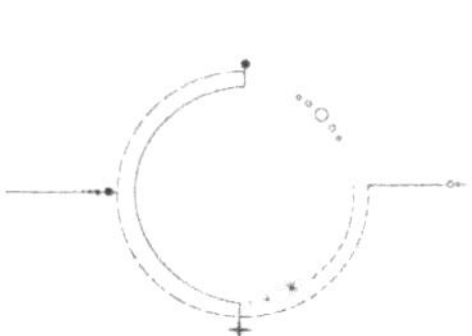

*D*ark grey clouds flickered with bursts of lightning, casting an eerie glow that pulsed through the sky as the storm raged beneath the skiff. Marius edged the ship closer to the top, eyes scanning for a safer entry point. The crackling of electricity from the storm scrambled the nav computer's readouts. With quick, deliberate taps, he adjusted the settings, trying to regain control of the fading system.

Above the storm, the sky was an indigo blue with wisps of cotton white clouds spattered across like paint streaks. Orinthia wrapped her hands into her seatbelt and waited for the eventual dive into the chaos below. She did not know Marius well, but was certain he would react without warning.

Within a minute, she was proven right. An opening appeared on the nav computer and Marius leaned forward on the yoke. Hard knocks of rain pelted the hull as they descended. There was little light other than the flashes of lightning that had yet to end. The storm fully engulfed them, and Orinthia saw none of the world below. She clenched her teeth and hoped Marius knew how far they had to go before smearing themselves against the planet's surface.

The seat rattled, threatening to come undone with each jolt. Orinthia gripped her belt tighter, willing herself to stay secured to the floor.

A series of numbers on the nav computer counted down in a rapid rate, jumping by the hundreds every few seconds. It was down to four digits, then three before Marius pulled up on the yoke and leveled out the skiff. They were still in the storm, but the free fall had ended. Streaks of rain crossed the window, creating silver lines against darkness as they hovered in place where Marius had stopped.

Again, he tapped a few more times on the nav computer, then shook his head. "The coordinates say we're right on top of where we're supposed to be," he said. "But the aerial map shows there's nothing but water and an empty cliff beneath us."

"Maybe they're hiding in an underwater city," Orinthia suggested in a dry tone, trying to keep from being sick.

"They'd still have to have somewhere to store their ships," Marius argued. "Marauders aren't that sophisticated. Even if they were, I'm not reading anything solid enough from up here."

Orinthia squinted and searched beyond the rain, looking for any sign they were in the right place. A succession of lightning lit up the area for more than a second. It was enough time to make out the shape of a cliff. "There." Orinthia leaned forward and pointed over Marius' shoulder. "Did you see it? There's a cave in that cliff."

Marius flipped a switch near his leg and eased the skiff forward. A beam of light cut through the gloom, illuminating what Orinthia had seen. As they neared, it became obvious why the marauders picked that location as their hideout.

Thick stones rose out from the sea, cut perfectly straight, creating pillars and columns along the cliff face.

The tops were uneven, like poorly built steps, followed by rows and rows. A hole like a mouth stood open before them, tall and menacing, but not wide enough to land the skiff.

"How are we going to get in?" Orinthia asked.

"The old-fashioned way," Marius answered. "We jump."

Orinthia let out a single laugh. "What?"

"The skiff won't fit," Marius said. He set the controls to hover and stood up. "And in this weather, our jetpacks will only last so long. So Dai can take us in close enough to bail out, then fly above the storm and wait for us to signal her back." Marius turned to Annatilla, "Understood?"

Annatilla nodded.

"Ward," Marius said, facing Orinthia and Cliff. "Get whatever you need and be ready to go in five."

Cliff was quick to follow the order. He rose from his seat and donned a thick black coat and filled the pockets with as many small weapons as possible. Once that was done, he strapped a belt to his waist and continued adding more armament of various sizes.

"We'll start by scoping out the area," Marius said, drawing Orinthia's attention to him. "If they're holed up inside, then there's a good chance they've taken the time to secure the entrance. Could be booby-trapped or under surveillance. Either way, keep an eye out and move slowly. Don't need you blowing our cover because you don't know what you're doing."

Orinthia rolled her eyes but kept her comebacks to herself. He could not care less about what she had to say, and there was no use in causing an argument that would only waste time. She was determined to prove her worth, whether he liked it or not.

"Dai, take the pilot's seat," Marius ordered. "Bring us in

as close as you can. Watch for the winds. I don't want to get sandwiched when we jump."

Annatilla swapped seats and her light hands flew across the console, flipping switches and turning knobs. The view outside spun and drifted to the side as she pulled the skiff parallel to the rocks. A gust of wind shoved them to the right, making her yank back to correct the action. Orinthia stumbled to the side with her jetpack in hand.

"Sorry," Annatilla said. "Better be quick. I'm not sure how long before we get tossed again."

Orinthia's pulse beat inside her ears like a drumroll, leading her launch like a high diver waiting for their performance. She pulled the collar of her jacket closed around her neck and zipped it up all the way. It was far from waterproof, but it would have to be enough to keep dry. With her jetpack secured, she signaled to Marius that she was good to go.

Cliff joined them and waited for Marius to give the order. The door opened in front of them. A blast of cold, wet air blew in. Marius shouted for them to jump, but Orinthia could only understand it by the moving of his mouth. His voice was drowned out by the roar of wind and water crashing around them.

Their leader leaped out and punched his ignition. He took a hard left and faced at an angle into the gale. Cliff was next to jump, who followed Marius' movements. With a glance back at Annatilla to make sure she held the controls steady, Orinthia took a deep breath and shot out of the skiff after the men.

She was immediately thrown to the right, and her hand slipped from the ignition. Her stomach lurched up to her throat as she dropped out of the sky toward the black sea. Orinthia pulled her arms in as close as she could and found the levers. Her thumbs pressed hard against the button and she shot up again. It took more correcting and she nearly lost sight of where the cave was, but eventually found where she needed to go.

The men were already out of the jetpacks by the time she reached them. Neither seemed worried that it had taken her longer to arrive. In fact, Marius looked annoyed she made it at all.

Orinthia landed on the solid ground and stepped forward, closer to the covering of the cave. It was not as much of a relief from the storm as Orinthia had hoped. Waves crashed beneath them, sending violent showers of foam inside and mixing with the torrent of rain. Water filled in from all directions.

Orinthia approached the men, stepping farther in, where it was almost dry. She placed her jetpack behind a rock next to the others, then removed her jacket and draped it over her pack to dry.

Cliff wore a glowing band on his wrist that softly lit up the space around him. He handed Orinthia one.

"Careful, there's a tripwire," Marius said with his visor covering his eyes. He pointed to a spot a few feet in front of him.

Orinthia turned her head to the side and squeezed the water out of her braided bun. She could not see what he saw, but tried to keep her eyes on where he indicated.

Marius moved forward, then took a wide legged-step over the trip wire. Cliff followed quietly behind, water dripping from his clothes.

With careful movements, Orinthia joined them. It wasn't until her right leg was in the air did she catch a tiny sparkle from the wire. She gave it another half foot of clearance before stepping down on the other side. The men did not wait to celebrate with her before heading farther down into the cave.

It was far from their only obstacle at the beginning. Marius led them around and over half a dozen more traps before they reached a set of tunnels.

"Which way do we go?" Orinthia asked in a whisper.

Neither of the men answered.

She shook her head and listened for anything that would set them in the right direction. But there was nothing. Not even an echo of dripping water or the chittering of bugs. It was deathly quiet and set Orinthia's skin tingly. "I don't like this."

"Let's go this way," Marius said, ignoring her statement.

Cliff gave her a long stare with his good eye, then followed their team-lead.

They stepped into the first tunnel. It was silent. Even the sounds of their steps were dampened. Orinthia's ears rang. The air was cold and heavy. She grazed the wall on accident with her arm a few times and it scratched like damp sandpaper against her skin.

Her and Cliff's bands made it easy to see what was around them, but anything outside of their circle of light was completely black. Marius, with his visor, did not have the same problem. He walked confidently down the path and moved with ease. It took ten minutes of winding through the wide tunnel before Orinthia's eyes adjusted at a gleam of light before them. Small at first, it blossomed into the warmth of artificial lighting.

Marius crouched down and made himself as low as possible. He waved for Cliff to stay back, but pointed at Orinthia to come closer. She lowered herself to the floor and crawled to him. They peered over a stone for cover and examined the scene before them.

An encampment filled the center of the large chamber, and Orinthia counted over fifteen different sized huts. There were animals penned up at the back of the room, and hover bikes stationed all around. At least fifty marauders roamed around from one place to another. Their voices reached them but did not flow down the corridor.

"How do we get down there?" Orinthia whispered.

Marius stayed silent for a moment. He tapped his visor and scanned the area. "We'll just have to find which way they came in."

THIS CHAPTER CONTAINS DEPICTIONS OF
PTSD, WARTIME TRAUMA, AND EMOTIONAL
DISTRESS, INCLUDING A COMBAT-RELATED
FLASHBACK. READER DISCRETION IS
ADVISED.

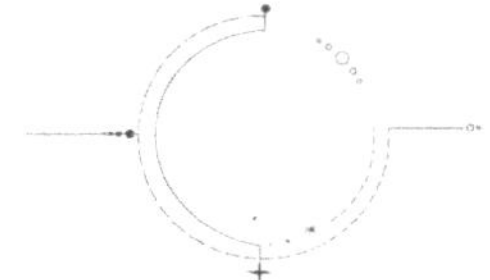

*M*ore than fifty captains. along with portions of their crews, converged on the *Fera's* decks. All for one purpose: to hear from Kos Rogue. Ignio called a meeting of his closest allies and most passive enemies. He prepared a round-the-clock feast in the mess deck for all who came. Never had so many marauders gathered together in the hope of creating alliances. It was an historic event.

Kos had laid out his argument, answered questions in public settings, and given scenarios where their aid would be beneficial to the fight. He offered what treasures he could and promised Adora's goods for the taking. It was an opportunity for not only riches, but a chance to unite against a common enemy once again.

In the end, he did everything he knew to do and was steadfast in his words and actions. The rest was up to the marauders, some of whom Adora had already approached.

Kos hoped his speeches had swayed them to his side. There was nothing left to do but wait while they deliberated with their respective crews.

The ship emptied as the conference closed. Each captain agreed to send word within the following days. The *Fera* was quiet and still, save for her own occupants. Kos continued to keep to himself aboard Mimi's ship. The talks had drained him and he struggled to stay in the present. He was tired, but his body and mind refused to rest.

The canvas bag Ignio had given him laid slumped beneath the cabin window. It'd been there since he received it, and he hadn't found the time to reminisce. Kos' brief search through the bag showed him enough and he wasn't in any hurry to dig more. But, boredom and mild curiosity nagged at him.

Kos leaned forward and dragged the bag closer to him. The tie came undone and he pulled the top open. Orinthia's photo was still on top. He took it out and gently set it aside. There were a few notebooks and journals he'd already seen, and he placed them next to Orinthia's photo on the bed. He found a gold-lined box that rattled when he moved it.

The lid slid open and inside were a handful of daggers. Unlike the ones he used regularly, these were older, lighter, and meant for speed more than strength. The handles still bore faint oil from the palms of those who owned them before. He closed it again and set it aside.

Going farther down, he found handkerchiefs folded into neat squares. They had been gifts from his aunt when he left for boot camp. Beneath those was a rusted pendant with no chain, and a dented coin from a port-of-call he could no longer remember.

Then, he reached something wrapped in cloth that had once been white. He didn't open it. He never had. But now, alone with his thoughts, Kos pulled back the edges and removed the frame from inside.

He stared at the image. Ghostly faces looked back. Memorabilia from before he was a navigator. The mission that took everything to survive.

There was nothing to hold onto. His mind was too spent and he had no will to fight it. The shadows of his old lives crowded in and took the last bit of strength he had. His eyes unfocused. Kos fell forward into the past.

His team moved in sync through yet another ship. Fifteenth for the month, maybe more. Kos had stopped counting. They were the best at what they did, and there was no rest when you were at the top of everyone's list. He moved on autopilot, shooting at anyone not in an EC Navy uniform who stepped in their path. His senses were sharp, but there was almost no use in trying to excel anymore. The itch never left, no matter how many bodies he stacked.

"Ship secured," a voice called over his comm. The words felt distant in his tunnel vision. "We found the Under Czar. She won't talk."

That perked Kos' attention. It'd been a while since he got his hands dirty. Everything had become quick and clean. Getting someone to squeal was more interesting than clearing a room.

Kos followed the directions on his HUD to the room where his commander held the Under Czar. He didn't know her name, and he never bothered to learn it. She was the fifth one since the war started sixteen years before. But if he had anything to do with it, maybe she'd be the last.

He had gained a reputation during his service. One that allowed him on high-profile missions. Kos Rogue was good at getting things done, and if it meant breaking someone for information, then that's what he'd do.

"Your weapon," the commander said, holding his hand out. "No need to get that close and let her sneak it off you."

Kos unslung his rifle and detached his pistol from its holster. He stepped into the room and faced the woman. Her silver hair pulled into two tight braids rested over her modified shoulders. Neither arm were ones she was born with, modified for who-knows-what purpose. The metal frame was see-through, filled with wires that mimicked muscle. She didn't look at him when he crouched beside her near the back wall.

"Do you have the authority to negotiate a surrender?" Kos asked, as he always did when first meeting a prisoner.

The Mod Bleyers had a strange structure of authority. Only certain levels of their leaders had the power to make major calls, and others were only powerful in name to bolster the appearance of strength.

He was met with silence. Kos clicked his tongue and retracted this armor, then nodded for the others in the room to step out. There was a pouch on his ankle. He bent down and took out a laser scalpel and ignited it. The thin line of light reflected off the woman's metal work as Kos faced her again. He placed the laser edge to the wires on her arm and pressed down. The smell of melting metal wafted up through his nose. In a few seconds, the mechanical arm was no longer attached to the woman and Kos held it in his hands.

"You're disgusting," the woman said in a thick accent Kos had never heard before. She spoke in a broken version of his traditional language, the one he learned to speak before he was old enough for a translator chip. Her accent, more than her words, caught him off guard, but only for a moment. Bright violet eyes bore into him. There was no fear of him, only hatred.

"This —" Kos held up the woman's arm, "— is disgusting. How much of you is biological? How much have you plopped out and replaced with steel and electricity?"

The woman kept her mouth shut. Her nose flared once as she took in a shaky breath.

Kos straightened and dropped the arm on the ground, moving to the other side of the woman. "You have three more chances to answer my question. Some of them are going to hurt more than the others. So, I'll ask again, do you have the authority to negoti—"

His question was cut off by a deafening explosion that rocked the ship.

The blast sent Kos crashing to the ground, his vision protected by his visor, but his clothes shredded by the debris. His ears rang with the sound of the ruptured metal and the groaning of the ship's hull. He sat up and looked around. Smoke circled in and surrounded him. There were no life signs outside the room.

In a single strike, his entire team was gone. But the Under Czar was still alive.

Kos' mind raced. The ship was clearly under attack, but from who? They'd secured the sector before boarding the Mod Bleyer ship. There was no time to think. His prisoner was still alive, and he needed to get her back to his own ship to continue questioning.

Kos scrambled to his feet, but his legs buckled under him. He yelled in pain, then forced himself up again. The scalpel was still clutched in his hand, the only weapon he could find in the mess. Kos undid the woman's restraints and dragged her out, ignoring the bodies of his fallen brothers and sisters as best he could.

He slowly made his way down the burning corridor. The woman's hand twitched in his, the only warning he had before she pulled herself free. She crawled to her feet and leaned against the wall. She looked at him for a second, eyes wide with terror.

The woman turned and ran back toward where they'd come. She only got a dozen feet before a second blast struck the ship. A gaping hole ripped through the side. The woman, bodies of his crew, debris, and smoke were sucked out with the rushing of oxygen depressurizing.

Farther away, Kos was thrown down. Flames curled around his legs, burning his flesh. He yelled, tearing his throat. With the scalpel still in hand, he jabbed it into the ground, and activated his armor tattoo with his free hand. His body screamed as it sealed beneath the protective barrier. Kos trembled as he used all his effort to drag himself through debris free-floating around him. He forced his way through to the next corridor, and pried open the failsafe to force the door to open. Once through, the backup sensors sealed the door behind him and he dropped to the ground.

There was no time to rest. Sirens blared around him. The ship was too compromised and whoever attacked them wasn't done. Another explosion rocked the ship. He had to get out. This was no longer a mission, it was a failure. He'd lost everyone he boarded with, and as far as he knew, he was the only one left.

No amount of training prepared him for that realization. That being two steps too far from an explosion was the line between life and death. That surviving was more than skill, but luck and timing.

He pushed the thoughts away, though they hovered in the back of his mind. There were two options before him: live to remember them, or die along side them.

Kos flipped through the schematics of the ship on his HUD and found a path to the escape pods. He stumbled, his legs barely able to hold him up, for minutes as the ship fell apart around him. He hoped he'd find more survivors along the way. But there were none. He was alone. As he reached the pods, he called out over the comm. "The ship's going down, is there anyone left?" Heartbeats passed, but no answer.

More missiles hit the ship. Yells down the corridors died down. Lights flickered and the ship groaned. It began to list as the thrusters either had given out or were disabled. The planet below pulled them closer and it wouldn't be long before it was in a free fall through the gravity field.

He called out again.

Nothing.

Kos swallowed hard, and he threw himself into the pod. He slammed the eject button and jettisoned away from the burning ship. Debris filled the porthole, and he watched as the vessel received more hails of cannon fire.

Half a Mod Bleyer fleet surrounded the ship he arrived on and the one he fled from. His ship fought back, but it was no use. Outnumbered and outgunned, the EC Navy vessel took on too much damage. A few escape pods managed to launch before the final blow, but not enough.

It was over. He'd lost. They had all lost.

The wreckage faded away from his mind. He was in the present, alone in his cabin. Tears silently trickled down his eyes and the picture from his past laid at his feet.

Heavy footsteps sounded as Thrutt stepped onto the ship. They stopped in front of Kos' cabin. Thrutt knocked twice. "Bud, you in there?"

Words failed to come to Kos.

"I had a feeling you'd be here," Thrutt said, stepping in and giving him a once over. "Lay down and I'll get you something to drink."

Kos didn't protest and followed Thrutt's directions. The

bed formed around him as he laid down. Scenes played across his mind's eye and he tried to push them out with other thoughts.

Thrutt came back with a hydro-sphere and a plate of light snacks. "You saw them again, didn't you?" he asked, moving across the room and leaning against the wall.

Kos sipped his water and stared at the giant's feet. His voice was airy when he spoke. "The last mission. The one before I was pulled from the field."

"That was probably the best thing to happen to you," Thrutt said. "They gave you new skills. Useable skills. Anyone can kill, but you learned to navigate. To chart the stars and forge a path through them."

"I was weak."

Thrutt came back to Kos and crouched down as best he could in front of him. "You got too good at surviving. It scared them. A man can only take so much before he turns on the handlers. They needed to keep you under their thumb. That's not weakness. That's power. But they made you feel like it was your fault."

Silence settled between them. Kos breathed, slow and ragged, but steadier than before.

Thrutt stood. "Rest. I'll be close." He left without another word.

Kos lay motionless, the photo still on the floor, and the past still fresh in his chest. But the present held steady.

And, for a while at least, that was good enough.

# 32

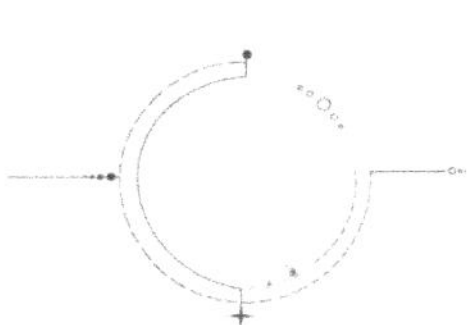

The jagged rocks dug into Orinthia's knees and no matter which way she moved, she could not find a comfortable spot. Marius had scolded her five times since Cliff left to scout a way down to the main chamber. Orinthia's nerves had not known stillness like in the corridor since before her new mod.

There was no life, no insect or skittering creature. Nothing but solid stone and Marius. She would have found comfort in it, if it were any other situation. But sitting perched above a group of marauders did not lend to ease.

"Stop squirming," Marius whispered with a hiss. "There's a lava tube or something right here and you keep nudging me closer to it."

"Look," Orinthia said, snapping back. "It's cold and damp in here. And I'm pretty sure my knees have permanent dents now." She rocked backwards so her weight rested on her feet, though that only made her toes ache instead.

"Cliff's been gone for half an hour." Marius checked his watch. "The walls are too thick to signal him back, so unless we hear him in trouble, we stay put so none of us get lost."

Orinthia rolled her eyes and turned her attention back to the chamber. Something about the way they moved unsettled her. She could not quite place it, but whatever they were doing was unusual. Their movements followed a circuit, back and forth, the same steps again and again. No one cooked. No one ate. No one rested.

Before she could think more on it, a prickle crept up her back. It started small, then grew like something was approaching. She turned, anticipating Cliff's arrival. As the sensation became more intense, she realized whatever it was, was too small to be Cliff.

Orinthia concentrated on the feeling and expanded her senses farther out. There was no sound of footsteps or rustling of clothes. Then, she heard the creaking of a blaster's hammer being pulled back.

With one hand, she reached for her own blaster and shoved Marius out of the way with the other. A bolt struck where his head had been a second before, throwing sparks at Orinthia's outstretched hand. She pulled it back and searched through the dark for the attacker.

Marius' yell echoed through the corridor, then softened as he fell down the tube.

Another blaster bolt fired at Orinthia. She let off a few of her own for cover, then connected with the stranger, pushing them back with her mod. Using the few seconds of distraction, Orinthia slammed on her light band and found the hole Marius had fallen through. She tucked her arms close to her body and rolled toward it. Her feet went down first, sucking the rest of her with them.

Rough, damp, sandpaper-like stone scratched at her clothes. The drop was steep and she had no way of controlling her speed. She slid for a full minute before the tube leveled out. A second before collision, Marius appeared in the light of her band and she crashed into him. The pair crumbled to the ground.

"What was that?" Marius yelled, shoving her off him.

"You didn't see him?" Orinthia asked. She checked herself for injuries then wiped her pants clean the best she could.

"Who?" Marius asked, his tone tight, lips curled.

"I thought it was Cliff, but the feeling wasn't right," Orinthia said. "Luckily I realized it when I did or you'd be a footnote by now."

Marius squinted at her. "That thing you can do?"

Orinthia undid her bun and rewrapped it tightly on top of her head. "Yeah. Like on the *Scow*. I sensed whoever was up there and it was unfamiliar. Smaller than Cliff, too."

"You can tell people apart with only your mod?" Marius tucked his chin to his chest and raised his eyebrows.

"Sometimes. The more time I spend with someone, the more I recognize the way energy comes off them. But really, it's more than that. Someone's mass, height, and the way they move are all unique and affect the way I sense them."

"So if I was in the middle of a crowd, you'd be able to find me?" Marius said in an almost teasing tone.

Orinthia set her hands on her hips and sighed. Explaining how her mod worked was a waste of time. They had to find a way out of the hole before someone else came looking for them.

"Maybe," she said. "I don't know. You gave off a different sensation than whatever it was on the *Scow*. And I could tell you apart from the bodies because you had a living frequency."

Marius smirked. "I give you a sensation, huh?"

Orinthia shoved his shoulder.

"Okay, so in theory, you'd be able to follow me if it were pitch black?" Marius rubbed his arm.

The idea of being blind made her heart jump. It was the last thing she wanted to do, especially with him. Everything outside the radius of her band light was completely dark. "I'm not doing that."

"You don't trust me?" Marius touched his chest in mock offense.

"You don't trust me," Orinthia said.

"Fair." Marius shrugged. "I'll let you keep the band on for now, but if I tell you to turn it off, you do it. Our cover's already blown."

"Why don't we just find Cliff and get out of here?"

"The mission comes first," Marius said, his levity dropping.

"A mission that we were sent on by a criminal." Orinthia tossed her hands out. "I didn't like this idea from the start. Look, I won't enjoy doing it, but I can probably use my mod to get Claven to talk. This is falling apart by the minute and we need to figure things out another way."

Marius put up a hand to shush her. "Stop. We're going through with this." He turned before she could respond and scanned the small chamber they fell into. "There's an opening over here. Saw it before you took me out. Might be tight, but I think it goes through."

"Can you be sure?" Orinthia asked.

"Why don't you use your witchcraft to see if you can *sense* anything on the other side?"

Orinthia shot a rude gesture at his back before stepping around him, extending her hand toward the faint opening revealed in her band's light. Closing her eyes, she focused, not on what she could feel, but on what was not there. Her arm trembled as she fought to hold it steady, seconds stretching unbearably. Just as she was about to give up, a flicker of energy sparked against her skin. It was small but unmistakable. There was a clear path all the way through.

She released her focus and collapsed to the ground, still conscious, but drained. Her knee ground over a sharp stone, tearing her pants.

"Whoa, what was *that*?" Marius asked, taking a step back.

Orinthia did not answer. Her head was clouded and she fought to stay awake. She patted her side and felt for a snack she brought for an emergency boost. It was warm from her body heat and reminded her of Kos. The caramelized filling beneath a crunchy layer of cookies did well to give her a pep. When it was finished, Orinthia stashed the trash back in her pocket and climbed to her feet.

She braced herself on the wall and regained an even breathing pattern. "The way's clear."

Marius twisted his mouth for a second. "I was kidding. Mostly."

"Well, it worked. So let's get this done so I can go take a nap."

He stepped in front of her and walked through the passage first.

They made it through in minutes. Orinthia stayed close to Marius and tried to clear her mind. They would soon be inside an enemy camp, and she needed her wits about her. The passage made a sharp turn and opened wide into a cone shape. Light filtered in.

Orinthia shielded her eyes with her arm and squinted until they adjusted to the change. There was almost no cover for them to hide behind and assess the situation. The pair ducked back into the passage and kept to the shadows as much as they could.

"Turn that off," Marius whispered, nodding at her wrist.

The ring of light disappeared, and darkness covered them. Orinthia pressed herself against the wall opposite of where Marius stood and examined the scenery.

The cavern was no longer quiet. The marauders knew they were there and moved quickly. Chatter and soft shuffling of boots echoed through the chamber, amplified by the cavern's acoustics.

A pinpoint of red flickered from the ridge above. Orinthia's eyes darted to the spot where they had been earlier, but the light was gone. She grabbed Marius' attention and waited to see if it would flash again.

"That's Ward," Marius said, some of the tension eased from his voice. "Okay, now we can get somewhere." He lifted his hand to his face and tapped his watch twice. It glowed red in response to Cliff's signal.

Before Orinthia could ask what it meant, Cliff tossed something into the cavern. A plume of blue smoke erupted from the center of the encampment. Marauders scrambled, shouting at each other.

Marius used the distraction to move in. He crept through the smoke, keeping low, and darting across the empty space between them and the huts.

Orinthia took in a full breath of air, then threw out her black blade. She followed a few feet behind Marius, but he crossed another direction out of her view.

Blaster bolts rained down from the ledge, dropping bodies where they stood. Return shots sliced through the space, flashing red and blue between stalagmites and makeshift tents. The air was thick with smoke, mixing with the dampness of the cave.

A bolt fired over Orinthia's head, just barely missing. She threw herself down and pressed against a crate, her chest rising and falling too fast. Her mind raced. This was not how she wanted things to happen.

*I have to do this,* she thought. *If I can't, then how will I ever kill Adora?*

Someone moved around the crate and stepped directly in front of her. He did not raise a blaster, just a long, chipped sword. A flicker of fire crossed his face, the kind only in people who liked to get close to their victims. The man lifted his sword to slash her, but instincts kicked in.

Orinthia was on her feet, slicing up and catching the blade midair. The black blade sparked as it ran along the marauder's steel. She twisted herself and kicked him out of her way, instead of taking a cutting blow. The marauder toppled through a hut.

She turned to find Marius, but a moment too slow.

A second marauder had a rifle level with her chest. Orinthia's breath caught. Time slowed. He was too far to strike with her blade, but her blaster weighed heavy. Her hand jerked up and she fired. The shot struck low in his abdomen, and he crumpled forward, gasping in pain.

Across the cavern, Marius moved like a ghost, clearing cover with rapid, precise shots. Orinthia watched him cut through the chaos without hesitation, each movement effortless and deadly.

He wore a smug grin on his face, confident in every move. But, the expression changed a moment later, replaced with wide eyed panic. Marius leaped forward, but a concussive blast caught him mid-jump, throwing him back out of view.

Orinthia's heart seized and she frantically looked for him. Her eyes fell upon the man who had thrown the grenade. He laughed as he raised his pistol toward her.

Burning beneath her skin, rage filled her. She reached out

for the man. He flew at her and met the black blade. His breath gurgled and she kicked him off the Tullian steel.

Victory was short lived. A blaster shot struck her in the shoulder. She yelled and ducked behind a smoldering tent. Her breathing was rapid, and she felt light headed. She fought through it, knowing Marius was still out there.

Orinthia risked a look around her position and found Marius no more than twenty feet away. She gritted her teeth and breathed through the pain, then turned her face up and yelled. "Cliff, Marius is down. I need cover." The words echoed through the cavern, breaking through the relentless blaster fire.

Half a second later, a layer of rapid fire blanketed her path, cutting off the marauders who had shot at her a second before. Orinthia ran as hard as she could and slid to Marius' side.

She crossed her arm up and recalled her blade. With trembling fingers, Orinthia undid her belt and wrapped it above the wound on his thigh. He let out a hiss as she tightened it.

The bleeding barely slowed before a voice called out.

"Hold your fire!"

It froze her to her core. Her body seized in place.

The firefight came to a halt, and a hush fell. Flames crackled and smoke continued to shift.

Each heartbeat brought clarity. These men they fought were not marauders. They were traitors. And Arsenio was there to lead them. It was his fight and they had been sold out.

Trembling, she turned her body while keeping pressure on Marius' leg and looked through the haze.

Arsenio stood above on the ridge, his blaster pointed at Cliff's back. Crackling of electricity danced around his other hand. Cliff laid limp at his feet.

Orinthia locked eyes with her brother as he stared down at her from his perch.

"I've won," he said, his nasally voice flowing around the chamber. "You've spent your whole life trying to escape us, Orinthia. But you should've known better. We always catch you in the end."

Orinthia's breath hitched, her chest tightened like a vise. The cavern shrunk around her, and the soot-laced air choked. For a moment, she was a little girl hiding under Uri's bed, curled up as small as possible. They always found her. They always hurt her. And now, Arsenio's shadow stretched long over her once again.

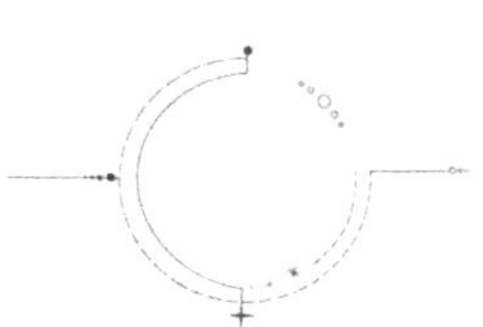

## 33

*S*moke curled through the cavern, the footsteps grew closer, and Orinthia stayed still. Her fingers gripped harder on Marius' leg and he yelped. The sound snapped her back to the present. She was not a child. She was a grown woman, and there were people who counted on her. The cave was not Uri's bed, and she was not alone.

Orinthia loosened her grip on Marius' wound and motioned for him to sit up. She refused to die hiding behind a dirty tent. If Arsenio wanted to take her out, he would have to work for it.

Marius put weight on his good leg and Orinthia stood up, pulling him with her. He draped his arm over her good shoulder and they looked for a clear path back to their tunnel.

"Don't let them escape," Arsenio shouted.

His crew dashed through the smoke and charged for them.

Orinthia dragged Marius through the maze of debris, her pulse hammering in her ears and body begging to rest. Every step sent a fresh jolt of pain through her aching limbs and the shot through her shoulder burned. But she forced herself to keep moving.

*Just keep moving.*

The sound of scuffling followed by a series of shouts caught her attention.

She turned just in time to see Cliff surge forward, rifle slamming into the back of Arsenio's legs. He stumbled. Eyes wide. Arms flailing. Then, Arsenio tipped over the ledge.

Orinthia's hand shot out in pure instinct, pure reflex, or maybe pure preservation as the face of her father flashed across her mind.

Arsenio's fall slowed unnaturally, like he had been caught by an invisible parachute. His body drifted instead of dropped, landing with a thud instead of a crack against the stone.

Her arm was still outstretched, fingers flared. Trembling.

Her stomach twisted.

*I saved him.*

Not because she wanted to.

Not because she meant to.

But because something inside her, some old, buried part, refused to let him die.

Even after everything, all the pain, the scars, the years of fear… she could not end him.

Cold sweats crawled up her spine. The urge to vomit surged, and she choked it back.

The men chasing them changed directions and dashed for Arsenio. Taking the opportunity to escape, Orinthia swallowed hard and pulled Marius the final distance to the tunnel. They disappeared into the shadows, leaving the cavern behind.

"You'll have to lead," Orinthia said, barely able to fill her lungs with air.

The pair stumbled through the dark, guided only by

Marius' visor. Both slow and weakened by the fight. It took them twice as long and multiple stops to get through.

Orinthia collapsed when he told her they had made it to the section they fell into. Her companion sat beside her and pressed his arm against hers. She was grateful to sense him through the dark.

He rummaged through one of his pouches, then something cracked. Marius sighed and took in several deep breaths.

"You okay?" she asked.

"Better, now," Marius answered. "Bleeding's stopped and should start healing up soon." He tapped her hand. "Okay, next thing. Let me see your band."

She undid the glow-band from her wrist and gave it to him. "What're you doing?"

"Cliff's still up there, and he's our only way out of this hole." A yellow glow lit up Marius' face. It was dusty and tired with bloody scrapes scattered across his cheeks. He pulled a knife from one of his pouches and opened the back of the band. "We got one shot at this, so I hope he's looking."

Marius punctured the battery pack with his knife and threw it up into the chute. It popped and flashed like lightning, then the room went dark again.

Silent seconds passed. The sound of electric humming jolted her senses. Something was coming, and there was a chance it would be from the wrong side.

A beam of light broke through the darkness, cutting like a lighthouse. The drone passed in front of Marius first, then Orinthia. Moments later, it shot back up the tube and disappeared. The room returned to eerie stillness. Orinthia kept her back pressed against the damp rock, fingers twitching against her now scuffed-up blaster. There were no voices, no movement.

Nothing.

Just the slow drip of water against stone and the pounding of her pulse.

Marius scooted back to her side. His breathing was controlled, but she could feel the tension flowing off him. He was ready to keep fighting.

She was not.

A faint scrape of metal on rock drifted across from her. Orinthia's grip tightened on her blaster. Her eyes darted in the thick darkness, desperate to see anything. The sound was smooth and deliberate. Boots hit the ground.

Orinthia was ready to throw up. She was too weak to sense who it was without pushing herself over the edge.

"Good move," Cliff said, turning on his light. "I almost walked out without looking down here. Ready to go?"

Relief hit Orinthia. A wave of tears trickled down her eyes, but she wiped them away. They were still in danger.

"Take Anton first," Marius said. "No matter what she wants to say, she's a civilian and we have a duty to protect her."

Orinthia, too tired to protest, rolled to her knees. If he was going to let her ahead, fine with her.

With practiced motion, Cliff wrapped the rope around Orinthia and lifted her from the ground. He fastened it across her chest and tugged twice to check the hold.

"Toss the rope down when you get up there," Cliff instructed.

That was her only warning. The rope lurched her forward through the chute. She ran her hands along the wall to keep from knocking her head on anything. The rope dug into her skin with each move.

Her ascent was slow, the winch pulling her inch by inch through the darkness. She tried to ignore the thought of the hole below. And it was not until she saw the glow from the opening above her did she take a breath of relief. Her muscles screamed as she hoisted herself onto solid ground and untied the rope from her body.

She was out, and now her crew needed her to send the rescue back. The rope unraveled from her hand.

Beyond the ledge, below her in the cavern, voices filtered out. Orinthia kept herself low and peered over. Smoke hung over the floor, and the figures scrambled to reorganize themselves. The battle had ended, but the hunt had not.

The winch hummed again. Orinthia scooted away and waited in the shadow. A minute later, Marius' voice grumbled beside her.

They sat in silence, processing what happened in their own way. Orinthia refused to let her head wander too far, afraid of what she may realize. She needed time to eat, to rest, to think. And more than anything, she needed Thrutt. Not his strength, but his steadiness. His wisdom.

A heartbeat later, the winch kicked on again, signaling Cliff's climb. Orinthia swallowed hard and waited.

THE TRIO TRUDGED BACK through to the entrance, stopping to listen for movement every few minutes. Nothing. Where their initial time was ten minutes through, it was twenty before they reached the original split. Marius held his hand to his side to stop the group from going on. Orinthia stumbled into him. He pushed his back against her and stepped away from the entrance. They moved a quarter of the way back before he stopped.

"What's go—" Orinthia began to say.

"They're waiting out there," Marius whispered. "Ward. Get her out. That's an order. I'll cover you for as long as I can."

"No," Orinthia said. "No, you have to come back with us."

"I trust you to finish the mission," Marius said. He set a hand on her shoulder for a long moment, then said, "Ward. Go."

Cliff slammed into Orinthia and lifted her off her feet. The wind rushed out of her chest and she could not yell for him to stop.

They ran in the darkness until Cliff unpinned a grenade. The flash burst behind Orinthia, casting light through the tunnel. Yells and blaster fire erupted throughout the passage. Orinthia covered her head the best she could, the wound in her shoulder aching with each move.

Cliff darted forward.

The room flared to life as Arsenio's men switched on their flashlights. The beams cut through the darkness.

Orinthia locked her eyes on Marius, who fired and ducked behind cover. He did everything he could to keep their attention on him. But it did little to stop them. The group broke off. Three stayed with him and another three followed Orinthia and Cliff.

Cliff continued to run. He pushed harder, huffing and grunting.

Orinthia strained for one last glimpse of Marius, but the shadows closed around him. With the last of her strength, she reached out for him in her mind, refusing to let him face the end alone. His frequency pulsed against her atoms, faint but real, like a flickering signal in the dark. She clung to it, staying with him in the only way she could. Then, in one heartbeat, the thread connecting them snapped. His energy faded, leaving behind only an empty mass. Nothing more.

The tears she held back broke through.

Cliff ripped another grenade from his belt and hurled it behind them without breaking stride. The dull clatter of metal was swallowed by blaster fire and pounding boots. The trip wires snapped. Explosions bloomed. Fire and thunder chased them through the dark.

The concussion hit like a shockwave, sending a wall of dust and rubble around them. Orinthia barely reacted. She was still with Marius. Not with her mod, but with her soul. All she felt was the absence. A hollow space where he had been.

Cliff barreled toward the mouth of the cave, bursting into daylight as debris rained behind them, sealing the others inside. The storm had passed, leaving a sky streaked with patchwork clouds. Bright light spilled over the rock walls, a poor reward for sacrifice.

As soon as they were clear, Cliff shouted into his comm, "Dai, we need a pickup, now!"

Orinthia moved on autopilot as Cliff set her down near the jetpacks. He threw his on quickly, but Orinthia fumbled with hers. Hammers beat the inside of her skull, but everything else was distant and muted.

Cliff guided her to the edge of the cave as the skiff swooped into view. The ramp dropped and, without hesitation, he grabbed Orinthia by the arm and jumped. It was a breeze compared to their arrival.

The door closed behind Orinthia and they zoomed away from the cliff, one passenger lighter.

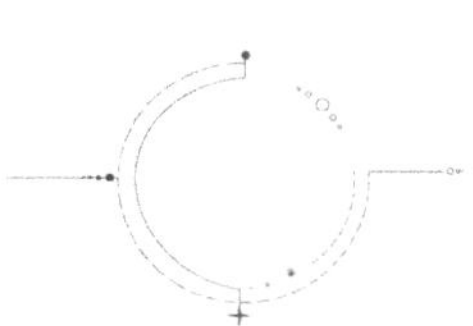

## 34

*T*ime drifted in quiet heartache.

Orinthia slipped in and out of sleep for a day, jolting awake with cold sweats and nightmares. When she could no longer close her eyes, she lay still, staring at the wall of her bunk and listening to the *Tertion's* engines hum.

The sound was no comfort to her. It only reminded her of everything she failed to do. She should have been glad to be back in a quiet place. But nothing about it felt good.

Her thoughts came in rushes and whispers, and her body ached from the inside out. But it was comfort compared to the lingering sensation of Marius slipping into death. She closed her eyes and tried to push it away, to sever the bond between them.

The memory burned like a wound in her soul. It held deep and unrelenting in her cells. The mod she had hoped would be a blessing was no more than another curse.

A slow but firm knock sounded on the door, breaking the spiral of guilt and regret. Orinthia did not move to answer. She did not have to. The door opened without her and soft footsteps tapped against the floor, coming to a stop behind her.

"Captain Solvay wanted to check in on you," Annatilla said in a hushed tone. "Are you well?"

"Tell him if he wants to know how I'm doing, he can come down here himself," Orinthia said, refusing to turn to look at the woman. "I'm not in the mood to play relay games."

"I have," Captain Solvay said from the hall. "May I enter?"

Orinthia shifted in her bed. She wanted to be left alone, but it was more courtesy than the old man had shown before.

Annatilla moved farther into the room to allow the captain space close to Orinthia. The woman blended in with the shadows, small and almost unnoticed even in her white suit.

"How are you feeling?" Captain Solvay asked.

She stayed quiet and stared at the wall again. *I can't tell them what I'm feeling. They wouldn't understand.*

"I already debriefed Ward, but this is something that needs more than one perspective," the captain said. "You were the last to be with Armitage. Is there a chance he could have survived? Ward mentioned the cave was a vast network, and it was possible there were multiple ways in and out."

Orinthia rolled her head on the pillow. "No. He was gone before the cave collapsed. I…" her voice trailed off, and she swallowed hard. She searched for a way to explain it. "I saw it. Adora's team had torches on him and I watched him fall. He's gone."

Captain Solvay made a noise in his throat. His aqua-rebreather bubbled. "I have yet to report to the Commissioner in hopes we had a chance to go back for Armitage. Now, we'll see how he wants us to move forward."

"No." She pushed herself upright, fury flickering beneath

her words. "We have to go back to the station. Get the information we were promised."

"Of course we're not going back," Captain said with a growl. "That traitorous scum double crossed us."

"All the better reason to see it through." Orinthia's eyebrows were pinched together and she threw her hands around while she spoke. "Marius died because of Claven. Whether or not he knows where Adora is, he knows something. He needs to answer for what happened and now we're not taking this on our knees."

"He lied." Solvay was almost shouting.

"He caused Marius' death." Orinthia slammed her fists into her bed. "You're taking us back."

"I am the captain," Solvay said, his machines bubbling faster.

Orinthia slid to the edge of the bed and stood. She braced her fingers against the wall to steady herself.

"And you're going to roll over and show your belly?" Her voice cracked. "How can you let that backstabbing space rat go free?"

She took a breath and stepped closer to Solvay. "You are Galactic Marauder Hunters. Messies. Remind them why they have to work so hard to destroy you. Take the *Tertion* back this time. Adora already knows we're searching for her. Let's be done hiding."

The captain stood silently, his head tilted up slightly to look at Orinthia. His eyes moved quickly over her face. He must have liked what he saw in her, because he cracked a smile.

"We are Messies," he said. "Sidera defende."

ORINTHIA WAITED for the warp engines to die down before entering the bridge. Her body ached, but her mind was lit with anticipation and rage. Whatever happened next, she would face it with the crew.

The captain nodded at her as she entered, then motioned for Talyon to hail the space station as it grew larger in the window.

"This is Captain Masood Solvay of the MHS *Tertion*," he said over the open channel. "By the authority of the Galactic Marauder Hunters, I order you to stand down and prepare to be boarded."

"Your authority isn't recognized," a voice responded immediately. "Be on your way or you'll be shot down."

Brul's cannon swung around and aimed at them.

Solvay stood with his arms tucked behind his back. He stood steady, unfazed by the threat. "Open fire."

Talyon keyed up their own cannon and sent two rounds across the black, making contact with the station's weapon. Pieces erupted in all directions.

"I am not asking for your permission," the captain said. "This is an order. Stand down or you will be turned to stardust."

Half a dozen ships undocked from the station and fell into a defensive pattern.

Talyon's hands flew across the panel, locking onto the closest few. She hovered, ready to attack when ordered.

Minutes passed, but neither side fired. Orinthia pinched her lips, no longer confident in her decisions to return.

The comm chimed and the voice said, "The Sheriff welcomes you aboard."

A wave of warmth washed down Orinthia's back.

"Take the skiff," Captain Solvay said, turning to Orinthia. "We'll stay back and provide cover if things go wrong."

*Which they always do,* Orinthia thought, as she gave him a curt nod. She left the bridge and joined the other two Messies in the jump craft. Marius' things still haunted the space. No one had the will to remove them yet.

The skiff thumped as they exited the ship and made the short distance to the space station. None of them spoke. Whether they were silent in reverence or anticipation, the quiet fell heavy on Orinthia's shoulders.

Annatilla maneuvered the skiff to the first open docking bay and secured the connection. The airlock hissed. "I'll wait here," she said, turning in the pilot's seat. "No need to show our full hand until we have to. Ward, you call in if you need backup."

Cliff grunted and tightened his grip on the rifle slung across his chest. He opened the hatch and pulled the ladder down, exiting first.

Orinthia set her hands on the middle rung to follow, but Annatilla stopped her.

She took a GMH coat off the back of one of the seats and tossed it at Orinthia. "Thought you might want to look the part after the speech you gave Solvay."

The fabric was still rough in her hands, but it weighed differently. Orinthia slipped it on and examined closer. The sleeves had been taken in and waist stitched to fit better. She could never be a Hunter again, nor did she want to, but the uniform was a flag waving as a warning to anyone watching.

"Thank you," she said.

Annatilla tilted her head and gave Orinthia a long look up

and down. "Adora's been one step ahead the whole time, hasn't she?" she asked. "Be careful. You don't know what events this might set off."

Her warning chilled Orinthia. *Maybe this will start something we aren't prepared for*, she thought. *But I'm tired of getting nowhere. Claven will talk whether he wants to or not.*

She lifted her foot to the lowest rung of the ladder and climbed out.

A small security troop waited for them on the platform. Each officer held a blaster ready to fire. Cliff stood with his aimed as well. One officer, a man in a bright orange coat, stepped forward and spoke up. "The Sheriff will only meet with one of you. He doesn't care which, but those are his demands."

"I'm going," Orinthia said to Cliff without turning to him. She took the golden blaster off her hip and handed it to the Messie.

"Fine by me," Cliff said, keeping his eyes on the group as he pocketed her blaster. "Don't care much for talking anyway."

The spokesman took Orinthia by the arm and pulled her through the crowd. Half the security team followed while the rest held Cliff at gunpoint.

Orinthia did not struggle as they escorted her to Claven's office. She met every eye they passed and set her jaw tight.

They stopped in front of the already open door and waited for Claven to wave them in. The officer shoved Orinthia through and stayed behind.

"Real brazen coming in here like this," Claven said, hitting a button under his desk. The door closed behind Orinthia, sealing them inside. Alone. He leaned back in his chair and folded his hands over his stomach. "Now, why'd you kick my front door in? Thought we had a deal."

Without moving from her spot, Orinthia lifted her hand and pointed at the desk. She shoved it aside and walked toward him, stopping where the table had been a second before.

"You had the deal with Marius," she said, looking down her nose at the man. "He's dead."

The old sheriff's eyes widened for a moment before narrowing. His gaze flicked from the desk, tossed by an invisible force across the room, then back to Orinthia. Suspicion hardened his face. "How'd a few marauders get the jump on a Messie?"

Orinthia threw out her black blade and set it an inch from Claven's chest. "They weren't marauders. Arsenio ambushed us. I'm only going to ask once and if you lie to me, I'll have you gutted before you take another breath. Did you know we were walking into a trap?"

"I don't work for Adora," Claven said.

The blade twitched against his shirt.

"No, I had no idea," he added, sinking deeper into his seat to avoid the edge.

Orinthia let the blade fall. He was telling the truth.

"Then tell me everything you know about the twins' plans," she said. "Or so help me I'll have the *Tertion* blow every ship you've got out of space. I'm done with the runaround. This ends now."

Claven nudged his chin toward her sword. "Care to put that away?"

"I will not," Orinthia said with ice in her voice. She may not have been able to let Arsenio die, but the part of her that felt Marius slip away? That part wanted revenge.

"She came to me, said we should stand together against the EC," Claven said, lips curling. "Said I wasn't looking to join a war. She just smiled. 'Can't have a war when you take them out from the inside.'" He mocked her voice. "Plans on cutting off the head and watching the galaxy scramble while the rest collapses around it."

Orinthia frowned. "What does that mean?"

Claven shrugged. "Didn't ask. I wanted no part of it. This station's paradise enough without risking a war with the EC. Don't need much else."

"So she just wants to watch them burn?" Orinthia twitched her eyes in thought. "Then the fleet's just muscle to backup the plan. That would mean…"

Her voice trailed off while the thoughts clicked. "I have to warn Kian. There are still people working for her inside the GMH. Maybe even the EC itself."

"Did you really think that wasn't the case?" Claven scoffed. "That she'd pull all her loyalists out of the EC's interests? Naive, aren't you?"

Orinthia ignored his quip. "Where is she? I can end this right now. Take her out before she even knows what happened. Even if she never said anything outright, I know you hear more than you let on."

Claven gave a dry chuckle. "There's always truth buried in rumors. Whispers of civil war trickling in from the outer zones. You listen long enough, you'll start to hear whats really going on."

Orinthia's eyes narrowed. "She's in the Lyngor system? Why?"

"EC can't touch her that far out, not without the risk of breaking treaties. Ain't no civil war, though. It's a rebellion. She's taken over the core planet, conscripting and recruiting whoever she can for her vengeance. They're not going as quietly as she'd hoped, though. The people are fighting back. But everyday she grows stronger. It won't be long until she strikes."

She raced through his words. The pieces snapped together one after another until the picture became clear. With the truth finally in front of her, her thoughts turned to the NCR.

Uri was not as safe as Kian had promised.

Spinning on her heel, Orinthia strode toward the door, saying nothing more to Claven.

It did not open. Claven's chair creaked behind her as he stood.

"You come into my house, threaten me, and think I'll let you walk without consequences?" Claven said, a tremble flowing from his voice.

Orinthia looked over her shoulder as Claven took a step forward.

His hand dropped to the blaster on his hip, fingers curling around the grip.

She focused on the desk and flicked her hand. The wooden table shot back into place, smashing into his legs and dropping him with a thud.

Facing the door again, she lifted her hand. Nothing beyond it would stop her from getting back to the *Tertion*.

— ✳ ✳ —

ORINTHIA HISSED through clenched teeth as she stepped off the skiff, one hand pressed to the bruise on her side.

It was only a short time before the security realized Claven was down. She had fought her way through the team waiting outside his office, then vanished into the crowd of residents. When she reached the bay, Cliff cleared a path, and together they sprinted for the skiff.

Fighter ships opened fire the moment they launched, but

Annatilla dodged every shot. It had been a short, wild escape, definitely not one she would tell Kos about.

Back on the *Tertion*, the Messies fell in behind Orinthia, their boots ticking against the grated deck as they rushed toward the bridge.

Annatilla broke off, hurrying toward the med-bay to grab a pack for Orinthia's wound.

The ship had come alive the moment they secured, thrusters screaming. By the time Claven's forces closed in, the *Tertion* had already jumped, leaving behind nothing but dust and silence.

Cliff moved ahead and opened the door to the bridge for her. They stepped in together. She glanced at the viewport, hoping Solvay had done as she had asked on her way back. With a quick sigh of relief, she faced the comm screen.

*Finally, I can catch a break.*

But Kian's face told her otherwise. His skin was a deep maroon. The background of the comm was different than the usual headquarters. He was aboard a smaller ship, and most of the bridge seats behind him were empty.

The relief vanished. Heat raced up her neck. She wanted to get the question out, but it choked in her throat. Her heart crashed against her ribs, afraid she already knew the answer.

"Orinthia, I'm so sorry," Kian said under his breath. "The GMH has fallen."

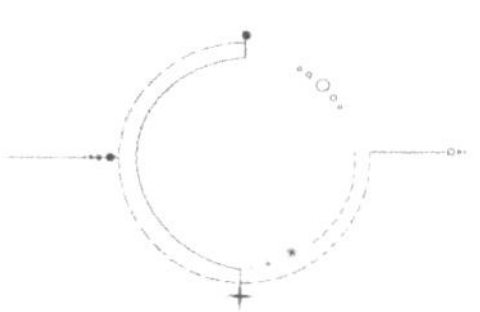

He was falling again.

Air rushed past him. Stone flew by. The world spun sideways and weightless. Then... nothing. The drop slowed like a dream, and when he looked up, she was there.

Reaching for him.

Arsenio's eyes flew open.

The ceiling above him was blank, rust red, and familiar. Unmoving. Like he had been for hours. His sheets were tangled around his legs, and his muscles ached from holding tension. The PortTab sat powered off on his chest.

Arsenio was unsure of what to believe anymore. Nothing made sense, but he knew what he saw. She caught him. But how?

The memory played on a loop in his head. He watched it from every imagined angle, trying to separate reality from emotion. It was no use. Something impossible happened, and his only clue was the sister he spent a lifetime trying to end.

He kept it secret from Adora. Where would he even begin? Aside from a brief report on his failure, Arsenio had not said a word to his twin. She was furious with him anyway, and both kept to themselves after he returned.

Yet, her voice popped into his head and broke the stillness of his room. *The GMH has fallen,* Adora told him. *Everything is in motion now. Time to bring them in.*

Arsenio did not respond. He simply flipped the tablet over, activated it, and sent out a message.

*Blaze through.*

Then, he tossed the PortTab beside him and dragged both hands down his face. Stubble had grown unruly. His usual clean-shaven face was patched with hints of a beard. His hair was uncombed and stuck out in all directions. He and his mirror had been strangers as of late, mostly by choice.

He should have responded, at least acknowledge he had followed through. But he no longer cared. His mind was elsewhere and he needed answers. Instead, Arsenio rolled out of bed and took the PortTab with him. He stood and strode into the hall.

The heels of his boots thumped under his feet with each step. His heart matched it. He took a turn he was not supposed to. Toward the room he was forbidden to visit. Uri's room.

Two guards waited near the door. They first looked at each other, then back to Arsenio. Neither moved.

"I'm going in," Arsenio said. "If you try to stop me, I will have you both executed on the lawn."

A breath passed. One of the guard's eyes flicked toward the hallway, toward the part of the compound where Adora kept herself. Another second beat by. They stepped aside and allowed him through.

Inside the room was cold. Refrigerated air was pumped

in, but it was to make the space uncomfortable. It was control. A tray of half eaten food sat at the foot of a mattress. Less than a bed, but a dingy half-folded case of padding on the floor. On top, under a thin sheet, sat his brother. The skin around his lips was cracked and dry. He was not getting cared for the way Adora had promised.

*Of course not*, Arsenio thought, shaking his head.

The two men locked eyes, but neither said anything.

A knot tightened in Arsenio's chest. If Adora found him in there, she would have them both beat. But, then why was he not allowed in? They were equals, were they not? The longer he stared at Uri, the less sure he became. It only nudged him closer to what he feared to believe.

Arsenio opened a note screen on his tablet and tossed it to Uri.

"There are things happening that I don't understand," Arsenio said. His throat rattled and his tongue felt fat. "You're going to tell me what you know."

Uri nodded and reached for the PortTab, then looked back at Arsenio to let him know he was ready.

Seconds passed while Arsenio thought of where to start. "Orinthia," he said. "What happened to her?"

Uri brought his eyebrows together, showing he did not know what he meant.

"She can do things now, can't she?" Arsenio asked. The words were strange in his mouth. Phrases like "power" or "ability" were silly in his mind, but that was all he could come up with.

Uri twisted his mouth for a moment. His fingers hovered over the screen, then typed into the tablet and turned it around.

*Yes, but only recently.*

"How?" Arsenio asked.

> *To save me. When she found Desidario, he*
> *only wanted one thing in return. To let him*
> *experiment on her one more time. And she*
> *let him.*
> *I don't fully know what it can do, and haven't*
> *had the time to find out. But she can sync*
> *with frequencies of things around her.*
> *Manipulate them and make them react to*
> *her will.*
> *How did you find out about it?*

Arsenio read over Uri's words slowly. Once. Then again. Each sentence twisted in his chest. She let him abuse her. Hurt her again just to save Uri.

Like she saved Arsenio. The thought crept up his throat with a sour taste.

"She did something to me," Arsenio said. "Not maliciously. I was falling, and before I hit the ground, I slowed. When I looked up, I saw her. There was a panic on her face. Like she hadn't meant to do it."

Uri cracked a grin and leaned back against the clay wall. He typed, then turned the screen toward his brother.

> *She's stronger than you think. Not because of*
> *the new mod, but what's inside her. You*
> *tried to break her. Desidario tried to break*
> *her. And she tried to break herself. But it*
> *only built her into something more. More*
> *caring. More brave. And someone who*
> *doesn't know how to give up, because she's*
> *already faced a world of hurt.*

Arsenio clenched his fists to fight the chill that ran down his arms.

The screen turned again, and Uri typed more.

> *Does it scare you? To know that taking me will bring Thia here and she isn't going to stop? It should. I've tried to keep her from losing control. Tried to protect what's left of her. She might've saved you once, but this changes everything.*
>
> *I'm not like her. I won't fight or struggle. But that's all you taught her to do. And now she's running on some DNA altering tech that our deranged father forced upon her. You'd better hope she finds Adora first and takes it out on her before she gets to you.*

There was a weight between them. Despite the cold, heat moved up his neck.

"None of that is part of Adora's plan," Arsenio said. He snapped the words out.

Uri tilted his head, eyes squinting a bit, waiting.

"*The* plan." Arsenio kept going. "Some daft sequencer's been feeding her dreams of grandeur. Told her how to take over the EC. If Orinthia was going to interfere with that plan, he would have warned her."

A handful of heartbeats passed before Uri moved the PortTab again. This time, no buildup. Just a single question.

> *Is keeping you deaf part of that plan?*

Arsenio stayed silent. The words coiled in his gut, burning. He blinked once. Twice.

The room was too bright. Too small.

His fingers twitched against his palm. His breath came in short, tight bursts. His head swayed, trying to grasp onto anything. A justification. A reason. Something to explain away Uri's soft accusation.

Uri typed again.

Arsenio tried to look away, but his eyes were locked on the screen.

> *I've seen the images. Knew exactly what I was looking at. It can be reversed. But I think you knew that, even if you didn't want to admit it. Have you even asked why she didn't push harder?*

The muscles in Arsenio's jaw tightened. His teeth ground together. He froze like the floor was swallowing his feet.

The weight of it all pressed down. All the years of loyalty and obedience. Only now did he see it for what it was.

A leash.

A cage.

They were not two hands holding the same stick. He was the stick. The tool. Manipulated and used just like everything else Adora touched.

"Why would she lie to me?" Arsenio yelled. "I've given her everything. My hands. My soul. I've done everything she's asked because I trusted her to do what was best for us."

The edges of his vision were white.

"I… I let her order me around. This was never a partnership. It was control. Over me. Over Orinthia. And I let her."

Arsenio shot a look to Uri. "How? How do I get back what was stolen?"

Uri lowered his gaze and typed again. Half a moment later, he turned it over.

> *The link between you two needs to be removed. It's severed the nerves, but if it's taken out, the nerves can be repaired. Not fully, and the longer this goes, the less effective it will be. We both know why she couldn't let you do that.*

"Because she couldn't control me anymore," Arsenio whispered. "Keep her voice the only one I hear, and I'll never ask for anything else."

His stomach twisted again like something inside was trying to crawl out.

Arsenio turned from Uri, pressing a hand to his chest, as if he could calm the storm beneath his ribs. There had been a time, a short while ago, that he thought her voice was a treasure in the silence. That he was not alone.

But, now, it was nothing more than a whip, forcing him farther into a game only she could see. He had always been alone. He did not even know who he was outside of her shadow.

There were no more rules. No more orders. Every choice he made would have to be his own. And she was going to see him.

The real him.

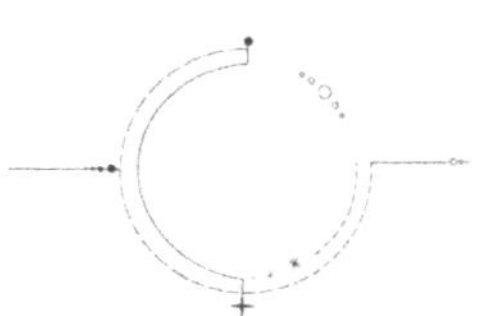

The *Fera's* bridge was too quiet. Kos had spent many hours in the room when he'd been quarter-master. Planning. Watching. Commanding. But it was no longer his ship. He was a visitor and nothing belonged to him.

Kos stood in the center of the room, out of the way while close enough to monitor what was going on. His arms were tucked tight behind his back, old habits sinking in. The count-down in his head ticked toward zero.

*Two minutes,* he thought. *Two minutes until we find out if we have a fighting chance or if this has all been for nothing.*

He forced himself to stay still, though his body was filled with electricity. His foot twitched and fingers tapped against each other while his pulse thrummed through his veins. There was nowhere else he needed to be, but he wished he were anywhere else.

Behind him, Ignio exhaled slowly, the sound cutting through the silence like a razor. Thrutt whispered something to him that Kos couldn't make out. The two men chuckled, then fell into stillness again.

*Sixty seconds,* Kos thought.

His throat was tight. It was not the waiting, he was good at that. It was the silence. The kind that stretched too long, that let his thoughts go where they shouldn't. He was still coming down from the last episode and the weight of it pressed on him. Kos clenched his jaw and focused on the stars ahead, the vast span of space laid out before him.

*Thirty seconds.*

He timed each breath and counted down. The first chime would soon come in.

*Three. Two. One.*

Two blips came over the comm. No words, just a prearranged signal that meant the sender would join their cause.

Kos held his breath. *That's one.*

Another pair of chimes sounded in the speakers, followed by more and more. He tried to keep track but lost count after fifteen.

Then, silence.

The comms officer looked back at her captain, who moved forward. Ignio leaned over the woman's shoulder, then said, "Give it another minute. More may come in."

Kos didn't like the tone in his voice. It was masked, but he caught the edge. Something was wrong.

No other ships hailed and the bridge fell quiet again. The comms officer shifted in her seat and handed a PortTab to Ignio.

"How many?" Kos asked, unable to stand another second of wondering.

"Twenty-six," Ignio answered, turning to face Kos. He cleared the few steps between them and handed him the tablet.

Kos read over the names of the ships that sided with

them. The realization fell onto Kos in a rush. His head reeled for a moment and he bit the inside of his cheek to keep him in the present.

He failed.

Orinthia wouldn't have the force she needed behind her. "This isn't enough," he said, shoving the PortTab back into Ignio's hand.

"It's twenty-six crews of marauders who'll fight with us," Ignio said. "You think they'd do that for just anyone?"

The bridge crew were half turned, watching the interaction between the two men. No one said anything, they only gawked at the scene behind them.

"I have nothing else to offer them," Kos said through tight teeth. "Nothing to make them see this is worth the effort."

"It may not be about what they can gain." Ignio crossed his arms. "They are making free choices, and whether or not you like it now, that was the option you gave." The captain relaxed his shoulders and let his hands fall to his side. "You're not Adora or the EC. You don't force people to fight your fight. That's what you promised them. These crews are standing behind you because they *want* to."

Kos' stomach dropped. *This isn't my fight,* he told himself. *It's Orinthia's.* Yet, with every move, every choice, the weight of it settled deeper, making it personal.

"It doesn't change that we need more firepower." Kos rubbed the side of his face. "I'll go out there. I'll have to find others who will stand with us. Adora has a lot of enemies we can reach out to."

Thrutt moved for the first time since the news came in. He stood beside Kos on the other side and turned so they faced each other. "Rogue, you can search the galaxy for the rest of your life and I don't think you'll feel like it's enough.

Look at what's in front of you. You have exactly what you need, stop focusing on what you don't have."

The words cut deep in Kos' chest, but he kept his face still. He took in a steadying breath through his nose. "We don't know what we're going up against. I haven't heard from Thia in days. We should've been doing something by now, not sitting around waiting for half our numbers to agree to fight with us."

Ignio and Thrutt exchanged long glances.

Every eye was on Kos and some murmured to each other.

"Walk with me." Ignio put a hand to Kos' shoulder and forced him to turn.

Thrutt followed behind them and they left the bridge. The three men walked a distance before they came to the lift and stepped in. It went up one level before opening to Ignio's cabin door. Inside, there was no food laid out on the table. No welcoming atmosphere to the room. Ignio didn't offer them seats, but led them a few paces in and stopped.

"There's more to this than fighters," Ignio said. His voice was even, but hinted at something Kos didn't have the patience to deal with in the moment. "Tell me what's going on."

Kos looked at the wall behind Ignio. Ahto's steel eyes stared back at him. Voices called out from the past, but he shoved them out. "I don't have the means to win."

Ignio shook his head. "No, that's not it."

"What do you want me to say?" Kos fought the anger building in his chest.

"The truth."

"The truth?" Kos shouted and gave a hard, single laugh. "The truth is Orinthia is out there, walking into a fight she can't win alone, and I don't know if I have enough to keep her alive. I don't even know if she *is* alive right now."

His words came out too fast to keep back. Each one hurt. No matter how many ships they had, it may not ever be enough. And that was too painful to think about. Kos dragged his hands down the sides of his face. His thoughts moved too fast.

Orinthia wasn't fragile, he knew that. She didn't need saving, as she reminded him many times. In some ways, she was stronger than him. But it didn't mean she couldn't be lost.

"I don't care if we win the fight," Kos admitted, his voice hiccuping. "I just want to make sure she survives it."

His confession hung in the air, heavy and real. Words he'd been too afraid to say or even let take hold in a full thought. Losing her would end him, and he wanted nothing more than to have her back with him. They'd been apart too long, and the distance wore on him.

Thrutt shifted.

Kos didn't look at him. He didn't want to see the soft eyes he knew he was getting. Ever kind, ever patient, ever loving Thrutt. Kos didn't want soft, he wanted fire.

"We can't control things like that," Ignio said, letting out a long sigh. There was a softness to his face, too. "I believe that this truly is about her, but your fear of losing her stems from something deeper. I've faced it, too. The death. The memories. The hurt. You'll never get over it. It will always be there. But you didn't survive a war to have it continue to defeat you everyday."

Kos scoffed. He didn't feel like he was surviving anything.

"Everything outside you is out of your control." Ignio straightened his back and lowered his chin. His words were smooth and practiced like he had repeated them multiple times a day. "You can't hold onto any of that. The only thing you have power over is inside you. These are your thoughts, secure them. They are your emotions, name them. You are your own man, be him. Every day. Every minute. Every time you feel yourself slipping, take control first. That's all you can do. And it is enough."

Kos inhaled a shuddered breath. Needles jabbed at him throughout his body, puncturing his emotional armor like a bubble. He'd held onto the past for so long, he didn't know how to let go. Blaming himself was easier than being alive by pure chance.

"Now," Ignio said softly, dipping his head. "Where do we go from here?"

Kos moved away from the men and walked to the picture window. He stared out, seeing millions of stars in front of him. This was where he belonged. If he had his own ship, he could do more. But that was also something out of his control.

Stars glinted and blinked at him. Somewhere in the cosmos was Orinthia. The waiting would soon be over. He'd go, too, all he needed was a course to follow.

"We prepare what we have, and listen for any signs we've missed," he said. "I don't know where Orinthia is right now, but she'll need us ready."

# 37

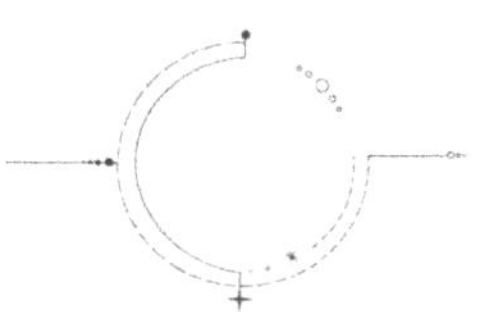

"Get the crates secured," Kos shouted to the droids and marauders darting around the hangar. "I don't want anything rolling loose during battle. That's the last thing we need, to be knocked off course from the inside."

They weren't his crew, they knew that and so did he. But, for the time being, they followed his lead.

The deck buzzed with energy. All hands were busy prepping for the days ahead. Every ship in their fleet was nearly ready to launch, Kos made sure of it. All he needed was the call to come, and he'd bring the weight of the galaxy with him.

Kos stepped onto Mimi's ship and checked the fuel levels for the fifth time that day. There was nothing left to do but wait for Orinthia to send word. He had no coordinates, no clear path back to her, just the lingering hope she'd check in soon.

They hadn't spoken in days, and been apart for longer. His heart ached to be close to her again. To hear her voice. To feel her soft touch on his cheek.

As if summoned by his desire, the comm beeped in his pocket. He threw his hand in and opened the device before it was fully out.

"Thia?" Kos barely got her name out before his joy was shattered by the sound of her sobs. His heart fell through his stomach. "What happened?"

"They took Uri," Orinthia said, choking on the words. "The GMH is gone. Adora has him."

Kos' mind reeled. He reached blindly for the pilot's seat, lowering himself before his legs gave out. "What?" was all he could manage.

"Everything's fallen apart." Her voice cracked, and more sobs followed. "I don't know what to do, Kos. None of this was supposed to happen. It's all over."

He forced himself to take a deep breath before the anxiety overtook his senses. A storm of emotions and thoughts tore through him.

"Hold on, hold on," he said quickly. "Tell me what's going on. I need to understand what we're dealing with."

Orinthia took in gasps of air and launched into the events of the last few days. The death of a Messie, her accidental saving of Arsenio, Adora's spies, and Uri's disappearance.

Kos stiffened. There was still the spy on her ship, the one Kian told him not to mention. He hadn't forgotten, but how was he supposed to have told her without putting her in danger?

And now? It wasn't the right time either. Not when she was barely holding herself together and alone. Not when the weight of Uri's abduction was already tearing her apart. She'd lose it and get herself hurt, or worse.

*One thing at a time*, he told himself.

"Kian doesn't even know when they took him," she said when she was done. "He called for a GMH-wide check-in to see who was still alive, and when they didn't respond, he realized it had been days since anyone heard from them last."

"Then how does he know they took him?" Kos asked, trying to piece it together.

"Another group stopped by, just in case they needed backup. One of the guards had been dead for a while… Uri and the other one were gone."

Kos cursed under his breath. "Okay, so what happens now? Does Kian have a plan for this?"

"He can't do anything." Orinthia's voice shook as she spoke. "The GMH is officially under EC control. Kian was ordered to regroup at the Moon base. He told us to go back, too."

Another string of unsavory words and phrases passed through Kos' mouth. He set an elbow on his knee and leaned his head onto his fingertips. "So that's it? The whole mission's a bust?"

"Solvay seems to think so."

*We risked too much for this to end in flames.* Kos turned on the ship's nav computer and placed his comm on the panel beside it. He typed in a search, waiting for Orinthia's signal to ping back.

*Error.*

"Are you in warp?" he asked.

"Yeah. Solvay's taking us to refuel before heading to the Moon," Orinthia said. Her words came through clearer, but still shaky. "I'm not going though. They'll arrest me, and I'll never get Uri back."

"Obviously not." Kos' fingers danced over the computer. "You're going to wait for me. I'll send Thrutt with the *Fera* to get ahead of it."

"I'll be gone before you get here."

His head snapped up and he stared at the comm. "What?"

"I don't care what I have to do to get another ship, but I'm not waiting anymore."

Kos lifted his hands and made a strangling motion toward her. "No. No, no, no. Think for a second, Thia. You don't know how to steal a ship. You don't even know how to fly one. What's your plan?"

"I don't have one." Orinthia snapped her words. "But I can't sit around and do nothing."

"Then wait for me," Kos said, almost shouting. He took in a calming breath and added, "Give me one day. I'll find you."

A long silence passed between them. "You promise?" she whispered.

"I swear it. I just need to know where you're headed."

"I don't know," Orinthia said, tears threatening her voice again. "This isn't my world. I thought I knew what I was doing, but I don't."

Kos straightened in his seat. His heart filled with a warmth he hadn't felt in a long time. He barely recognized it as pride, love for what he could do, and doing something he was good at other than killing. "But it is my world."

He swiped at the tattoo on his palm. The holographic map flickered to life before him. "Where were you last?"

"A space station. Brul Station."

Kos pinched the image to zoom out. "What system?"

"I don't know." Orinthia paused. "But it orbited a planet called Hedphin. Two suns. It was an Old Earth station. Really old."

Kos' fingers moved with precision, skimming through binary systems, discounting ones he'd been to before. *There.*

"Found it," he said. "Now, let me work backward." His mind filtered through Solvay's possible choices. *He'd pick somewhere safe, out of the way. With little marauder activity.*

*Maybe even a Navy outpost.* His gut settled on one. "I think he's taking you to Chazet."

"How do you know?"

"Because this is what I did for half my life," Kos said, entering in the data on the nav computer. "Doesn't matter. I'm leaving within the hour. Where's Adora so I can send Thrutt?"

"Lyngor system," Orinthia said. She let out a breathy laugh and sniffed. "The rumors of civil war were her. We've seen it the whole time, and I never put it together."

"Sure, why not?" Kos let out a dry, humorless chuckle then sighed. "At least we know now. Listen, as soon as that ship lands you get off and wait for me. I'm going to push as fast as I can. Just. Wait."

Orinthia was quiet for a moment. Long enough that Kos had to check if the comm was still connected. "Thia?"

"I'm here," Orinthia said. She had stopped crying, but he could hear the strain in her voice.

"Are you okay?"

"No," she whispered.

"I know," Kos said. He closed his eyes and pictured her in his arms, comforting her like she'd done for him many times. "I'm coming for you, I promise. Nothing is going to stop me from getting to you, understand?"

"This feels like Caytoo all over again," Orinthia said.

"Just don't run off with any strangers and you'll be fine," Kos lightly joked. "Really, stay put. I know how you get."

"Okay," Orinthia said.

"I love you. More than anything, I love you. They're just words, but I'll give everything to show you."

Orinthia gasped. Her voice seemed farther away, like she'd turned her head away from the comm. "There's someone at the door. I have to go before they see the comm."

Kos took his comm off the panel and held it, wishing it were her in front of him. "See you soon."

The line disconnected and he was left in the stillness once again. The weight of the galaxy fell on his back. He wasn't totally sure he could actually make it to her in a day. But he needed her off the *Tertion* before he lost her.

Kos set the comm on the panel again and rushed to his cabin. He pulled out his favorite coat from his kit bag, the one he'd worn when he left Buscoch. The breast pocket was heavy, and he unzipped it.

Freya's data chip sat at the bottom, untouched since he placed her there. Once in hand, he returned to the control room and climbed under the panel to insert the chip. It took a minute to find the right port, but the chip fit securely and he pulled himself out again.

The cockpit lit up as all the lights turned on at once. Then they dimmed until only one was left blinking.

"Freya, can you hear me?" Kos asked.

There was no answer. Only the blue light near the yoke continued to blink.

Kos bent low and looked for wires he could reconnect and move around. He tried a few and called out to Freya each time. There was no reply. He stood up again and sighed.

The light continued to blink, but as he watched it, he noticed a pattern. "Freya?"

Two long blinks.

Kos smiled. "You're there?"

Again, two blinks followed by a long pause before staying blue.

"Thia's in trouble," Kos said. "I need you to find the fastest route possible to a planet called Chazet. Use as many or as few jumps as we need to. Then calculate how hard we can push the ship before we blow the drives."

The light flashed rapidly.

Kos imagined Freya giving him an earful, mildly thankful she could not speak to him. "Look, this isn't your ship. I haven't found one for you, yet. But that's not the point. We need to get to Chazet by tomorrow. Whatever you have to do, you do. Got it?"

The light did nothing for a second. Then, it slowly blinked her affirmation.

"Good," Kos said. "I'll be back in a few minutes. There're a few things I need to take care of, but as soon as I'm on board, we need to leave." He did not wait for her reply before he darted out of the ship and ran to the mess hall where he'd find Thrutt.

The stone man was on his feet before Kos crossed the room. They needed few words to know when something was wrong. "Tell me," Thrutt said, his voice steady and measured.

Kos ran through the details, saying only what really mattered: Orinthia was about to do something reckless and he needed to save her. "You have to get the fleet there. Thia's not going to let me take her anywhere else, so we'll be right behind you."

Thrutt's eyebrows pinched together, not in anger but in thought. He was reworking the plan and fitting pieces into place. "Where am I taking them?"

"Lyngor system," Kos said. "Most likely the capital planet. She's been behind the war brewing out there, so expect to be met with forces. Tell Ignio what he needs to know and get the others going as soon as you can. I'm not sure what we'll find, but none of this can be good."

"Call me as soon as you get Thia, and keep her safe," Thrutt said.

The weight of his words settled deep in Kos' bones. He was no longer Thrutt's priority, and hadn't been for a while.

But he was okay with that. They knew where the other stood. Kos was thankful to have someone who cared about her as much as he did. He knew that if anything ever happened to him, she'd be taken care of.

"I'll bring her back," Kos said.

"Keep yourself safe, too," Thrutt said. He set a heavy hand on Kos' shoulder and pulled him into a crushing hug. "See you when this is over."

## 38

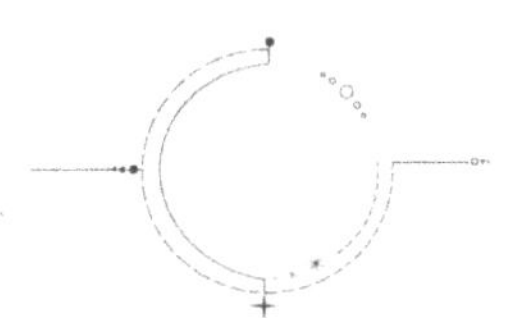

Orinthia stuffed her comm under her pillow before moving to answer the door. She took a deep breath and wiped her eyes. The door slid aside to reveal Annatilla standing with her arms crossed behind her back. She wore a straight look on her face, no hint of what was on her mind showed on her features. The two women stared at each other for a moment. Orinthia waited for her to say something, but when the silence got to be too much, she asked, "Is the captain looking for me again?"

Annatilla shook her head and stepped forward. "Can I come in?"

"I guess," Orinthia answered slowly, but the woman was already inside.

Annatilla glided through the space, examining the bare walls and disheveled bed. She turned on her toes like a dancer and faced Orinthia, lacing her fingers in front of her. "How are you dealing with everything? First Armitage dies, then your brother goes missing. Not to mention the whole reason you're even here was to catch Adora, and now we're being pulled away. That's a lot to carry on your own."

The statement stung. It was hard to hear all her failures lined up one after another, not that she needed a reminder. "It is. Why are you saying this?"

"I wouldn't go quietly." Annatilla shrugged, her face still placid. She added slowly, "Then again, there isn't much of a choice when you don't have a way out."

"Look, I'm tired," Orinthia said, placing her hands on her hips. She exhaled the frustration from her chest. "I haven't fully recovered from the cave, and I'd like to get some rest before we make land. So, sorry if this feels short, but just get out what you have to say."

A soft smile crossed Annatilla's mouth and she tilted her head to the side. Her large eyes stayed on Orinthia. "I'll take you to her."

Orinthia's breath caught. The offer struck her hard in the gut, almost sending her back. It was the last thing she expected to hear from the Hunter. Orinthia took a moment to collect herself before responding.

*Kos is coming for me,* she thought. *He told me to stay put. But, if I can leave faster, then it would be better, right? Then again, Kos would be upset I didn't listen. It would hurt him that I didn't wait. Is it worth it?* She let the question linger. *He knows I have to do this. Saving Uri would be worth it, yes.*

"How? The skiff isn't fast enough," Orinthia said, filling in the gaps with reasoning. "And jumping ship during a warp would tear it apart anyway."

"We'd have to wait until we refuel," Annatilla answered with a shrug. "Steal a ship. Find the fastest one in port and commandeer it." She said it so simply and with so much confidence. Like there was no risk involved.

Orinthia let out a laugh. It was her plan before calling Kos, but with flare. Annatilla actually had the power and authority to commandeer a ship. And she knew how to fly.

The idea was starting to look brighter. Except for the part where Kos was going for her. She hesitated.

*Kos can still meet us at Lyngor,* she thought. *I can call him and tell him to change course. It wouldn't be hard. I think.*

"Okay, we'll do it." For the first time since they left Brul, Orinthia felt hope. A fire lit in her belly.

Annatilla sat down in the desk chair and crossed her legs, scooting in like she owned the space. "Perfect."

"What are you doing?"

"Don't worry about me," Annatilla said. "You go ahead and rest. I'll stay here so we can sneak out as soon as the ship lands."

The fire died down a little. If Annatilla did not leave, Orinthia would not be able to call Kos without revealing her comm. "You're just down the hall. I'm going to pass your room when we land. Get ready whatever you need before we leave."

Annatilla smiled and patted a wide pouch on her hip. "Already did. Got it right here. My suit takes care of most things, so traveling is pretty easy for me."

Orinthia twisted her mouth. She could not tell Kos about the change of plans without being exposed. It was almost ridiculous to keep it hidden, given they were about to break the EC's orders together. But she could not risk losing her only link to Kos. He would have to use it to find her once they were in Lyngor. She learned her lesson from Celso smashing the last one. At least for the moment, the comm needed to stay secret.

—✳ ✳—

ORINTHIA LAID ON HER SIDE, trying to ignore Annatilla's tapping on her tablet. It was rhythmic and constant, enough to prick at her nerves in the otherwise silent room. She covered her ears with the pillow, and the comm touched her forehead.

*I need to call Kos,* she thought.

It had been a long trip made up of interrupted sleep and wild dreams. Orinthia had no peace in her body. Her mind was in a haze and thoughts out of place. Deep in her soul, she knew she made the wrong choice, but she did not know how to get out of it without blowing Kos' arrival.

The landing gear groaned as it locked into place, the ship shuddering under the strain. It had been too long since they touched solid ground, and the ship felt it. That was the signal they needed to step into their plan.

Annatilla stood and stretched her thin frame. She shot Orinthia a grin like a silent cue.

Orinthia kept an arm beneath the pillow until Annatilla turned her back. Then, once out of view, she slipped the comm from its hiding place and buried it in the pocket of her coat laying on the floor. The cold metal pressed against her palm for a moment. Her heart thumped in regret. Kos was coming for her and she had not told him the plan had changed.

She inhaled and threw on the modified GMH jacket, masking her feelings, and followed Annatilla.

They paused at the doorway, and Annatilla leaned her head out. After a heartbeat, she curved around the wall and moved into the hall.

The women ran together, leaving only inches between each other. Orinthia's pulse drummed in her throat as they moved. The ladder was feet away. Annatilla reached it first and climbed up with a speed Orinthia had not seen before. It took Orinthia a few seconds longer, her muscles still fatigued. They reconvened on the top deck.

A moment later, Annatilla froze. She put a hand to Orinthia's shoulder and shoved her into a nook. Shadow covered them.

The skittering click of Talyon's boots echoed through the corridor. They were light and graceful, unlike the thumping of the captain's boots following behind half a minute after.

The captain and his XO stopped. Orinthia's skin crawled. The air was hot around her. She pictured them turning and seeing her and her accomplice in the crook of the wall. But they did not. Instead, the bay doors slid open and a rush of frigid air swept in.

Annatilla stayed still for seconds longer, then nodded for Orinthia to follow. They kept close to the wall, walking on the balls of their feet to make as little noise as possible. No one met them on their way to the exit. The door remained open and escape was looking possible.

*First step down,* Orinthia thought. *How many more to go?*

The chilled air coiled around Orinthia's body, cutting through the coat like knives. A heavy scent of fuel and damp metal came with it. It was strange, almost sterile.

Annatilla moved first, stepping onto the ramp like the breeze itself. Orinthia, less agile, followed. Cold mist from the melting snow bit at her face, making her shiver and her steps falter. She threw her head to the side, looking for Solvay and Talyon.

The officers had made their way to the front of the ship and spoke to a dockhand. Neither of them noticed two-thirds of their crew slipping away.

Orinthia turned her focus forward. The spaceport stretched out around them, a massive semi-enclosed structure designed to hold off the worst of the storm from the frozen planet. Dozens of travelers and dockworkers roamed between ships.

Overhead, a red heating grid pulsed along the open framework, casting a dull glow that kept ice from overtaking the walls. Melted water dripped steadily from the beams, pooling along the grated floors before being whisked away by cleaning droids. Beyond the barriers at the edge of the port, a blizzard raged, snow whipping violently against the shields.

A sleek silver ship fluttered in, landing half way down the hangar from the *Tertion*. Orinthia watched it from the side of her eye as she kept up with Annatilla. It landed with ease and purred with a high-pitched whirr as the engines died down.

"There's a fast looking ship," Annatilla said, pointing a few meters away.

Orinthia left watching the new coming ship and searched for where Annatilla mentioned. The ship did not look like much at first. It was sleek and narrow, almost too small to be useful. There were no weapons she could see, but the more Orinthia stared, the more she understood why Annatilla would pick it.

Everything about it read "speed". The hull was in perfect condition, without bulky plating like the *Tertion* or a freighter. Just clean, sharp lines like it was built to slice through space.

As they reached the ship, Orinthia bent low, as if trying to admire its make. She ran her hand over the hull and swayed her head back and forth.

Halfway around the ship, Orinthia brushed a nearly invisible seam in the metal. Her heart thumped into her throat. She froze, caught off guard by something else. A sharp tingle against her skin, familiar and strong, called out to her.

Orinthia spun in a half circle, the room blurring around her in such speed that she almost fell over.

*Kos.* He was there. He had made it like he said they would.

"We don't need to steal this," Orinthia said, not looking at Annatilla. "I have a ride for us." She stood on her tiptoes and frantically looked at every face. There were too many people. Her skin was humming with life and matter. She lowered herself again and closed her eyes, concentrating on the sensation she had a moment before.

His frequency.

*Kos,* she thought again, as if trying to send herself to him. Her mod was only at a fraction of what it had been before, but she pushed on, willing herself to feel him.

At the edge of her senses, no more than fifty feet away, she found him. Her eyes flew open. Standing near the silver ship that had landed just before. Her cells were alive. She weaved her head back and forth until she saw him.

Kos' dark hair pulled into a tight bun on the back of his head. He looked weary as he spoke to one of the dockhands. She took a step toward him, but Annatilla grabbed her arm.

"It's okay," Orinthia said. "My friend's here. He can take us to Adora."

Annatilla's grip stayed tight. She leaned in and spoke close to Orinthia's ear. "You're not going anywhere but on this ship," she said. Her voice was as chilled as the air around them.

Orinthia shot her a look, eyes locking onto the woman's face. The usual softness was gone. Her angelic features were set like stone. Her large eyes darkened beneath a furrowed brow. She angled herself back, and opened the panel to activate the doors of their soon-to-be stolen ship. A gap parted behind her like mouth waiting to swallow them both.

"What are you doing?" Orinthia asked, struggling to get free. It was no use. Annatilla's mechanical hand locked on her wrist like a cuff.

"Get on the ship. Now." Annatilla reached across her waist and undid the pouch. She pulled out a black cylinder. A red light blinked on the side.

"Anna—" Orinthia's protest was cut off.

"Adora wants to kill you herself, but I'm not afraid to become a martyr. This will take us both out, and every living thing in this port."

Orinthia's stomach lurched. Her mind raced to find a lie, a blip of humming, anything. It came up empty. She was serious. Orinthia twitched her fingers toward the grenade, but Annatilla smiled a wicked smile.

"Don't try it," she said. "I know all about your special talent. That's my job, to interpret what people aren't saying. I've known since you and Armitage got back from the *Scow*. If my hand comes off the spoon, the grenade goes off. I don't think you're that good to react fast enough."

Orinthia called her vile names under her breath. She focused her mind on Kos again, working out how far away he was. It was too much of a risk. He would get caught in the blast if she tried anything. She looked for him again. The crowed shifted for one precious moment.

Kos turned in time. Their eyes met, and reality folded on itself. The noise, the chaos, the cold, it all fell away.

"Kos!" Orinthia shouted, letting her voice carry across the spaceport.

Annatilla slammed the grenade against her ribs and yanked Orinthia backward. She stumbled up the ramp until they stood inside the ship. Using her knee, Annatilla hit the switch. The doors sealed in seconds.

Through the narrow gap, Orinthia watched Kos lunge

forward. He shoved against the bodies in his way. His mouth formed her name, and his eyes were wide, in pain.

The seal locked into place. Kos was gone.

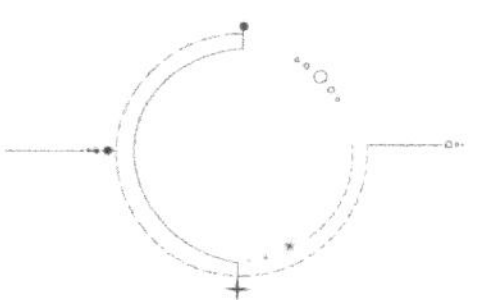

os didn't know what made him look up. Maybe it was instinct, a shadow in the corner of his eye, or just luck. Whatever it was came just in time to watch Orinthia scream and get dragged onto a ship he'd never seen before. Panic filled her eyes, reaching across the spaceport and grabbing him by the heart.

He jumped forward, pushing himself as hard as he could through the sea of travelers. As soon as he moved by one, another fell into their place, like shoveling water out of a stream.

They were so close, but each step seemed to take a lifetime. He called out to her, his voice drowned out by the rushing of blood through his body. Did she hear him? Did she know he was coming for her?

The doors snapped shut, cutting them off from each other. He pressed on until he was close enough to touch the hull. His hands beat the steel, searching for a way to force the doors to open again.

Vibration rippled through the vessel as it lifted off. Kos didn't wait, he spun around and darted back to Mimi's ship, pulling the blaster from his hip. He waved it in front of him, cutting a path through onlookers scrambling to get out of his way.

His feet beat up the ramp and he shouted at Freya before he cleared the entrance. "Freya, get a lock on that ship that's taking off." Kos skidded in and set the blaster on the console. He flipped switches, turned dials, and typed in commands on the nav computer. The ship lifted and the bay door hissed closed.

Kos maneuvered through the spaceport and out into the storm. Visibility was low and the white ship blended in with the snow. "Do you have it?" he asked.

A red dot blinked on the nav screen, pulling farther away from the center. "Calculate where it's going to jump. Thia's on there."

Numbers ran down the side of the computer screen. The dot disappeared. For a single second, Kos' heart froze, sending a shock through his body. His ship lurched forward, warp gathering around him before they had broken atmosphere.

The chase was on.

Kos stared at the the streaks of light before him. His mind raced to make sense of the minutes that had passed.

*She was right there,* he thought. *She was right there.*

The light faded around him. He fell backward into a tunnel, heavy darkness drowning him as he crashed. Kos gasped for air, clawing at nothing with feverish swings.

*This is inside of you,* a voice echoed in the distance. His voice. *Be the man you need to be. You are stronger than your fears, act like it.*

Air filled his lungs, and he took in long gasps. *Use the fear and anger to press forward,* his thoughts continued. *You know where she's going. Focus on what you have to do to get her back.*

The shadows lifted slightly. He saw the ship clearing around him. *This is not who you are. You don't quit. You don't back down. You protect people. Now get up and get the job done.*

Kos fell forward, bracing himself on the console. Strands of hair stuck to the sides of his face as he heaved in and out, drawing in gulps of air. Nausea made a pass through his body, but he worked it down. He'd made it through in one piece, and for the first time he didn't feel like he was dying.

It took a few minutes before he felt close to normal again, but he wasn't any worse off than be had been before. Kos sat down and took in a steadying breath.

*This is going to hurt,* he thought as he reached for his comm. It was heavy in his hand as he debated who he would call first.

His heart wanted to reach out to Orinthia, to hear whatever happened on Chazet was a misunderstanding. But the terror in her eyes told him the truth. She was under duress. And if she had her comm hidden, calling her would only lead to its destruction. He wouldn't be able to find her once he landed.

Calling Thrutt was not ideal, either. Kos was supposed to protect Orinthia. To keep her safe and bring her home. Even the thought of confessing he lost her again sent a knife through his core.

But he needed to talk to someone. He needed advice on how to move forward.

The comm blinked steadily for a moment until it connected on the other side. Thrutt's voice came in clear and filled the small cockpit.

"How're things going?" Thrutt asked with enthusiasm.

Kos swallowed hard and choked over his words. It took a few attempts to get the whole sentence out. "I don't have her."

There was a pause. "What do you mean?" Thrutt asked. "She hasn't shown up yet?"

"No, I found her." Kos lowered his head into his hand. His mind played back the moment. The crowd shifting. Their eyes meeting. The relief followed by panic on her face.

Then, the woman. The one in the spacesuit. He recalled Kian's introduction on Buscoch. *Annatilla Dai*. She had stood too close to Orinthia, moved too quickly, and pulled her on the ship with more vigor than necessary. Like it was the plan the whole time. Kos' stomach twisted.

"And?" Thrutt said when Kos hadn't added any further information. "Where is she then?"

"Gone." Kos sat up and rubbed his face. "One of the Messies loaded her onto a ship in a hurry. She was trying to get out of there with a quickness. But Orinthia saw me. She called my name. She wouldn't have left on her own unless she was being forced."

Thrutt took a second longer to respond. "Do you think she was arrested?"

"No," Kos said flatly. "There weren't any cuffs, so this couldn't be anything official. They're going to Adora."

The thought gnawed at him. Whatever the reason, Orinthia would've fought her way out if she had a choice. She didn't go quietly toward anything.

Kos slammed his fist against his knee. "I shouldn't have listened to Kian. There was a spy, someone feeding Adora information, and I kept that from her. She should've been warned. And that woman, Annatilla Dai. She was someone Thia told me she trusted. I let this happen. I could've stopped it."

"She's smart," Thrutt said. "Don't discredit her just yet. If this Dai is working with Adora, then we know where they're going. Not much has changed."

"Everything has changed," Kos shouted. "She was supposed to be safe. I was supposed to keep her safe."

"You can't control everything, Kos." Thrutt's voice rattled the speakers on the comm.

It worked to shake Kos' mind clear. Only a handful of times had Thrutt yelled at him, mostly in his teenaged years. But each one of the times were justified. Kos bit his lower lip and glared at the comm. Just because Thrutt was right, didn't mean he was happy about it.

"What are you going to do about it?" Thrutt asked, his tone more even, though an edge lingered.

"How far are you from Lyngor?" Kos asked, flipping his palm up to open the map.

"Half a day at most," Thrutt said.

Kos fidgeted with the image. His thumb hovered, twitching slightly as he chewed his lip. Then he found it. A hidden route threading straight through the path of a dwarf star's gravity well.

"I think I found a way to get there sooner," Kos said. "But you're not going to like it. And neither will Mimi if she finds out what I might do to her ship."

Thrutt sighed. "What's the plan?"

"A star jump," Kos said.

"You'll be pulled into the star before you can make a full turn," Thrutt said.

"Not if I plan it right," Kos said, his hand moving to the nav computer. "It's the only way I can shave off time. Freya can handle it, even in this ship. I just need the right angle first."

He glanced down at the light. It blinked rapidly. Kos

chose to believe she was congratulating him on his brilliant plan and not calling him every name in her dictionary.

"No," Thrutt said flatly.

Kos looked at the comm. His eyebrows pinched together. "If I can get there faster, I can—"

"You'll make things worse." Thrutt's voice was sharp, cutting through Kos like a knife. "Or, you could die. Do you think that just because I've been worried about Thia that I stopped caring about you? I cannot physically keep you from doing this, but I'm telling you not to."

Kos' nostrils flared and he took in a deep breath, filling his lungs with cool, recycled air. "I can't just sit here."

"Yes you can, and you will," Thrutt said. He didn't raise his voice, but there was weight behind his words. "Think it through. What happens when you show up and she's not there yet? If you get there before her, you have no way of knowing which planet they land on. You'll waste more time waiting than just staying on the course you're already on."

His fingers were spread wide, ready to punch in the coordinates that would send him head first into a star. The more he repeated that in his head, the less sure he felt. It was risky, even for him. Every possible way it could go wrong flickered through his mind. Every warning sign he'd ignored in his desperation to hold onto some shred of control.

"You have to trust the plan. Your plan," Thrutt said.

Kos dropped his hand to his side and threw back his head. Thrutt was right. He was always right. "What am I supposed to do, then?"

"Wait. That's all you can do." Thrutt's words were even and strong.

*Waiting feels like a surrender when I was so close to getting her back.*

"You have to give up this idea that you're the only one

who can solve this," Thrutt added. "We're all behind you. This fleet came together because of *you*, Rogue. Not Thia. For you. Let them do what they came to do."

"Fine." Kos exhaled sharply, his chest rising and falling too quickly. His hands curled into fists, the comm made a sound like it would snap if he squeezed any harder. He lifted his head and set his jaw askew.

"But the second I find her, I'm done taking orders. You told me to figure out what kind of man I'm going to be. I'm going to be the man who will burn down a planet to save the only thing that makes this life worth living."

## 40

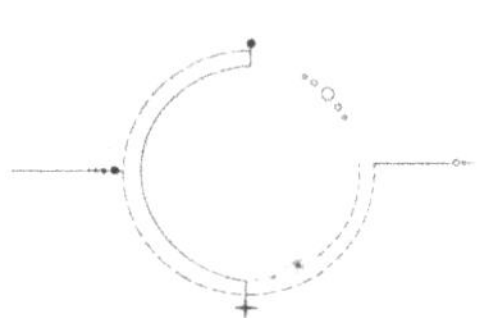

*H*ow do I keep falling into these traps? Orinthia asked herself as she watched the light blink on the grenade clenched in Annatilla's fist.

*I have all this power, but I'm still fooled every time. She didn't lie, not once. Or if she had, it was flawless and a performance that would've put Desidario to shame. But why? What does Adora have on her that she'd not only betray me, but everything she stands for?*

Annatilla sat with her legs stretched from the pilot's seat to the one across from her, ankles crossed and fingers scrolling through her PortTab. Her other hand swayed, propped up at the elbow on the arm rest, waving the grenade like a reed. She looked up at Orinthia and grinned.

"You got a face that says you're thinking too hard," Annatilla said with an easy lilt in her tone. "Ask me anything you'd like. Secrets don't really matter at this point. I know you want to."

Orinthia adjusted herself. Her back ached from sitting hunched on the steel floor. She dropped her arms over her bent knees. "What is she promising you?"

A soft coo of a laugh passed through Annatilla's helmet speakers. "Oh, sweet thing. Adora's not giving me anything. I'm not doing it for her."

The words hit like a slap. "Then why? What's all this for?"

Annatilla set her feet on the floor and turned the chair to face Orinthia. She leaned forward and pressed her forearms on the seat cushion. "I'll let you in on a secret. There's a good portion of us that don't really like Adora all that much. We're doing it for him."

"Arsenio?" Orinthia let out a breathy laugh. "He's nothing but another pawn."

"Exactly," Annatilla said with a curt nod. "He doesn't truly see it, but we do. And he deserves so much more. He has a vision of what the galaxy can be. We're going to fix it together. But you're in the way."

"Ew, gross," Orinthia said, scrunching her face. "You're in love with Arsenio?"

Annatilla curled her upper lip and pulled her head back. A fire burned across her cheeks. "He's so much more than that. I'm fully devoted to him. He saved my life and I owe him everything. Love is trivial compared to the reverence he deserves."

"You're nuts," Orinthia said. "They are the worst people in the galaxy. The only thing they deserve is the business end of a blaster."

Annatilla leaped to her feet before Orinthia had time to react. The back of her hand cracked across Orinthia's face. Pain shot up her skull. Her ears rang, skin burning from the force. The cool air stung against the raw wound.

Until that moment, Orinthia had forgotten Annatilla was cyborg. Now, there was no mistaking it. She hit the floor hard, landing on her side. Her vision flashed white, then dark.

For a moment, there was nothing. When she came back, Annatilla was crouched beside her head, looking down at her.

"You're not as weak as they make you out to be," Annatilla said, though there was no hint of compliment in her words.

Orinthia pushed herself up and moved away from the woman. Her ears continued to ring and her thoughts were foggy. She touched her cheek where she had been hit and felt the jagged edges of a cut. "Well, they're wrong about a lot of things."

"You lived with them." Annatilla stayed where she was, balancing perfectly still on the balls of her feet. "Saw what they're capable of everyday. But you're nothing like them. Why?"

"Because I have a conscience," Orinthia said, working her jaw.

"Enough of your quips," Annatilla said. "I want real answers."

Orinthia narrowed her eyes. "I don't know how more of a real answer I can give. They're sick. Maybe my father broke them too hard. Maybe they were born like this. I don't know. But I'm not like them, because I'm not."

Annatilla's expression stayed the same, but something shifted in her voice. "You could've been."

The words filled Orinthia's clouded mind. She played them over and over. Claven had accused her of being Adora, too. Was she?

*No, I'm not.* Orinthia shook her head.

"Yeah, I could've been like them," Orinthia said, her voice quiet and even. "It would've been easy. Giving in to the hate that was already there. Letting the anger take over."

A flash of heat rolled through her, remembering her

younger years full of spite and bitterness. A hunger to fight anyone and everyone. Who she was just a year before.

She exhaled, pushing the emotions out. "I was close to it, too. But I was never good enough for them. Because I hated myself more than I hated anyone else."

There was a long pause. Orinthia found Annatilla's eyes and focused on them. No matter what she did or said, Orinthia would refuse to break. "But I found people who care about me, and not what I can do for them. They showed me I am worthy of love without the exchange of service or how much I can take a hit. And that's why I'm not like the twins."

"You're never going to see them again," Annatilla said, raising to stand.

"I've been told that before." Orinthia gave a single shoulder shrug. "Even if it's true this time, I know I've won. Because they can kill me, but they can't take away the bond I've formed. Adora has loyalty based on fear and power. I have loyalty forged through camaraderie and trust."

"I'm not afraid of them," Annatilla said. "Arsenio earned my devotion when he made me like this. He's given me everything and I give it back to him."

"Who are you, really?" Orinthia asked. She waved a hand up and down at the woman. "Before this. Before they twisted you into a blind servant."

Annatilla stared, long and cold, at Orinthia. The silence tricked Orinthia into thinking she actually heard the ticking of the light on the grenade. For a second, not more than a blink of an eye, something cracked through Annatilla's resolve. It was gone before Orinthia could read what it meant.

"Batra Ghest."

The name lingered in the air. Orinthia ran it through her mind and tried to place where she had met the woman before.

It took her longer than she was proud to admit, but realization cleared in moments.

"But you died," Orinthia said. Her stomach flopped. "It was the first funeral we did as Hunters. You and six other officers. The only time we ever lost that many at once."

"I did die," Annatilla said. She looked down her nose at Orinthia. Her voice came out slow and hard, like each word disgusted her. "That body is gone. Everything about her is gone. I barely have her memories."

She paused and the glint of worship passed over her face again. "But Arsenio pulled me from the ashes and made sure I had a life. He remade me into perfection."

Orinthia scoffed and shook her head. "He's more like my father than just his face, then. Though I doubt he actually remade you on his own."

"Desidario helped him, yes," Annatilla said. "They pulled connections and favors to save me. But it was at Arsenio's word that he did it."

For the first time, Orinthia let Annatilla's words settle. Desidario had his hands in everything. Every single thing in her life. She looked away from the woman and focused on the ground. It should not have bothered her as much as it did, knowing that he gave someone else the gifts she had previously thought were reserved for their family.

The knot in her chest grew into a sting, flowing through her nerves. She did not want his love. She did not need it. But it was knowing that he helped Arsenio when he came to him, even if it was for his own gain.

*What did Arsenio have to exchange?* she thought. *Or did he give him this act freely? Am I the only one who had to earn his blessings?*

Orinthia took in sharp breaths, fighting the tears of hurt and anger. Nothing she did would ever be good enough for any of them. And now Desidario was dead. There were thousands of words left unsaid. Thousands of hurts unaccounted for. But to Annatilla, he was as much of a god as Arsenio. The pain he caused Orinthia was life to Annatilla. They could never see the same people through the same eyes.

She settled into resolve and relaxed her shoulders. This was not a desperate act like it had been for Celso. There were no conflicting emotions to pull at. The twins had Annatilla locked in, fully devoted, and ready to give it all for them.

"If Arsenio has such a great plan for the galaxy, and Adora wants to tear it apart, then why does he follow her still?" Orinthia asked.

Annatilla brought the grenade near her face and twitched her fingers. She grinned at Orinthia's flinch. "He needs her to level it so he can rebuild it. We're not foolish enough to think this will save people. He's not looking for redemption."

"Then what is it?" Orinthia asked, frustrated. "I've never known Arsenio to stand up for anything. He's always followed Adora's play. This is new for him."

"It isn't, though," Annatilla said. "You think Adora's the dangerous one? She is. But even she knows she can't do this alone. She burns everything down and when the galaxy is nothing but ashes, Arsenio is the one who will reshape what's left. They balance each other. You see him as her shadow, but he sees himself as the foundation. You can't have one without the other."

"This is complete madness," Orinthia said. "Do they want the responsibility of ruling the galaxy? That's a lot, even for them."

"Of course not." Annatilla waved her hand, brushing away the question. "She's reckless. That's why we follow Arsenio. Adora will be a legend for the ruin she leaves in her wake. But not Arsenio. Arsenio will make sure there's something left when the fire burns out. He'll be the man who rebuilds the stars."

"And then what, *you'll* rule?"

"I'm merely a footnote in his history," Annatilla said. "He'll find someone better for that job. The EC will continue as it always did, unaware of the power shift. But the twins will be calling the shots from the background."

Orinthia leaned the back of her head against the wall. Annatilla was wrapped up in the twin's aspirations, there was no point in pressing the issue further. She took in a lung full of air and settled in for the last bit of the trip. Her eyes twitched to the nav computer to see how long they had left.

"I'll tell you when we get close," Annatilla said, stepping to the side and blocking Orinthia's view. "You get there when we get there." She leaned back and pressed a button. When she moved again, the nav screen was off. Annatilla returned to the pilot's seat and went back to reading her PortTab.

Orinthia swallowed down the irritation, her fingers curled around the edge of her coat and pulled it closer around her. The comm was still in her pocket. In Annatilla's arrogance, she had not searched her. Orinthia's mind wandered to Kos. He was there, feet in front of her. If she had been a second faster, maybe she could have reached him first.

Her heart ached. He looked exhausted. She wondered if he had slept at all since they had been apart. The pain wound up her spine and she forced it out.

*He's coming for me,* she thought. *I know he'll be right behind us when we land. And he would've called Thrutt, too. I'm not alone this time. My friends are coming.*

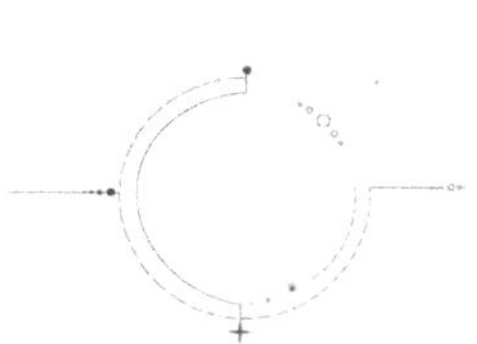

## 41

*O*rinthia stared at the wall for so long, she started to see shapes that were not there. There were no clunky engines of the *Tertion*. Nothing to keep her mind occupied during the long trip. Two days, maybe more, she could not tell. Annatilla fed her packaged snacks from the galley and made her use the bathroom with the door open. Emotional torture layered over the stress of not knowing what came next.

A soft chime broke the quiet. Annatilla straightened in the pilot's seat and flipped switches with practiced ease.

"We're here," she said, with no tension in her words.

Before Orinthia could brace, they dropped out of warp. Proximity alarms shrieked. The blackout screen rolled back from the windscreen just in time for a streak of cannon fire to flash across, leaving a white hot trail in its wake. Orinthia watched with mouth and eyes wide open as the blast struck another ship in the port side.

Annatilla reacted with ease. She yanked the yoke back, rolling the ship over crippled cruisers and diving toward a dusty red planet below. Blaster bolts slashed past their nose, burning lines in the dark.

Orinthia sucked in a breath and covered her head with her arms as the ship rocked from an ion burst. Impact sensors wailed. The hobby craft was not designed for combat, its shields only rated for low level asteroids and space debris. Outside, laser missiles zipped through the battlefield, explosions blooming like miniature suns.

There was no telling who was fighting who. The chaos was more than Orinthia's mind could grasp in the moment. Annatilla, however, was unbothered. She weaved without a flinch, slipping between fighters and dodging clouds of flak. The controls hummed under her command, responding with a precision that only came from experience, or recklessness.

A warning light blinked red on the console. Something was locked on them.

With a grunt, Annatilla twisted the yoke and rolled the ship out of the way. The missile streaked past, colliding instead with a cruiser in the distance. They made it through the dogfight without any real damage, other than Orinthia's nerves.

The planet's surface loomed closer, a vast stretch of crimson filled the view as they broke through the atmosphere. Deep reds, oranges, and browns dotted large sections of land. Orinthia could not make out what was liquid and what was solid earth. As they neared their destination, what she had assumed was desert, was thick forests and high mountain ranges.

In minutes, the thrusters cut and they slowed to a gentle landing speed. The luxury liner was worth its money. Unlike the *Tertion* or even *Freya*, there were no bumps or jolts as the landing gear lowered. The craft touched down like a feather and lowered itself with a whisper of a sigh.

Annatilla stood and pulled a pin from the pouch on her hip. With a light touch, she replaced it in the grenade and set it back inside.

Taking the opportunity, Orinthia jumped to her feet, bringing both arms up to toss out her blades, but Annatilla gripped her wrist. In one move, she twirled Orinthia around and pulled her arm up so her fist was between her shoulders. Pain shot up her muscles and the joints felt as if they would separate.

Without a word, Annatilla pushed her forward, shoving her from the cockpit into the corridor. Orinthia dragged her feet, buying every second possible.

*Kos will be out there,* she thought. *I have to give him as much time as I can.*

She was not going without a struggle. Orinthia took in slow breaths and pictured the latches on Annatilla's helmet. She was tired, hungry, and in pain, but she pushed through it. The image was fuzzy, but she focused anyway. Her pulse thudded in her ears and she reached for the memory of cold metal. It took several long seconds of effort.

Then she found it. Solid and real against her hand she had not moved. In one swift motion, she flicked her fingers. A sharp *pop* snapped through the tight space as one of the latches came undone.

Annatilla gasped, then growled in anger. She threw her hand to the latch and closed it again. With a kick to the back of the leg, she shoved Orinthia down onto her knees.

She braced for her shoulder to dislocate, pinching her lips and taking in deep breaths through her nose. Instead, Annatilla planted a boot firmly against her lower back. Before she could react, a sharp twist wrenched through her arm. Something shifted with a sickening pop.

White-hot pain tore through her elbow, sending a shockwave up her arm. She panted through the pain, her mind struggling to focus on anything but the searing agony. There had been many fractures and dislocations as a fighter, but that did not make it any more bearable.

Annatilla let go, and Orinthia's arm fell limp to the side. "Don't be stupid," she said. "Get up."

Bile filled Orinthia's mouth. She spit it on the ground and stayed on her knees. *Is it broken?* she thought, trying to move her arm. *No, maybe not. Dislocated? I hope it's just dislocated.*

Fingers tangled in Orinthia's hair near the scalp, yanking her upright. Each step brought a flash of agony. Orinthia clutched the top of her arm to keep it from swinging. She hissed between her teeth.

The air was hot as they approached the ramp. It had a metallic scent, like junkyard rust. Microparticles of dust hung in the air, drying Orinthia's mouth and making it feel like sandpaper. She pinched her lips together and drew short, shallow pulls through her nose. An auburn light filled the entrance, Orinthia squinting as her eyes adjusted to the color. Her vision cleared through tight blinks.

And there she was. Adoracion.

A hot, liquid-like rush went down Orinthia's spine. It came from inside her, seeping out of her cells. Fear.

Adora stood in front of a small group, not as large as the one on the *Mathias*, but just as well-armed.

Orinthia forced her chin higher, though she trembled. Each step she took was deliberate and slow.

The moment her boots hit solid ground, a soft whirr stirred above. She barely noticed it was there, until someone shouted.

"Incoming vessel!"

She looked up, scanning the sky. A stream of blaster fire

erupted from Adora's guards, aiming for a sleek silver ship angled for their direction.

*That's the same one from Chazet,* Orinthia thought. *Kos.* Her heart leaped. She had been right. He did come for her. The ship tipped to the side, revealing the pilot's outline.

Kos let out a line of blaster fire, cutting between Orinthia and Adora. Rocks and dust kicked up, followed by hollering and stamps of confusion. They were distracted.

Using the cover, Orinthia threw herself against Annatilla and twisted free from her grip. She bolted for a line of trees in the distance, clutching her useless arm against her side. Every step sent a fresh wave of pain and nausea through her body. But stopping would get her killed. Even over the cover fire, she heard Adora yelling orders for them to ignore the enemy ship and kill Orinthia.

Orinthia's teeth ground together as her feet beat the dirt. Faster and faster, the trees formed around her. The ache and throbbing became too much, and though she had not made it very far in, she had to slow down. She weaved in and out of the thick woods, going as deep as she could before stopping to rest.

Breath rasping in her throat, she pressed her back against the rough bark of an oxblood tree trunk. Ember leaves drifted from the high canopy, swirling in a slow descent, their colors shifting like dying coal; red, orange, black, then red again. Long shadows stretched and danced as they fell. It would have been peaceful if she was anywhere other than hiding for her life.

A layer of sweat formed over her skin, collecting the tiny particles of dust like fabric. It itched. She slid down and tried to steady her breathing, sending out her senses as much as she could through the mist in her mind. No one had followed her, at least not yet. The thick foliage swallowed every sound behind her, wrapping the woods in a suffocating hush.

She reached into her breast pocket for the comm to call Kos, but froze. A flash of presence prickled against her skin. It was small but unmistakably Annatilla. The woman stalked closer, no more than twenty feet away.

Orinthia's pulse hammered as she looked for a better hiding spot. Nothing. There was not enough cover between her and the next tree in any direction for her to move. She exhaled with a sharp huff. There was no room to run and she was being hunted.

As quiet as falling ash, she braced herself with her good arm and rose. The world tilted slightly, but she held steady, listening for the right moment. Heartbeat after heartbeat passed. Then she sensed her.

Orinthia pictured the brittle leaves scattered across the ground and hurled them backward with a snap of focus. She looked back to see if it had worked. Smoldering litter rained down around Annatilla.

Through the chaos, Orinthia darted forward. A blaster bolt screamed past her head, sending splinters of bark into the air as it struck the tree beside her. Another two followed, missing by inches.

Veering hard to the right, she cut across the path and ducked behind another trunk. The moment she stopped, her stomach lurched. A ferocious burning shot through her arm, seizing the rest of her body, and sending her doubled over as she vomited. She wiped her mouth with the back of her GMH coat sleeve, gulping in ragged breaths.

In the midst of her discomfort, she almost missed the footsteps coming in front of her. Orinthia glanced up and stared down the barrel of Annatilla's blaster pistol.

Orinthia pulled herself straight. Each breath stretched like minutes as she held herself together the best she could.

Annatilla fired. No warning. No hesitation.

Time slowed. Orinthia was caught between a yell and a cry. Sparks exploded from her chest. She staggered, bracing for the sear of a blaster bolt, waiting for the pain and warmth of blood.

It never came.

Her hand trembled as it found the wound. Dry. The comm hand taken the hit. Her only link to Kos had saved her life.

She coughed as the air returned to her lungs from the blow to her chest, but adrenaline surged through her. A second chance. Even with exhaustion weighing her down, she managed a dozen steps before her legs gave out. She hit the ground. Anguish, hot and constant, coursed up her arm. The burn in her throat from screaming hurt almost as much.

Footsteps approached behind her as she rolled to her back. Annatilla's shadow blocked out the light peeking in from above.

"I'm really surprised you've kept that coat on this long in this heat," she said, stopping at Orinthia's head with her blaster poised to end her. "At least I'm told it's hot. I can't feel much inside this. But you made it easier to find you, so thanks."

Orinthia blinked hard.

"You really are so compliant now, aren't you?" Annatilla asked. "Slap a few orders in front of something and you just do whatever you're told. I thought you would have thrown a fit about having to wear it. Never did I dream you'd keep it with you everywhere you went. There was nothing you did that I didn't hear."

The words tangled in her fogged mind, processing

through the sludge. Then, slowly realization hit her. There was something in the coat. Annatilla had used her pride against her.

"Yes, even your marauder fleet." Annatilla fake whispered. "We were very prepared for your friends when they got here." She leaned forward and put a hand against the side of her helmet where her ear would be. "If you listen real close, you can almost hear them dying up there."

Orinthia took a deep breath, drawing strength from sheer determination. She rolled to her knees, legs wobbling beneath her, but she stared Annatilla down. With a deep breath, she stood. The women were only feet apart. Whatever Orinthia did, she knew it would have to be quick.

Annatilla scoffed and retrained the blaster to Orinthia's head.

With a grunt to conjure up power, Orinthia lifted her good arm to her chest and threw out her blade. They locked eyes. A tense, unspoken beat stretched between them.

In a flash, Orinthia took one step to the left, causing Annatilla to aim that direction. Then, in the middle of her movement, she spun to the right. Her blade swung up, catching Annatilla across the chest in a swift line.

The spacesuit tore like a tissue beneath the silver blade. Annatilla dropped her blaster. Her hands flew to the hole and pressed the edges together, desperately trying to close the gap. Wires and raw, red flesh peeked out through the opening. She drew in air with shaking gasps as she fell to the ground, still helplessly trying to save herself.

There was no blood. No entrails. Just the flapping of gloved fingers against plastina fabric.

Orinthia stepped forward, staring down at Annatilla. Her shoulders rose and fell with each heavy breath as she watched the woman fade. She swung the blade up again, recalling it back to a normal arm.

In the puttering silence, she shrugged off the Hunter coat, and tossed it over Annatilla's twitching body.

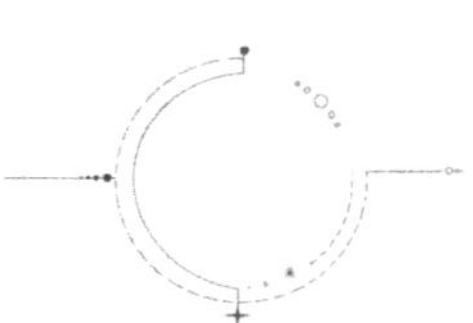

## 42

*A*s Kos peeled out of warp, he flew straight into the middle of complete chaos. The battlefield roared to life around him. Blaster bolts streaked through the void. Ion bursts crackled against failing shields. Pieces of debris moved in slow-motion through zero gravity. Warnings flared across his console, including a rapid, never ceasing blue light near his hand on the yoke.

He barely spared any of them a glance. His focus was locked on a single vessel, weaving dangerously through the firefight ahead.

"Freya, keep a lock on that ship," Kos shouted. "Whatever you do, don't lose it." Her nose angled down, following their prey's trajectory.

Kos' hand flew to his pocket and yanked out the comm. It blinked a handful of times before Thrutt answered.

"Some party you got going," Kos said.

"'Bout time you showed up," Thrutt replied. People barked orders in the background. Alarms rang in the distance.

"Look, keep all fire off the two incoming crafts," Kos said, skipping the banter. "We're the two smallest ones out here and will be ripped to shreds. I'm the one in the back. Thia's aboard the white hobby craft ahead of me. Just need long enough to get landed and then I can get her."

"Get an eye on those ships that just showed up," Thrutt said. His voice was quieter, as if he pulled the comm away from his face to talk to someone on his side. Then, louder, he asked, "What's the plan?"

Kos let out a breathy laugh. "Survive? I don't know. I've run some ideas through my head, but most of them depend on very specific factors. Nothing I can control. So, right now, I'm just going to make sure they make it through this and work things out as they come."

A streak of white crossed his path. He pulled up and rose above it, gritting his teeth.

"Cutting it close, don't you think?" Thrutt asked.

Leveling out again, Kos adjusted to keep in line with Orinthia's ship. "Yeah, but there's not much to work with. Can you spare some people my way? I'll need ground support for whatever I run into."

"Had some on standby just in case," Thrutt answered. "I'll tell Ignio to get them out. Where am I sending them in case you get separated?"

Kos tucked the comm under his chin and tapped on the nav computer. He read off the coordinates Freya calculated.

"Okay, I'm going with them." Thrutt paused. "Be careful. I'll find you down there."

An alarm blared in Kos' ears. He didn't have time to say goodbyes. The only thing he could do was grab the yoke with both hands and dive straight down. The comm fell from his chin-hold and clacked closed near his feet.

"Freya, show me a clear path through this," he said.

The nav computer ran several lines of code before settling on a solution. It gave him a speed and angle he'd have to match in order to make it free in time. "Alright, let's go."

Kos leaned side to side, swaying through the mess around him. Orinthia's ship dashed past the battle toward the planet. It grew smaller in the viewport and almost disappeared.

Again, a warning signal went off.

"Freya, chaff," Kos ordered.

Bright lights flew out from all sides of Mimi's ship. They caught the missile, but the blast wave sent Kos forward. The artificial gravity generator inside Mimis' ship stuttered under the pressure, just long enough for inertia to take over. His feet lifted off the ground for a moment and he forced all his weight against the yoke. Space spiraled for a full three rotations before Kos corrected the fall. He pressed on until he, too, was free from the firefight.

KOS BROKE THROUGH THE ATMOSPHERE. Heat washed over the ship as he made his descent. The white vessel cut across the sky, too far ahead. He pushed the yoke forward, willing his ship to drop faster. They were minutes ahead of him, but he knew Orinthia may not have long to spare.

The forest below split open into a clearing, revealing a compound with towering walls. At its opening, beyond the enclosure, stretched a landing pad. It was lighter in color than the rest of the land, but easy to make out even at his distance.

He banked, circling wide for a better view. Figures lined up near the white ship that stood out against the deep red of everything else. They were armed and waiting.

Movement caught his eyes. Two figures stepped out of

the ship, one being shoved from behind. Even from as high as he was, Orinthia's hair stood out.

Within seconds, the platoon shifted, and blaster bolts fired up at him.

Kos pulled the yoke to the side and swung the ship around. He adjusted his angle more, then moved this thumb to the auto-blaster, Mimi's only weapon aboard the ship. After a moment to steady himself, he pressed down on the trigger. A controlled burst of fire struck the ground in a line as he flew by. Dirt and debris kicked up, and he hoped it was enough to give her an opportunity to run.

With a sharp turn that made the cockpit tremble, Kos went back for another pass. A singular person broke from the group and ran toward the trees. The white GMH coat told him who. Again, he laid down cover fire, giving Orinthia the best chance she had at escape. He watched carefully as she disappeared into the woods.

Five dots appeared on the radar, two behind him and three ahead. Kos pulled up and rocketed straight into the sky, drawing their attention to him. The ship could take the force, but shook from the effort of quick maneuvering. He bit into his bottom lip and climbed as fast as he could before leveling out. In one swift turn, he faced the two closest to him. His thumb hovered over the trigger as he put the first one in his sights.

Before he locked onto a clear shot, the ship erupted in flames. Larger chunks tore apart from the blast and hurtled back to the surface. Kos snapped his gaze to the second ship, unsure of where the attack had come from. It was just enough time to watch it detonate the same as the last.

The comm on Mimi's ship beeped. Kos took a moment to catch his breath before activating the call.

"Someday I'll let you fight your own battle," Thrutt said over the speakers.

Kos loosened his hold and relaxed into the seat. "Right now, I'm just glad to have some luck. We made some ground, but I lost Thia again. She took off into the forest. I have to get down to find her."

"We've got your back," Thrutt said. "I'll keep a ship up for cover and the rest of us will follow you."

"Take out as much of the ground crew as you can before we settle," Kos said, already turning to go back to where he last saw Orinthia. With a second to breathe, Kos retrieved the comm that had slid around during the fight. He activated the device and set the it beside the nav computer, waiting for Orinthia's to ping her location back.

*Error*, the computer responded.

He tried again.

*Error*.

"What's wrong?" Thrutt asked.

"I can't track her comm," Kos answered. He jabbed in different codes and options, trying to force the outcome he wanted. Nothing worked. He cursed loudly. "It must be broken." His free hand slammed against the console, sending a sharp sting up his wrist. Again and again his efforts were no use. No matter how hard he tried, how much work he put into it, he still lost her.

"Land, now, Kos," Thrutt said. His voice cut through Kos' anger. "Get down there and look for her. We'll take care of everything else."

"What if —" Kos started to say.

Thrutt interrupted. "Stop. Whatever those next words were don't matter. She's down there, alone and scared. This is what we've come here to do. Now go get her."

Kos clenched his teeth until his jaw trembled. Then, he let

go. He wouldn't stop looking for her until he knew for sure. And if anything happened to her, there'd be more than enough people to take his rage out on.

"I'm going." Kos set Freya to land the ship. He was out of his seat and by the door before they had fully settled. With his blaster in hand, Kos swiped at his armor and stood ready to fight whatever was waiting for him outside.

The ship thumped as it touched down. Kos jammed his hand on the lever and jumped out as soon as there was room for his body. His HUD scanned the area as his feet carried him with speed. Tall, blood red trees surrounded him in seconds. He searched for any signs of life, anything to give him a direction to run.

Harder and harder, he pushed through the leaves and plants, jumping over what he could and going around what he couldn't. An opening formed to his left. He merely glanced at first, but almost fell over as a flash of white cut against the red.

A sharp pain clamped around his chest, stealing his breath as he slid into a turn. Leaves scattered around his feet, caught in the force of his momentum.

*No. No. That can't be her. It's not.* He tried to convince himself the white coat on the ground was not Orinthia.

His feet barely touched the forest floor as he ran. Branches snapped against his arms, lungs burning from breathing recycled air. He had to be wrong.

*It was just a trick,* he told himself. *A light cutting in through the trees. Anything.*

*Just not her.*

He made it back to the opening and slowed, shaking with each step. The back of his mind told him there was something not right, something he was missing. But he only noticed the flatline across his HUD. He swiped up and took off his armor.

With a trembling hand, he grasped the coat and threw it off the body.

A wave of relief crashed against him, making him stagger back. It was the woman, the Messie who took Orinthia.

Annatilla laid crumpled on her side, hands loose in front of her near a gash in her spacesuit. She did not move or make a sound. Kos let her be. He'd get no answers from a dead woman. But the clean cut in her suit told him everything he needed to know. Orinthia had been there. She was alive, at least long enough to do this.

Kos kept his HUD down and looked for signs that would lead him in the right way. He bent low and looked for tracks, blood, anything. More curses slipped through his teeth.

"Mimi would've found her by now," he said to himself. "I have no idea what I'm doing." He stood again and opened the map reader on his HUD. Several paths calculated at once, branching out in different directions. Most led nowhere.

Except one.

Kos stared at the highlighted route, watching the line move until it ended at the compound. His stomach twisted. *That's it.* He took off in a sprint. *She's going back.*

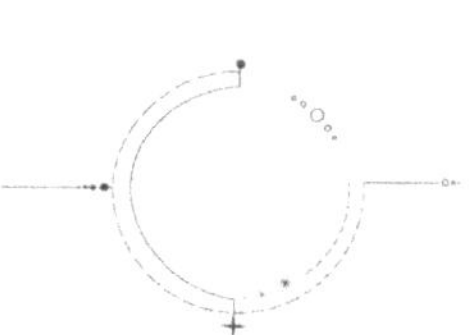

## 43

Burnt orange blended into burgundy and maroon in the sky as the sun touched the horizon. Orinthia sat under a tree and leaned her head against a trunk. Bark tugged at her hair. Her body trembled, not from the temperature, but from exhaustion. She had very little left to give, yet she was still so far from her goal.

Rest was not easy, either. The air was too thick and hurt her lungs. Her arm burned and swelled. The skin almost matched the color of the dusk settling around her. All she wanted was to close her eyes and sleep. But she could not. There was no safety in the woods. Someone would soon find her, and she knew the respite could not last long.

The compound lay ahead about half a mile away. From her hiding spot, Orinthia heard blaster fire echo out across the open space. It was faint and sporadic, and she could not tell exactly where it came from. She only hoped it was her friends, and that they were winning.

Her head bobbed a few times. Despite the circumstances, as the sun lowered, the atmosphere bordered cozy. She tried to imagine laying in bed on a warm summer night, with windows wide open to allow the fresh in air. It was not a place she had been before. Her apartment windows did not open. Nor was it Mimi's too-humid house. The room only existed in her mind, the one she had made up for her and Kos to live in once they were free.

Peaceful. Safe. Together. That was all she dreamed of.

A branch snapped somewhere behind her, breaking the perfect moment in her head. She bit her lips to keep silent, though her blood rushed around her body in a torrent. With what little effort she could give, she searched out the source of the sound, praying it was some native animal. The sensation trickled around her. One she had been so close to a lifetime before.

Orinthia tried to call out, but her voice failed. She coughed and swallowed sandy saliva before trying again. "Kos," she said. Her words croaked. Hot air rushed from her nose as she blew out, gathering the will to get to her feet. It took more than one try, but she staggered up.

The feeling grew potent, he was near. All she had to do was follow it. She stumbled through the forest, a newfound force pushing her on. Then, in the dying light, he stepped into view.

They both froze, only for a moment, then ran to each other. Kos closed the distance first. He threw his arms around her, but she yelled in pain. Frantically, he let go and moved back. His eyes darted all over her body, looking at her through the visor over his face.

"What happened?" Kos asked. He gingerly took her arm in his hand and looked at the injury.

His words were smooth in her ears. She could not feel the heat of his hands on her swollen appendage, but the touch was enough. He was there with her.

He was real.

"Kos," was all she managed to get out. Thoughts rushed through her head in a dizzying speed. She gripped his hand with her useable one and held as tight as she could.

Kos steadied her with one hand, and the other went to his pocket. He pulled out a ration bar and set her back on the ground. "Eat this." Orinthia did as she was told, finishing the snack in a few bites. It was bland and dry, but having something in her stomach was better than hunger pains.

Again, he examined her arm. "It's not broken, but it's bad." He looked around the woods then down at himself. Without hesitation, he pulled his shirt where it tucked into his belt and cut the hem with his dagger. The fabric tore unevenly, but he kept going, slicing off a long strip.

"I need to call Thrutt to pick you up," he said, standing. "But let's take care of this first."

"No, Uri's still inside," Orinthia said. The sun was low and only stray rays lit the land.

Kos snapped two long branches from the tree above, stripped the limbs with practiced movements, and slid them under his arm. Then he twisted at the waist, reached behind his head, and undid the ribbon from his hair. The strands touched the top of his shoulders, curly and uncombed.

He crouched in front of her again, lowering the makeshift supplies into her lap. "Someone else can go find him. Now hold still. This is going to hurt, I'm sorry."

With slow and easy movements, Kos took Orinthia's forearm and met her eyes. She hissed from the pressure and clenched her jaw, then gave a pinched nod.

His hands trembled. "Just keep breathing, okay? Don't tense up. It makes it worse." Kos adjusted his grip and held his own breath. With one sharp tug, he guided the joint back into place.

A white-hot flash tore through her, worse than the initial

dislocation. She gasped, choked on it. Tears sprung to her eyes before she could stop them.

The pain did not vanish, but it shifted. There was less fire, but a deeper, gnawing ache that radiated through her marrow.

Kos did not look at her face. He kept his head low and worked as quickly as he dared. "This is for padding," he said, wrapping the fabric around her swollen arm. "Can you hold it steady for me?"

Orinthia did her best to keep still, even through the ache pulsing up to her shoulder. She bit into her lips and made as little noise as possible.

Kos took both sticks and set them on either side of her arm. He wrapped the ribbon around the sticks and secured them to her arm.

"That will keep it sturdy enough for now," Kos said. "I'll get you a med pack as soon as we're back on the *Fera*."

"I'm not going," Orinthia said. The light was almost all gone, but she could see him in the shadows.

Kos cursed, bringing his eyes to hers. "Yes, you are. This is over and you barely survived."

"I can't let Adora win," Orinthia said. "She'll bring everything down and we'll have nothing."

"Run away, right now." Kos took her good hand in both of his. "Please, just leave with me. We can take Mimi's ship and get as far away as possible. You're going to die here if we don't."

"I can't," Orinthia said again, emphasizing each word. She gripped his hand, trying to show she had some fight left, even if it was almost a lie.

"Why not? Tell me." Kos's voice rose dangerously close to a yell. "Why does this mean more than living? I've fought my way across the galaxy to get to you. I've never asked anything from you, never shoved my love in your face. But

I'm tired, and worn out. All I want to do is see tomorrow with you next to me. Why can't we just do that?"

Orinthia let his words hang between them before answering. Tears welled up in her eyes and she drew in a broken breath. "Because it'll all mean nothing if we lose."

She paused and looked at the ground. Tears trickled down her cheeks. "All the work we did to get to Elendoras, losing *Freya*, Marius dying, the hurt you've been through… it will be thrown away with nothing to show for it. I can't walk away because in a sick way this has been the best time of my life. You've fought for me. You've loved me beyond anything I could have dreamed of. Kos, you stood up to marauders to bring me an army. How can I leave when you've risked so much to get me here?"

She sniffed and whimpered for a second before continuing. "I shouldn't care about the EC, and really it isn't the Confederacy itself that I'm worried about. But the twins want to destroy the foundations and build it new. They are evil, and many more people will die in the process. I know nothing of war, but I know you. I see what it's done to you. As much as I wish I could go back in time and save you from that life, I can't. But I can stop someone else from living that reality. At least with this. There will always be another war, but this is the one I'm trying to prevent. This is as much for you as it is for me."

A sapphire moon rose, shedding soft light through the canopy. Ethereal streaks fluttered down, making the ember leaves glow. The dust reflected in the rays and sparkled like stars in the darkness. Kos' face was clear in the moonlight. He bit his lower lip and stared at her.

Orinthia stared back, hoping he understood the weight behind her fight. She was not just fighting for Uri. He was her brother, and she loved him. But the real battle had always been for Kos. So they could be free and live the life he deserved. If throwing herself on the pyre would grant him salvation, she would do it without a thought. Kos was the light and warmth of her life. The sun that lit her way. She loved him completely.

"Whatever you say, I'll do," Kos whispered. "I'm in this deep." He leaned in and pressed his lips to hers. His mouth burned, but she did not care. It was her favorite feeling, one she had missed while apart. Each kiss was soft, but desperate. They needed each other. Two halves of a whole person. She vowed in her heart to never leave his side again.

Kos pulled away, pressing his forehead to hers. His visor was still down, and she saw lines of code across the glass, like Annatilla had on hers.

Orinthia's stomach twisted for a moment. She did not like killing. It was not as easy as she had hoped. Saving Arsenio was instinctual. Killing him and Adora would take sacrifice and strength she was unsure existed inside her.

"We can't get anywhere with you like this," Kos said, moving to sit beside her. He placed his hand on the side of her head and made her rest on his shoulder. "Sleep while you can. I'll keep watch."

"There's no time to sleep," Orinthia protested. "I have to —"

"If you want to convince me you're able to keep going, you're going to have to rest first. You can't walk two feet without collapsing, and that's not going to help anyone. We're a team, now. Please listen to me for once."

Orinthia surrendered with a sigh and nestled closer to him. It was hard to argue when being near to him, in the quiet and stillness of the night, was more than she hoped for. Death may soon come for them, so she might as well hold on to their time together while she could.

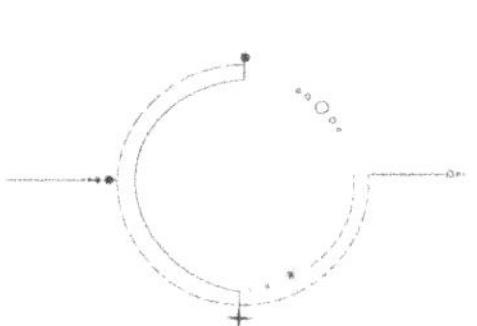

Silver moonlight bathed the forest. An occasional breeze sent leaves spiraling through the breaks in the trees. Orinthia laid peacefully on Kos' shoulder, breathing slow and steady in the silence of the warm night. Even with the occasional blaster fire echoing across the way, she slept on.

Kos trained his focus to hear every noise, watch every shadow, and notice any shift of movement. His HUD scanned what his eyes missed, giving readouts of his surroundings. They were safe for the moment, but he didn't let hope linger. He wasn't a fool to think they weren't looking for her.

The occasional ship flew overhead, kicking up dust as it moved to and from the landing pad at the front of the compound. From their cover, Kos couldn't be sure who the vessels belonged to. His mind wandered to the battle above the planet. There hadn't been time to see which side was winning. All that mattered was the woman beside him, and now he had her. Yet, their journey had long to go until it ended.

A silent ping lit up the corner of Kos' HUD. A message

from Thrutt rolled across the display. They'd taken the court-yard, but the interior was still unsecured. It was a clean way to keep Kos updated without waking Orinthia.

Beacons from the broken compound rotated far across the clearing. Alarms or searchlights, Kos couldn't be sure from his position. But the light passed through the gaps in the trees in flashes, reminding him how close the threat really was.

Kos took stock in the sounds around him. No engines. No hover bikes. No rovers. Just the ships. It told him their enemies were most likely moving on foot. That would make them slow. Predictable.

Kos set his hand on Orinthia's leg to wake her. He regretted stealing her rest, but knew their cover wouldn't last long.

Orinthia stirred, then her eyes flew open. She gasped and looked around until she faced Kos. Her shoulders relaxed, but her chest still rose and fell quickly as she regained her normal breathing. "How long has it been?" she asked, rubbing her cheek where her face had pressed against his arm.

"An hour," Kos said. He leaned in and kissed her fore-head. "I'd give you all night if I could. But we're eating away at our luck."

A long yawn, followed by quick coughs and a hiss passed from Orinthia. She scrunched her face and held her arm close to her body. "I feel like it was minutes."

"I know." Kos frowned, running through ideas of how he could help her better. All his medical supplies were on Mimi's ship. He hadn't thought of anything but getting to this moment. A hand of guilt settled on his chest.

"We're fine," Orinthia said with a strained smile. "It'll be okay soon."

Kos nodded. He could only hope she was right. "Thrutt

said they've made some good ground. No backup yet, though. For either of us."

"Has he found Uri?" Orinthia asked.

"No. They haven't made it far inside. It's harder to clear a building than taking out enemies in the open."

"Then we should get going." Orinthia put a hand on Kos' shoulder and forced herself onto her feet. She took long breaths in and bit into her lip.

"Let's set some rules first," Kos said, wiping his hands after he joined her. He turned and made her look him in the eye to be sure she understood how serious he was. "You do not leave my sight unless I tell you to. Then you run fast, far, and don't look back for me. If I say stop, you stop. If I say move, you move. This is my world now. You have to listen to every command I give, no matter how harsh it sounds. Stay behind me and keep your head down, got it?"

Orinthia gave him quick nods.

"I'll do my best to get you to Uri," Kos said. He reached out and brushed her cheek. "But if we have no other choice, no chance to save him or stop Adora, I'm making the call and getting you out."

Orinthia opened her mouth to argue.

Kos continued talking. "I'm sorry, but I have to keep you safe. Lastly, if anything happens to me —" he swallowed hard and tightened his jaw, "— you keep going. Thrutt will find you."

A breeze caught Orinthia's hair and tossed the strands out of her face. The moonlight kissed her hair, turning silver into iridescence. Kos let his eyes linger over her features, taking a mental snapshot. She was his, and he would do everything to keep her alive.

He took in a long breath, breaking his gaze from her face

before he had a change of heart and forced her off that awful planet. "Let's move."

His hip opened and he pulled out the golden blaster. With quick and light steps, Kos moved ahead of Orinthia and crept toward the edge of the trees. In the open, he saw the damage clearer. Smoke drifted from downed ships. Silhouettes of bodies laid still like dark mounds. Vehicles were turned over and some dug into the ground. The compound walls had chunks missing, exposing the inside like a cavity.

Kos motioned for Orinthia to follow as they cut into the open. They made it to the first disabled ship. His pulse kicked faster as several blaster shots came out ahead. He pressed himself against the ship and waited for more.

Slowly, he edged around, looking for the source. Nothing. *Must've come from inside,* he thought, continuing forward again.

They made it a few more feet before a beam of light curved around and landed on them. Caught in the spotlight, Kos pushed Orinthia back and they dashed for cover. A hail of blaster fire pocked the dirt. High pitched thumps followed as they struck the overturned rover they hid behind.

Boots pounded against the dirt. He tapped his visor and recorded the sound. *Four enemies.*

Kos glanced at Orinthia. Her eyes were narrowed, and determination was written on her face. His finger twitched against the trigger as he calculated the positions of their opposition. Between heartbeats, he jumped up and braced himself on the edge of the craft. Two shots struck the first of Adora's men, sending him to the ground. Kos swung around and hit the second with another two to the chest.

His vision blurred. The tunnel formed around him and his body moved on its own. There was no sound. No screaming. Just a void.

Kos yelled, a heavy solid grunt. He took hold of his surroundings and forced himself back. His shoulders heaved up and down. Moonlight washed his memories away, revealing the present. Their enemies laid dead beyond him. He'd made it through and won against them and his mind.

He looked down at his side. Orinthia stared up at him, her hand on his leg. She hadn't left him. There were no harsh lines on her face. Only understanding and care.

The spotlight shone on them again, making him hit the floor beside her. There was nowhere to go. He looked at his pistol. "This isn't going to take out that light."

Orinthia rotated her head, scanning the area. "Look, there's a rifle."

Kos followed her gaze. The spot she pointed out was too far, they wouldn't make it without being seen. He sighed and handed her his blaster. "Think you can cover me?"

Orinthia nodded and rolled to her knees.

He dashed, ten feet ahead. Sliding to a stop, Kos reached out and caught the barrel of the fallen rifle. As he raised it, he dropped into position. The spotlight burned in his sights. He braced his arm against his knee. With a steady breath, he fired.

The light burst into a shower of sparks. Gunfire continued to rain down. Kos adjusted his aim. The turret flared red against the dark sky. He fired again. A spark and crack. Then silence.

Kos slung the rifle over his shoulder and rushed back to Orinthia. He took a second to catch his breath, then reached for her hand. "Come on."

They kept low, moving quickly. The gunfire died down, but Kos knew it wouldn't be for long. He scanned the path ahead, looking for a direct way inside.

Movement blinked on his HUD to the right. Kos whipped

around, pushing Orinthia behind him just as a blaster bolt tore through the air where she had stood.

More of Adora's forces popped up out of the wreckage.

Kos returned fire, shuffling back until they reached a good cover spot. They crouched down behind a hover bike. It wasn't much, but it would have to hold long enough to come up with a way out.

He tapped a message to Thrutt, letting him know they were nearing the compound. A second later, a reply came across.

*Need backup?* It read.

*Might soon. We're on the western wall,* Kos responded.

A bolt ricocheted off the bike's seat. Kos turned and fired, using his HUD to lock on target.

Orinthia grunted behind him, followed by scuffling, a sharp gasp, and boots scraping against the dirt.

Kos spun, his heart hammering.

One of Adora's Hunters had her. An arm locked around her chest, and he was dragging her up.

Kos moved, but Orinthia was faster. She jammed the golden blaster under the man's chin and pulled the trigger. The shot cracked through the night.

The guard collapsed with her in tow. Orinthia shoved him off, rolling to her side, gagging. Her bad arm cradled tight with her blaster still clutched in her good hand.

More blaster bolts bounced off the surrounding debris. Kos barely registered it. "Hey, hey, look at me." He kneeled beside her and cupped her face.

She shook. Her breathing was sharp and uneven.

Dirt kicked up as bolts smacked the ground. It would be seconds before someone got a clean shot.

"Bury it. Just for now." His voice was low but firm. "Push it down and move forward. You can fall apart later, I promise.

But not here." He wanted to laugh. Burying it never did him any good, but it was all the advice he had for her.

Orinthia's lips pressed together. She nodded, trembling.

Kos saw it in her eyes. Uncertainty, hesitation, and heartbreak. He wasn't sure if she could pull the trigger on Adora. If she faltered and lost her nerve, he would do it for her. Always for her.

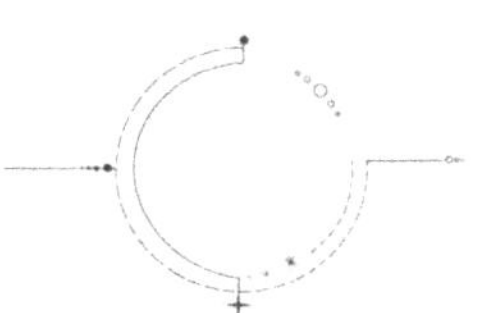

## 45

*W*hite dots still burned in Orinthia's eyes, blurring each time she blinked. Metallic, thick air graced her tongue with every short breath. Her body ached. Her arm throbbed. Kos' brace had come loose and the sticks hung on the sides, only held on by the bottom ribbon. She could not move.

Kos fired over the hover bike, saying something she did not understand. His voice was muffled in her head as it raced to clear the image of the dead man. He grabbed her shirt and hoisted her to stand.

"Move," Kos said in her ear, cutting through her haze.

They darted across the way, nothing but moonlight to light their path. It was quiet for a moment. No one came after them as they made it to a larger hiding spot.

"We've got about twenty feet to go." Kos leaned against the hull of a skiff and tapped his visor. His breathing was deeper, but still controlled. His body worked through the motion of the battle, not struggling against it.

Unlike Orinthia, who gasped beside him. She braced a

hand on the skiff and set her head against it. Her legs wobbled beneath her. The nap had not worked as well as she had hoped, and every part of her screamed for her to let go. But she would not. Whether it was adrenaline or sheer spite keeping her going, she did not care. She only hoped it held long enough to get the job done.

Kos touched her injured arm and examined the splintered brace. "That didn't last long."

Orinthia tilted her head. The sticks jutted out like bones under the dim light. "Can you fix it?"

"I don't have anything left." Kos sighed. He tugged at the bottom ribbon, letting the sticks fall. "You're going to have to move slower."

Orinthia let out a sharp, breathless laugh. "That'll get us killed."

Kos ran his hands over his pant pockets, then shook his head, muttering curses. "I didn't think this through."

Orinthia rolled herself and stood shoulder-to-shoulder with him. "There's no time to worry about it, anyway. They're going to keep coming, and even if we had the time, we're still too far in to run back now."

He stared at her for half a minute, running his lips over his teeth, then muffled a sigh. "Ready, then?" Kos lifted the rifle into ready position and inclined his head as a silent order to move. He did not wait for the answer before curving around the skiff and jogging forward.

Orinthia's gait was uneven and awkward as she held her wounded arm close to her side. Lightning shot up her arm, rattling her bones like a live wire. She could sense nothing around her through the fire growing in her mind.

The blaster in Orinthia's hand grew heavier with each step. Twenty feet could have been a thousand at the point. It felt so far away, even as the opening in the wall laid clear ahead. There was no more cover. No more second chances. If they got caught, it would be a stand to the death.

She could not read Kos' mind, but she knew he was thinking the same thing, maybe had been for a lot longer than she had. He tightened his grip on the rifle and moved his head in sweeping motions.

A pang of guilt hit her. This was not the life she wanted for him, yet he continually threw himself at it. For her. Always for her. *Once we get out of this, I'm going to make it up to him,* she thought. *I don't know how, but I have to.*

Kos slowed and moved to the right, placing his back against the wall, near the gap. He leaned his head in and looked around, then tapped the side of his visor. "I can't find a clear path," he whispered. "They shored up the yard to keep anyone from coming in this way. Mines and e-wire. It's a sloppy job and parts look unfinished, but I can't risk hitting the wrong spots. I don't have the time or tools on me to deal with all that."

"Then how do we get in?" Orinthia asked. Her elbow throbbed and she stifled a groan.

Moving away from the gap, Kos turned and scanned around them. "Thrutt said they secured the entrance. We can go that way and walk right in." He tossed his chin forward and started walking along the outside of the wall.

The pair kept close to the wall, hiding in what shadows they could find. Blaster fire came less and less, and Orinthia wondered what it meant. How many were still holding strong for the twins? Did they all believe they were doing the right thing, even as so many were dying?

They had only made it a few feet before freezing. Frantic footsteps broke the silence, louder from somewhere farther down the wall, near one of the other damaged sections.

Kos turned first, swinging the rifle and shifting Orinthia behind him.

Her heart was in her throat. She threw her eyes around in the dark, searching for the source, waiting for a dozen guards to appear and gun them down. She held her breath, not daring to move, in fear she might scream.

Instead, a young man, maybe younger than Orinthia, though it was hard to tell in the night, burst from a tiny gap. He skidded to a stop, nearly stumbling over the rubble, and his hands flew over his head. A rifle hung loose from a strap around his shoulder, swaying with the sudden halt. His eyes squeezed shut, head turned away, like he was bracing to be shot.

"Wait." Orinthia put her hand on Kos' elbow to stop him. "Look at him."

The man's arms shook. He shrunk down, making himself a smaller target, or melting from fear. Either way, he was not a threat.

"Please, I just want to get out," he said, his voice trembling as much as his body did.

From deep in her clouded mind, Claven's words came back to her.

"Are they making you fight?" she called out.

The man nodded.

"Answer out loud," Kos barked.

"Yes," the man said, shrinking more. "They've taken over my home and forced us to join or die."

"He's telling the truth," Orinthia whispered.

"Drop your gun and get out," Kos ordered. "If I see you again, no second chances."

The man's rifle clacked to the ground as he threw it. In a flash, he dashed through the wrecked vehicles toward the forest.

"There's probably others like him," Orinthia said, watching him grow smaller in the distance.

"And plenty more that agree with Adora's ideals," Kos said, moving back the way they were headed. "We can't let everyone go just because they may or may not want to be here." He took a step forward, but Orinthia reached out to stop him again.

"Can we stay here for a minute?" Orinthia asked, placing her back against the wall. "I just need to breathe for a moment."

Kos came around and crouched for a better look at her face. "Is doing this really worth it? We could probably make it to Mimi's ship and get out of here."

Bracing her good arm on her knee, Orinthia thought about his question. Every muscle ached, and she no longer had feeling in her feet. If she closed her eyes for too long, she thought she would pass out then and there. Leaving, running away and letting Thrutt wrap things up, would be a relief. A year ago, she may have taken him up on it. And even in that moment she had every excuse to turn tail. But she could not. People she cared about sacrificed too much to get her there.

"You don't need to answer," Kos said with a sigh. "I can see it on your face. Take a second to rest, then we'll move on." He brushed his fingertips against her knee and stood.

Energy bolts ricocheted in the distance, bounding off metal into stone. Another echoed from inside the compound, reminding her of what little time they had. Rest would be her reward for getting the job done.

"I'll follow you," she said, straightening with a moan. Golden blaster in hand, she touched Kos' back again.

The same chest tightening feeling crept up, like it had a few months before on Elendoras. She pushed it out. *This time is different,* Orinthia thought. *I'm going to end it once and for all.*

Together, they moved in unison along the perimeter at a jog. Orinthia had no concept of time through her weariness and she did not know how long they went before Kos slowed down.

"There's a shallow ditch that could give us some cover," he said.

Orinthia looked over Kos' shoulder. A berm popped out of the ground and curved back down. It was larger than she had expected.

Kos climbed over first, then slid down, kicking up dust. He turned and held up a hand to catch Orinthia.

She counted to three to steel her nerves and followed. Going up was easy. It was the drop that nearly broke her. Only a foot off the ground, it should not have mattered. But the impact shot through her, rattling her already battered body. She bit down on a cry and panted through her nose.

Ignoring the stare Kos gave her, Orinthia forced herself to keep moving. *No turning back,* she repeated to herself. Their feet crunched the rocks and rubble below.

Old pipes sat unburied in some places along the base of the trench. They oozed out a thick, dark brown substance, turning the red sand into maroon mud. It smelled of copper and reminded Orinthia of the way blood tasted after a hard hit to the mouth. She spit out the feeling and turned her eyes away.

Pieces of the wall had collapsed into the ditch, which forced them to climb over to get around. Other sections were reinforced with long, patchy grey and black boards which were splintered from years of exposure. It was not hard to see how Adora managed to overtake the planet. Everything seemed to be holding on by mere threads as it was.

*Still*, Orinthia thought, *this is a poor proof of concept. She may've taken out a backwards dustbowl, but with just a handful of marauders, we've managed to push back. The EC has none of my respect, but even then they'd sweep right through here and clean her out.*

A wild idea crossed her mind and she came to a halt.

Kos took a few more steps before he slid to a stop. His rifle swung around as he looked for the cause of Orinthia's sudden actions. "What's wrong?"

"What happens when the EC crosses into a territory that isn't theirs?" Orinthia asked, her mind slowly working through the pieces that fell together.

"It depends," Kos answered slowly. "If they have permission then there'll be guidelines to follow. Uninvited... it might be seen as a threat or invasion."

"So if the EC were to come here with warships to stop the twins —"

"It could be treated as an act of war." Kos finished Orinthia's sentence.

Her stomach twisted. "That's how they plan to topple the Confederacy. They didn't intend to take a fight to them, but to draw the EC into something they had no chance of winning."

Kos nodded then cursed under his breath. "And if they don't, the twins can keep expanding until they become too big of a problem to ignore. Either way, they get with they want."

The whole matter finally made sense. Why Kian was so insistent on the GMH handling the situation. But not just the GMH. One wild, misfit crew and a marauder. Small enough that if they were to be found out, it could be played as a misunderstanding or even they went rogue. He was standing in the middle, a one man barrier holding the EC at bay to keep the galaxy from falling into another war.

A breeze picked up, sending red sand trickling down the sides of the ditch like grains through an hourglass. Orinthia felt each of them drop, like tiny pin pricks across her skin. Her senses were alight. A last wave of energy coursed through her as if waiting for the right moment to surface.

*You're not alone, Kian,* Orinthia thought. *We're standing beside you. I'm not going to let you down, not this time.*

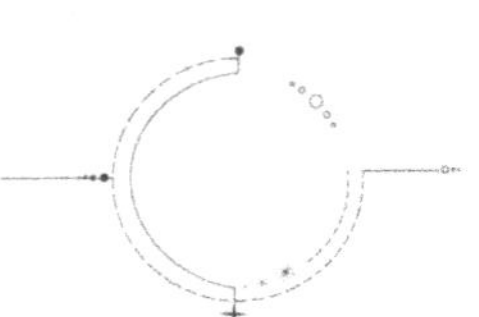

## 46

"There isn't much farther to go," Kos said, readjusting the rifle and facing forward again.

They moved quicker than before. Orinthia braced her arm close to her body, but found the pain was at least tolerable. She worked in her mind what she would do or say once they reached Adora. That was cut short, however, when Kos held up a hand and took a few steps back.

"It gets pretty narrow up ahead," he said. "The ditch pinches at the front and goes through a culvert under the main entrance. We need another way around." They backtracked a dozen feet to a less steep spot.

It took more effort than she would have liked, but Orinthia leaned on Kos' strength as he helped her climb out. She held his hand longer than necessary, soaking in the last moments together before they faced Adora. "Thank you for bringing me this far. I wish you weren't here, but I'm glad to not be alone."

Kos lifted her hand to his lips and gave a gentle kiss. He let it drop without saying anything and shouldered the rifle once again. With a sharp nod, he continued onward.

From their new position, Orinthia saw the landing strip ahead. Annatilla's stolen ship sat deserted at the end closest to them. The ramp was still down, waiting for someone to return it to its owner.

There was another ship, only a silhouette in the dim light, farther down. It was larger than Annatilla's, closer to freighter size but without the bulky sharp angles. The wings curved up halfway down the length and formed into gentle slopes. Moonlight reflected off the wide cockpit window, but the body was matte and swallowed every trace of illumination.

A little ways in front of the second ship were the compound's front gates, wide open like they had been when Orinthia first arrived.

Orinthia's heart tapped against her chest. The warm breeze dried the sweat building up on the back of her neck. They were nearly there. Images of slashing Adora down the moment they found her crossed Orinthia's mind. She did not deserve the right to speak for her actions. But, Orinthia knew it would take more finesse than she was capable of in the moment.

Kos stepped a few paces to the right, avoiding a mound of dirt. He was a few feet away from it by the time an orange glow flowed out from the side. He skidded to a stop and stood his ground, rifle at firing position.

Orinthia stayed behind him and moved to the side for a better view. She lifted her blaster and waited to see who emerged from the hole in the ground.

A shadow spilled out, stretching long until it reached the end of the light. A small figure followed behind it.

The air escaped Orinthia's lungs as she watched Adoracion Anton dust herself off.

Adora froze mid-wipe and swiveled her head to face the

pair of guns aimed at her. The tunnel's light lit her face, catching her red scar and the smirk beneath it.

"Disappointed, but not surprised," she said, voice smooth like polished stones. "Of course it's you who made it out of those woods, not Annatilla. She was tactical, but not much of a fighter. Still, shame to waste the talent."

Orinthia's mind seized. Her hand trembled with a flurry of unnamed emotions. She ached to pull the trigger and end her where she stood, but the strength to do so failed her. "Shut up. Shut up right now."

"Why?" Adora let her hands fall to her sides and she straightened to face them better. "You going to shoot me? Or have your pet do it?" She flicked her attention to Kos. "Little ship rat trailing fleas. No wonder she keeps you around. Makes her feel better about herself.

Adora lifted her palm toward Kos. Before she could get a dart out, Orinthia squeezed the trigger on her borrowed blaster. From unsteady hands, the shot missed, kicking up a puff of dust behind her sister. With a sharp jolt, Adora jumped to the side and snapped her aim toward Orinthia instead. The angle was off, and the dart struck just in front of Orinthia's feet.

She did not wait. Using the distraction, Adora spun and broke into a full sprint toward the farthest ship.

The first shot came from Kos. Blaster bolts cut the air around Adora, sizzling past as she pressed harder into her sprint. Both he and Orinthia followed her. Kos fired again, one bolt catching her in the arm.

Adora cried out and stumbled a few steps. Still moving, she twisted and loosed another dart toward him.

Orinthia was slower, her injury dragging her pace, but she reached out with her mind. Adora's energy crackled like white light through her mind. Slowly, Orinthia curled around her sister's legs. With an exhale, she yanked back and noticed a shift in the connection as Adora fell forward.

Kos reached her first and held the rifle level with her chest.

Blinking fast, Adora rolled over. Confusion flashed across her expression. It did not last. Rage overtook her features. She kicked up hard, knocking the rifle out of his hands and then surged to her feet.

By the time Adora was fully up, Orinthia had reached them.

Aiming at Kos again, Adora raised her hand.

With a yell from pain ripping through her, Orinthia swung up her injured arm and called out her black blade. Before Adora could get another dart off, Orinthia brought the blade down and sliced through bone and muscle, severing Adora's hand from her arm.

A chilling screech ripped through the air. Adora stumbled back and clutched her bloody nub to her chest. Her eyes were wide, face twisted into a blend of rage and terror.

Orinthia stepped closer and set the tip of her sword on Adora's collar. She lowered her gaze and spoke in as even a tone as she could manage. "Make Arsenio bring Uri out here right now."

Adora's eyes narrowed. Her shoulders and chest rose and fell with shallow gulps of air. "I've already told Arsenio to kill him."

There was no hum in Orinthia's head. It punched her in the gut and all strength she had stored failed. The blade slipped down Adora's chest and sliced through her shirt, leaving a thin trail of blood exposed. She lost her grip on the blaster and it fell as she took steps back.

Kos retrieved the rifle and set the muzzle to Adora's head. He shot Orinthia glances, waiting for the command to end it.

But she could not think. Adora's words had shaken her to her core. She felt nothing. No anger. No sorrow. No heat.

Just emptiness.

"How could you do that?" Orinthia muttered. "He loved us."

"Because I knew it would hurt you the most," Adora screamed. "I hate you."

Each pump of Orinthia's heart sent fresh pain through her. She wished for the ground to open up and swallow her, crush the feeling out of her soul. It hurt more than she thought anything could. All her plans, every thought she had fell apart. She failed Uri.

Seconds trickled by like minutes. The world around her was on fire, every atom reached out and pressed against her. She was drowning under the pressure.

Her breath caught. Just as she slipped beneath the weight of it all, one light surged to the surface, a bright star. Strong. Alive. Like an elastic band snapping back into place, Orinthia broke through the shock and turned.

Two men walked up and behind them, climbing out of the hole Adora had a short time before.

Relief crashed into her, raw, staggering, and overwhelming. It struck her as hard as the grief had, but in reverse, ripping the breath from her lungs with such force she almost fainted.

Uri. Alive.

The light of him blazed through her haze, drawing closer, and real.

Arsenio held a blaster to Uri's head and did not waver in his pace.

"Drop your weapons and step away from her," he shouted. The words were pronounced with effort, but the intent was clear.

"Do it," Orinthia said to Kos, recalling her blade and moving away from Adora.

Kos grunted and unslung the rifle. It clacked to the dirt a foot in front of him. He stepped toward Orinthia and stood half an inch in front of her.

The men were close, no more than a few yards away.

Orinthia glanced down at the golden blaster. She connected with it in her mind. It wobbled, but she waited. They had to be right on her to get a clear shot with her non-dominant hand.

*One shot for him, one for her,* she rehearsed in her mind, picturing the timing with each second.

Arsenio came into clear view. The moon was directly ahead, lighting the runway like a blue sun. A breeze sent loose dirt rolling across the ground. And there was hatred in his eyes, the same look Adora had given her.

On Orinthia's mental mark, she yanked the blaster off the ground, and held out her hand to catch it, taking her eyes off her brothers for just a moment.

A flash of light popped and blaster bolt ripped through the air. The surrounding air froze as she searched for the pain ripping through her body. When there was none, her ears waited for the sound of a body dropping. It happened in half a second. The blaster had barely made it to her hand.

The sounds traveled around them, bouncing around the open space. There was more than her voice in the mix. She snapped her eyes to Uri, expecting to watch him crumble lifeless to the ground. Instead, she followed his gaze to Arsenio who held his arm straight out in front of him.

Another beat passed. A thump sounded behind her. Orinthia continued to turn until she saw what her mind could not make sense of.

Adora laid on her front, face buried in the dust. She did

not move. Like a light switch, the energy from her shut off, leaving a solid lump on the ground.

Orinthia tore her eyes away from the body at the sound of a blaster clacking to the ground. Arsenio placed his hands behind his head and stared ahead.

Uri rushed to Adora and knelt beside her. Gently, he touched her. "She's dead."

"What just happened?" Orinthia asked, not daring to look away from Arsenio.

Kos took his golden blaster from Orinthia's hand and moved to Arsenio.

"The truth," Uri said, standing straight and coming around to look at Orinthia. He pulled her into his chest and held her tight.

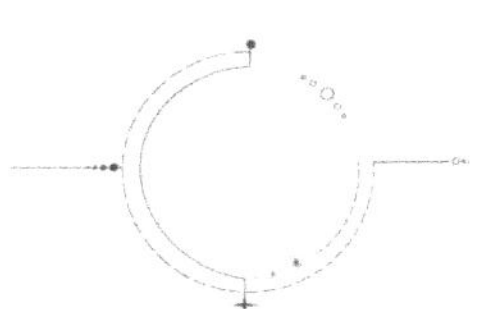

## 47

If there was anything Kos had learned in the short time he'd been with Orinthia, it was to never expect an Anton to follow the set path. But this? This made no sense. He stood with his blaster level with Arsenio's eyes, mind racing. Adora was his twin and co-conspirator. And yet, Arsenio had been the one to pull the trigger.

Kos had thought he understood their roles. Adora was the hand pulling the strings. Arsenio played the dutiful enforcer. And Orinthia was the outlier and wild card, the unpredictable one.

He couldn't have been more wrong. They were all as insane as the next. It was no wonder they were constantly at each other's throats. The bloody ending was always meant to happen, and they all needed to be as far apart as possible.

There was no time to dwell on it, though. Only four people knew what happened, and they were still in a very active war zone.

Kos blinked hard, shaking the thoughts loose. Tapping his visor, he contacted Thrutt. His comm beeped beside his ear.

Messaging would take too long, and they needed to get out, fast.

"Adora's dead," Kos announced as soon as the line connected. "We need backup to get to the ship."

There was a long pause from Thrutt's end. A few pops of a blaster filled the silence. "So she did it, then?"

"No," Kos said, eyeing Arsenio, who had not flinched or swayed since surrendering. "The brother." He glanced at Orinthia from the side of his eye. She was too far for him to reach, and he wished Uri would drag her away from the body. Her breathing was steady, but her face was unreadable; too still, too blank.

"Uri?"

"The other one," Kos replied, returning his focus to Arsenio.

"Oh. That's unexpected," Thrutt said, his voice pitched higher. A grunt and another set of blaster fire sounded in the background. "What happened?"

"I don't know." Kos gave a slight shake of his head, more reflex than answer. "But this isn't the place to figure it out. Meet us at the landing strip. I'll patch you the coordinates. Mimi's ship is on the north side of the compound and we'll need cover."

"Copy," Thrutt said. "We're on the move. Stick tight."

The line went dead.

Kos switched the blaster to his other hand and fixed his stance. He regretted not having something to secure Arsenio's arms with, but that had not been part of the plan when they set out. They weren't meant to take prisoners. He wondered if he should shoot him there, too. End it all and give the galaxy, and Orinthia, peace.

*Something isn't right,* Kos thought. *What if this is part of some sick plan? What if killing her was exactly what Adora wanted?*

Bile trickled up the back of his throat. He hated not having answers, and hated being manipulated even more. There was no good path to go down until they heard from Arsenio.

"Why aren't you saying anything?" Kos barked at the man. "You just killed your sister. Where's the remorse, or explanation?"

Uri cleared his throat and stepped closer to Kos, pulling Orinthia with him. His voice was low, but clear. "Kos, he's deaf."

The words landed like a misfired shot; sharp and unexpected, but not enough to throw him off his feet. Kos' breath hitched for half a moment, his grip tightening on the blaster. It only added to the mystery. As the moment of sudden shock passed, unease took its place.

"The chip connecting his and Adora's thoughts was dislodged when Thrutt broke Orinthia out of prison," Uri added without prompting.

Kos let out an abrupt, hefty laugh. The irony was beautiful. Poetic, even. It didn't explain anything, but it didn't need to. Arsenio was trapped in his own mind, just like they had trapped Orinthia in fear for years. Now he was alone, with no one left on his side.

A rush of running footsteps cut through the night, jolting Kos' senses alive once again. He looked around and realized he was the only one armed. Orinthia could barely stand, and he had no idea if Uri had ever fired a gun in his life.

The steps kept coming. Too many for him to fight on his own. His focus snapped to Arsenio, the only tool he had left. Kos yanked Arsenio and spun him around, slamming the barrel of his blaster against the back of his head, and placing him between the newcomers and those he was trying to protect. His grip was iron-tight, dragging Arsenio into position so whoever came out could clearly assess the situation. If they decided to start shooting, he'd make sure Arsenio took the first hit.

Kos' comm beeped, but he had no freehand to answer it. A second later, words popped across his HUD. "We're coming out, don't shoot."

The tight coil of his nerves loosened, but his grip on the blaster stayed firm. His heartbeat thundered, and his body still expected a fight that wasn't coming. With a slow exhale, he released Arsenio's shoulder with a shove. He kept his focus sharp, however. They were far from secure.

Thrutt was the first to pop out of the gate, sweeping his gaze over the flightline before leading the rest of the crew forward. They moved quickly, closing the distance until forming a loose half-circle around the group. Low murmurs passed between them, whispers carrying through the tension.

The stone man took hold of Arsenio's arms, locking a pair of cuffs around his wrists. He cocked a brow at Kos. "Didn't know we were taking souvenirs."

Kos clicked his tongue and shook his head. "I don't know what to make of any of this. But we can't leave him."

"Then let's move," Thrutt said. He tilted his head behind him.

"Wait," Uri said. They all turned to look at him. "What about Adora?"

Kos scoffed. "She can rot here. That's what we came to do."

He glanced at Orinthia, who held herself together beside Uri with her head low. She was bloody and dirty, her clothes were torn and hair a mess. Still, he couldn't read her expression. It was placid, in shock. She hadn't looked at Adora, not even a sideways glance since she died. Nor had she spoken. He wanted to hold her, remind her she was free, and this was what they were fighting for, but it was not the place. First, they needed to get off this planet and leave it as nothing but horrible memories.

Uri shook his head but kept his thoughts to himself. He, however, did look back at his younger sister. Whether he was saying his goodbyes or reliving moments in the past, it didn't last long. He faced Kos again and gave him a slight nod.

"Move out," Thrutt said, taking the lead. He put Arsenio into the custody of one of the marauders. At his order, the crew of half a dozen men fanned out around the small group, keeping a tight formation as they jogged.

Kos took up the back, close to Orinthia. She winced a few times, but stayed quiet.

They made it to the entrance of the tunnel and went around.

The two closest marauders kept their weapons trained on the opening until they were fully past. It was quiet for the first leg of the trip. There were no guards out until they reached the wrecked vehicles again. Four of Adora's people moved through the debris, checking the bodies of their fallen comrades. One popped up first and fired a few rounds toward the crew.

Kos stepped in front of Orinthia, activating his armor. His vision began to go bright, swallowing up the scene before him. A blaster bolt bounded off his bicep as the plating locked in place. It was enough to anchor him into the present. He shook his mind free, trying to keep Ignio's words in the forefront of his mind.

The marauders made quick work of the attackers, leaving only one standing by the time they reached the mess. He darted behind a hover bike, firing blindly, his gaze flicking to Arsenio, careful not to hit him by mistake.

Without missing a beat, two of the marauders peeled off from the formation, flanking him from the opposite sides. A handful of shots cracked though the night, ending the fight. None of them paused. The group pressed forward, weaving through the wreckage, scanning for any sign of movement. The last thing they needed was another ambush.

Kos' HUD read the distance to Mimi's ship. They only had a quarter of a mile to go. Once they passed through the last set of downed vessels, there would be no more cover until they made it to the ship.

The moon was behind them, dimming the light on their path. Kos focused on the readout and watched the numbers drop with every step. Orinthia panted hard behind him, pain filling her voice. His heart pinched. There wasn't time to stop and carry her out like on Elendoras. They needed to keep moving.

Mimi's ship came into view as they rounded the compound wall. Seven hundred feet and they were clear.

A barrage of blaster bolts cut across their path, pressing them back. Kos searched and found two gunners stationed at the top of the wall. He shouted for them to be taken out, joining in the fire. His HUD lit up the gunmen, but at that distance, his pistol had little effect other than cover fire.

One of the marauder's shots hit its mark, and the rifleman toppled from the top of the wall. In return, a marauder near the front of the group took a hit and collapsed. The back and forth lasted a full minute, taking another two marauders. Finally, the last rifleman fell forward and hung halfway over the ledge.

Thrutt did not wait for anyone else to show up before

leading the crew the short distance to Mimi's ship. He reached it first, and keyed in the code for it to open. Then, he waved the rest in, bringing up the rear once everyone was inside.

Kos led Orinthia and Uri into his cabin and told them to sit tight. He swiped up on his armor and recalled it as he ran to the cockpit. "Freya, get us out of here." He sat in the pilot's seat, and Thrutt joined him. "Take us to the *Fera*."

The loading door thumped closed and sealed. In half a minute, they were off the ground and angling toward the sky. Kos typed in the preflight checks, making sure they wouldn't blow up as they left the atmosphere, then gave Freya the okay to ascend.

He allowed himself to sit back and breathe for a moment. His nerves were alight, feeling every piece of fabric touching his skin. They had made it, but he couldn't shake the tension in his chest. The hours he had lived through were as close to war as he'd seen in years.

Darkness crept around him in the stillness. His adrenaline running high, playing tricks on his mind. He closed his eyes and focused on all they accomplished. They were safe. They were alive. He did his duty for the woman he loved, and not some thankless government. There was honor in his actions, not senseless killing.

His pulse ticked down with each passing assurance. No voices yelled out to him. No deep waters dragged him under. He had won the battle against himself.

When he opened his eyes again, they were in space. Skirmishes went on in the distance, but nothing like what he had come in to. Freya plotted a course away from the fighting and made a long way around. In twenty minutes they cleared the distance, and the faint outline of the *Fera* came into view.

Kos activated the comm, keying up the *Fera's* code. "Captain Ignio. This is Kos Rogue, requesting permission to come aboard."

# 48

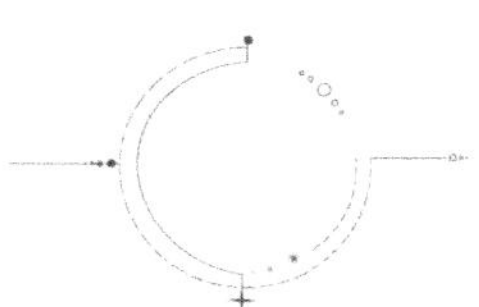

The *Fera's* landing bay opened wide, the light casting a glow like a morning star to call old sailors home. Mimi's ship slipped through the threshold, its silhouette swallowed by the illumination before settling into the safety of steel. The landing gear exhaled a low, mechanical sigh, echoing the sentiments of those inside the silver vessel.

Whatever happened next, it was out of Kos' hands. There was only one role left for him to play, and he planned on perfecting it for the rest of his life. It took some effort to get out of the pilot's seat, but after a long stretch, he headed to his cabin.

Thrutt followed behind him, but kept far back enough to not crowd them. He stood in the hall with his arms crossed and watched from the distance.

Orinthia sat on the bed, her back pressed against the wall and her feet hung over the edge. She faced him as he stepped in, and she gave a solemn smile. Her arm was in a proper sling with a med pack tucked under the fabric. The swelling had gone down and her coloring started to return to normal. It was good to see her comfortable and in decent spirits.

Kos leaned against the doorframe and smiled back at her. Like hers, his smile didn't reach the corners of his eyes. But he was happy, at least as happy as he could be in the moment.

"What happens now?" Uri asked, standing and moving closer to Kos. "What are they going to do with Arsenio?"

The bit of levity he had vanished at the mention of their prisoner. They had stuffed him in the other bunk room, with the rest of the marauders keeping an eye on him. He would've liked a minute more of a breather before dealing with it, but the moment was gone.

"I have to let Kian know we have him," Orinthia said, speaking for the first time since the incident. "The EC would've sent a fleet out by now. They have to know what they're coming in to."

Kos bit his bottom lip and thought for a minute. Adora was dead. Arsenio was captured. There was no one making plays anymore. Sure, they probably had generals or commanders of some sort, but everyone who made big picture calls was gone. Their people were still following old orders, unaware their leadership had collapsed.

"Arsenio needs to call them off," Kos said. "Send his people running. It won't solve all the problems, but as long as the EC doesn't come in guns blazing, they have a better shot at talking down the situation if the system's government catches wind."

"How do we do that?" Orinthia asked, scooting to the edge of the bed. The blanket bunched up around her as she awkwardly moved. "He can't hear anything, and the only one who could talk to him is dead."

"I've been able to talk with him the whole time," Uri said.

He looked around the room. "What did you do with his PortTab?"

Kos reached into the pocket on his thigh and pulled out the small tablet. "Kept it in case we could get any information off it. Why?" He passed it to Uri who held his hand out.

For a moment, the man didn't answer. He pulled up a screen and began typing something. A minute later he turned it around for the others to see. "It takes longer, but this is how I've talked to him. He answers me out loud and then I write more for him to read."

"Do you think he'll talk to us?" Orinthia asked, lowering her voice.

"I don't know," Uri said. "But we can try. He's going to be in as much shock as the rest of us, even if he was the one who killed her. That connection is gone now. And he knows it."

Kos ran his tongue over his teeth. "That's a lot of hope for someone who has tried to kill everyone in this room."

Uri shrugged. "It's all we have. I just know that I was able to get him to talk to me before. And I think that's why he killed Adora."

Just when Kos thought he had reached the end of surprises, he was hit with another. "You told him to kill her?"

"No, of course not." Uri held his hands up and shook his head frantically. "He had questions I answered, most of which he didn't like. Look, we can talk about it later. One problem at a time."

"He's right," Orinthia said. "We have to at least try to get him to call off the rest of their forces."

Kos straightened off the door frame and fanned out his fingers, waving for them to step across the hall to the other room. Thrutt stepped aside and came closer to where Kos stood. When they were through, Kos turned and joined them, standing beside Orinthia. He knocked on the door with a bent finger. "It's Rogue, let us in."

The door slid open and three marauders faced them. They each stood with their rifles loosely at their side, but within reach if they needed to react quickly.

Beyond them, secured to the bed frame and sitting crossed legged on the floor, was Arsenio. He did not look up as they entered. His eyes focused where their feet were.

With a message already written on the tablet, Uri stepped closer and crouched in front of his brother. There was no response for a second, then Arsenio's head moved up to face Uri better.

"And if I don't?" Arsenio asked. His voice came out slightly different than before, too even or too rehearsed. The edges of the words were soft, his breath control more forced, like forming them by mouthfeel and memory alone. His usual nasally tone didn't help the matter, either.

"Can you type out what I say?" Orinthia asked, coming closer. She did not lower herself to their height and kept a pace behind Uri, careful not to get too close.

Uri held up the tablet and pointed out an icon. "Just talk and it'll write it out for you."

"There's nothing left to lose," Orinthia began, keeping her head turned in a way she did not look directly at Arsenio. Her hand hung clenched at her side.

Kos slid closer to her and pressed his fingertips against her fist.

"Your people vowed to die for your cause, and they will unless you call them off," she continued, drawing in a deep breath. "Annatilla told me everything. How you want to rebuild from the ashes. You can't rebuild a ruined system from inside a prison cell and you'll crumble along with it. Adora's used you your whole life, and now she's gone. If the

EC comes through here, your people will die in her name. And that means she still wins."

Uri turned the PortTab back for Arsenio to read. It didn't take long for Arsenio to look away, his lips curling into a snarl. There was a long silence. Kos wondered if he was going to shut them out completely.

"Broadcast the phrase 'Skitlan Majorica'," Arsenio said, to no one specifically. "It's a retreat code."

"He's telling the truth," Orinthia said. Her voice held steady, but something had shifted, an edge Kos couldn't place. It wasn't doubt or hesitation. Just a flicker of something old and wounded. Whatever it was, she buried it fast.

Kos turned to Thrutt. "Did you get that?"

Thrutt nodded. "Skitlan Majorica," he repeated. "Has no meaning to me, but I'll have Tryn spread it across all open channels and frequencies." For a large stone man, he moved with ease and dashed from the ship into the bay. His steps thumped until they disappeared down the hall inside the *Fera*.

Kos addressed the other marauders. "Wait outside the ship. We'll get you when it's time to transfer."

The marauders nodded and followed the order without question.

He waited for them to be fully off the ship before he spoke again. "Now, somebody better start explaining what happened down there. I'm not sorry she's dead, but I also don't like being left in the dark."

Uri sighed and rose to face Orinthia and Kos. He held the tablet out for Kos to take and glanced back at Arsenio for a second, then back to the pair. "He finally realized what we've all seen the whole time. That Adora was in full control of his life."

"But how?" Orinthia asked. "What did you tell him?"

"Ask him yourself," Uri said, nudging his chin toward the PortTab. "He deserves to have his own voice for once."

Kos pressed the record icon and placed the tablet closer to Orinthia.

"Why did you kill Adora?" she asked. "What did Uri tell you that was powerful enough to make you turn on her?"

Kos lowered the tablet to Arsenio's level and set it in front of his face.

Arsenio let out a sharp, choked laugh and shook his head. "We were supposed to be a team, a double-edged sword with nothing between us." His lip curled again and his eyes narrowed. "But in reality I was nothing more than a puppet. She pulled my strings, lied to me, used me, just like she did everyone else."

He paused and blinked for a hard second. His voice rose. "Everything I knew was an act!" His restraints banged against the bed frame as he lurched forward. "And the one thing that connected us, made us the unstoppable force I believed us to be, was my prison in the end. She told me there was no way to regain my hearing. That I'd be deaf for the rest of my life. It was hard at first, but I accepted it. I was comforted knowing I still had my sister."

Orinthia flinched, but steadied herself.

After a few shallow breaths, Arsenio swallowed hard and straightened his spine. His voice was lower, cold and even. "That snake purposely kept me locked away to keep control of me. I could hear again. All I had to do was have the mod removed. But no, she couldn't give up her leash."

"So, —" Arsenio looked Kos in the face, a shadow of a smile danced around the edges of his mouth "— I freed myself. I took away the only thing she truly cared about. Herself."

Kos held Arsenio's gaze, but even as battle hardened as

he was, he couldn't deny how shaken he was by the revelation. And not just the story, but Arsenio's reaction to her death. It was cold and sick.

Arsenio shifted his gaze and looked at Orinthia. "In the cave, you saved me from falling. Why?"

The air in the room was thick, tension was high for everyone inside. Kos watched Orinthia, waiting to see how she'd react to his question. She owed him nothing and had every right to ignore his query.

Orinthia extended her hand and took the tablet from Kos. "I should have let you die for all you did to me. Don't think it was mercy. Whatever reached out for you was not me. Some part of Desidario, maybe. This was another one of his curses he saw fit to give me."

Arsenio read the message and nodded slowly. "He always favored you above the rest of us. His precious baby girl with her mother's face."

A surge of energy pulsed through the room from where Orinthia stood. She gave a heavy grunt, and Arsenio slammed against the bed frame with a single thud. With the tablet still in her hand, she said, "You can keep his favor, because if that was his love, then I want no part of it."

The tablet dropped in his lap. She stormed out of the room and kept going down the hall. Kos took off after her, catching her as she stepped onto the ramp.

One marauder pushed himself off the hull of Mimi's ship and gave Kos his attention.

"Take him to the brig," Kos said, tossing his head back toward the opening.

The marauders filed in, one after another, and disappeared inside the ship.

Kos led Orinthia by the hand, not speaking or forcing her to say anything. There was no point. His only job was to catch her when she fell, be it emotionally or physically. They walked silently down the corridor, letting muscle memory lead him to the lift. It moved up several levels and opened to a wide hall.

Together, they walked through the large opening onto the observation deck. Kos pressed a button on the wall, and the ceiling opened, slowly exposing the expanse of space. He led her to the steps and sat her down, pulling her head to his shoulder. They both looked up and watched as speckles of light danced across the sea of black.

"You changed my life in this room," Kos said, keeping his voice as soft as possible. "Each time we met in here, you shed new light into my darkness. I didn't know it then, but I needed you from the first time you fell into my life."

Orinthia snorted a laugh.

Kos smiled to himself. "It's over now. You're not under their shadow anymore. Pick a star, and we'll fly that direction, exploring every planet and system from here to there."

"I want somewhere to call home," Orinthia said, adjusting so she could look up better. "The most peaceful place we can find. Where no one knows us and we can decide who we want to be."

Kos leaned in and kissed the top of her head. They were both covered in sweat and dust, but he ignored it, content to have her with him again. "That was my idea all along."

"But we would've been living in fear. Now, every move we make is because we want to, not out of necessity."

"I can live with that," Kos said, leaning his cheek against her head.

*Peace,* he thought, watching the speckled void. *I'm working on it, but we'll find it together.*

Their moment of calm was interrupted by Kos' comm beeping in his pocket. He considered ignoring it, but the call kept coming in. With a sigh, he stretched out his leg and fished out the device.

"Whatever it is, can wait," he said after he flipped it open.

"Thia's needed on the bridge." Thrutt's voice wasn't upset, but the words came out quick. "It's the GMH."

49

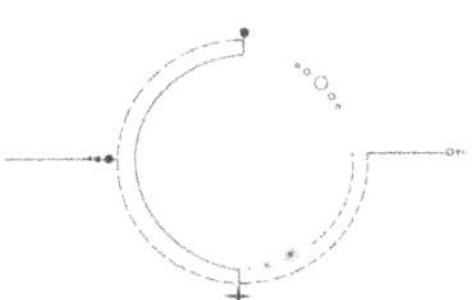

For a few stolen moments, Orinthia almost believed they were done. The fight, the pain, the ghosts, none of them could touch them in their solitude. She had all she needed. Stars above, Kos beside her, and the knowledge she was finally free.

But, the GMH found her. Again. They called, and she answered. Orinthia alone walked the line between worlds as marauder and Hunter. She was not a hero, nor a villain, just something caught between the two. And perhaps she had been blind to think she could truly live a life of her own.

In the stillness, she knew it would always be her burden to bear. That was the cost of caring, the weight of choosing to stand for something greater than herself. So, she served those who had served her and made her way to the bridge, where she was needed once again.

Still in her tattered and bloody clothes, she carried herself with as much poise as possible. Thankfully, no one stared too long as she and Kos entered the room. It was the first time she had seen the *Fera's* bridge, and it was larger than she expected. There were two rows of control panels, one along the front beneath the curved window, and one in the center that split in two. Each had their own set of screens, dials, knobs, and an assortment of things Orinthia had no clue about.

In the middle of it all stood Thrutt and a tall alien man who was a foot shorter than him. He had strange tattoos on his face which would have sent a shock of fear through Orinthia if she had not been exhausted. A monocle eyepiece moved in and out quickly as she stepped forward. Though he stood straight-backed and commanded the room, there was an air of compassion about him.

The man gave a bow at the hip as she approached. "It's good to see you again, Thia."

Orinthia nodded and blushed, not remembering where they had met before. "Thank you for your help," she said, covering her embarrassment. "All of this. Believing in me and Kos —"

Ignio held up a hand to cut her off. "I appreciate the gesture, but it will have to wait. Right now, we need your assistance." He turned to face the windscreen and motioned for her to come closer.

Kos moved with her, but kept a few paces back.

"We don't want trouble with the EC," Ignio said. "No more than we already have, that is. However, it seems they are unaware of our involvement. A Galactic Marauder Hunter ship has appeared on our radar, and is broadcasting a stand down order. I fear if the ship does not tread lightly, they will be attacked by one of our less reasonable comrades."

"And it would start more than anyone signed up for." Orinthia finished his thought. "The GMH is gone, so I think I know who it is. Have they announced themselves?"

"Captain Masood Solvay of the *Tertion*."

Orinthia placed a hand to the side of her face and rubbed her eyebrows. "Yeah. Thought so. Patch me in. I'll talk to him."

Ignio turned to a female comms officer and gestured for her to pull up the screen. In a moment, the orange captain stood before them, hard faced and arms crossed behind his back.

Solvay opened his mouth to speak, but the words caught in his throat. His expression shifted and the rebreather around his neck bubbled loud. "Anton. What is this? Where is Dai?"

With a calming breath, Orinthia worked out the best way to explain what happened on the planet below. How would she be able to make betrayal palatable? "We have custody of Arsenio," she started, choosing to lead with the best news.

"Adora is dead." She paused. The words struck the center of her chest. "So is Annatilla."

The captain froze on the screen, unmoving as if it had glitched. If it was not for the bubbles moving in his rebreather, Orinthia would have had the connection checked.

"Annatilla's dead?" The words came out slow and careful, like saying them would cause him pain. His eyes snapped to Orinthia, narrowing. "How?" The single word was as good as an accusation.

"She was a traitor, Captain." Orinthia pulled herself straight. "She'd been feeding the twins information the whole time."

"What evidence suggested this?" Captain Solvay asked, his words sharp. "How did you learn this truth?"

"For starters, she had a grenade to my head for over two days," Orinthia said, filling her voice with weight. "Then it became pretty clear when she came out and told me herself."

She wiggled her injured arm. "Annatilla did this to me. And, Adora was waiting for us when we landed. I think that's proof enough."

Solvay muttered a few phrases Orinthia's translator did not understand. He shook his scaly head and hissed. "What about the twins? We've spent weeks hunting them down only for you to come back and tell me you only have one in custody while the other is dead? How did you manage all of that?"

"Look around." Orinthia waved her hand in a wide stretch. "Only a few hours ago, this place was a war zone. We barely made it out. The marauders took charge and kept Adora's forces back. While it raged up here, she was trying to flee, but Arsenio got to her first."

A well of anger burned in her stomach at how much it ached to talk about her dead sister. She blew out the pang and continued. "He turned on her. Put a bolt in her before we could make an arrest. Now, we're taking him back to the EC to face the consequences of his rebellion, just as I was ordered to when given this mission."

"You will transfer him over to me this moment," Solvay said. "I will not have marauders handle such a delicate matter."

Orinthia lifted her chin and stared Solvay in the eyes. Her irritation found a fissure and she let it spill through. "These marauders have saved the Earth Confederate. They've defended it better than the GMH ever has. Every one of those ships is full of sailors who volunteered to fight and deserve the respect they earned. Many of them had served the EC once before, without the fame or glory, and have done so again. Arsenio is not leaving their custody. I trust them more than any EC fleet to get the job done right."

Solvay's jaw tightened. "I can order you to do it. You're still under my command."

"I don't do well with orders, Captain." Orinthia barely blinked. Her voice was steady, but there was no mistaking the warning behind it. "It's in everyone's best interest to let us do what we do and take him back ourselves."

The old captain's eyes scanned the room behind Orinthia. He growled and twisted his mouth before speaking. "I'll inform Commissioner Roldross of your departure."

"Thank you." Orinthia bowed her head in response. "Once we've reached Earth's sector, we'll turn Arsenio over to you. Until then, he's ours."

Captain Solvay's face did not change from the scowl as he bowed at the hip. The screen cut off before he straightened and the connection dropped.

A silence settled over the room, heavier than before. No one spoke.

Orinthia turned, expecting to get an earful for volunteering their services without prior approval. Instead, she was met with a room full of marauders on their feet.

Not a single hard look sat on their faces. No glares of disproval. Several of them exchanged glances, a few more nodded at her in unspoken solidarity. And in the center of them all were Thrutt and Kos. Her world had gone full circle.

The crew of the *Fera* had once voted against her on mutiny charges. But there she stood, facing an arm of the GMH for them, preaching their loyalty and honor.

No one needed to say it, Orinthia had spoken enough for them. The marauders would stand with her.

She swallowed hard and turned to Ignio, trying to block out the silent standing ovation she received. "Sorry to spring that on you without a discussion first. I don't trust Arsenio to get to the NCR safely when his people are still close by."

Ignio tipped his head, a smile tugging at his lips. "It's been a long time since anyone outside our ranks saw our worth. We're honored to serve you and will follow your lead." He reached out to Kos and beckoned him closer. "Now, please rest. You've earned it. We've got a long way to go and you have no need to worry anymore."

Kos took Orinthia by her good elbow, wrapping an arm around her waist. He gave Ignio a long, knowing nod before turning away, leading her toward the exit.

Thrutt followed in silence, his heavy steps the only sound as the doors slid shut.

— ❋　❋ —

THE FIRST FEW days on their trip home were filled with sleep and eating. Kos requested meals and had them sent up to Orinthia's cabin to share in private. He forbade her from doing most things, except rest. Even Thrutt and Uri were barred from entrance more than once. It hurt her at first, to be kept away from them, but Kos' company made up for it.

He had not said it in so many words, but their time apart had taken a toll. The solitude was as much for him as it was for her. If he was not eating or sharing stories with Orinthia, he was snoring soundly in a cot he had brought into her room. She had wondered if he had slept so much in his life.

By the third day, she was well enough to leave her cabin, at least by her standards. She and Kos strolled through the ship. He lead her through passages she had not seen before and humbly bragged about features he designed to make systems run smoother, or small adjustments he had done to make life easier for the crew.

Orinthia had no idea what any of it meant, but she loved

listening to him talk. There was a beauty in his passion she hoped to see more often.

Uri was less than thrilled to be back aboard, however. He said so over dinner the night before they reached Earth. "At least I'm here mostly on my own accord this time. I can't say I'll miss it once we land."

"I'm just glad we're finally all together again," Orinthia said, looking around the room at her patchwork family. She had all she needed. Except one thing. "Too bad I wasn't able to grab any of my stuff before we left, though. There wasn't a lot, but I'd like to have had my mom's picture back."

Unannounced, Kos leaped from his seat and ran out of the room.

The three left behind glanced at each other, each having a varying level of surprise on their face. He was gone for over ten minutes before coming back in, skidding to a stop with a cream colored canvas bag in hand.

It took a moment for him to catch his breath, then he dug inside. After a few seconds, Kos pulled out a frame and handed it to Orinthia from across the table.

"There was so much going on that I completely forgot about this," he said.

The metal was cool in her hands, and she ran a finger across the image. Her mother, with all the emotion a photo could capture, smiled at her. The surrounding light illuminated the glass and reflected her face beside Jeana's. A deep, forgotten ache filled her chest, longing for a memory she did not have.

Uri leaned over and examined it closer. "I've never seen this before. Where did you find it?"

"In Father's room," Orinthia said through her breath, not daring to think about the time. "I knew Adora would be too afraid to look in there, so it was often my favorite hiding spot."

It was hard to push away Arsenio's words while staring at almost identical images of herself. One with long auburn hair, the other with sliver. She passed the picture to Uri and scooted her seat back. The chair legs made a dull scraping sound. "You keep it. I've managed this long without it, so you can take care of it for a while."

Her brother motioned to protest, but Kos interrupted.

"How about we call it a night?" he suggested. "We'll be making the transfer tomorrow and should all get a good rest."

Thrutt was the first to stand, clearing his throat to emphasize Kos' insinuation. "Come on, brother —" he gestured to Uri, "— we have much to get get ready for."

Orinthia forced a smile and wished the pair a goodnight. She had never wanted to be away from either of them as much as she did in that moment.

Alone again, Kos crouched beside her and took her hand in his. "I'm not sure what happened, but I'm sorry."

"They just keep ruining things, don't they?" Orinthia let out a snorted laugh.

Kos scrunched his face. "Who? Thrutt and Uri?"

"The twins," Orinthia said. "I so badly wanted that picture back, but when I saw her, all I thought about was Arsenio's claim I was the favorite because I look like our mother. How selfish is that? I was punished just as much, if not more sometimes, as they were. That's not love. He never loved any of us."

Standing, Kos pulled Orinthia to her feet and held her in his arms. "This is love," he whispered into her hair. "And I'll show you everyday until you believe it. If there was a way to take away those memories, I would. But we're stuck with the past that made us. The only thing we can do is build our future, like we planned."

Tears threatened to well up, but she had enough heartache over the last few weeks. She refused to let her emotions take hold, at least for the moment.

"Okay." She rested her head on his chest. "Whatever comes at the end of this path, we face together. Tomorrow, we start the rest of our lives."

## 50

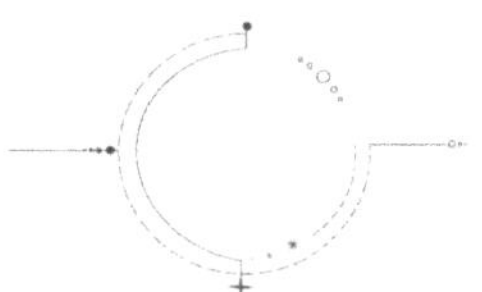

*A* signal trilled through the ship's speakers, alerting the crew they were about to drop out of warp. Orinthia sat with her legs crossed at the edge of her bed, wiggling her foot over her knee and staring at the floor. The bittersweet scent of leather polish hung in the air. Clothes from rejected outfits lay in piles on the floor. Her hair was pulled into the tightest braid possible, having been done and undone several times just to keep her hands and mind busy.

She had tried to sleep, but too many thoughts filled her head where dreams should have been. In the stillness of the ship's morning cycle, all she could do was wait and hope the EC would hold up their end of the deal.

Technically, she accomplished her task. They did not need to know her intention was to kill Adora, especially when she was not the one to pull the trigger. That should have brought her peace.

It did not.

Kos, too, was more tense than he had been in days. Change loomed on the horizon, and they could only hope it leaned in their favor. He tugged at the sleeves of his maroon coat and smoothed a hand over his beard.

"Do you want to see it?" Kos asked, gesturing to the shaded window across the room. "We should be close enough to get a good view of Earth by now. It's been a while since you were home."

The skin around Orinthia's ear warmed. She set both feet flat on the floor and joined him. At Kos' touch, the shades rolled up and cool light slid in through the growing gap. Crafts and satellites orbited like ants around the planet. Vast cloud systems spiraled over the continents, and deep blue oceans stretched across the surface. It was as it had always been.

Beautiful.

"I never get tired of seeing it," Kos said, placing an arm around her shoulder and leaning against the glass. He pulled her close to rest on his side. "There are billions of planets and systems out there, but this is the one we all started from. I wasn't even born here, you know? My aunt lived here. When she took me in, it's where we stayed. And where we met Thrutt."

Orinthia set her chin on his chest and looked up to better see his face. "Do you ever wish you could clone yourself and live two different lives? This one, and one where things turned out how they were supposed to?"

Kos kissed her forehead. "I used to. But this is how it should be. I'd suffer through it all to find you again."

Her ears burned hotter, moving down her cheeks to her neck. "Kos Rogue, I have too much to get done for you to talk like that."

With a smirk, he kissed her one more time and pushed himself away from the window. "Let's get to it, then. Sooner this is done, the sooner we can live again."

Fingers intertwined, they made their way to the loading bay where Thrutt, Uri, and a handful of marauders stood beside Mimi's ship. Arsenio was cuffed between two marauders, flanked by another two with rifles at the ready.

"Solvay's been comm'ing in every two minutes," Thrutt said as a greeting. "If we keep him waiting any longer, I worry he may try to board and claim Arsenio himself."

"That wouldn't be a surprise at all," Orinthia said, rolling her eyes. "Get him in then. Let the *Tertion* know we're on our way."

At her suggestion, four of the marauders stayed behind. It was best not to cause undue panic on either side. Thrutt and Kos headed to the cockpit, while Orinthia and Uri remained with the others to keep watch over Arsenio.

Within a minute, the ship lifted and exited the belly of the *Fera*. Orinthia could not see out, but she pictured each step in her mind. The void of space stalling them. The slow drift into emptiness. Then, the turn as they angled toward their destination.

Their flight lasted ten minutes. It was the silence that wore on her. Out of everyone, Arsenio was the only one who looked at peace. He swayed with each bump and jostle but kept his gaze steady, staring at something no one else could see. It was reminiscent of ancient dethroned kings being led to execution. An eerie calm in the midst of a storm.

An ache tugged at Orinthia's core. Something she could not name, or maybe did not want to. She stood with her back against the wall and arms crossed, watching her brother, her tormenter, and wondered if they had ever shared a tender moment. He was different than his twin. The shadow to her light. The glove in her hand. His voice was never his own.

Yet, there he was, the one who survived. He and Orinthia were never more the same than in that moment. Both free of their bonds, and though he was going to prison, it was the choice he made for himself.

She did not fool herself into thinking he saved her. There was no debt between them. Just mutuals who overcame the same enemy.

The thrusters hummed as the ship slowed, followed by a thump and a hard rock. Hissing came from the front of the ship, signaling their airlock connection to the *Tertion*. Uri stepped aside and joined Orinthia as the marauders moved around them toward the hatch.

Arsenio's cuffs tinked against the rungs as he climbed up, announcing his exit from the ship. He disappeared through the hole in the ceiling and stepped onto the *Tertion's* deck. The two armed guards stayed on Mimi's ship while Orinthia led everyone else aboard the second ship.

There was a noticeable difference between the two vessels. Orinthia had almost forgotten the rusted smell of the air, so thick she could taste it. The familiar sounds of the old engines hummed through the walls. It was not a comfort to be back, but the feeling was close enough.

Orinthia took a moment to center herself before turning. An unexpected presence lingered in her mind. She looked back to see not three, but four Galactic Marauder Hunters waiting to receive their prisoner.

Kian, in his commissioner's uniform, stood out from the others. His skin was bright purple, and his mouth was pressed into a thin line.

"Do you ever do things the way you're supposed to?" Kian asked, making an exaggerated hand wave toward her.

"You told me to get them." Orinthia shrugged. "There was never an agreement on how."

"Fair," Kian said with a sigh. "But the amount of spinning

I had to do to convince the EC not to blow you out of the stars is —"

"Well worth it." Orinthia ended his sentence. "Now, take him. But remember, if you lose him again, I'm no longer in business."

A flash of maroon rolled across Kian's skin before quickly retuning to the violet hue. Without a word, he signaled for Cliff to receive the prisoner.

The larger man stepped forward and loomed over Arsenio. He grabbed the cuffs by the center chain, gave a sharp tug, and pulled him across to the GMH's side of the ship. Arsenio stumbled slightly but did not resist. Cliff positioned him with stiff precision, standing tall at his side like a wall.

"Thank you," Kian said, his voice low but firm. "I know this wasn't the ending anyone expected, but it was the one we needed."

Captain Solvay's rebreather bubbled faster for a second in the silence. He jerked his eyes, glaring at the men behind Orinthia.

"What about my pardon?" Orinthia asked. A warmth moved down her arms, sending a tingle through her hands.

"Well, that will be taken care of when we land," Kian answered. "You need to testify before the Council, and there will be a review, then —"

"No." Orinthia said, clenching her fists together. Static built up around her skin. Her chest tightened and it grew harder to breathe. "That wasn't the deal. I returned him and I get a pardon. I'm done working for what I'm owed."

"This is how it works," Kian said. "The GMH is gone, and I don't have the authority to hand out pardons anymore. That's for the EC to decide now."

"I went through fire to get him." The static pulsed against

her knuckles. "I didn't come back just to beg in front of a council."

Kian exhaled and adjusted his collar like it was shrinking. "Just come with me. Once we get to the NCR, I can pull some strings to get you in front of someone who matters. A signed testimony, a handshake, something. But at the end of the day, it's the best I can offer."

"She's not going anywhere," Kos said from behind Orinthia. "There was already one traitor aboard this ship. I'm not risking leaving her unwatched again."

"This is not a marauder ferry." Captain Solvay hissed.

Kian held up a hand and gave a slow blink. "Shut up, Masood. I'm so tired of this. Rogue, come along. But we need to move. We're running late as it is."

Solvay muttered under his breath and turned on his heels, leading his crew and Arsenio away.

"I'll take Mimi's ship down," Thrutt said, patting Kos' arm. "Meet you at the diner."

Uri scooted closer to Orinthia.

"And you're coming, too?" Kian asked.

"Might as well," Uri said.

Thrutt descended through the hatch, sealing it shut behind him.

Kian stepped forward. He met Orinthia's guard but did not flinch. His shoulders relaxed. "You've earned more than the EC will ever understand. I'm going to do whatever I can to make them see that."

Orinthia loosened her fists and nodded. They gave each other tight smiles before Orinthia escorted her small crew to her old cabin to wait.

—✳  ✳—

THE PACK ORINTHIA had brought from Buscoch laid on her bed, stuffed with nearly everything she arrived with. Her two companions stood against the wall, moving their arms in and out of crossed positions, shifting feet, and clearing their throats.

"Can't wait to be back in a real bed," Orinthia said, breaking the silence. If the banging of the ship's engines and clanking of pipes could be called silence, that is. "And it will be nice to have you back again, Uri."

There was a quick shuffle behind her, like Uri had been startled by her statement.

"Yeah, for a while at least," he said, sniffing.

Orinthia looked over her shoulder, holding a pair of pants she was halfway through shoving into the pack. "What does that mean?"

Seconds ticked by. Uri looked at the wall above her bed.

"Answer me." Orinthia tossed the pants aside and faced him. She had never demanded anything from him before. But she was weary, stretched too thin, and tired of being left in the dark.

"Everywhere I go, I'm used against you," Uri said, drawing out his words. "Desidario, the twins, even Kian baited me to keep you straight. We need to be apart for a while. Truly apart."

The words smacked Orinthia in the chest, digging into her core. Her cheeks flushed and her arms went cold. "And you're blaming me for that?"

"No, no, not at all." Uri stepped closer, but she pulled

back. "I love you too much to continue putting you in danger to rescue me."

"Then stay with me," Orinthia said. Her throat grew tight. "Stay where I can keep you safe."

Uri looked over his shoulder at Kos, who looked away, then faced her again. "You're living a life I'm not prepared to be part of. And it isn't a bad life, *for you.* This is what I've always wanted you to have. To be loved. To find a form of peace. To be somewhere you belong. I don't fit into this world you're building. And that's okay."

"Why am I constantly punished for saving you?" Tears dripped down the sides of Orinthia's face. Her breath shook.

"This isn't a punishment." Uri moved closer and took her by the shoulders. "You've given me a second chance at life. You've showed me that I was not who I thought I was. And now, I don't even know who that is. It's exciting."

The ship thumped and rocked, sending them swaying for a moment.

"Before the twins escaped, I was doing some digging," Uri said. "Someone contacted me who knew our mother."

The air rushed from Orinthia's lungs. Her legs wobbled and she grasped Uri's arm to keep her up.

"No-Mods," he continued. "They're out there. And I'm going to find them. Maybe they can help me find answers."

"Wouldn't No-Mods hate everything you are?" Kos asked. He moved to stand near the pair. His hands hung loose at his side.

"They don't hate tech," Uri answered. "But they under-stand the dangers of misuse. Part of what they do is help safely remove mods. Or, rehabilitate those who have been been injured by too many."

Orinthia glanced at Kos. He bit his lower lip and flared his nose.

"You're one of a kind, Uri," she said, swallowing hard. "How will they give you an answer?"

"I can't guarantee they can. But Mother believed in their cause. Even if I can just learn about why she sided with them, it would be a place to start. I was programmed with her memories, but I don't know anything about her."

A wave of nausea rolled through Orinthia, curling up in her spine. "Why does every win have to come with a loss?"

"I was going to wait to tell you," Uri said, letting her go. "It won't be right away, though. And we'll spend time together before we leave. But I am leaving."

"We?" Kos asked, cocking his head and narrowing his eyes.

Another long silence passed. "Thrutt's going to accompany me."

Kos cursed, and threw his head back, dragging both hands down his face. "You wrapped him up in this?"

"No, I didn't," Uri said. His voice hardened in defense. "I was asking how best to tell Thia, and he offered to go. We both knew how she'd worry, and this way I won't be going alone."

He blew hard and ran his fingers through his hair. "Look, you two are starting a life together. We can all see it. Thrutt and I will only get in the way or make things awkward. Neither of you know how to survive without moving at full throttle. And now we've all reached a lull in the chaos. It's time to find out who you are when fighting isn't the only option."

There was little comfort in his words. The future was happening a lot faster than she had planned for. Orinthia looked up at Kos and their eyes met.

His face softened and he gave her a few short nods. They

would figure it out together. Forever was a heavy word, but she was ready to see where it took them.

THE *TERTION* TOUCHED down in the NCR. A tremble passed through Orinthia as she stepped onto the top deck and waited for the others. Fresh, dry air rolled in through the cargo bay doors.

She moved to the opening. White sunlight stung her eyes. All feelings of homesick were dashed away as Orinthia looked over the arid desert. No trees for miles. Nothing but beige sand and blue mountains.

*This can never be my home again,* she told herself. *Not when there is so much more out there. Kos and I will find somewhere, even if it takes us a few tries. It will be ours and no one can take it.*

When Uri and Kos joined her, they moved outside and watched as Arsenio was transferred into the custody of no fewer than fifty armed EC officers. There was no great fanfare, no cheering or uproar at his return. Not even a slew of social net reporters vying for the story. Just a long, weighted stare between siblings. Arsenio held Orinthia's gaze until the moment he was turned away and led into an armored hover car.

Kian closed the doors, sealing in the prisoner, and knocked twice on the side. In a swift motion, the car lifted and sped through the sky toward the capital prison.

They all watched as it was joined by another group of armored EC vehicles.

When each one was just a dot against the blue, Kian moved to Orinthia.

She looked at him. His coat was undone and moved to the side.

"Spent the journey back arguing for this." He pulled a PortTab from his coat and flipped the screen around. "Even got Solvay to swear on your behalf. You won't have to set foot in a court, as long as you keep yourself out of trouble."

"Kian." Orinthia choked on a lump in her throat and read over the pardon orders. She knew he likely sacrificed more than he would ever admit to. "You've been a good friend to me. I won't forget this. Thank you for giving me the chance."

"You believed in me when no one else would." He placed the PortTab back in his coat and took in a deep breath, dramatically sighing with his entire body. "Let's take a walk." Kian stepped away before anyone could respond.

The three exchanged glances but fell in line beside him, not saying anything.

The flight line was quiet in the mid-day heat. No other ships docked or departed. They were alone in the empty EC port.

"Shame, really," Kian said turning toward the hangar at the end of the strip. "We lost a lot of good assets during all this. I'm not sure how many ships Adora's people took when they left. It'll probably take us a few months to sort it all out. Even then, things can get miscatalogued and documents shuffled around."

He tapped his watch against a panel, unlocking a wide gate that slid open in front of the group. Beyond, in the hangar row, sat half a dozen vintage star-class vessels. The type GMH captains would have fought for a chance to command.

Kos made a popping sound with his mouth and let out a slight whimper.

Then, Kian turned around and walked toward the way they came.

Orinthia furrowed her brow and watched the Galoric, waiting for an explanation.

Kian, already several paces away, glanced over his shoulder and waved his hand to push them forward. "Look, just don't take anything I'm going to regret."

He strode away again leaving the gate wide open, and the possibilities even wider.


**Get a free bonus short story at TheShortWriter.com**

ACKNOWLEDGMENTS

I've made so many amazing new friends while writing *The Fallen Hunters*. Each one of them holds a special place in my heart and has made this author journey a little easier. Most of them I've never met in person but encourage and support me, make me laugh, and give great advice. These friends live online in the Thread community as both authors and readers. You all are the best, and I can never repay the support you've shown me. I hope you all become best-selling authors with movie deals!

Next is, of course, my husband. He helped me through some really dark days while drafting and editing, talked me out of throwing away the book, and walked through plot lines. Being an author, especially one who doesn't get out much, can be lonely. He's given me the grace to cry, laugh, and gush along the way, and I wouldn't have gotten this far without him.

While editing the prologue of the second draft, I realized this book was incomplete without Arsenio's POV. But, seeing as he was a deaf character, I wanted to do him justice. In walked Blair Wynters. We met on Fiverr when I was searching for a sensitivity reader for Arsenio and I could not have been happier with what we made together. They were the first to read each of Arsenio's chapters, and the feedback I got was not only constructive but illuminating. We both learned a lot through the process and I think this book would have been lesser quality without it.

# ABOUT THE AUTHOR

Lorena Para (1990-present) was born in Southern California. Her parents moved to The Land of Enchantment (New Mexico, USA) in 1993, where she lived until high school graduation in 2008. She moved back to California and attended college. While working on her bachelor's degree in Elementary Education, she met her husband. They live together in a small mountain town tucked away between Los Angeles and Fresno, along with their two children, dogs, chickens, ducks, and hobby homestead.

Lorena is a fan of writing science fiction, dystopian, and post-apocalyptic genres. She finished her first self-published series in 2020 and is currently working on an expansive space pirate series.

When she isn't writing, she is running a small handmade sticker business, homeschooling, her daughter, playing video games, and consuming all forms of Star Wars media.

Stay up to date by joining her newsletter crew at:
TheShortWriter.com

facebook.com/theshortwriter

instagram.com/theshortwriter

pinterest.com/theshortwriterLP

goodreads.com/theshortwriter